Harry's Game

First of the Few

Harry's Game

First of the Few

Karl Jackson

Alpaca & Goose
2019

Harry's Game - First of the Few, is a work of historical fiction based on events that took place during the Battle of France in 1940. Any names, characters, places, events, or incidents within the story are either the products of the author's imagination or inspired by similar actual events and used in a fictitious manner. Any references or opinions related to any organisations or entities exist only within the fictitious realms of the story, and any resemblance to actual persons, living or dead, is purely coincidental.

karl@harrysgame.com

Book design & Illustration by Karl Jackson

First published – November 2019 by Alpaca & Goose

www.alpacagoose.com

First Edition

ISBN 978-1-9162651-0-3

www.harrysgame.com

‘Friends’

Dedicated to the men and women whose stories became legends, and whose actions saved the world.

Chapter 1

Lazy Days

Spring had been odd, to say the least. Britain and France, among others, had been immersed in war since the previous year; but other than the older people venting tiresomely about their hatred of all things German, and how this time they'd give the 'Boche' an even bigger beating than the last, you wouldn't really know there was much of a war on. Certainly not in rural France. At times there was an air of unease, but it had mostly subsided since the army was first mobilised and sent to sit on the border, where they languished with little to do for months on end. Boredom and frustration at the inaction had become the biggest talking point, and any suggestion of the Germans actually crossing into France hardly put a dent in the casual French swagger, which at times bordered on arrogance. This attitude was held equally by both the general public and grandstanding politicians; and buoyed up by the ever so persuasive news reporters, who seemed to spend every waking moment making stirring, and at times quite ridiculous, speeches on the radio.

In the unexpected warmth of the May afternoon, two girls were sunbathing on the grass beside an old Nieuport biplane, enjoying the gentle breeze and half listening to yet another pompous broadcast.

"Do you think they'll come?" Harriet asked, as she stared upwards and watched the meandering stream of small fluffy white clouds glide across the azure blue sky above. She was as English as they came, with a voice almost absent of regional dialect except for the faintest hint of Yorkshire, which still clung on tightly despite her having lived in France for the last nine years. It was just about the only thing out of place in the idyllic little French aerodrome. "The Germans, I mean. Do you think they'll come here?" she continued, as she lifted onto her elbows and looked over at the Tricolore flapping proudly in the breeze, at the top of the flagpole by the rickety old canvas hangar. "I mean, they could. Couldn't they?" She looked down to her friend lying beside her.

"Do you ever stop?" Nicole sighed. Her hands were locked tightly behind her head, and her eyes remained closed. In contrast with Harriet, her accent was unmistakably French.

"I was only asking… No need to bite my head off, moody..."

"I'm not biting off your head; I just have better things to occupy my mind. As have you, my very pale English rose." She opened one eye and smirked. "Relax and enjoy the sun. You need it on your skin more than anyone."

"You make it very hard to like you, Nicole," Harriet replied with mock scorn, as she laid back on the sweet smelling grass, and went back to staring at the sky.

"Nonsense, Harriet. I'm delightful," Nicole giggled.

"Don't call me that!"

"Why not? It's your name, after all."

"Because my name is Harry!"

"No, your name is Harriet. Harry is the name of a boy, and you're not a boy!" Nicole teased, leaving Harriet to roll her eyes and groan in frustration. Both she and Nicole had spent the day fixing an oil leak on the engine of the old French army Nieuport biplane they were lying beside. When they'd finished with the oil leak, they decided to roll down their overalls, kick off their plimsolls and spend what remained of the warm May afternoon doing a little sunbathing. It was a perfect isolated spot; they just had to keep an eye out for the return of Nicole's grandfather, Claude, who owned the Nieuport and for whom they were supposed to be working.

Harriet had moved to France with her mother and father in 1931. Her father was a businessman who worked mostly for the British government, in a roundabout way, as a business adviser at the consulate in Reims; while her mother did everything a good English housewife of her social standing should. Made jam, kept the home, managed the staff, and threw celebrated parties for influential politicians and businessmen; she was the perfect host and very well respected. Not that Harriet got to see much of that side of life, having spent most of her time at a French boarding school; which is where she'd met Nicole, the girl destined to be her best friend, confidant, and tormentor in chief. School life had been a horrible experience at first. Some of the more elitist French girls had bullied Harriet mercilessly, and they weren't at all keen on having a shy little English girl in their school, especially one with such a poor grasp of the French language. Even some of the professors were horrible to her much of the time, sometimes because she was English, sometimes because they just enjoyed being cruel, or so she'd assumed. Nicole hadn't stood for any of it, though, and six months into their first year at school together she'd threatened the head girl over the bullying and been involved in several fights. She'd also become embroiled in a blazing and most public argument with her professor, who she'd called 'an elitist short sighted moron with no appreciation for Harriet's talents', while forcefully questioning how such a feeble minded person had even become a teacher in the first place. As eleven year old girls go, she was undeniably feisty. A friendship was forged in the fire of the school, which was to last for many years. They grew close, and they spent most of their holidays together, usually in the country with Nicole's grandparents, Claude and Magritte, where Nicole had lived most of her life since being orphaned. It was Claude, Nicole's grandfather and long retired wartime fighter pilot, who had taught both Nicole and Harriet how to fly in his old Nieuport. The very Nieuport he'd flown against the Germans in the Great War, and which had been sold off as obsolete by the French government around the same time he'd retired. Two useless old flying machines put out to pasture together; Nicole's grandmother would frequently say.

Harriet loved to fly, though it drove her father to distraction. He wanted her to be more proper, a young English woman who would marry well and raise a family, and Harriet wanted nothing of the sort. There would be the most ferocious arguments almost every time they met. He would bluster about all he'd done to give her the right start in life, and how she was ungrateful and childish with her dreams of being an 'aviatrix, like that damned Amy Johnson', who he frequently referred to as 'ridiculous' and 'manlike'. Harriet would bluster back twice as hard. She'd spent enough time watching Nicole direct scathing and debilitating fire at anyone deserving of it, and she'd picked up some useful tips which only escalated the arguments further. The more her father pushed her to be a respectable housewife, the more Harriet upped the ante, to the point where she'd committed to becoming a flying missionary, spreading the word of women's rights and equality as she flew around Africa in her very own aeroplane. Things frequently got out of control, and Harriet's mother was often left playing the part of the peacemaker, with the unenviable task of trying to negotiate an uneasy truce between the warring pair. It was on the most recent peacekeeping mission that she'd got both parties to agree to Harriet going to Geneva in Switzerland after finishing school, and training to be a nurse. It was a profession which met the class requirements of Harriet's father, just, while allowing Harriet to do something other than being a housewife. It wasn't perfect, but it stopped the arguments, and Harriet even managed to convince Nicole to go with her. Secretly, Harriet's mother agreed with her daughter, and she was more than a little jealous of the freedom Harriet had ahead of her.

Harriet left to finish school the following day, and from there she went straight to the countryside to stay with Nicole. The sunny days sped by as they helped Claude service the Nieuport so they could fly again before heading off to Switzerland, and their adult life of responsibility and service. They'd changed a cracked cylinder over the previous days and finished replacing the fuel lines that morning. All that was left to do was clean up; something which Nicole declared to be a waste of perfectly good sunbathing time, so as soon as Claude had left to run errands, she'd made the decision to down tools for the day.

"But they could come..." Harriet said again as she watched the clouds

"You're relentless." Nicole sighed.

"Apparently, the expeditionary force the British have sent to Belgium is the best equipped army the world has ever seen, so Father says. Over a quarter of a million men."

"Then what do you have to worry about?"

"Well, they're in Belgium. What happens if the Germans don't come through Belgium? What if they come straight into France?"

"Then the French army will stop them, I suppose. We have a very big army too, you know. The way you go on at times, you'd think the British won the last war by themselves!" She jutted out her elbow and gave Harriet a playful nudge. "You're not the only ones who can fight, eh Harriet?"

"I told you not to call me that!" Harriet bellowed, as she rolled and pounced on Nicole. They laughed and fought, rolling around the luscious green grass and through a slick of fresh oil that had dripped from the Nieuport's sieve like engine. It wasn't the first time they'd fought. Fighting and wrestling had become a frequent feature of their time both at school and at home. It always started with Harriet being excitable about something or another, and Nicole replying with disdain. Sooner or later it would escalate into a fight until one or the other yielded, usually Nicole, who did so out of her professed boredom at her friend's infantile behaviour. Which, as now, resulted in Nicole being tickled until she yielded with more congruence.

Their giggles and screams were drowned by the thundering roar of an engine passing so close that the ground vibrated, followed by a large shadow which blocked out the golden sunlight as it passed overhead, and plunged them into unexpected shade. Harriet, who was now sitting on Nicole and tickling her ribs, stopped and tilted her head back to look up at the uninvited disturbance. "A Hurricane!" she gasped, as the brown and green camouflaged fighter of the Royal Air Force flew over them. "Nicole, look! A Hurricane!" she yelled, excitedly. She hadn't seen one before, not close anyway. A few days earlier a squadron of them had passed over, somewhere in the clouds, but this was the first time she'd seen one of the powerful machines so close. Nicole wriggled and turned to watch, then quickly climbed to her knees as it turned tight and came back towards them with its wheels down. They looked at each other excitedly.

"It's landing..." Nicole said excitedly. "Do you think he's lost?" The Hurricane bounced a few times before settling on the grass and rolling towards the girls, who knelt side by side with mouths open. "Merde!" Nicole gasped quietly, as the Hurricane swung to a stop twenty feet or so in front of them. "Clothes!" she said as she stood and pulled up her overalls. "Harry, clothes!" She dragged her friend to her feet and pulled up Harriet's overalls. Harriet looked at her with confusion, then quickly realised she was showing more flesh than a young lady should, and blushed as she tried to make herself at least half presentable. The engine cut and the girls stood in silence while putting on their plimsolls, and listening to the few hisses and clunks coming from the airframe, which now it was standing in front of them looked somewhat worse for wear. The canvas fuselage was ripped open in several places, and oil was streaked from engine to tail. The canopy slid back, and a cloud of greyish white smoke billowed into the air, accompanied by a deep barking cough.

"Bloody hell!" a very English voice ranted from the cockpit. The pilot scanned his surroundings, then turned to look at the girls. "Well if you're not going to help, you can bugger off!" he bellowed at them. "I hardly need a bloody audience!" The girls looked at each other, then ran to the Hurricane, and Harriet bounced up the wing to the cockpit and looked inside. The pilot was gripping his left leg, which was bloody and shaking like a leaf as he tried to steady it with his equally bloody hand. She could see daylight through the side of the cockpit. Bullets had passed through both airframe and pilot and shattered some of the instruments as they passed through. "Parlez-vous Anglais?" he asked, as he pulled off his flying helmet to reveal his sweat soaked sandy blond hair, which matched his large smoke stained moustache. He was an older man, older than her by a good few years, and powerfully built with broad shoulders and a square jaw. "Well?" he demanded. "Come on, girl. Parlez-vous Anglais?"

"What? Yes, of course," Harriet replied, as she gave her head a shake. "Are you OK?"

"What the bloody hell does it look like?" he blustered.

"There's no need to be rude!" Nicole chastised him as she joined Harriet on the wing. "She's as English as you, of course she speaks English! We just didn't expect your ugly face to disturb our day!" He raised an eyebrow in surprise. It was clear that he wasn't used to being spoken to that way.

"Fair play. No harm intended, old girl," he said to Harriet. "I've had a bugger of a day, and to top it all some German decided I didn't have enough holes in me, so kindly donated a few bullets..." He looked down at his leg briefly. "Don't suppose you'd help me out, would you?" He looked sorrowful, and his tired emerald eyes pleaded as he unfastened his harness and held out his shaking bloody hand. The girls did as he asked, and helped him drag his bloody body from the Hurricane and sat him on the wing, where he tilted his head back and gasped a few deep breaths. "Flight

Lieutenant Anthony Sullivan, Auxiliary Air Force," he said as he composed himself. "Sully to friends."

"I'm Nicole, and this is Harriet," Nicole said confidently.

"Thank you both for your help. I'm obliged to you."

"You're welcome," Harriet replied. "What happened?"

"I'll be back!" Nicole said as she turned and ran off the wing. Harriet watched her run off towards the hangar, then turned back to the pilot.

"Did you get one? A German, I mean?" she asked excitedly.

"Of course I did!" he replied, sounding hurt that it would ever be questioned. "You don't think I'd let somebody do this to me and not give them a punch on the nose in return, do you?" He gave her a wink then looked up at the sky. "Unfortunately, he had a few of his pals with him, the same buggers that knocked down the rest of my chaps. I saw Jumbo get out, and Sergeant Smith put down in a field somewhere. Still, they got all of us..." He groaned as he bent his leg, and blood pulsed out of the hole in his thigh in a thick surging wave. Harriet instinctively reached out and put her hand tight over the wound. He gritted his teeth and nodded. "That's it, good girl. Push a bit harder, and you'll keep me alive yet."

"What else should I do?"

"You're doing it, old girl. You're doing it... Now, what's an English girl doing in the middle of France?"

"I live here..."

"Well that's unfortunate," he gasped through gritted teeth, as Nicole arrived with the first aid kit from the Nieuport and pulled out a bandage. Between them, they busily dressed the leg wound, and his hand. They'd been practising on each other since they'd both decided to train to be nurses, and they felt confident that they could stop most of his bleeding.

"Why?"

"Why what?"

"Why is it unfortunate that I live in France? I quite like it here."

"Because the whole bloody German army is heading this way," he barked with a frown. "The buggers came through the Ardennes and smashed right through the French army at Sedan. We've been doing all we can to hold them back and give the army a chance to do something, but we've been overwhelmed. I lost my entire flight just today, and it's the same story across the front."

"Oh..." Harriet's smile faded as she listened to his words.

"Anybody with any sense is making a run for the coast. You should probably join them," he continued, as Nicole pulled a dusty long necked brown glass bottle from the first aid kit while they talked. She twisted at the cork until it popped and gave it a sniff, then raised an eyebrow and turned down the corners of her mouth in a typically French way and shrugged.

"Brandy," she said matter of fact.

"Brandy?" Sully repeated, looking hopeful.

"Brandy," Nicole confirmed before handing it to him. He smiled and took a mouthful.

"Bloody good brandy," he said with a sigh of contentment.

They were disturbed by a horn sounding repeatedly, and the girls turned to see Claude's truck bouncing along the dirt track and into the field, leaving a cloud of dust in his wake.

"Friend of yours?" Sully asked as he swigged more brandy

"My grandfather," Nicole replied. "This is his airfield."

"I see..."

The door flew open, and Claude jumped out before the wheels had stopped turning and quickly sprinted towards the Hurricane.

"Allemande!" he shouted. "Germans!"

"Where?" Sully asked as Claude came to a halt by the wing. He stopped suddenly and looked around, then stepped back as he realised there was a Hurricane in front of him.

"Who is this?" he asked Nicole in French.

"Flight Lieutenant Sullivan, Auxiliary Air Force," Sully replied. "Had to put down in your field after being shot up by an angry German." Claude looked at the girls, then back at Sully. "Your girls have been patching me up and feeding me your brandy... Hope you don't mind, old boy?" Sully looked at the girls. "He does speak English?"

"I speak English," Claude replied. "We must go; we all must go right now. The German tanks are thirty minutes from here." He clapped twice and gestured the girls off the wing, and they dutifully complied. "Come, pilot. You too."

"Now hang on!" Sully protested. "The only place I'm going is back up there." He gestured to the sky with the brandy bottle. "We're going to need every Hurricane and pilot we can get our hands on if we're going to slow the Germans down. Now, if you have a few pints of oil I can borrow I'll get on my way." He slid down from the wing and put weight on his leg and instantly screamed out. "Bugger!"

"You can't fly," Claude said with a look of confusion.

"Of course I can bloody fly!" Sully protested before trying again to shift himself, getting as far as half standing before he realised that neither his left leg nor his left arm was working all that well. "Bloody Germans!" he yelled, before rolling onto his back and looking at the trio staring at him. "Well you got me out of the damned thing, the least you could do is put me back in it!" he raged. The girls stepped up onto the wing to help as Claude stepped forward.

"And then what?" Claude asked. "Your throttle is on the left side; how will you use it when you can't use your hand? And if you do get up, how will you control the rudder when you can't use your leg? Besides, you'll bleed to death and fall out of the sky before you get to your airfield." Sully looked furious and hopeless.

"But we need aeroplanes!" he protested. "We lost three today that I know of, and one yesterday. How will we fight without aeroplanes?"

"I don't know, but if you want to live, we should go," Claude shrugged in response.

"Leave me here... I'll burn her rather than let the Germans get their hands on her. You girl, Harriet, reach in and grab the flare gun for me, won't you?" Claude nodded, and she jumped up to the cockpit, her overalls half unbuttoned, and sleeves rolled high, showing her skin covered in a filthy mixture of black oil and red blood. "Hang on, this is your airfield, isn't it?" Sully asked.

"Yes," Claude replied.

"Do you fly?"

"Of course I fly, why would I have an airfield and an aeroplane if I didn't fly?"

"You fly her."

"What?"

"You fly her. They won't miss me, I'm past my best anyway, but they can use another Hurricane. Get my map will you, Harriet, there's a good girl. I'll show you where the airfield is. It's not so far away, and once she's started, she's like any other aeroplane to fly really."

"No!" Claude replied instantly.

"Oh come on, old man," Sully blasted as Harriet handed him the map. "Nothing to be scared of, the Luftwaffe will have likely buggered off home for beer and medals by now anyway. Hide in the clouds, and you'll be there in no time."

"Scared?" Claude replied as he puffed out his chest. "Seventeen Germans. That's how many I shot down in the last war. Seventeen! How many have you shot down, Englishman?"

"OK, OK, I'm sorry..." Sully put up his hands in surrender. "I was out of line, I know. I'm just keen to get the kite back to somebody who can use it. I know you're not scared."

"I'm not. I have a wife and these girls to get to safety. I can't just leave them."

"OK, old boy, I understand. You'd better get going; I'll burn her once you're on your way."

"Come with us. We'll take you west to your army."

"Oh, that's OK. Your girls have done a first class job of patching me up, but I can't see me lasting that long without a doctor. Best you get going."

"You're sure?"

"Yes, of course. I can't stand the bloody army anyway. I'd rather give myself up to the Germans and end up in the bag, better that than spend time with that lot of smelly old trench dwellers." He winked and smiled confidently. "Off you go, and thanks for the brandy. Oh, I can keep the brandy, can't I?"

"You can," Claude replied. They shook hands, and he flicked his head towards the girls for them to get to the truck. "Good luck, Flight Lieutenant."

"Bet I could fly it," Harriet said as they walked away.

"Not as well as me!" Nicole replied.

"You wish you could fly as good as me."

"Please... You're a child. When you've grown up, you can try and fly as well as me," Nicole said dismissively. She was three months older than Harriet, a fact she frequently used to taunt her when they bickered, often acting as though she was many years older instead of only a few months. It was a very effective approach; Harriet bit every single time. Nicole had found lots of threads to pull that would annoy Harriet, and her age was just one of them.

"You're pilots?" Sully called after them, his voice low and serious. The girls stopped, turned, and looked at him. He had the slightest hint of a smile on the corner of his mouth, twitching the tip of his moustache upwards.

"Yes," they replied in unison.

"No... No, no, no," Claude said as he worked out what was going on. "They're too young."

"It's a ferry mission. Drop it off at the airfield, and our chaps will get you back to wherever you want to meet. It won't take you half an hour to get there."

"Not that!" Claude argued as he nodded at the Hurricane. "It's too big. Too powerful. That they can fly." He pointed at the Nieuport. "That, yes! A Hurricane? No. They're not good enough."

"She is," Nicole said as she put her hand on Harriet's shoulder. "You know she is, Grandpa, she's a natural pilot, you even said so to Grandma." Harriet blushed and looked into Nicole's eyes. "It's true; she's the best, better than me. I bet she could get it back OK if the Flight Lieutenant showed her."

"Impossible!" Claude was shaking nervously. "She's too young," he said as he looked at Harriet. "You're too young. I must get you to your parents."

"I don't even know where my parents are," Harriet said. "Reims, maybe? We can't go to Reims."

"No, you can't!" Sully said. "Not if you want to stay out of a prisoner of war camp!"

"Claude, I'll do it!" Harriet protested.

"No." Came his simple reply.

"You don't get to say no!" Harriet said as she straightened her back and squared her shoulders while pushing her chest out. "I'm British, and I'm a pilot, and that means it's my duty to get that aeroplane back into the fight!"

"Merde!" Claude hissed.

"Come on, Grandpa, let's help her get ready," Nicole said with a smile.

"She may not be my blood, but you are," he growled at Nicole, "we'll talk about this later, with your grandmother."

"Yes grandpa," Nicole bowed her head obediently and sneakily winked at Harriet.

"And don't believe I didn't see that! I was a great pilot; I have perfect eyesight, and I see everything." Claude helped Sully to his feet and leant him against the cockpit, while Nicole rolled down Harriet's sleeves and helped her dress properly. Buttoning her overalls closed like a mother tidying her daughter on her first day of school.

"You'd better be as good as I think you are," she whispered.

"I am," Harriet whispered as she tried to stop herself from shaking as much on the outside as she was on the inside.

"No games. Fly careful and get home to England. We'll get word to your parents that you're safe."

"I'll come back."

"No... You need to get home."

"What about you?"

"I'm French, and this is my country. I'll be safe here."

"But I'll miss you..."

"Don't be ridiculous; I won't miss you." Nicole scowled. "I've seen your annoying face every day for more years than I can remember, and I need a break!" She hugged Harriet tightly, then kissed her on both cheeks.

"Oh, do come on!" Sully boomed. "If you take any longer, the Germans will be marching up Whitehall before you've finished saying your goodbyes!" He took off his sheepskin flying jacket and wrapped it around Harriet. It was a little bloody and very smoky, and so big that it buried her, but it felt comforting in a way. "You'll need that," he said as he zipped it up.

"Be lucky," Nicole whispered in Harriet's ear before giving her a final kiss. She gave her friend a boost up onto the wing, and helped Claude fasten the parachute onto her. Sully put his flying helmet on her head and tried to smooth her hair out of the way, leaving a few wispy strands waving around her face.

"That'll have to do," he said as he fastened it. "Sorry it's a bit damp, I got a sweat on in that last scrap." She nodded and forced a smile as he leant beside her and talked her through the controls. He gave the best advice that he could on how to fly the aeroplane, and reminded her once more about the undercarriage. The only aeroplane she'd ever flown had a fixed undercarriage, and Sully was keen to point out that many a pilot had forgotten about the wheels and landed on their belly. "That button's the gun. Don't touch it," he bellowed as he pointed to the brass button on the control stick. "I can't imagine there's too much ammunition left, but nobody wants to get shot up unexpectedly," he said with a frown. "Now, if things do go a bit wrong and Jerry turns up, you need to drop to the deck and run and keep going west. I've already pulled the plug so you'll get the best you can out of the engine if you open the throttle fully, and if the shooting starts you need to bail out right away, don't get mixed up with any of that nonsense, just flip upside down and unfasten your harness. You'll pop out like a cork from a Champagne bottle," he smiled. "Just make sure you're high enough, a few thousand feet at least, and don't forget to pull your ripcord." He tapped the large D shaped handle tucked under her armpit. Harriet nodded while going through the instruments and touching everything in turn as he identified it. "You can read a map?" Harriet nodded again. He took a pencil from his boot and marked the airfield. "Fly twenty minutes full speed and turn here, then ten more minutes and you should see the airfield, you can't miss it, there's a huge old mansion house surrounded by tents. Land there and they'll look after you, and give them this." He pushed his card into her hand.

"How will I know when to turn?" she asked. "I don't have a watch." Sully looked at her and smiled, then pushed up the bloody sleeve of his cream coloured roll neck pullover and unfastened his white faced pilot's watch from his shaking left wrist, then reached down and put it on Harriet's wrist.

"There, now you look like a proper fighter pilot," he said warmly. "it's a good one, you know, a proper Swiss pilot's watch. Look after it, and it'll look after you." Harriet nodded and smiled nervously. "OK, good luck old girl," he said as Claude helped him from the wing, and Nicole quickly replaced him at her side.

"Do as he told you," she said firmly. "No messing about!"

"I won't mess about..." Harriet smiled nervously. "Nicole, can I do this? I mean really, can I fly this?"

"Of course you can. It's just a faster version of the Nieuport." She tapped the canopy confidently.

"Come on. You need to get out of here before the Germans turn up," Sully shouted.

"I'll see you again," Nicole said.

"Not if I see you first," Harriet replied with a smile. Nicole nodded, and Harriet started the mighty Merlin engine after a shout of 'clear prop.' The engine roared into life and fire spluttered from the exhausts, along with a cloud of blue smoke.

"Bonne chance!" Nicole shouted as she jumped down and left Harriet to the cockpit, which to Harriet suddenly looked huge. The Nieuport was prehistoric in comparison. All the dials, the levers, everything was so confusing. It would be overwhelming for a young girl if she wasn't already overwhelmed by the task ahead, that is. Harriet fought the fear and swallowed it deep down inside, then wiped her already sweaty forehead, put her trembling hand on the throttle and pushed it forward. The Hurricane strained, ready to move, and she was rolling the second she released the brakes.

"I can't see a bloody thing," she said out loud as she rolled forward at an ever increasing pace. She backed the throttle off and felt the Hurricane slow, then she remembered the instruction to wiggle the tail a little, and did so. Throttle forward, and she rolled again, swinging gently left and right so she could see where she was going. At the end of the field, she turned into the wind and powered up. Nicole waved, and in reply, Harriet did something like a salute, then pushed the throttle forward until she felt the Hurricane sprint across the grass with bumps and bounces enough to shake her in her seat. It was much more powerful than the old Nieuport, or anything else she'd ever experienced. She released the throttle briefly and pulled her harness straps as tight as they'd go, then grabbed it again just as the Hurricane hit a dip in the grass and bounced into the air. 'Catch it,' she whispered to herself, then gently pulled the stick back towards her and felt the cushion of air under the wings. She'd done it. She'd caught it, and she was flying the mighty warbird. Speed, height, and a turn, then a low level flypast of those she'd left on the ground, and a wiggle of the wings before looking forward and skimming the treetops as she headed west towards safety.

Chapter 2

Making an Entrance

The absolute terror of flying such a colossal aeroplane kept Harriet focused for the first few miles. The ground was passing fast, much faster than it ever had in the Nieuport; and as much as the vibrations of the mighty beast made her smile, they also made her nervous. She'd never flown anything like it. Excitement soon got the better of fear, and the temptation to experiment was impossible to resist. The natural aptitude that Claude had noted when teaching her came to the fore as she pulled back on the stick, launching the Hurricane at a hole in the fluffy white clouds. She couldn't help but smile as she was thrown tight against her seat by the roaring Merlin engine, which with the canopy still pushed open for an easy exit was filling her ears with a noise that was surprisingly enjoyable. Even the exhaust fumes that slipped into the cockpit as they were dragged along the fuselage by the speeding slipstream were not entirely unpleasant; they just served to remind her that she was doing the thing she loved more than anything else, she was flying! After threading through the hole in the clouds she pulled the stick left and spiralled as she climbed in a slow and thrilling roll, then reversed it the other way before she levelled off just long enough for the speed to pick up again, and for her to feel the smile on her face reaching all the way to each ear. Once level and cruising she checked the map, compass, and Sully's watch to make sure she was still on track and hadn't got so carried away she was heading in the wrong direction. She smiled as she saw that she was right where she should be, and making remarkably good time. The gauges were showing the engine as running hot, though, and she suddenly remembered Sully asking for oil when he first landed, something that she'd forgotten in the excitement of agreeing to fly his aeroplane home. She found herself wondering whether the German that had shot him up had hit the engine, too. She throttled back a quarter and took the pressure off the engine, then dipped the nose a little to try and help it cool after the strain she'd just put it under with her antics. She blushed a little and chastised herself for being so reckless, "bloody fool, what were you thinking? It's a ferry job, not a jolly!" She did this a few times, then let herself smile again when the little devil on her shoulder reminded her that she was in a single seat aeroplane somewhere above the scattered clouds. Who would know what she'd done? Let alone care? A check of the gauges showed the temperature easing, so she throttled back a little more and felt the pitch of the vibrations deepen. She could then settle into doing the job she'd been tasked with, which included thinking through the calculations needed to adjust her flight time based on her new speed.

It didn't take long for Harriet to arrive at what could be her destination, though it had taken longer than she'd expected due to an almost urgent need to keep the speed down, so the engine didn't overheat. Through the broken fluffy white clouds she could see the mansion house Sully talked about, or at least she thought she could. She checked her map, it was the only mansion house in the area, and the woods to the south were exactly where they should be, as was the lake. She'd done it! She did a wide circuit to the left with her wing dipped so she could see below. There! Hurricanes! All lined up in a neat row along the tree line with ground crews crawling over them like ants, refuelling, rearming, fixing, and whatever else needed to be done to keep them in the fight against the advancing Germans. The Germans! She'd let her mind wander again, and been more engrossed in the fun of flying than the reality and danger of her situation. She was delivering a warplane to the Royal Air Force so they could fix it up and get it back into the fight against the Germans, who were reported to be making their way across France without much to stop them. She went through her pre landing checks as she lost altitude and prepared to turn on to her final approach. She went out a distance, a good few miles further than she needed to in a long wide arc, her theory being that the longer she had on approach, the longer there would be to get rid of some of the speed and altitude she'd been holding on to before trying to land. Speed was still a bit too fast, height about right, flaps, the temperature was still a bit on the high side, but she was almost on the ground, so she didn't need to worry too much about that. She folded her map and stuffed it under her thigh, then went through the landing checks again, trying to remember everything Sully had told her. The canopy was already open; it had been the whole time as Sully was quite insistent it should be so she could bail out without hindrance, should she need to. She pulled the stick back a little to take care of the speed, then eased it forward again and looked out ahead to gauge her distance to the seemingly endless grass lawn to the front of the mansion, which appeared to be the landing strip. As she did, she noticed something glinting in the sunlight. It was a small group of Hurricanes on landing approach, three of them altogether, one of which was smoking quite badly. All three were about ready to land, slowing, rocking slightly, and wheels hanging below ready to meet the rapidly approaching ground. Undercarriage! All that time flying a Nieuport had been great, but it had a fixed wheel undercarriage and that hadn't prepared her for the retracting wheels of a Hurricane! She chastised herself again, loudly, "bloody idiot trying to land without wheels! Some pilot you are!" She looked around the cockpit urgently, where was it? There were so many dials, switches, and levers that her brain was struggling to pick out the undercarriage lever. She clenched her teeth, already blushing with embarrassment at the thought of the massed ground crews pointing and laughing at the idiot trying to land without wheels. With frustration she accepted she was going to have to go around the circuit again, to give herself time to remember how to get the wheels down. She angrily pushed the nose down to counter the throttle increase that she needed to regain speed and altitude for a circuit. As she did, the Hurricane to the left of the formation ahead started spitting black lumps from its left wing just as it touched down, while the ground ahead and behind jumped into the air in spurts of mud and dust. A flash of yellow and orange flame streaked from the engine. Seconds later the Hurricane spun into the ground and buried its nose in a fountain of dirt, before erupting into a ball of flames. Harriet's heart raced, what had just happened? Had the pilot lost control? Had something broken away from the wing? She dipped the nose further and dipped her left wing to get a better look as she leant her head out of the cockpit, and her stomach squeezed tight as the reality of the situation dawned on her. A few hundred feet behind the two remaining Hurricanes, both of which were now bouncing along the ground having touched down, was a spread of four German fighter aeroplanes, Messerschmitt 109s with bright yellow noses flying in loose pairs and chasing the British aircraft with their guns blazing. Harriet couldn't breathe for a moment. She reached up to pull the oxygen mask from her face so she could gasp in some air, but it had never been on. She couldn't breathe because she was suddenly in the centre of a battle, and she was terrified. More bullets slammed into the second Hurricane, which was already swinging hard right to avoid the stream of concentrated fire directed at it. Harriet looked down at the control stick. She was gripping it so tight that every nervous shiver was being sent directly from her spine through her hand, and into the Hurricane's wings. She looked at the brass button on the control stick. She had to, didn't she? How could she do anything else? She was the only one that could, and the only one that should, there was nobody else. She lined up the sight with the lead Messerschmitt and aimed just ahead of it, the way Claude had talked about when he told his stories, then with a soft slip left to line up she pushed the button. The entire Hurricane shook violently, and the smell of cordite filled the air while streaks of bullets ripped the Messerschmitt apart, right down the centre from nose to cockpit. The shock of the guns firing made her tense and pull on the stick. Without releasing the gun button the left wing dipped, and she swung wildly to the left, her stream of fire going with her and zipping in a line right through the cockpit of the second 109, and only when it had burst into flames and she'd flown through a ball of smoke and fire did she stop firing and level out. She quickly banked right, noting the pair of Hurricanes had landed and split from each other; and were now bouncing in different directions, trailing smoke as they went. The leading pair of 109s were downed in a matter of heartbeats, and the rear pair had split and climbed fast, left and right. Instinctively, she pulled the stick left and back until her fist was punching into her guts and squeezing against the tightness she was feeling inside. Her Hurricane pointed towards the closest Messerschmitt 109 and gave chase as if it knew what she wanted without her having to ask. She banked a little tighter and gave a short burst on the guns, the bullets skipped just ahead of the fleeing 109's nose, and the pilot spun viciously to the right and into a steep dive towards the now smoking airfield below. Harriet followed, slamming the stick hard right and pushing down, and gasping at how the solid beast of an aircraft responded and threw her against her tightened harness. She turned so hard that she felt like she was entering a darkened tunnel as blackness narrowed her vision to a small cone straight ahead, a cone fixated on the yellow nose of the diving 109. The sky was littered with clouds of black smoke and orange fire, and brilliant white streaks of burning bullets flying in every direction. She gulped in the stinging smoke filled air coughing from the engine and focused, the darkness brightening slightly as she took the depth from her turning dive. She banked left, spun, and followed the 109 into a full throttle almost vertical climb to the clouds as the engine stopped coughing and ran smoothly again. She pushed the fire button again and watched the 109's rudder feather as small pieces of it splintered off in its wake. She was getting close. The 109 tipped and started to loop over to escape her, she followed suit and pulled the stick back into her stomach, feeling herself roll backwards as the engine started to stutter, and the sky flew by as once again her vision darkened. She could only just see through the sweat which was streaming down her face from under her flying helmet and stinging her eyes, as the 109 rolled out of the top of the loop into another diving turn. She had him. Just a little further to line up, and... Her Hurricane suddenly shuddered, and a hole appeared in the canopy frame just to the left of her head. She was sprayed with sparks, as a chunk of metal flipped up above her and disappeared in her slipstream. A cloud of black smoke billowed from the engine as it coughed again, and she looked into the small mirror just above her. A yellow nose was diving down from behind, and its guns were blazing. She'd been so caught up in chasing the 109 in front of her she'd forgotten there was another. She rolled hard left, and another stream of bullets narrowly missed the cockpit, a couple just scraping the underside of the left wing as she rolled. A push on the stick and she was in an inverted dive for the ground, and this time the engine failed, a yellow streak flashed before her eyes, and she hit the guns one more time, pulling right and giving the engine a chance to catch up, it stuttered back to life, and she thundered away with the guns until a cloud of black smoke filled the sky, and the 109 dived towards the ground. She dived after it, closing until she watched it go down, staying right on the tail of the smoking wreck and pulling straight up at the last second to avoid it as it skidded along the ground. She dipped her wing and saw the chasing 109 overshoot and pass underneath her, then dived back down and sat right on his tail. She was so close she couldn't miss. With a push of the button, the 109's wing ripped, and a fine cloud of petrol filled the air in a white haze and soaked her Hurricane. Another burst and her guns clicked empty, but it didn't matter, the 109's left wing was already burning fiercely. She followed it as the pilot increased speed and pulled it into a steep climb, feathering the flames until they just about dulled. It wasn't a minute after the climb started that his propeller fluttered. He levelled, opened his canopy, and flipped upside down. Seconds later, he was falling through the sky, and Harriet pulled a wide banking turn, watching as the pilot's parachute opened, then she quickly looked around for any other aircraft. There was nothing. Just her. The ground below was thick with black smoke, but she could still just about see the landing strip. Her engine coughed again, and she looked at the oil gauge. The temperature was off the chart, and the pressure was dropping. There wasn't that much fuel left, either. Another look around and Harriet did what few landing checks were possible. The Hurricane was hanging on to life by its metaphorical fingertips. The gauges were in every range they shouldn't be, and the engine was coughing and choking, so all she could do was scrub off speed and height, and this time remember to lower the undercarriage, which gave a reassuring clunk as it locked into position. She lined up, lowered the flaps, eased the throttle, then bounced onto the ground with a welcoming thud. A lick of flame lashed the cockpit from the engine, and she cut it immediately, assuming there was less chance of dying in a fiery ball of flames if the engine was cut and the fuel shut off. The quietness was deafening as the airframe creaked and bounced along the grass. She pulled the brake lever, lightly at first, then with more purpose until the Hurricane lurched, swung to the left and came to a halt. She was down.

Chapter 3

Arise, Sir Harry.

"Come on, Sir. Let's get you out of here," the rough voice of a Londoner barked as he leant into the cockpit and snapped the release of Harriet's harness. She looked up through the smoke at his big grey moustache, which was the defining feature of his rugged face. He was a giant of a man, or so he seemed as he towered above her in smart grey overalls with three stripes and a crown on the sleeve. He wiped the smoke from his eyes, then reached into the cockpit and grabbed her with his shovel like hands. In one hard jerk he had her off her seat and out onto the wing, then quickly dragged her away from the Hurricane, which was now surrounded by airmen with fire extinguishers. Once at a safe distance, she was allowed to drop to the ground. She dropped to her knees and coughed so hard that she felt like an entire lung was trying to make its way out of her mouth. She felt sick, and between the coughs, she retched and shook uncontrollably. "It's only a bit of smoke, Sir. The doc is on his way over, he won't be long," the same voice reassured in a calm and confident tone, before suddenly increasing a few decibels as he yelled across the field. "You lads, get that Hurricane stripped as soon as you've got the fire out, I want an assessment and serviceability plan in an hour!"

"Yes, Chief!" came the assorted replies.

"Bravo, Sully! That's the way to show them, old boy!" a very well spoken Squadron Leader roared excitedly as he arrived by the Chief's side and looked down at Harriet's coughing carcass. "Four of the buggers in one shooting match, you'll get another DFC for this, I'll make sure of it!"

"Bloody fantastic!" another young officer added as he and a few other pilots ran over to join them.

"The Hurricanes didn't come off too good," yet another pilot contributed as more of them gathered to watch Harriet choke. "Poor buggers likely didn't even know what hit them."

"It'd have been worse if Sully didn't get here in time to give the Hun a bloody nose," the Squadron Leader said. "I dare say they'd have beaten up the entire field and we'd all be walking home if it wasn't for him!" He leant down and took Harriet's shoulder, and guided her as she turned over to look up at the gathered crowd now surrounding her and chattering excitedly. "You're not Sully..." He said as the group fell into silence, leaving only the distant shouts of the ground crew to fill the thundering quiet.

"No, Sir. I'm not," Harriet coughed. Her face was filthy with smoke and sweat. She could be almost anybody, except a big blond man with a thick golden moustache, which is the person the gathered pilots were expecting to see.

"Well, lad. Who the hell are you?"

"It's Sully's kite, alright," one of the other pilots added.

"Harri..." Harriet started coughing before being able to finish. "Cornwall," she spluttered as she sat up, took the offered handkerchief and wiped her mouth and stinging eyes.

"Harry Cornwall?" the Squadron Leader asked while looking around the circle of shrugging pilots, none any the wiser.

"Maybe one of the new chaps they sent over when the scrap started, one the replacements?" one offered.

"One of the new chaps or old guard matters not, you've certainly earned your spurs today! So, where's Sully? Any news?" the Squadron Leader asked.

There was an audible gasp as Harriet pulled off the sweat soaked leather flying helmet and released her hair, letting it fall around her shoulders as she shook her head and ran her fingers through the sweaty knots. She unzipped the oversized jacket and opened the top couple of buttons of her overalls to feel the cooling air on her smoke smeared skin.

"Bloody hell!" came one remark

"I say..." came another.

"That's certainly not Sully," came yet another.

"Going to fill us in on the details, old girl?" the Squadron Leader asked once he'd composed himself.

"Harriet Cornwall," she said as she looked around at the gathering of men surrounding her with their mouths open in amazement. "Mister Sullivan crash landed at our airfield a short while ago. He was injured, shot in the leg and hand and couldn't fly back himself, so he asked me to bring his aeroplane here so you could use it in the fight against the Germans."

"You're a girl," one of the younger pilots uttered.

"Yes, Sir. I know," she replied. The pilot stood next to him rolled his eyes, while slapping his friend around the back of his head in mock chastisement. "Here, Mister Sullivan said I should give you this," she handed the Squadron Leader the card Sully had given her as she'd left.

"Well, Miss Harriet Cornwall, it's a pleasure to meet you, I'm Squadron Leader Barnes. What say we get you cleaned up and something to drink? Then we can talk about what just happened here."

"Thank you, that would be wonderful," Harriet replied. "I don't suppose you'd have a lady's room I could use?"

"I think we can sort something out," he said with a laugh. "Alright you lot, the show's over. Johnny, get a section in the air and have a bit of a nose about, will you? I don't want another episode like this. It should damned well never have happened in the first place, and will somebody find out what the hell that bloody French ack ack squadron was doing letting the Germans in the back door like that?"

"Yes, Sir," two officers replied before turning to their duties. The buzz of an engine in flight filled the air as Harriet composed herself, and she joined the gathered airmen searching the darkening late afternoon sky.

"There!" Barnes shouted as he pointed to the speck in the distance. "Now's a good time, Johnny, before whatever that is turns up and starts shooting. Everyone else take cover!"

"Gold Section Scramble!" the young officer, Johnny, yelled as he ran off towards the parked Hurricanes a few hundred paces away.

"Come along, no time to chat!" Barnes took Harriet by the arm and started running towards the mansion house. "Chief, get your lads off that crate until the threat passes. They can fix it later!"

"Sir!" the Chief replied. "Ground crews take cover!"

The whole airfield buzzed into life as men ran about their duties, shouting instructions and commentaries as they went. Harriet ran alongside Barnes, and he dragged her through the main doors of the old stately home, which she immediately noticed to be very well presented, and not the place she expected to see the RAF. She followed him up the stairs to a large reception room with a balcony that overlooked the field and landing strip. A few airmen were in the room, some looking out of the windows, others were doing paperwork at one of the few ornate dark wood desks strewn around the perimeter of the room. Barnes strode over to the large full length windows and stepped out onto the balcony, and Harriet stood by his side as a pair of Hurricanes bumped quickly along the grass strip, racing to intercept whatever was heading towards them. The buzzing grew louder, and Barnes put his hand to his eyes to block the lowering sun. They stood in nervous silence as the scrambled Hurricanes reached the speck, circled, then fell into formation to escort it towards the airfield. The speck was getting bigger, it was a biplane, which she didn't expect. As it got closer, she made out a flash of light blue livery against the silhouette of the fuselage, and as it reached the grass strip runway, a figure waved deliriously from the back seat. It couldn't be... could it? She rubbed her eyes and looked again. Old Number thirteen! It was Claude's Nieuport, and unless she was very much mistaken it was Sully in the back seat, but whoever was flying? As the three aircraft passed, she saw a flicker of blonde locks from the front cockpit.

"A turn up for the books," Barnes said, as he watched the procession head downwind for their final turn. "Looks like we're safe for now." He turned and strode across the room. "Where do you think you're going?" he asked as Harriet followed at his side.

"With you," she replied confidently.

"Oh?"

"That's my friend's aeroplane that just flew in, and I'm pretty sure it's my friend flying it." He didn't reply or send her away, so she walked as quickly as she could to match his pace, and smiled excitedly to herself as they walked over the grass to meet the Nieuport. There was something wrong, though; the picture ahead wasn't right.

"Bloody hell..." Barnes gasped. "Chief, get the crews ready!"

"Where's the undercarriage...?" Harriet asked nobody in particular, as her brain put the picture together. The escorting Hurricanes roared overhead and flew off with a wiggle of their wings to say goodbye, then hurried off to continue their patrol, leaving the Nieuport to drop closer and closer to the grass with just a pair of short jagged stumps hanging where the wheels used to be. She held her breath, they both did, as the stumps kissed the ground, lightly at first, then dug in as the fuselage pitched forward and the propeller struck the ground, sending lumps of mud and grass flying in every direction. There was nothing that could be done to control the aeroplane once it had touched down. It was just a case of waiting for it to do whatever it was going to do, which fortune dictated would be a straight plough forward until the nose was half buried, and the propeller was nothing more than a shattered mess, and the rest of the previously pristine light blue biplane had shuddered to a silent halt. Smoke and steam, and a fine rain of mud and grass surrounded the creaking aeroplane. Harriet stood and stared; she was wide eyed as the ground crews rushed in with fire extinguishers and axes, then she smiled as she heard Nicole's familiar voice.

"Thank you, but please remove your hands. I can walk perfectly well by myself!" Nicole appeared from the wreckage along with Sully, who was being carried on a stretcher.

"Comfortable, are we?" Barnes asked as the stretcher bearers carried Sully towards them.

"Now, now, Barney. Don't be like that," Sully replied. "I see you found your way here alright," he said as he acknowledged Harriet. "Got my kite here in one piece, I hope?"

"Just about," Barnes replied, as Nicole strolled over to join them. While walking, she casually removed her tatty old flying helmet almost exactly as Harriet had done, but with a sultry flair which stopped everyone in their tracks and demanded they look while she shook out her tousled blonde locks. "Your friend?" Barnes asked Harriet, who nodded in reply and smiled excitedly. "Looks like you've had a spot of bother," he continued as he looked back to Sully.

"This?" Sully asked as he lifted his slung arm and looked down at his splinted leg. "Yes, I suppose you could say that, but you should've seen the other bloke!"

"Get one?"

"Did I? Went down like a streamer, he did. Unfortunately, his pals didn't see the funny side, and the humourless arses saw fit to give me a slap before running off home. Ended up piling in at an old French field where I met these fair maidens," he smiled at the girls in turn before looking around the airfield. "Looks like you've had a spot of bother yourself old boy, Fritz had a pop at the airfield? I saw the wrecks of a couple of 109s back there."

"Something like that..." Barnes nodded. "It's good to see you, Sully," he said with a warm smile as they shook hands. "You men get Mister Sullivan to the doctor," he instructed the airmen holding the stretcher.

"Yes, Sir," the airmen replied, before carrying Sully on his way.

"Thanks, old boy, we'll talk later. Thank you, girls. My life is yours!" Sully called as he was carried off. Nicole was now standing by Harriet's side, and Barnes looked at them both.

"You two have earned a rest," Barnes said. "Get yourselves inside and talk to the Chef. Tell him I sent you, and he'll get you some tea and a sandwich.

That should sort you out," he smiled. "Come and see me when you've cleaned up a bit, and we'll talk about what happens next."

"Thank you," they replied in unison. He nodded politely, then turned away and headed back to the mansion house.

Chapter 4

Together Again

"What happened here?" Nicole asked as they sat on the grass with the tea and bread supplied by the Chef. He'd suggested, in the politest way he could muster, that they vacate his kitchen as he had an entire squadron to feed after sundown; so they took their things out in front of the house where they could sit picnic style and watch the busy airfield go by while they talked. "Did the Germans attack?"

"Kind of," Harriet replied as she bit into the bread. It was surprisingly fresh, and the sliver of cheese on top of it was soft and creamy, and a little smelly, just how she'd come to expect French cheese to be. "Anyway, how are you even here?"

"Grandpa thought that Sully's injuries were worse than they looked at first, so he decided it was important to try and get him back here to see a doctor and had me fly the Nieuport. Secretly I think he wanted to get me further from the Germans, too. We left not long after you."

"Will he be OK? Your grandpa, I mean?"

"I don't know," Nicole shrugged. "I hope so. He was nervous, I haven't seen him so nervous before, I think he was worried for me, and you of course. He set us off and said he'd collect grandma, and then they'd go to Reims to let your parents know you were safe."

"I'm sure they'll be OK," Harriet said with a forced smile. She wasn't sure at all, but she wanted to try at least to reassure Nicole. "So, what happened to your wheels?" she asked, quickly changing the subject.

"We met a German on the way here, and I had a little accident," Nicole replied with a slightly guilty look on her face.

"I see..." She was going to ask for details but thought better of it. "I'm happy you're here."

"Thank you, me too," Nicole replied with a forced smile. "Two hours ago, we were sunbathing, now look at us..."

"What do you think will happen now?" Harriet asked. She was nervous, and a little scared by all that had happened, but she was also a little excited.

"With what?"

"With us? With the war? Do you think it's as bad as it seems?"

"I don't know," Nicole shrugged. "Maybe the army will stop them, and it'll be all over, then we can go back to normal life."

"Nurse school, you mean?" Harriet asked with a frown of disappointment.

"I suppose," Nicole smirked. "Though I find flying aeroplanes in a war much more exciting."

"Me too!" Harriet giggled, then leant close to Nicole and whispered in her ear "I shot down a German."

"Shut up!"

"I did, I promise!"

"You can just about hold an aeroplane straight and level in the air. The only way you'd take down a German is if you crashed into them!"

"You're horrible!"

"I'm your friend, as much trouble as that brings me, and I wouldn't be much of a friend if I let you make up stories about shooting down Germans. Especially when we're sitting on an airfield and surrounded by fighter pilots, proper pilots!"

"I'm beginning to think it's a shame the Germans didn't get to our airfield before you left," Harriet rolled her eyes. "Maybe they'd go back home if they'd captured you and had to listen to your harshness."

"You'd miss me…"

"I'd enjoy the peace and quiet."

"That hurts me."

"'Ere, you two,'" a gruff Corporal shouted as he walked across the grass from the mansion. "When you've finished gassing, the boss wants a word!"

"You English are so charming," Nicole muttered to herself as she drained the tea from her cup.

"Quite..." Harriet added. "The boss?" she asked the Corporal.

"Squadron Leader Barnes, the tall, dark haired man you met earlier," the Corporal said with palpable frustration, "He's waiting for you up in the Ops Room."

"Ops Room?" Harriet shrugged questioningly.

"Give me strength..." the Corporal sighed. "The big room upstairs with the balcony?"

"Oh. Oh, yes, thank you," Harriet giggled.

"Bloody girls," he muttered as he wandered off. "No business on an air station."

The girls dropped their mugs and plates back in the kitchen, to the disgruntled thanks of the Chef, then headed back up the wide staircase to the balcony room, the Ops Room. Barnes was standing in the middle of the room facing a pair of pilots. Both were clad in smart black leather jackets, blue trousers, and black flying boots, and they were flanked by a couple of armed airmen. The room had an air of stale smoke and Barnes had a smirk on his face as he noticed the girls and beckoned that they join him, which they did.

"What is this?" one of the pilots asked in a very strong German accent. He was a little taller than Harriet, and maybe about the same age as Barnes.

His hair was golden, although now darkened by smoke, as was his face, and his white and blue silk scarf. The other pilot was much younger and not quite as confident as the blond. He was scratched and cut, and had his arm in a sling.

"Ladies, allow me to introduce you to Major Erwin Von Rosenheim of the Luftwaffe," Barnes said. "The Major is a veteran of Spain, Poland, and now France, with some thirty seven kills to his name."

"Thirty nine..." the Major corrected. Barnes nodded and smiled politely.

"Thirty nine," Barnes repeated before continuing, "and the young man to his left is Lieutenant Hummel, his number two."

"Hello..." Harriet said nervously, having never met a German pilot before. Nicole simply flicked her hair and dismissed them both, as only a French girl could.

"A pleasure to meet you, Fräulein," the Major said with a polite and smart bow of his head, something replicated by the Lieutenant. "Squadron Leader... These are your secretaries, perhaps?"

"Not at all, old boy," Barnes laughed as he slapped the Major on the shoulder. "I present to you, Miss Harriet Cornwall." He held his hand open towards Harriet.

"I'm afraid I don't understand, Squadron Leader?" the Major raised an eyebrow

"Miss Cornwall," Barnes continued, barely able to contain himself. "The Major has asked to meet the pilot that shot down his entire flight unaided, himself included,' he smiled before lowering his voice to a half whisper for comedic effect. "By the way, he was the chap who you chased around the sky and forced into his parachute." Harriet felt a blush spread across her face as the situation unravelled, and she was able to make sense of what was going on.

"I don't think I understand the English humour today, Squadron Leader?" the Major said softly, not entirely sure of what to say, or even what to think.

"No humour, old boy. You asked to meet the pilot who shot you down, and here she is."

"Sie ist ein Madchen," the Lieutenant said. The Major looked at him and nodded, then turned back to Harriet.

"He said that you're a girl," the Major translated.

"I am..." Harriet replied. "Though maybe I look like I need reminding of the fact, people seem to be telling me I'm a girl an awful lot today," she said with a frown of disappointment. The Major stared at her for a moment, then looked at Barnes once more and received a genuine nod and a shrug. It seemed to do the trick and provide the Major with the reassurance he apparently needed to believe what was happening. He stood smartly to attention and saluted. Harriet blushed some more, and Nicole smirked.

"An honour to meet you, Fräulein Cornwall. My compliments on your flying," he said politely.

"And mine on yours," she replied, quite unsure of what else she could say.

"I don't think your compliments are truly deserved, Fräulein. After all, you shot down four very experienced combat pilots on your own. I acknowledge your superiority, and perhaps young Hans and I are lucky that our war is now over, I don't think I'd like to meet you in the skies again," he said with a smile. Harriet blushed some more and didn't know where to look. She was only saved from the awkwardness by the arrival of another pilot entering the room with a confident air. He was a Sikh. Tall and elegant looking with a neatly trimmed beard and moustache, wearing an RAF blue turban, and carrying his brown sheepskin flying jacket and Mae West life jacket.

"You asked to see me, Sir?" he asked in a very well spoken English accent, which had only the slightest hint of his native Punjab.

"Ah yes, just one moment Raj," Barnes said warmly before turning back to the Germans. "Now, gentlemen. Headquarters have asked that we send you back to England post haste, so you'll be taking a very cramped ride in the back of one of our Lysanders this evening. I assume you're not going to give my pilot any trouble?"

"You have my word as a gentleman," the Major replied, "I think perhaps we've both had a bellyful of being shot at today, and maybe we shouldn't test our luck any further." He gave Harriet a knowing half smile while removing the blue and white silk scarf from his neck. On closer inspection, she could see that it was patterned with blue and white diamonds, and an intricately embroidered edelweiss flower hiding in the corner under the smoke and filth of battle. "Miss Cornwall," the Major continued, "it is customary for a downed pilot to surrender a memento to his victor in recognition of their skill. Sadly, Squadron Leader Barnes has already relieved me of my pistol, so all I can offer is my scarf." He handed it to Harriet, who with a nod of encouragement from Nicole took it and smiled politely. "My daughter made it for me before the war started. She's a little younger than you, but looks not too different, in a way."

"Oh... Oh, I can't," Harriet protested as she tried to hand it back to him.

"I'd be insulted if you didn't," the Major smiled. "You've already shot me out of the sky, and that's about all the insult I think I can stomach today. So, if you wouldn't mind?" Harriet nodded and smiled and blushed once again.

"OK, Sergeant. Escort these gentlemen down to the aeroplanes, would you?" Barnes instructed the airman guard before shaking the hands of the German pilots.

"Sir!" the armed escort barked, and with his colleague, they led the German pilots from the room.

"How's the hand?" Barnes asked the Sikh pilot.

"I've had worse playing cricket," came the confident reply, while he lifted and rolled his bandaged wrist and left hand as if to show it still worked.

"Flight Lieutenant Rajinder Singh," Barnes introduced the officer to the girls. "On loan from the Royal Indian Air Force, and one of my Flight Commanders." Singh stood smartly to attention and gave a small bow. "Mister Singh is one hell of a pilot and an absolutely terrible liar." The girls looked on nervously, not sure where Barnes was going with his dialogue. "He was flying that smoking Hurricane you saved from the Major and his flight when a cannon shell almost took off his hand. The doctor has patched it up, but I'm pretty sure it hurts like hell."

"It's quite tolerable, Sir," Singh replied with a smile. "Nothing more than a sprain."

"Are you going to be able to fly?"

"Oh, yes, Sir. I can't see why not."

"I suppose we'll see..." Barnes frowned, not entirely believing his young pilot. "Anyway, what happened on your patrol?"

"We ran into about thirty bombers over the Ardennes, Heinkels," Singh replied, as he walked over to the large map of northern France which had been pinned to the wall. He waved his hand over the Ardennes forest; a place Harriet and Nicole knew all too well from their walking holiday the previous summer. "They were heading south east and slightly below us. They hadn't seen us, so I led the flight in line astern. I took down the lead aircraft with a two second burst, and he went straight into a dive, I saw him crash. Then I pulled up a little and put another two second burst into the belly of the aircraft behind it, which went down the same way. As I passed through the formation, I saw them break in all directions. Unfortunately, Flight Sergeant Wilkes got caught in their crossfire and went down over the forest, there was no parachute I'm afraid, but he did get one of them before they got him. Pilot Officer Harris got one and shared one with Sergeant MacDonald, who got two."

"Five out of thirty, that's not a bad show, Raj."

"Yes, Sir. We didn't want to let them go," Singh smiled. "They seemed pretty shaken by our attack and turned back towards Germany.

Unfortunately, I'd taken a hit to my engine, as had Mister Harris, so I made the decision to turn back instead of giving chase."

"Sensible decision, Raj," Barnes gave a supportive nod. "I think it's fair to say you'd done more than enough."

"Thank you. Sadly, we didn't see the fighters that jumped us when we were landing..." Singh looked at Harriet for a brief moment before continuing. "Though we wouldn't have been able to do much if we had. My aeroplane was at its limit, the engine had seized right before I touched down, and Mister Harris wasn't able to turn and get out of the way."

"Yes... A shame about Harris, he's a good man."

"He is. He was hit in the leg and couldn't get out of the cockpit when his Hurricane spun into the ground and caught fire," Singh explained. "His burns are pretty bad, but the doctor seems to think he'll live, especially now he's heading back to England." Harris had been the first Hurricane shot down by the German attack that Harriet had interrupted, and the pilot whose Hurricane had burst into flames as the 109's cannons ripped through its wing and stopped it in its tracks.

"Sergeant MacDonald?"

"Not a scratch. Again."

"Luck of the devil, that one."

"Very much so."

"Puts you and old Grumpy MacDonald on the same now, doesn't it?" Barnes asked mischievously.

"Not quite, Sir," Singh replied with a degree of irritation. "He's a half kill ahead."

"Ah yes, that's right. Both aces now, though?"

"That's something," Singh rolled his eyes in disappointment.

"Well, talk to Cas later, and we'll get the combat report written up. You're sure that wrist isn't bothering you too much?"

"No... No, I'm fine," Singh replied with a pained smile, while once again rolling his wrist. "It's just a bit stiff."

"If you're sure? I don't mind releasing you and sending you back with one of the Hurricanes that needs a workshop overhaul. You could escort the Lysanders back over the Channel, then drop the Hurricane off and get your wrist looked at properly before bringing it back? I'm sure we'll still be here." Singh shook his head and smiled confidently, as the sound of engines starting drifted through the wide open balcony windows. "Last chance?" Barnes offered while turning and stepped out onto the balcony, followed by Singh and the girls. Down on the airfield the German pilots were having their hands tied, before being helped into the waiting Lysander. They could just make out Sully and Harris squeezed into the rear of the aeroplane next to it. When all was ready, the Lysanders were released by the ground crews and crept forward to line up with the end of the runway. Sully turned and waved a tired and mournful wave as they started their bouncing taxi across the grass strip. They lifted into the darkening sky and turned out of view, the sound of their engines dulling as they quickly raced into the distance, heading home with their precious cargo.

"Told you I shot down a German," Harriet whispered to Nicole as they watched.

"You didn't tell me you shot down two!" Nicole whispered forcefully in reply.

"That's because she shot down four," Barnes said, as he watched the patrolling Hurricanes circle the airfield. Nicole's eyes opened wide as he turned to face them. "Now, let's not pretend that any of us think you're safe here, or that this little spat is going to be over in a couple of days so you can go back home to your families, wherever they are," he said with a voice of concerned authority. The girls stood almost terrified, as though they were being chastised at school. "The truth is that we're in a bit of a spot," he continued. "Word is that Jerry has given both the British and French armies a huge bloody nose, and I can't imagine they're going to stop at that.

They've got us on the run, and they know it. The air forces haven't fared much better, either. Over half the French Army Air Force has already been wiped out, and most of our squadrons out here have had a bit of a pasting, to say the least, as you've seen today; but we've got to keep flying otherwise the Luftwaffe will have total air superiority, and the army will be totally buggered." He took a drag off his cigarette and put a hand on his hip. "The two of you were supposed to be heading to England on one of those Lysanders. Unfortunately, that's no longer on the cards, largely thanks to your own efforts in shooting down the Major and giving us a couple of valuable prisoners who took your places on the bus home. Anyway, my point is that as of now I have a number of Hurricanes in various states of repair, and fewer pilots than I have aeroplanes. That wouldn't usually be a bad thing as it's always good to have spares, but if we have to get out of here in a hurry, it'll mean leaving perfectly good aeroplanes behind. So... I'm going to have to do something against my better judgement. Until we can work out what to do with the pair of you, I wondered if you'd both be on standby to work as ferry pilots?" Harriet and Nicole smiled at each other. "Now, don't get carried away! You won't be going anywhere near a German. Again..." he boomed. "We have a reserve airfield picked out should things get a bit dicey around here, and all you'll be required to do is fly the kites from here to there. That's it, simple." He looked at them questioningly, and they both nodded excitedly in agreement. "I thought that'd be your answer," he smiled. "I'm not entirely sure if I'm allowed to do this, but I'll get the Adjutant to talk to Headquarters when he's back and square it away somehow. He'll appreciate the challenge," Barnes smirked to himself before continuing. "Well, we'd better get you up to speed; it's obvious that you can both fly, and you've already had a trip in a Hurricane. How many hours have you both got in the air?"

"A little over three hundred," Harriet replied.

"Four hundred for me," Nicole added with a half smirk aimed in Harriet's direction.

"Not a bad total," Barnes nodded. "So I don't think we need to teach you much about flying, more familiarisation with the Hurricane. I think you'd be able to take care of that, Raj?"

"Happy to, Sir," Singh replied.

"Good. I'll get word back to command that you're here, and put out a request for word of your families if you give us the details. The Adjutant will go through the navigation with you both so you can find your way around the local area. I'm assuming you can both read a map?"

"How do you think we got here?" Nicole asked dismissively. Barnes nodded and conceded her point silently.

"Thank you, in that case, for both offering to help, and for what you did today. Mister Singh will look after you, in the meantime, I'll sort you some digs. If anyone asks, let's just say that you're ferry pilots with the Air Transport Auxiliary, for now. I'm pretty sure they have lady pilots."

"Thank you!" they replied in unison, then left the balcony with Singh.

"Oh, Harry?" he called after them. Harriet turned and looked at him. He reached behind his back and pulled a pistol holster from under his jacket. "I think you've earned this." She looked for a moment, then took the holster and pulled out and examined the shiny black Walther pistol with its gleaming gold grips embossed with silver and gold edelweiss flowers. "Careful with that, the Major told me it was very expensive." He gave her a wink. "Now the two of you stay out of trouble. Learn your aeroplanes, read the maps, then come join us for supper later."

Chapter 5

The Not So Still of The Night

"So, you're the one I have to thank for my being here?" Singh asked as they walked through the main door, and out towards the scattering of bell tents which sat on the lawn between the house and the grass runway.

"Excuse me?" Nicole replied.

"Your friend, I'm told she shot down the Germans who attacked us while landing, and in doing so saved my life."

"Ah... Yes, that's her," Nicole said as she rolled her eyes and gave Harriet a nudge as she blushed once again. An automatic and uncontrollable response which Harriet was both acutely aware of, and increasingly frustrated with.

"You have my thanks," Singh said while briefly making eye contact and giving her a polite nod, though nothing that could be mistaken for a smile.

"You're welcome," Harriet replied nervously.

"Your names?"

"Harry... Harriet Cornwall," Harriet half stuttered, still almost uncontrollably nervous.

"Nicole Delacourt," Nicole replied nonchalantly, maintaining her air of detached indifference.

"A pleasure to meet you both. As you heard, I'm Flight Lieutenant Rajinder Singh."

"Charmed, I'm sure," Nicole replied dryly, drawing a look of disappointment from Harriet.

They walked to a pair of Hurricanes which were set a little apart from the others. They were surrounded by a horseshoe of sandbags stacked to just below shoulder height and topped with camouflage netting raised above the emplacement with poles.

"Sergeant Kaye?" Singh asked the airman holding a long wrench in place at the front of one of the Hurricane's engines. The airman winced as he pulled on the wrench, and nodded at the long legs stretching out of the cockpit, clad in blue trousers and flying boots.

"AP?" the airman shouted. "AP!" he repeated louder when there was no reply.

"What?!" came the irritated reply as the young female engineer lifted her head and torso out of the cockpit and glared at the airman, who then nodded at Singh and the girls.

"Mister Singh..." The airman pointed. She followed his gaze, looked at Singh and then the girls in turn, then back at Singh.

"Sir?" she asked, not any less irritated.

"Sergeant Kaye, I have a job for you," Singh replied formally, yet politely.

"I have enough of those, Sir," she replied curtly, then looked back into the cockpit, appearing to dismiss Singh. She fiddled impatiently with something then looked back. "Let me tighten the throttle cable, and I'll be down." She leant into the cockpit again, and Singh looked at the girls briefly, looking just slightly impatient and a little bemused by the non commissioned officer making him wait while she finished her work. Harriet looked at Nicole, who raised an eyebrow in reply; both were surprised to see a female mechanic. Kaye finished a couple of very long and awkwardly silent minutes later, then ran down the wing and jumped to the ground before walking around the wingtip and standing in front of them. She gave the airman a nod, "You can finish off tightening it." With her hands on her hips, she looked expressionlessly at Singh. "Yes, Sir?" She was a tall and fearsome looking woman with a strong yet elegant jaw and piercing hazel brown eyes which she squinted slightly while focusing. Her chocolate brown shoulder length hair was scraped back into a short ponytail which held it out of her face.

“Ladies, this is Sergeant AP Kaye, one of our senior aircraft engineers,” Singh said. "Sergeant Kaye, this is Miss Cornwall and Miss Delacourt, they're Air Transport Auxiliary pilots, and they're attached to us temporarily.”

"I'm not sure how this affects me?" Kaye shrugged.

"They'll be ferrying our spare Hurricanes to the reserve field, should we need to withdraw from the area in a hurry," he continued.

"Yes?" AP asked.

"Yes, and I was hoping you'd get them started with a crash course on the Hurricane, so to speak. I'll be back in a while to take them through the flying side, but I'd be grateful if you could run them through the technical aspects of the aeroplane? Nothing too in depth, just what they need to get from a to b." He asked in such a way that couldn't be refused, and Kaye rolled her eyes and pursed her lips, and fired a look of irritation at the girls.

"I have a lot of work to do on these two Hurricanes if I'm going to get them airworthy for tomorrow," she protested.

"I'm sure it won't take up too much of your time, Kaye. I'll be back before long." Singh said as he turned to leave. "Ladies, Sergeant Kaye will look after you until I return." He quickly marched out of the sandbagged hide before she could protest any further.

"It seems everybody is keen to let somebody else look after us today," Harriet said to herself as they watched him leave.

"That's because we're in the middle of a war, and nobody has time to babysit," Kaye replied, pulling their attention back to her.

"Carburettor isn't going anywhere, AP," the airman said as he removed the wrench.

"Get the cowlings back on," AP barked. "We'll need to give them a test later." She looked at the girls for a moment, then shook her head in disappointment. "Well, let's get started."

"Yes, let's," Nicole replied, almost sarcastically.

"If you pay attention you may be able to land your aeroplane properly next time, instead of piling it nose first into the ground and hoping for the best," Kaye fired back at Nicole.

"I had no wheels!" Nicole said defensively.

"Not my problem," AP replied. "Now, the Hurricane is a bit more technical than that bucket of bolts you flew in here," she continued as she frowned at Nicole, who for once was desperately biting her tongue. "There's a lot to learn if you're to get it to the reserve field in one piece. Instead of scraping to a halt in a ball of flames," she went on while switching her frown to Harriet.

"I don't really think that was my fault," Harriet protested, "the Germans shot me up pretty bad..."

"Yes, I saw, but he only got his shot on you because your engine spluttered and you were distracted trying not to stall, weren't you?" AP stood with her hands on her hips while she waited for the reply.

"What? How would you even know that?" Harriet asked as she blushed.

"Because it's a fault with the Merlin engine, the marvel of modern engineering that powers the Hurricane, and the Spitfire for that matter. The collective geniuses at Rolls Royce designed it with a carburettor that has a large float chamber, instead of it being fuel injected like the Benz engine in the 109. That means when you perform certain manoeuvres, you risk flooding or starving the engine, and that makes it stutter and eventually stop. Which is why you dropped away, and he got his guns on you. Flying is about more than the stick and rudder, ladies; it's about knowing your aeroplane. Now follow me, and I'll show you around. Unless either of you has any more excuses that you'd like to bore me with before we start?" The girls looked at each other before shaking their heads. Sergeant Kaye was young looking, but she was venomous and thunderous, not the type of person anyone would dare trifle with. She guided them around the Hurricane, pointing out everything they needed to know both inside and out, and having them repeat it back to her, with the occasional question to check they were paying attention. She had another pair of mechanics running around tidying up the aeroplanes before sending for an armourer who checked the guns over while she continued her teaching. Finally, as Singh returned, followed by an airman with an arm full of kit, a fuel bowser turned up and refuelled both Hurricanes.

"Finished?" he asked.

"It'd take a lot longer than that," AP replied, "but they're all yours."

"Thank you, Kaye," he replied. "The CO said they should get comfortable with these two aeroplanes. I'm told that you've got them both serviceable?"

"They're better than serviceable, I've been working on the carburettors to stop them failing," AP said, almost a little hurt at the suggestion that she hadn't gone above and beyond.

"Is that an authorised adjustment?" Singh asked with a frown.

"Of course it's not authorised!" she replied dismissively. "Anyway, they're probably the best Hurricanes available to the squadron now I've finished them, and I'd prefer it if they went to experienced pilots."

"And I'm sure the CO will consider that when our replacement pilots get here. Has the Chief signed off on your modifications?"

"Not yet."

"I see... Are they safe to fly?"

"Have I ever released an aeroplane not safe to fly, Sir?"

"No... No, you haven't Sergeant Kaye. OK, let's get a few circuits done before last light. We'll talk about the modifications later, but for now let's get these two strapped in." Singh turned to the girls and handed them both an off yellow Mae West life jacket, then gave Nicole a worn and tarnished brown sheepskin Irvin jacket and matching flying helmet, both of which smelled ominously of smoke. "Their previous owner won't be needing them." Nicole frowned in mild distress at the thought of what may have happened to their previous owner. The airman also had a couple of pairs of brand new RAF issue fleece lined black flying boots, which the girls quickly changed into right away. "OK, let's get you fastened in, there are parachutes on the wings. Kaye, would you help Miss Cornwall?"

"Harriet, isn't it?" AP asked as she looked her in the eyes.

"Harry to friends..." Harriet replied nervously.

"Well, Harriet, it's your lucky day," AP said, making Harriet frown a little at her decision not to call her Harry. She was led around the wingtip, where AP pointed to the large letter H painted on the fuselage of the Hurricane. Harriet's face lit up. "H for Harry..." AP said before helping Harriet into her parachute harness, then into the cockpit where she was strapped in tight.

"Do you remember everything I told you?" AP asked.

"Yes, I think so," Harriet replied as she fought the butterflies in her stomach.

"Don't think so, know so!" AP corrected. "Be confident! If you're not, the aeroplane will bite you, or the enemy will kill you. Own it or be owned!"

"Yes. Got it," Harriet replied as confidently as she could. "Now, if you'd be so kind as to jump down off my aeroplane. I wouldn't want to take off with you hanging on to the wing," she added with a growing sense of confidence dragged from deep within.

"Don't get too carried away," AP said as she finished pulling the last strap tight enough to make Harriet wince. "This is my aeroplane, and you make sure you bring it back to me in one piece!"

"Yes, Ma'am!" Harriet replied.

"Sergeant," AP corrected.

"Excuse me?" Harriet asked.

"Sergeant AP Kaye, aircraft engineer, Women's Auxiliary Air Force," she said sternly as she removed her flight boot from the cockpit ledge. "Don't call me Ma'am, I work for a living!" She turned and jumped off the wing.

Harriet looked around the cockpit at the many instruments and levers, and thought through what she'd just been told in her whirlwind lesson on the controls of a Hurricane. It had been significantly more in depth than the urgent briefing Sully had given her a few hours earlier, but still nowhere near what she needed to make her as competent as she'd like to be. She did, however, very clearly remember the warning that touching the undercarriage lever when not in the air would have her grounded, in all ways imaginable. AP's words still rattled in her ears, 'confidence!', 'Own it!' She looked out of the cockpit at Singh and AP as they stood talking while a gaggle of airmen came into the Hurricane pen and buzzed around the aeroplanes. As was typical for Harriet, her mind started to wander from the task immediately at hand. She found herself thinking about AP, a young woman who was obviously a very talented engineer, so gifted that the RAF let her maintain and repair their front line combat aeroplanes. It impressed Harriet, but more than that it intrigued her. Her father had told her repeatedly that girls can't and don't join the RAF, yet here she was being told what to do by not just a girl, but a girl with rank, and a skill. In addition, she'd been told she was a temporary ferry pilot in the Air Transport Auxiliary, as though girls flew all the time, and Barnes hadn't even questioned it. Harriet's outlook on life had already changed immeasurably, despite having only been involved in the war for a few short hours. How was she going to be able to accept being anything less now that she'd tasted a different life? How would she tell her father she wanted to join the Women's Auxiliary Air Force?

"Anytime today!" AP shouted, breaking Harriet's daydreams and pulling her back to the golden light of the late afternoon. She looked over and the engine of Nicole's Hurricane, marked with a large letter P, was already roaring, and a pair of ground crew airmen were guiding the wingtips as she edged forward out of the Hurricane pen. "You'll need your engine running if you're going to fly. I know we didn't cover that in our brief, but I expected it'd be something an experienced ATA pilot already knew," she said with a look of disappointment. Harriet blushed, nodded, and chastised herself silently in that order while she prepared the cockpit.

"Clear prop!" Harriet finally shouted, to which AP rolled her eyes and raised her hands in the air while looking around as if to suggest Harriet was simply delaying the inevitable by shouting a warning to clear when there was nobody there. Harriet became more flustered, then took a deep breath and calmed herself before starting the engine, all while repeating to herself 'be confident! Own it.' The Merlin turned over then spluttered into life, firing a beautiful cocktail of flames, sparks, and blue smoke from the exhausts. AP pulled the start lead from the plug on the fuselage and pulled the trolley starter away, before climbing up the wing, reaching into the cockpit and flicking a switch. She briefly looked down at the pistol holster Harriet had stuck in the top of her flying boot to keep it safe and stop it digging into her ribs while sitting. Her expression didn't change; she looked Harriet in the eyes and spoke as quietly as she could while remaining audible.

"Don't break my aeroplane!" AP warned as she took hold of the tip and waved ahead. Harriet nodded and let the Hurricane ease forward, then followed Nicole in taxiing to a holding spot at the end of the grass strip. AP left her and, with the airman from the other wingtip, they walked over and joined Nicole's crew. Nicole looked over and smiled excitedly, her eyes were wide with anticipation and showed brightly through the darkness of the smoke and filth smeared across her face, smoke which she hadn't yet been able to remove from her face since crashing the Nieuport. Harriet smiled back, then rubbed her face and saw the black smoke on her fingers. She was just as filthy, coated with a paste of sweat, smoke, and cordite from her earlier altercations. Singh rolled up in his Hurricane and took his place to Harriet's left.

"OK, for this flight we'll be identified as Black Section," Singh said over the radio. "I'm Black One. Cornwall, you'll be Black Two and Delacourt Black Three. Understood?"

"Black Three, understood," Nicole replied.

"Black Two, understood," Harriet added, frustrated that Nicole had replied ahead of her when there was an obvious order to these things. In her mind, anyway.

"OK, let's get going," Singh instructed. The three aeroplanes roared as their throttles were pushed open, and steadily they bounced down the grass strip three abreast. Harriet felt herself smiling again. It was a smile that stretched wide across her face as she pushed the stick forward a little to lift the tail, then bumped and caught the air beneath her wings and felt the unmistakable sensation in her stomach as she pulled back on the stick and floated up into the bumpy and choppy air. The cool breeze, the warmth of the sun, and the smell of the engine was like nothing else. Since her very first flight when she was eleven, she'd loved taking off into the liberating solitary freedom of the air, and experiencing it in such a powerful beast as a Hurricane just made it better. They spent thirty minutes doing circuits, flying around and around, approaching, landing, taking off again, climbing, turning, flying straight and level, all of the basic flying they'd need to do to get their aeroplanes to the reserve airfield. The pair of Hurricanes that had been patrolling the area even joined them and flew in formation, making Harriet smile even more as the five aeroplanes moved through the air as one, until the patrol gave them a wave before leaving again to continue their guard. "I think that'll do," Singh said eventually, a phrase that Harriet knew would come but still made her heart sink. "Follow me in." He led them down, and for the final time they touched down, but this time they eased the throttle back instead of throwing it forward, and under Singh's orders taxied back towards their Hurricane pen and the waiting ground crews who pushed the aeroplanes back into their sandbagged homes once the engines had been cut.

"See, I brought it back safe and sound," Harriet said confidently as AP appeared on her wing and helped her unfasten the harness.

"Good!" AP replied bluntly. "Anything I need to worry about?"

"Only the compass, I think."

"What's wrong with it?"

"I don't know... I was hoping you'd be able to tell me," Harriet said with a frown. "It kept swinging wildly for no apparent reason, and at times showed the opposite direction entirely to that we were flying in. I checked with the others, and it was this compass that was faulty."

"OK... I'll add it to the list," AP sighed. "Anything else? Engine running, OK?"

"Fine, or as far as I could tell."

"Out you get, then," AP said and held Harriet's arm as she stood, then stepped back to let her out of the cockpit and immediately climbed in and started tinkering.

"Bye, then..." Harriet muttered and walked off the wing, with a small jump down to the grass.

"Leave your parachute on the wingtip," AP shouted after her without looking out of the cockpit.

"Isn't it incredible!" Nicole asked excitedly as she put her arm through Harriet's, and they walked away from the aeroplanes and out of the pen.

"It's better than incredible!" Harriet exclaimed, at least as excitedly as Nicole.

"So when this is all over, and we get home," Nicole continued, "how are you going to tell your father that you want to be a pilot again?"

They both laughed as they joined Singh, who was strolling slowly in the same direction to allow them to catch up with him. They walked together to the operations room, where Barnes was talking to a pair of pilots wearing uniforms distinctly different to those of the RAF.

"Well?" Barnes asked Singh, turning his attention from his guests for a moment.

"They'll do," Singh replied.

"Good. Hopefully, we won't need to use them," Barnes said, before turning back to his guests. "Mister Singh, this is Lieutenant Hugo Romain of the French Armee de l'Air, and Lieutenant Lech Popowo of the Polish Air Force. They've just arrived via the German lines; would you show them to the Mess and get them somewhere to sleep? They'll be staying with us for the night."

"Yes, Sir. Gentlemen?" Singh invited.

"Get something to eat and get some rest," Barnes told the visitors. They were smart, but scruffy looking at the same time, their faces and uniforms showing the wear of battle. Each carried a small grey bag holding what few possessions they could escape with, and the Pole had a short stubby barrel held tightly under his arm. Both nodded in agreement with Barnes' instructions. "Mister Singh is one of my Flight Commanders. He'll get you squared away. We'll talk about getting you to where you need to be in the morning." They shook hands and left with Singh, who gave the girls another polite nod as he left, passing another officer who was heading into the room. "Good timing, Cas. Any luck?" Barnes asked the tall, golden haired older looking man, who was wearing the pristine and unmistakable officer's uniform of the RAF. Though unlike almost every other officer they'd met so far, there was no sign of flying gear other than the pilot's wings on his tunic, which appeared at first glance to be a little different to those worn by all of the other pilots. Harriet looked a little closer as he crossed the room, and both casually and skilfully threw his grey blue peaked cap on the hat stand without even looking. His wings, which sat above a row of medal ribbons, were slightly different in shape, though almost unnoticeably so; and they had the letters RFC instead of RAF in the centre, denoting the Royal Flying Corps, the predecessor of the RAF, and identifying the wearer as a pilot who had flown in the last war.

"Not much," Cas replied. "The Mayor spent his time demanding to know how we intended to defend his town if the Germans come, and subsequently wasn't really in the mood for talking about keeping the roads clear for our vehicles should we have to pull out in a hurry."

"I see..." Barnes said. "Well, we'll just have to do our best if, and when the time comes, I suppose."

"I managed to pick these up, though," Cas said as he pulled a bottle from the small crate he was carrying. He had a glint of mischief in his cobalt blue eyes as he passed it to Barnes.

"Champagne…" Barnes' eyes lit up. "1921 Bollinger, very nice," he said approvingly, as he inspected the bottle.

"Six of them, actually," Cas replied as he put the crate on his desk. "In this crate, at least."

"Should I ask where they came from?" Barnes asked.

"Believe it or not, the old priest from the town church," Cas casually replied. "We met him by the side of the road. The wheel on his cart was playing up, snapped a spindle by the looks of things, so we gave him and his cargo a lift in the truck."

"His cargo?" Barnes raised an eyebrow.

"Forty one crates of fine Champagne, thirty five of which are now being buried in an old tunnel in the woods along with a few other bits and pieces," Cas smirked. "He was quite sure that the Germans will be here before the week is out, and he wanted to keep his investment safe. His gratitude for our help came in the form of a few crates, and a blessing, of course."

"Of course… That explains why you took so long..."

"Quite... Blessings can take a while," Cas said quite casually, as though it was something he was involved in every day. "That and the town's more than a little chaotic. Lots of civilian refugees moving through. French, Belgian, Dutch, even some French army units. All heading south and west."

"Great, the roads are going to be a nightmare!" Barnes sighed.

"That French air defence unit has cleared off, too. The one at the farm down the road that was supposed to be looking after us."

"Yes... I sent Warrant Officer Peters over there a while ago to have words with their commander. Nowhere to be seen. Which explains our little run in earlier."

"Oh?"

"Four of the yellow nosed bastards sneaked in at treetops and shot up Raj's flight as they were landing,"

"Bloody hell, everyone OK?"

"We lost Wilkes to enemy fire over the Ardennes, along with Sully's flight, and Harris when they were jumped on landing. His Hurricane went up like a Roman candle, he'll live, but he was badly burned. I've sent him back to England in the Lysanders, along with Sully and a couple of Germans who dropped in. Thanks to these two," Barnes nodded in the direction of the girls. "Which leads me to the next matter."

"Good afternoon," Cas said politely, one eyebrow raised inquisitively.

"Good afternoon," the girls replied.

"Cas, meet temporary ferry pilots Harriet Cornwall, and Nicole Delacourt of the ATA," Barnes said. "Ladies, Flight Lieutenant Salisbury, or Cas to practically everybody who's ever met him, which seems to be most people I can think of, somehow. Cas is the Squadron Adjutant. He makes sure everything around here gets done the way it should be, like registering temporary ferry pilots with Headquarters, so they know who you are and how much to pay you."

"A pleasure," Cas said warmly, as he shook their hands while looking questioningly at Barnes. "I wondered who in the squadron had taken to wearing Chanel." Harriet blushed slightly, while Nicole suppressed a smirk.

"I gave their details to Corporal Wilson to be processed," Barnes continued. "You may want to have a talk with them after you've talked to Raj, they both have combat reports that'll need filing, and you'll probably need to talk to Headquarters and discuss how this all works. I'm sure you'll be able to square it all away."

"I'll get on that..." Cas replied with a smile.

"For now, I wonder if you'd take them to Section Officer Finn? They can room share with her in the old coach house. They'll need some hot water and a chance to clean up, and they could probably do with a few bits and pieces from the stores if you can find anything useful."

"I'll take care of it."

"Food in the Mess in an hour, ladies," Barnes said. "Section Officer Finn will show you the way. I'll see you later."

"If you'd like to follow me?" Cas asked with a smile, before leading them through the house, across the courtyard, and to a blue wooden door which Cas knocked on firmly. "So, combat reports?" he asked while they waited.

"I'm not sure you'd call it that, really," Harriet said coyly.

"I forced down a Messerschmitt 109," Nicole added confidently. "I took off his propeller, and he crash landed." Harriet stared at her in silence. "What?" Nicole demanded innocently.

"What?" Harriet echoed.

"You're staring at me," Nicole frowned.

"When did you take the propeller off a Messerschmitt?" Harriet asked. "And how? Hanging out of your cockpit with a wrench?"

"Don't be ridiculous." Nicole replied dismissively "I flew my undercarriage into his propeller."

"Deliberately?" Cas asked, mesmerised at the conversation.

"Of course deliberately," Nicole replied in disgust. "I'm not an idiot! He was trying to shoot us down, and we had no guns, so I did what I could and used my undercarriage to shatter his propeller. I saw his face, and he was very surprised," she said with a giggle, while Harriet and Cas continued to stare at her in disbelief. She noticed their faces and shrugged again. "What? Ask Mister Sullivan, if you like. He was with me at the time."

"Mister Salisbury?" the stern looking woman who opened the door asked as she stood before them dressed in RAF blue. She was pretty, with dark eyes and blonde hair tied in a neat bun, though the sternness of her expression hardened her looks. She didn't smile, but her firmness was different from AP's austere and distanced lack of emotion, it felt cold.

"Section Officer Finn," Cas greeted her almost jovially. "We have two young guests from the ATA who will be staying the night, and the CO thought it better they bunk with you."

"Oh... I see..." Finn replied, not appearing to be overly impressed with the idea.

"There you go," Cas said to the girls. "Let's talk about combat reports later. I'll have some hot water sent over, and you can get yourselves cleaned up before supper. Section Officer Finn will bring you down to the Mess," he said with a smile, before turning and marching off, and leaving the girls faced with the cold looking woman, who was in the middle of switching her look from icy to disdainful. She stood back and gestured the girls to follow her, which they did, up the narrow stairs to a white walled room above the old coach house. There were two beds, both neatly made, one of them with a few bits and pieces laid on and around it. A rope had been rigged across the corner, along which several different items of clothing were hanging.

"I'm afraid the two of you will have to share," Finn said as she pointed to the spare bed.

"That's OK," Harriet replied. It hadn't been the first time they'd shared a bed. Cold winter nights at the school practically demanded it.

"And don't touch any of my things!" Finn snapped. "The bathroom is through there. I've finished so use it as you will."

"Thanks," Nicole replied with a heavy dose of sarcasm.

"You're welcome," Finn said abruptly, as she sat at the desk beside her bed. "I'm afraid I wasn't expecting visitors, but I do have a report to finish writing before supper, so I'd be grateful if you could keep the noise to a minimum."

"English hospitality," Nicole mumbled.

"Excuse me?" Finn asked, without turning to look at them. Harriet shook her head at Nicole, she'd known her long enough to see an argument when it was coming. Nicole shrugged and threw her jacket and flying helmet by the bed, Harriet followed suit, and they both headed for the bathroom, which was almost the same size as the bedroom but much less appealing. A tin bath and a bucket stood in one corner, and a line was strung from wall to wall, holding what they could only assume to be Finn's laundered underwear.

"Her underwear is as cold and uninviting as she is," Nicole half whispered, sending Harriet into a fit of giggles. "It's true. I bet she's not married."

"Neither are we!" Harriet managed to counter through her giggles.

"We are young and beautiful," Nicole said as she flicked her hair.

"She's not ugly." Harriet offered in Finn's defence.

"Maybe not on the outside..." Nicole replied with the raise of an eyebrow.

"Stop it!" Harriet giggled. Another knock on the door downstairs had Finn letting out an angry sigh from the next room before scraping her chair loudly across the wooden floor and stomping down the stairs to answer.

"Hot water, Ma'am. For the ATA pilots." A northern male voice announced.

"I'm not sure why it would take quite so many of you," Finn replied with annoyance. "Upstairs," she barked. A clatter of boots on wood followed, and four airmen formed a queue at the bathroom door, each carrying two oversized buckets of steaming hot water.

"Mister Salisbury's compliments, Ma'am," the leading airman said as politely as he could manage. He was a big man with a Newcastle accent, or somewhere close to that area. "In the bath, Ma'am?"

"Oh, yes. Yes, thank you," Harriet replied as she pulled Nicole out of their way, and let the airmen pour bucket after bucket of steaming hot water into the bath. The tall Geordie then handed a couple of towels embroidered with the letters C.A.S. in the corner, and a bar of soap to Harriet. "Thank you so much, Mister?"

"Grieves, Ma'am. Leading aircraftman Albert Grieves," he replied humbly.

"It's very kind of you, Mister Grieves, Albert, thank you to all of you," Harriet smiled. "Unfortunately, we don't have much to offer by way of thanks."

"Oh, no Ma'am," he protested, "just doing our jobs."

"When you've finished, Grieves," Finn hissed from the next room. Grieves and the others smiled then quickly left to be replaced in the doorway by Finn, who listened for the door to close downstairs before turning back to the girls. "It's clear that the two of you have no idea about the Royal Air Force or the behaviour expected of those in it, so I'll give you a head start. For some reason, the CO saw fit to invite you to stay, though the temporary nature of this act may yet be his saving grace. As such, you are to live with the officers, and you should behave as such. That means you don't offer anything 'by way of thanks' to enlisted men, it's their job to serve, and you never call them by their first names, ever. Understand?"

"Oh, I understand," Nicole said in the tone that usually signalled the pending arrival of a volume change.

"Finally, for now, this is an RAF unit," Finn continued, "and I'm your superior officer for the duration of your stay. You'll behave like ladies and officers, maintain the discipline of the service, and set a good example to the section of WAAFs I have here. You'll also call me Ma'am, and you'll do as I say, when I say, and show me the respect that is afforded to my rank. Which includes not passing nasty schoolgirl comments about my underwear. Are we clear?"

"Perhaps I should make something clear for you, lady!" Nicole snarled. She stepped forward, her voice already raising a few decibels as she moved towards Finn, who squared her shoulders and pushed out her chest in an attempt to assert her authority.

"Not now..." Harriet said as she stepped between them, and put her hand on Nicole's shoulder. "Come on. We don't want the water to go cold after those nice men went to the trouble of bringing it up here for us." Harriet had developed a way of talking to Nicole that calmed her almost instantly, using a softness and gentleness which took the sting out of Nicole's anger. It had been used to successfully diffuse many potentially damaging situations, some of which would undoubtedly have led to them both being expelled from school. With her other hand, Harriet started to close the door.

"There... A bit of English decorum," Finn continued as the door was closing. "Maybe if you French had a little more discipline, your country wouldn't need our help to save you from the Germans, again." Harriet pushed the door closed with a click.

"I'll punch her in the face," Nicole blustered angrily.

"I know," Harriet said softly, "and she'd deserve it. But let's save it for when we're leaving. It's almost dark out, and we kind of need somewhere to stay."

"Tomorrow I'll punch her in her stupid English face."

"Careful," Harriet added jovially, "the English outnumber you at the moment."

"It's people like her that led to a revolution in France," Nicole said, still not able to let it go. "The stuck up, pompom snob!"

"Pompous," Harriet laughed.

"What?"

"Pompous. I think you mean pompous. A pompom is a woollen ball like your sailors wear on their hats."

"Stupid English language," Nicole blustered, fighting to hide a smile from her face, which was soon followed by a giggle. "Well, maybe she's a woollen ball, too. She has all of the charm and personality of one." They both giggled and started to kick off their flying boots so they could get ready for a bath.

"You didn't tell me you'd crashed into a 109."

"I could hardly compete with your shooting down four of them, could I?"

"It's not about competing," Harriet laughed. "How did it happen?"

"It's all such a blur," Nicole said with a shrug, "Grandpa insisted that I should fly low to avoid the attention of any Germans, and I thought we had until a pair of them saw us. They were so high above that I thought we'd passed by unseen, but in a light blue aeroplane you're always going to be a target, I suppose." She dropped her overalls to the floor and stepped out of them. "There, my underwear is much better, don't you think?" she asked confidently.

"Get in the bath!" Harriet said with a laugh as she stepped out of her overalls.

"Even yours is better, though I had to educate you some time ago."

"Nicole, bath!" Harriet insisted. Nicole sighed then pulled off her underwear and stepped into the large steaming metal tub. Harriet stepped in behind her and felt the searing heat climb her legs. "Gosh, it's hot!" she gasped.

"Let's sit together," Nicole offered, and Harriet nodded in agreement. "Three, two, one, sit!" They both sat, and a small tidal wave of hot water lapped them both and spilt over onto the wooden floorboards. Both gasped and grabbed at the sides of the tin bath.

"Let it go. Let it go," Harriet repeated as she felt her skin burn. Finally, her nerves accepted the heat, and she relaxed her muscles while Nicole did the same. She reached into her lap and pulled the soap from the water and rubbed a lather in her hands before passing it to Nicole. "So, the German?"

"Yes... He dived on us," Nicole continued. "I didn't think we had a chance, not in the old Nieuport anyway, and neither did Sully. He told me to land on the road through the woods so we could run and hide in the trees. Like he could run anywhere. I ignored him, of course, he'd have been a dead goose if I'd landed, the German would have shot him to pieces before he could ever get out."

"Dead as a duck…" Harriet corrected, instantly wishing she hadn't.

"What?"

"Never mind. So, what did you do?" Harriet's eyes were wide open with excitement.

"I used the only thing the Nieuport had, slow speed. I could turn tighter than the German who couldn't fly slow enough, so he had to make longer passes to try and get me, then he would overshoot and have to come around again. I did it enough to frustrate him, then one time he passed me I dipped over a ridge, and he shot over me very fast, and by the time he'd swung around to come back at me, I'd dropped to the road between the trees out of sight. When he came over the ridge, I pulled up hard and spun the undercarriage into his propeller."

"You must have been so scared!" Harriet exclaimed. Her heart was pounding just hearing the story.

"A little," Nicole smiled. "More for Sully than myself, though. I could land and run, but he would be dead."

"What happened next?" Harriet asked, wanting to hear the full story.

"He went straight down into the trees. We almost did, too, but I'm an excellent pilot," Nicole said in her usual confident manner.

"Of course…". Harriet rolled her eyes.

"Of course," Nicole agreed, "he hit us with one of his bursts and the cylinder we changed this morning seized again. Anyway, I got us back, just, the fuel leaked, the oil leaked, everything leaked!" She handed the soap back to Harriet, who'd started scrubbing the filth from her face. "It was a good day for luck."

"Yes."

"And for amazing French pilots."

"Yes..."

"Though you still have three more than me," Nicole said with frustration. She leant forward and rinsed her face in the quickly greying water before laying back against Harriet and sighing. "Four Messerschmitt 109s... Now that's the work of an amazing pilot."

"I had a good teacher," Harriet smiled.

"We both did, the best," Nicole agreed. "I hope he and grandma are OK."

"I'm sure they will be. They lived through the last war, and that was the bad one. This one won't be anything like that."

"I think you're right," Nicole sighed.

The girls relaxed and washed and enjoyed the heat of the bath, which was thick with grime and dirt, but still a comforting place that neither was in a hurry to leave. Much to their disappointment, their moment of normality in an otherwise exceptional day was eventually shattered by a hammering on the bathroom door.

"Yes?" Harriet replied. The door opened, and Finn stood looking at them both as they lounged against each other in the bath, unable to shift the look of displeasure from her face.

"I'll be leaving for supper in a few minutes," Finn announced. "If either of you intends on eating, you'd better wrap up whatever this is and get dressed. I'm not waiting around!" She turned her nose in the air, then left them and closed the door.

"I hate that woman," Nicole snarled before standing up and stepping out of the bath. She grabbed a towel and threw the other to Harriet, who was now standing and joining her. They dried and quickly dressed again. Their clothes were grimy, but at least their skin felt clean. Once they were dressed, they checked each other over for tidiness, tidied and tied each other's hair, then stepped out of the bathroom. Nicole stood confidently in front of Finn, who held herself equally boldly, not to be outdone or belittled by some poor mannered young French girl.

"Remember what I told you both," Finn hissed. "We have a duty as officers, even though neither of you looks the part." She eyed them with contempt as they stood in their overalls, flying jackets, and boots, before turning on her heel and heading down the stairs. "Are you coming?" she barked, and the girls quickly followed her out into the cooling evening air. They followed her through the courtyard and to a large, noisy room at the front of the house which had a decorated handmade wooden sign on the door identifying it as the 'Officer's Mess.' Finn marched in confidently, and the girls followed. Inside were many of the squadron pilots, and some other officers, some in army green but most in blue. The large reception room was scattered with couches and chairs around its perimeter, and a long table down the centre. Most of the officers were seated at the table, and except for Cas, they hadn't seen them enter the room. He looked at them from his place next to Barnes at the opposite end of the table.

"Gentlemen," Cas said as he stood. Barnes followed, as did the rest, all turning to look at the girls as they entered the room, and in doing so totally ignored Finn in her sharp and pristine uniform. He nodded at a young officer who turned and approached them with a bounding stride. He was a handsome young man with golden hair and dark eyebrows, and his green eyes smiled as he stood before them.

"Gus Williams," he said as he held out his hand, which the girls shook in turn. "Let me take those jackets, will you. It's a bit warm in here, and you'll melt otherwise."

"Thank you," Harriet said after they'd introduced themselves and wrestled with their jackets. Gus took them, and another officer stood from a couple of places along from where Gus had been sitting. He had dark hair and grey blue eyes and was ruggedly handsome. He was wearing an RAF officer's tunic with small 'Canada' shoulder titles.

"Come on you fellas," he said in a North American accent. "Shuffle down and give these ladies somewhere more welcoming to sit." The officers made space and switched seats, and the Canadian gestured for the girls to take the chairs he'd cleared about halfway down the table.

"You're very kind, thank you," Nicole said politely.

"Not at all, Ma'am. Logan Maxwell, or Max to friends, it's a pleasure to make your acquaintance."

"Here we go..." The officer sitting across the table chirped. "Yank hospitality at its finest."

"Hey!" Max replied with a frown on his face. I'm Canadian, remember?"

"And I'm a Chinaman," the very well spoken English officer that had been mocking replied almost dismissively. Max smiled, and the room descended into laughter. Cas nodded, and everyone sat down and returned to their jovial conversations at the same time as the glasses in front of the girls were quickly topped with red wine by Max. The well spoken English officer who made the witty Chinaman comment was sitting opposite and wearing a turquoise blue cravat, he leant forward and smiled. "Just watch yourself around the colonial," he nodded at Max. "He'll pour you glass after glass of wine while telling you stories of wonder and delight from the new world with the rugged charm only a colonial can. Then, at the end of the evening, he'll have relieved you of your purse, your jewellery, and anything else of value you may own, leaving you with nothing more than a headache from the wine and his increasingly unbelievable stories." The surrounding officers burst into laughter.

"Something you've learned from experience, Archie?" Gus asked, to the amusement of the others as he returned to his seat.

"More times than it's comfortable to admit, old boy," Archie replied. "These days, I just pay him at the start and forego the tedious stories." More laughter ensued.

"Sir Archie Russel," Max said as he gestured at Archie with his glass. "Lord of the Manor, and proud owner of most of North Yorkshire."

"Well, I think we're quite safe," Harriet replied with a shy but confident smile. "We're wearing everything we own and don't have a purse between us. Even the jackets and boots are borrowed."

"Is that so...?" Archie asked as he sat back and looked at them both with a degree of consideration. "Sir," he called over to Barnes, who immediately acknowledged him. "Would you mind if we were excused for a couple of minutes?"

"Sitting down in fifteen, Mister Russel," Barnes said, after looking around the room and giving Archie a nod.

"Very good, Sir," Archie said as he stood. "Right, come on, Yank. You too, Gus. Ladies, would you join us for a moment?" The men stood, and the girls looked surprised. With a nod of reassurance from Cas, they both stood and followed the three pilots out of the house. "Gus, off you go to the WAAFs, meet us in our tent in a couple of minutes," Archie ordered. Gus smiled and quickly ran off into the night. "Step into our humble abode," Archie opened the flaps on one of the tents to show a group of beds and kit bags. "Right, you ladies wait there," he instructed, then he and Max went to their beds and pulled kit bags from underneath each. A minute or two of rummaging while the girls stood silently and watched, and the men returned to them. Max handed Harriet a silky smooth, light blue shirt of the highest quality and a pair of RAF blue trousers. Archie presented similar clothes to Nicole.

"Sorry, Ma'am, mine aren't quite as fancy as his, what with me being a colonial and all," Max said with a wink as Harriet took the clothes from him.

"They'll be a little on the large side," Archie said to Nicole, "but if you give me a moment." He returned to his kit bag and rummaged some more before returning with two black leather belts. "There, those should do you."

"Who on earth carries spare belts to battle?" Max asked

"Who on earth doesn't?" Archie replied. "Be a good chap, Yank, and grab that sailor's knife you have. I expect we'll need to poke holes in these belts."

"Please don't, it'll ruin your belts," Harriet protested.

"Oh, don't be silly," Archie countered. "There are plenty more where they came from."

"Sure, he'll just have the servants run up a few more," Max added as he returned with his folding knife, which had a large spike laid out from one end.

"Preposterous!" Archie hit back. "They're staff, not servants. Anyhow, measure up, and we'll poke the holes." As they worked, Gus pushed the tent flap open and stepped in excitedly. "Get anything?" Archie asked.

"Did I?" Gus replied. "Daisy was most supportive." He held out a lipstick and a small tin of powder.

"You're sweet on her, huh?" Max teased.

"She's sweet on a tall American pilot," Gus countered.

"Canadian," Max corrected his young friend.

"Oh, shut up, the both of you," Archie said, as Nicole held her jacket up so he could pull a belt around her waist. He pulled it tight and marked it, then passed it to Max for holing before doing the same with Harriet. He then handed Harriet the makeup. "Right, you ladies have approximately seven minutes to get changed and get back to the Mess. Don't be late, or the skipper will be irritable. He likes to start on time." The trio of pilots left the tent and pulled the flap closed, leaving the girls looking at each other a little in shock. They smiled, then giggled, then quickly changed into their loaned clothes.

"It's so soft," Harriet said as she pulled on the light blue shirt and felt it against her skin. She'd never felt anything like it.

"Stop daydreaming," Nicole replied. "We only have minutes!" She pushed the tails of her oversized shirt into her pants to pull it in, then fastened her trousers and fed the belt through the loops. Harriet did the same and pushed on her flying boots while Nicole untied Harriet's hair, scraped her fingers through it, then tied it in place with a piece of canvas tape. Harriet returned the favour while Nicole applied lipstick, then dabbed soft pink powder from the tin onto her cheeks, before turning and dabbing Harriet. "There," she said as she stood opposite Harriet in the flickering lamplight. "Beautiful!" Harriet blushed and held Nicole's hand. Her French friend knew all there was to know about glamour and had done her best to teach Harriet over the years, despite her best efforts to be a messy, oily, mechanic and pilot. It made her blush to hear anyone say she was beautiful. "We should run." Harriet nodded, and they left the tent and ran back to the Mess. Harriet knocked and then entered.

"Gentlemen... And ladies," Barnes said as he stood, nodding and raising an eyebrow at Finn who was slow and almost reluctant to stand. The room went silent as everyone looked at the girls as they walked back to their seats. Barnes nodded, and everyone sat down and continued their conversations. He gave Archie a nod and a smile, then went back to his conversation with Cas and Singh.

"With thirty seconds to spare," Archie said.

"I don't know how to thank you," Harriet said. "We'll wash them and return them to you tomorrow, I promise."

"Not at all, old girl," Archie replied. "Our gifts to our guests, it's the least we can do." The others agreed.

Before the conversation could progress any further, the door opened, and a couple of airmen brought in the food. Chicken and mushroom in a creamy sauce with boiled potatoes, the Chef had created something special.

Harriet found herself relaxing, though not as much as Nicole who was enjoying the company of Gus and a couple of the other young pilots. The girls were the stars of the show, and pilots jostled for position as they attempted to woo them with stories of their flying. Harriet was polite to a fault, but Nicole was a little more flirtatious. She was able to keep the pilots hooked by laughing and giggling and playing to their egos, almost begging to hear more about their daring adventures. Finn was furious throughout. She sat close to Barnes and engaged in polite conversation while studiously ignoring the young fools at the centre of attention. The wine flowed freely, and spirits were high, but before things escalated the conversation was disturbed by the sound of metal tapping on glass. Everyone fell silent and turned to look at the top of the table as a pair of airmen filled glasses with Champagne.

"Ladies and Gentlemen… If I could pull your attention this way for a moment, I have a few points of order before we step away from the table..." Barnes said as he stood. "Firstly I'd like to thank Cas for somehow laying his hands on a couple of dozen bottles of Champagne in the middle of a war!" He waved his glass upwards, and the gathered officers slapped the table in applause, something that took Harriet and Nicole by surprise and fascinated them both. "Second, I'd like to welcome our French and Polish friends," more table clattering, this time with the girls joining in, and much tipping of glasses to the proud and blushing Frenchman, Hugo, and Pops, the smiling Polish Officer, both of whom were sitting further down the table. "Settle now..." Barnes continued as the table slapping subsided. "I know that you've had a rough ride as of late, and we're missing a few friends that we'd started out with, but I want you to know that you're all doing a first rate job. HQ are more than impressed with your efforts, as am I, and it's an honour to fly with such brave and tenacious pilots." A cheer went up, and the table slapping resumed. Barnes waved his hand downward to quell the noise before continuing. "Before I release you to enjoy the rest of your evening there's one final matter I'd like to address, that of our guests from the ATA." He tilted his glass at the girls, and everyone's eyes followed and fixed on them. "I'm sure the rumours have done the rounds, I've even heard a couple myself, so I'd like to set the record straight. Between them, Third Officers Cornwall and Delacourt accounted for five Messerschmitt 109s this afternoon." A quiet gasp passed around the room. "Flight Lieutenant Sullivan, late of this parish, told me before he departed for home how his pilot, Miss Delacourt, evacuated him. After a German patrol jumped him and shot him down, resulting in him being badly injured, this courageous young woman volunteered to return him to us in an old unarmed Nieuport from the last war. During the flight, they were set on by a 109 some twenty miles from here, and old Sully ordered his pilot to land and save herself by running into the woods. An order Miss Delacourt repeatedly chose to ignore; instead deciding to use her superior flying skills to run rings around the 109, before flying directly at him and using her undercarriage to ram his propeller and send him into the ground. Thus, saving her aeroplane, temporarily, and Sully's life." There were gasps of surprise from the gathered pilots. "She then proceeded to control the landing of her crippled aeroplane safely at our airfield, preventing any injury or loss of life." Nicole was blushing. For the first time in her life, she was speechless, and bright red under the gaze of the assembled officers. "Not to be outdone," Barnes continued. "Miss Cornwall volunteered to transport Sully's damaged Hurricane here, and after a brief introduction, she was able to fly it safely across country. Where she discovered a flight of four 109s were in the process of jumping Raj's flight as they were landing, having come in at treetops to beat up the airfield." The pilots stared at Harriet as Barnes talked, making her nervous and embarrassed to be the centre of attention. "Instead of doing the sensible thing and getting out of trouble, as any of us would," Barnes continued. "Miss Cornwall chose to attack the Germans, knocking two down in her first pass, then engaging the other two in aerial combat and besting them both, including a very distinguished Major with over thirty kills to his name! Delivering us from the certain loss of more Hurricanes and their pilots, and whatever other mischiefs the unhindered Germans could have rained on us with nobody to stop them..." Harriet was shrinking into her chair as he spoke. "So, ladies, if you'd be kind enough to stand, so we can embarrass you entirely." The girls dutifully stood, both blushing. "Three cheers for the ATA. Hip, Hip, Hurrah!" Three loud hurrahs were followed by a loud cheer and lots of slapping of the table. Barnes winked mischievously and took his seat. The girls quickly followed, and both gulped their Champagne, bottles of which were rapidly being deposited on the table.

The evening progressed, and the Champagne flowed. There was lots of singing and dancing, and even more laughing. It would be difficult to know there was a war going on in the same country. Pops had even brought out the large keg of vodka he'd arrived with, much to everyone's delight. Nicole was the life of the party, much to the scorn of Finn, who kept to herself before finding a reason to leave and turn in to bed early.

"Are AP and the others not joining us?" Harriet asked Max halfway through her third glass of Champagne.

"Sadly not," he replied. "They're a great crowd, but unfortunately they draw the short straw in all of this. We pilots do the easy part, we just climb in and fly where we're told, but they have to be up all hours fixing the aeroplanes and getting them ready for us. That's the hard part. You should see them strip down an engine and rebuild it. It's genius."

"So, they're working?" Harriet asked

"Some maybe, but certainly all of them will be from before first light when we go on standby. Anyway, they wouldn't want to socialise with us Officers. They've got more class and better taste."

"Especially when that snapdragon Finn is around," Archie added. "The loathsome snob, she's the very worst type of officer. She treats the other ranks like dirt, and God alone knows why. She's hardly royalty herself."

"Yeah, that's true," Max continued. "She's in charge of the WAAFs attached to the squadron, and she rides them hard. Won't let them socialise with the men, certainly not with the officers, and she wouldn't let them within ten feet of a bottle of booze."

"Well, that's just not fair," Harriet said. "In fact, that's horrible."

"That's Finn," Max shrugged in resignation.

"Is there any more Champagne?" Harriet asked

"Why?" Max asked with a chuckle. "You planning on making a night of it?"

"Well, I heard Cas say there were a few crates," Harriet replied. "I just wondered if there were any spare bottles?" Max smiled, and Archie gave him a nod and wink.

"Meet me at the front door in two minutes," Max said, before standing and hurrying from the room.

"Give them these, too. Would you?" Archie asked as he put a couple of packs of cigarettes on the table in front of her. "And this." He pulled a bar of Swiss dark chocolate from his breast pocket. She nodded and pushed them into her pockets as she stood.

"Thank you so much," Harriet said as she pulled on her jacket.

"Not at all. It's like needling the snapdragon from a safe distance. Honestly, I kind of enjoy it," he laughed. "Off you pop, Max will be waiting."

"Nicole, I'm going for some air," Harriet said, disturbing her friend briefly. Nicole nodded and laughed and continued to flirt with Gus, Johnny, the young Scottish pilot sent to shoot her down earlier, and Hugo and Pops. She was confidently laughing at the right moments and leading them into trying to impress her, which they were competing to do, though they'd also gone down the route of flattery and praised her repeatedly for her action against the German. Harriet rolled her eyes at the display, then slipped out of the room. Max was waiting by the door with a couple of bottles of Champagne.

"All yours," he said as he pushed them into her hands. "The WAAFs tent is around the side of the house. You can't miss it."

"Thank you again," she said with a smile.

"No problem," he smiled.

Harriet walked off into the silver blue last light of the day and immediately had to stop and steady herself. The Champagne had gone straight to her head, and her legs, as had the smooth yet potent vodka that Pops had brought with him. When he'd escaped Poland, he'd brought with him several bottles of the vodka his family used to distil from potatoes, but once in France he found an old Calvados cask to decant the bottles into, for ease of transport, which had given the vodka a uniquely sweet and distinctive taste and made it very easy to drink. She took a deep breath and composed herself, then continued around the building until she found the circular bell tent with distinctively female voices coming from within. She opened the flap and looked in to see five young women sat around a flickering oil lamp in the centre of the tent.

"Hello..." she said softly, not wanting to disturb the women from their conversation. They were all in uniform; some wearing skirts, some trousers and boots.

"Hello," a blonde girl who looked a similar age replied. "What can we do for you?" She had a distinctly southern accent, unmistakably a Londoner.

"I'm sorry, I don't want to disturb..." Harriet said, tempted to back out of the tent.

"Don't be silly, come in," the blonde Londoner insisted. Harriet smiled nervously and stepped into the tent. "Ma'am..." the WAAF added. "You're that ATA Officer who shot down those Germans, ain't you?"

"Yes... I brought you these. I wanted to say thank you for lending us your make up earlier." She held out the Champagne, and the young WAAF smiled and took one of the bottles and looked at it.

"Now that's a thank you," she said while eyeing the Champagne thirstily. "Though you didn't have to, it was our pleasure. Mister Williams said you'd arrived here with nothing, so it's the least we could do."

"Oh, there's these, too," Harriet pulled the cigarettes from her pocket and handed them to the nearest WAAF.

"You can come again," the blonde replied with a laugh. "I'm Corporal Wilson, Ma'am," she said as she straightened up. "Pleasure to meet you. These are Marten, Green, De Kuiper, and Lancashire." She pointed around the tent and each in turn nodded and smiled with a polite 'Ma'am'.

"Doesn't anybody in the RAF use first names?" Harriet asked with a frown.

"We do... When officers aren't around, Ma'am."

"Well, I'm Harriet Cornwall, Harry, to my friends, and I'm hardly an RAF officer so I wouldn't mind at all if you called me Harry."

"Only if you have a drink with us, Harry?" Wilson waved the bottle and raised her eyebrows questioningly, and Harriet smiled. The cork was popped, and an upturned box was pushed in front of Harriet for her to sit on. She was given a tin cup, and Wilson started to pour. Harriet stopped her quickly.

"Only a splash, I've had more than enough already. Besides, I brought it for you." Wilson smiled and filled the everyone's cups before taking her seat.

"Well, Harry. I'm Daisy. That's Sally Martens, Jenny Green, Suzy De Kuiper, and Adele Lancashire, who we call Lanky. Cheers," they all clinked their tin mugs together and repeated the cheers before taking a drink. "Bloody hell that's good!" Daisy said, as her eyes widened with delight. She handed around the cigarettes, which were declined by Harriet, and they all lit up. "It's like bloody Christmas," she said, and they all laughed.

"I didn't realise there were so many girls in the RAF," Harriet said. "I didn't expect to see any of you here, especially in the middle of a war."

"There aren't enough of us," Daisy replied, much to the amusement of the others. "In fairness to the RAF, they recognised a long time ago that women have the skills they need. Sally and Jen are drivers, Suzy looks after the parachutes and other safety equipment, Lanky's an armourer, and I'm a signaller. All critical jobs which women can do as good as any man, better in some cases, and it frees up the men to do the fighting. Something the RAF ain't that keen on letting us do."

"Aren't you scared? Of being killed, I mean? The Germans aren't that far away."

"Were you scared when you shot down the Germans earlier?"

"I don't know..." Harriet frowned. "I don't suppose I thought about it that much."

"It's the same for us. We've got a job to do, that's all. The CO was told by HQ to evacuate us when things started getting a bit heated a few days ago. He told them he'd let us make our own decisions and we chose to stay. He caught hell for that from above... Still, we're part of this squadron and we have jobs to do. If we'd have gone home, it wouldn't have been right. The lads don't get to go home, so why should we? Besides, who else would do our jobs? We'd be leaving the squadron short, right when they need everyone they can get."

"You're right, I suppose," Harriet shrugged and sipped her Champagne.

"Of course I am," Daisy said with a mischievous wink. "Old Sharkey didn't agree, though. She was furious." The others giggled.

"Oh?" Harriet asked

"Yeah... She was all for leaving, had her bags packed and everything," Daisy explained. "She couldn't wait to get back home to England, where she could live in a place with flushing toilets and running hot water, but she was backed into a corner when we voted to stay. You see, there's supposed to be a WAAF Officer with any section of WAAFs, and if she left there wouldn't be one, and the CO would have had to order us home with her. She wouldn't dare do that because she'd have been in a bad light with him, and that wouldn't do for her career. Rumour has it that the CO offered to let her go, and he was going to give AP a field commission, so we still had a WAAF Officer if we stayed without her."

"Why on earth didn't she just leave?" Harriet asked as she sipped more Champagne.

"Because she hates us more than she hates being here, AP more than the rest of us, and she just couldn't bear the thought of being responsible for AP being commissioned," Daisy sighed.

"Daisy!" Suzy whispered forcefully.

"What?" Daisy asked. "I'm not saying anything the rest of the squadron doesn't know. Old Sharkey's a right cow."

"I'm sorry..." Jen said to Harriet with evident embarrassment.

"Oh, don't be, please," Harriet said, keen to reassure her new friends. "I've met her. We even have to share a room with her, and she's already told us in no uncertain terms what she thinks of us."

"She would," Daisy continued. "You're younger than her, you're officers, and you've got a rare skill for women, you're pilots..."

"Why do you call her Sharkey?" Harriet asked with a knowing smile.

"Sharks have fins…" Daisy laughed. "They're also ugly, dangerous, and nobody really likes them much," she laughed some more, as did Harriet the others. "Anyway, enough about her... What's it like?"

"What's what like?" Harriet replied.

"Flying?" Daisy said, and they all leant in towards Harriet excitedly.

"You've never flown?" Harriet asked in genuine surprise, having assumed all people in the RAF would fly at least some time.

"Not even as a passenger in a Lysander," Daisy shrugged, and they all shook their heads.

"Oh... I don't know how to describe it. It's like being free, I suppose. Truly free. The vibration of the engine, the noise, the smell, it all wraps around you as you float weightlessly on a cushion of air. Like you're away from all the troubles of the world, especially up above the clouds. You really should try it sometime."

"If only... You're the only female pilot I've ever met, and I don't think they'll be in a hurry to send the likes of us up in the air, it's unheard of. How did you learn to fly anyway, you can't be any older than me?"

"I have my friend to thank for that, Nicole, the other pilot who came with me," Harriet replied. "Her grandfather was a pilot in the last war, and he started teaching us years ago. He was adamant that women should learn to fly and fix their own aeroplanes, he said the future would be different, and gender wouldn't get in the way of ability."

"Wow." Daisy gasped. "I'm surprised the old boy network didn't have him strung up for such heresy. Good on him, though, I wish I had somebody like that in my life when I was growing up."

"You can fix aeroplanes, too?" Suzy asked.

"I suppose..." Harriet shrugged. "He made us learn before he'd let us fly solo, so we could do our own repairs and get home if needs be."

"Don't tell Sharkey that," Daisy said with a giggle. "She'll hate you even more."

"Speaking of fixing aeroplanes, where's AP?" Harriet looked around the tent.

"Working," Daisy replied. "As I should be soon, I'll be on watch in the Ops Room in an hour."

"She's not happy with the engine on one of her Hurricanes," Lanky added. "She'll probably be up there all night. I'm going to go up and join her in a minute. I've got some guns to work on before tomorrow."

"Can I come?" Harriet asked.

"Yeah. I'll get my coat." Lanky stood, and she threw on her long blue greatcoat.

"Goodnight," Harriet said to the others. "Thank you for making me feel so welcome."

"Thank you for the Champagne and smokes," Daisy replied. "Visit anytime. You'll always be welcome."

"Goodnight," the others added, and Harriet walked out of the tent with Lanky.

"Why does Finn hate AP more than the rest of you?" Harriet asked Lanky as they walked.

"Because she's good, " Lanky replied. "The CO would have promoted her by now if he could. Finn frustrated it, though. She's had AP up on charges a few times, usually for insubordination."

"That's horrible," Harriet frowned.

"That's life in the RAF," Lanky said with a smile. "Don't get me wrong, it's a good life, it can be exciting, and we get to do things other women wouldn't even dream of. I mean, who gets to come to France and repair machine guns on Hurricanes? We get to see things and do things, and the girls are great, it's just the politics."

"Like Finn?" Harriet asked.

"Yeah..." Lanky nodded. "Get the wrong boss, and they can make your life hell just because they don't like the look of you. That and the pay."

"Oh?"

"We get paid more than the girls back home, so I'm not complaining too much," Lanky continued. "It's just that we get paid a third less than men who do the same jobs."

"What?" Harriet asked in shock.

"Yep," Lanky replied. "Take Daisy, for example. She's a Corporal, a watchkeeper, and a signals specialist. She can read and send Morse code better and faster than anyone else in the squadron, she can set up field telephone networks, and she practically runs the operations room when things are hectic. Corporal Jones, Billy, he does a similar job but isn't as sharp, and gets paid a third more just because he's a man. It's just not right."

"It isn't, I agree."

"What about you, if you don't mind me asking? Do they pay you the same as the male pilots?"

"I've really no idea... I don't even know how much they'll be paying me yet."

"Oh... I'm sorry. You mean you haven't been paid?" Lanky said uneasily, feeling a little embarrassed.

"I mean that this morning I was changing the cylinder on an aeroplane engine and planning to go to nurse school in Switzerland. Tonight, I'm on an RAF airfield and wearing somebody else's clothes, drinking Champagne, and being called Ma'am," Harriet said as she looked at Lanky, and the pair of them laughed.

"AP!" Lanky called as they reached the Hurricane pen.

"In here," came AP's reply from the bell tent behind the position. They entered to find AP sitting on a box and rubbing a metal tube with sandpaper. "Come to look at that gun?" she asked without looking up.

"Yeah, I'd liked to get it finished before the morning so that I can focus on the other aeroplanes. They'll probably be up on sorties again at first light, and they'll need it. What's that you're doing?"

"Most likely..." AP shrugged. "The fuel wasn't flowing right. If I rub the line down a little at the join, it may get a better fit."

"Oh, I brought somebody to see you." Lanky added. AP looked up at Harriet, then went back to focusing on her task.

"Bit late for visiting isn't it, Ma'am?" AP asked dismissively.

"I wanted to bring you something," Harriet replied. "A thank you from both of us for teaching us about the Hurricane."

"Just doing my job, Ma'am."

"Well, I wanted to all the same," Harriet said, choosing to ignore the coldness she was faced with, "and please call me Harry." She held the second bottle of Champagne in front of AP.

"I don't drink on duty, Ma'am..." AP replied after briefly looking up at Harriet. "Thank you, though. Maybe Lancashire can take it for the others to share?"

"Maybe..." Harriet handed it to Lanky who'd just pulled off her coat. Lanky smiled warmly at Harriet, trying to reassure her against AP's bristly reception. "Then maybe you'd like this instead?" Harriet pulled out the chocolate and offered it. "And the name's Harry. If you want to call somebody Ma'am you can go and talk to Section Officer Finn, but I'm Harry," she said with all of the confidence she could muster. AP looked up with the slightest of smiles on her face, just the corners of her mouth turning up as she looked at Harriet through narrowed eyes. She paused for a moment, then took the chocolate and put it on the cot next to her.

"Thanks, Harry," she replied, then got on with her work.

"What is it you're doing?" Harriet asked after another couple of minutes of silence. AP dropped her head in disappointment, then sighed before looking up.

"The fuel feed into one of the cylinders on the Hurricane you were flying was blocked by a bent fuel line, which explains the misfiring you reported after your flight. The replacement doesn't fit in the cylinder properly, so I've rubbed it down, and now I'm polishing it, so the fit is snug. After that, I need to overhaul the cylinder. It's going to be a long night, so unless you've got any more questions?"

"I could help if you'd like?"

"You?" AP laughed.

"She changed the cylinder on that old Nieuport that crashed earlier," Lanky said as she rolled up her sleeves. "Didn't you?"

"I did," Harriet said proudly, as AP stared for a minute.

"OK, we'll see... Haven't you got a gun to fix?" she asked Lanky.

"I certainly have." Lanky danced off out of the tent with a smirk on her face.

An hour later and Harriet was under the tarpaulin rigged over the front of the Hurricane to keep the light from escaping. A blazing lantern helped her see while up to her elbows in oil and grease helping AP with the engine. She followed AP's instructions without question, and despite being a little lightheaded from the Champagne, she managed every task without complication. AP didn't say as much, but she was impressed. She didn't let up, though, and worked Harriet hard, continually testing her with tasks, while Lanky lay on the wing fiddling with the guns. A little after midnight, Harriet and AP were talking through the intricacies of the Merlin engine when Lanky hushed them.

"What is it? AP asked

"Listen..." Lanky replied. The pair joined her in craning their ears upwards to listen to the distant drone of engines.

"Ours?" Harriet asked.

"Maybe" AP replied. "They're coming from the east so it could be a raid heading home, but I'm not convinced. Put the cover over the lamp" Harriet did as she was told, then followed AP and Lanky out from under the tarpaulin. They all looked up into the starry sky in the direction of the droning. Searchlights lit up the sky in the west as the skyline flashed again and again, and the not too distant sky filled with explosions as thuds and booms of all sorts rattled the air.

"What's over there?" Harriet asked.

"The French army supply warehouses," AP replied. "There's a rail depot in the town, and they supply the whole region from there." The droning bombers passed over the pitch dark airfield heading for the town to join the raid. Harriet was nervous. It was the first time she'd seen a bombing raid.

"Poor bastards," Lanky said as the three stood side by side and watched.

"Better them than us," AP said. They watched the skyline flash and illuminate for a while in silence. There weren't really any words that could be put to such a situation, so she uttered the only ones she had. "We should get back to work..."

Chapter 6

The Cold Light of Day

Harriet's eyes opened wide as the sound of a roaring Merlin engine filled the air. She stared straight ahead at the brilliant white light shining in her eyes and warming her face, and it took a moment for her to realise where she was. Her first thought was that she was at school, but her dormitory bed felt very different. She blinked and rubbed her eyes, moving her hand from beneath the grey blanket pulled up around her shoulders. As her eyes focused, she could see sunbeams filtering through the blue smoke which was blowing from the Hurricane in the pen beyond, and swirling around its tail. Another look around and she recognised AP's tent, which was pitched in the trees behind the Hurricane; she was in a cot wrapped in blankets, with her jacket thrown over her and her flying boots placed neatly by her side. She sat up with a groan, everything ached, including her head. She pulled off the blanket and slipped her feet into her soft fleece boots before standing and walking forwards towards the tent flap, coughing at the petrol fumes ticking her throat as she walked through the gap in the sandbags and made eye contact with AP, who was sitting in the cockpit of the Hurricane. She jumped on the wing and climbed up to the cockpit. AP throttled back and idled the engine then gave Harriet a small smile from the corner of her mouth.

"I thought you'd appreciate the alarm call," AP said with a laugh. "Wouldn't want you to miss breakfast."

"Is it working?" Harriet asked as she nodded in sleepy, yet reluctant gratitude for the alarm call.

"You're awake, aren't you?" AP replied, still laughing to herself.

"I meant the engine," Harriet frowned.

"It is so far..." AP confirmed. "Get yourself off to the Mess and have breakfast, you'll need to check in with the CO anyway."

"What about you?"

"I had mine at first light." She turned back to the cockpit and increased the power again. Harriet nodded and turned to head off for breakfast. AP throttled and called after her. "Harry..."

"Yes?" Harriet replied, choosing not to look back.

"Thanks for your help last night, you made the job much easier, and quicker."

"You're welcome," Harriet said as she continued forward and jumped off the wing. She didn't turn or look back at AP, waiting instead until she'd left the Hurricane pen and was on her way across the grass strip in the misty gold and purple light of dawn, before letting herself smile at being appreciated by the most difficult of mechanics. Her happiness was short lived, though, the columns of black smoke climbing into the western sky soon reminded her of the previous night's bombing. She also remembered sitting on AP's cot for a few minutes rest when they'd finished the engine overhaul, they were going to share the chocolate and then she was going to return to her bed in the coach house above the stables. She remembered eating a few squares of chocolate, and her eyes feeling heavy, but that was it. She blushed a little at the thought of having passed out in the tent, as her inner voice tried to reason that it had been a particularly hectic day, while she walked through the house and into the Mess to join the gathering pilots, who were significantly less boisterous than the night before. All were dressed for flying. Some in Irvin jackets, others in their blue tunics, and all carrying or wearing their faded yellow Mae West life jackets. Pleasantries were exchanged, and tea was poured. Just as the boiled eggs with bread and butter were being served Nicole made an appearance looking a little concerned, a look which quickly switched to annoyance as she locked her eyes on Harriet. She was suitably pleasant to everyone, then took a sip of tea before growling at Harriet in a low voice.

"And where were you last night?" Nicole demanded.

"Miss me?" Harriet asked with a mischievous smile.

"I was expecting you!"

"Sorry," Harriet said with a shrug.

"Corporal Daisy told me you went to the aeroplanes."

"I did."

"All night?"

"Yes. I was overhauling a Merlin engine with AP, and it was great fun." Harriet said excitedly as Nicole rolled her eyes. "What?"

"You chose that and left me alone all night with that... that snapdragon woman!"

"Oh, Nicole... What did you do?"

"Nothing..." Nicole smirked mischievously and left Harriet doubting her reply. They were joined by the rest of the officers and conversation picked up as the eggs and bread were eaten, and tea was drunk. Their dark and tired eyes were soon sparkling once again.

"Hey, Yank," Archie shouted boisterously.

"What's up, your lordship?" Max replied.

"Now, now, Yank, don't get your manners in a muddle," Archie said. "I merely wanted to offer you a deal."

"Oh yeah, what's that?" Max asked suspiciously.

"If I don't make it to tomorrow, you can have my breakfast egg."

"That's pretty kind of you. If I don't make it, you can have mine."

"What about me?" Gus asked. "What do I get?"

"To be quiet and eat your egg! There's a good chap," Archie replied casually. "You're far too young to be trading breakfasts." Max gave Archie a wink, and they both laughed.

"You're right, I suppose," Gus replied. "I still have my youthful reflexes, and the Germans will get both of you long before they get me. I'll have both of your eggs."

"The confidence of youth," Max laughed.

"Yes, but it's such a shame about his lack of charm," Archie added. "Though I suppose that only comes with age." The others laughed and continued with their breakfast. "Has anyone seen Pops and Hugo this morning? I hope the vodka isn't keeping them in bed."

"They left a few hours ago," Barnes said as he entered the room. "Gone by car to join a Polish squadron attached to the French.

"Unfortunate... I quite enjoyed that Calvados vodka." Archie said with a frown.

"Shame that you can't handle it, Archie my boy," Max said with a smirk.

"Alright, enough of that," Barnes interrupted them before they could go any further. "There's a bit of a flap on, and we're wheels up in twenty minutes. So, finish off and get yourselves out to the courtyard for a briefing. Same for the rest of you, come on."

"Early start," Archie said before pushing the last of his bread into his mouth and swilling it down with tea. The rest of the pilots did the same, and everyone left the room with Harriet and Nicole following close behind. They stood at the rear of the courtyard, where the Sergeant pilots met with their officer counterparts and greeted each other while mingling. The Chief was there, too, along with a couple of his non commissioned officers from the ground crews.

"Right, listen up," Barnes said as he stood in front of them with Cas by his side. A large chalkboard had been mounted on the wall with an impressively intricate map drawn on it. "Two German armoured divisions hit the bridges here a while ago as you know." He pointed in the direction of the Ardennes forest. "The French have been back and forth with them, but this morning they've secured a bridgehead, and there are reports of huge columns of armour and supporting infantry racing up to cross the bridges here and here." He waved at the board. "If they get through, they'll be able to race straight across France." He drew a line across the map to the coast, "and cut off the entire British Expeditionary Force which is currently fighting its way out of Belgium." There were gasps and mumbling among the pilots. "Command is going all out on this one. Every bomber we have serviceable in France is currently being armed and assembled to form a massive raid against the bridgehead. The plan is to flatten everything. Tanks, trucks, bridges, the lot! And it's our job, along with the other fighter squadrons over here, to keep the Luftwaffe off their backs long enough for them to do their work. Subject to everything going to plan, we may even get released to attack targets of opportunity once the bomber boys have done their jobs and we've got them safely out of the area. The priority, however, is to get the bombers in and out. This is a full force effort, so we're all going. Flight Commanders check the maps and update your pilots on the forward fields we'll be using to refuel and rearm." He rechecked his watch. "Wheels up in ten minutes. Good luck, gentlemen, let's make this a good one and see if we can stop the Huns in their tracks!" The Flight Commanders gathered around the chalkboard, as the rest of the pilots hurried from the courtyard. "What's the score, Chief?" Barnes asked.

"Eleven serviceable and combat ready," the Chief replied, "and Kaye and Lancashire worked through the night to get two more ready for flight testing this morning."

"Good show, Chief," Barnes said as he gave him a warm slap on the shoulder. "If things get out of hand today, we may need those spares. What about the rest?"

"Two are write offs, Sir. We've been cannibalising them for spares."

"You'd better get them stripped down and ready to go in case we need to move. The other two?"

"We're going to start on them today and see if we can get at least one in the air."

"OK, good luck. Thanks, Chief, and thank those two for their work last night," Barnes said, before joining and Cas and walking behind the Flight Commanders as they headed for the arched exit from the courtyard.

"Where the hell do you think you're going?" Barnes asked as the girls walked by his side.

"Only to watch them take off..." Harriet replied innocently.

"Damn right only to watch them take off," Barnes said. "Cas, these two trouble causers stay on the ground unless we need to evacuate to the reserve field. Got it?"

"Got it, Sir," Cas said with a smile.

"You've already used up your nine lives," Barnes said to Harriet. She blushed a little as Nicole smirked. "I don't know what you're smiling at," he said to Nicole, "God only knows how you managed to fly that bucket of bolts here without it falling out of the sky, and it's probably thanks to God that you didn't!" Nicole just smirked more. "Anyway, stay on the ground. Cas, if we're not back by this evening for some reason, get them back to Blighty as planned."

"Yes, Sir. Good luck." Cas said.

"Thanks, Cas. See you later." Barnes said as he shook hands with Cas, before jogging off to join the rest of the squadron. Cas stepped forward and stood between the girls, the three of them watched in silence as engines roared into life and pilots climbed into their steeds ready to fly into action. Ground crews strapped the pilots in and held the wingtips as they guided their charges before letting them free to roll. The pitch of the engines changed, and the first flight took off, and then the next, and then the next until all of the Hurricanes were climbing neatly into the afternoon sky. As one they banked to the left, and they were gone, to battle.

"Nothing quite like the feeling, is there?" Cas asked

"Of watching them go?" Harriet said.

"Of being left behind..." Cas replied as he watched the black dots get smaller. "The funny thing is, you know, at the end of the last war I was just relieved to have made it out alive. The last few months were a slog, and we lost lots of good men. Most days it was a flip of a coin as to whether or not you came back, and by the time we'd finished, I never wanted to fly another combat mission again... Yet here we are. All that and what wouldn't I give to be going with them?" He gave Harriet a warming smile, which creased the corners of his eyes and turned up the ends of his mouth. "Chief," he called as the Chief Technician walked past.

"Sir?" the Chief replied as he quickly changed direction and walked over to Cas.

"You've got the two Hurricanes ready for these young ladies to take over to the reserve field if needs be?"

"Yes Sir, the two they took up yesterday with Mister Singh, they're both prepped and ready to go."

"Very well... Fuel? Ammunition?"

"Full tanks, Sir. We haven't reloaded, though, I didn't see the point as they haven't been through air tests yet, and they're not ready for fighting."

"I see. Have them dragged out and brought to ready, would you? Have their ground crews with them, I want them out of here sharpish if the Germans turn up."

"Yes, Sir."

"And Chief, maybe rearm them, too. I know they're only being ferried, but I'd hate for these two to get in a fix with a stray Jerry and have nothing to fight with."

"Good idea, Sir. I'll get on it."

"Good show, Chief. Get your other crews on with stripping the lame ducks."

"Sir." The Chief marched off and barked his orders at the ground crews.

"Let's get up to Ops," Cas said to Harriet and Nicole. The girls nodded and followed him back into the house, where airmen were shuffling papers and keeping busy, and one appeared with a tray of tin mugs filled with steaming sweet tea. The girls took a mug each then went out on the balcony to enjoy the morning air.

Cas daydreamed a moment and couldn't quite help wondering how long it would all last. He'd been through the Great War, the war to end all wars, and he'd seen the reality of mechanised superpowers going head to head on the battlefield. The British Expeditionary Force, hundreds of thousands of men, were in full retreat from a superior German force that had marched its way through Europe without slowing. Likewise, the French army, the biggest standing army in Europe, had been steamrollered. No, this wasn't going to be over in weeks, or if it was, Cas knew for sure he wouldn't be on the winning side. He'd genuinely wished he could have taken off with the rest of the squadron, and deep inside he knew it was for more than one reason. He wrestled with the idea, of course, because it wasn't the English way, but deep in the places gentlemen of his standing didn't talk about at parties, part of him at least hoped that he'd be killed in combat. Get the bullet he didn't see coming and die doing what he loved, flying. Better that than another long and dragged out war of attrition like the last.

"Flight Lieutenant Salisbury?" A young army officer asked as he entered the Ops Room with his Sergeant by his side. They were dirty looking, and certainly not fresh off the boat.

"Yes?" Cas replied as he was dragged from his cycle of thoughts.

"Captain Evan Thomas, Seventh East Yorkshires," the officer introduced himself as he took off his helmet. "And this is Sergeant Oliver," he introduced the man by his side, who had the most fantastic looking moustache with waxed and twirled tips, which wouldn't look out of place on a pilot.

"What can I do for you, Evan?" Cas asked as they shook hands.

"I think it's more what I can do for you...?" Evan replied.

"Call me Cas."

"Cas... Yes, well, division sent my company and me down here to give you chaps a hand," Evan explained.

"Oh? Fly aeroplanes, do you?" Cas asked mischievously while raising an eyebrow. He tossed his hat onto his desk and headed out onto the balcony with Evan and Sergeant Oliver in tow. The girls stood quietly in the corner and watched the newcomers intensely, each desperately hoping for news from the front.

"Not at all," Evan laughed. "Apparently, you're in need of anti aircraft defences, and division would like us to keep out any Germans that wander in this direction, so you can keep supporting our chaps up north."

"And they've sent us a whole company?" Cas asked with a hint of sarcasm.

"Reinforced company." Evan corrected.

"Of course..." Cas said with a smile. "Well let's just hope that the Germans don't send too many of their chaps to wander in this direction. Until recently we had a French anti aircraft battery assigned to us; their Headquarters was in the farm down the road. Unfortunately, they pulled out sometime yesterday and left the door open for the Germans to stroll right in, which they did, and shot down one of my fighters." They shared the remaining cigarettes from Cas' pack. "If you don't mind me saying, Evan, it doesn't look like you chaps just arrived off the boat from England?" He looked at Evan's dusty and almost ragged uniform, and his Sergeant's dusty and torn jacket, which begged how he'd managed to keep his moustache so pristine. Evan looked down at himself and shrugged almost shyly.

"No... Not quite."

"Been in a scrap?"

"Yes..."

"What's it like? At the sharp end, I mean, how are we doing? Are we giving a good show for ourselves?"

"I'm not sure I'd put it that way, exactly."

"Then how would you put it?"

"Well, the reason you have a reinforced company, is because that's about all there is left of the Seventh Battalion."

"What? How?" Cas asked with a frown of disbelief.

"They hit us like a hammer on glass..." Evan stopped and looked at Cas. He looked uncomfortable in his own skin. "Truth is we're only here because we were the air defence company and positioned in depth. The first we knew the battalion had been overrun is when German tanks rolled through the hedges of the farmhouse we had dug in around. It was all we could do to get back to the river and the second line defences. I lost a lot of the company just trying to get away, but a few lads from the other companies made it back somehow, too, and I inherited the lot..."

"What about our artillery? Our tanks? Surely we had something to throw at them?"

"We did... Sergeant Oliver here was leading the Mortar Platoon, which is where my company took most of its losses. I had my platoon dug in to defend them, for all the good it did."

"Tanks get you?" he asked Sergeant Oliver.

"Stukas dive bumbers," Oliver replied. "We got a couple of tanks and a big handful of their infantry, then the rest pulled back and left the Stukas to fall on us. It was like a swarm of flies there were so many."

"My God..."

"Yes, we could have done with God's help."

"I don't doubt it."

"So, you see, we're here because we were the fastest runners when the Huns turned up, so to speak." Evan continued. "Not exactly the Coldstream Guards, who incidentally were putting up a bloody good fight when we last saw them." Evan seemed to shrink as he talked. At over six feet tall, he was a commanding presence, but as the story went on his shoulders hunched and his head bowed with shame.

"You can pack that in, boy!" Cas scolded him harshly. Evan sparked a little and lifted his head. "I was here for the last war, and I can tell you that there's many a hero laid in the fields of France and Belgium because he was too brave, too stupid, or too bloody unlucky to turn and run when the opportunity presented itself! I can guarantee you that to a man, if given the opportunity to do it all again, they'd be running alongside you. You hear?"

"Yes... Yes, Sir!" Evan straightened up.

"Now you listen to me. You and your men are highly trained infantry soldiers, and we can't go throwing those away for pride and honour. It's exactly that sort of thinking that got us into such a bloody mess in the last war. No, you did absolutely the right thing. You got your men out so you could regroup and fight another day, fight properly, and give a good account of yourselves."

"Yes, Sir." Evan smiled and pulled back his shoulders, filling the balcony with his presence, while Sergeant Oliver smiled confidently with a gleam in his eyes, seeming keen to get another chance to fight.

"That's better," Cas said as his warm and fatherly smile returned to his face. "When did you and your chaps last have something to eat?"

"I don't remember... Yesterday, I think? Maybe?"

"Right, get yourself set up around the airfield then have your lads go down to the kitchen. Tell Chef I've said for him to feed and water you all." Cas looked out over the airfield. "You can see the sandbagged pens along the tree line where we keep the aircraft, and we keep the ammunition and spares over in that barn. The tents down here and around the back are accommodation, and this building is our Headquarters. The grass strip you see rolled flat is the runway. I'll let you decide where's best to set your guns up."

"Yes, Sir. Thank you, Sir." Evan replied, confidently. Cas winked again and flicked his head to gesture Evan to leave. He took the last drag off his cigarette and threw it into the sand filled bucket, then he and Oliver left Cas on the balcony.

"Oh, Evan?" Cas called after him.

"Sir?"

"If any Germans should wander in this direction, be a good chap and keep them off my airfield, would you? At least until I manage to get my aeroplanes away."

"You can count on us," Evan said with a big smile. His soldiers joined him, and they left Cas to look up to the northern sky. No sign of the squadron, of course, they hadn't been gone long, and it was unlikely they'd even got as far as meeting the bombers yet. He daydreamed, for a moment more, thinking back to his time in the previous war. He'd been a young infantry officer at first, and he'd seen his share of blood and gore in the trenches at the battle of Ypres. Over one hundred thousand casualties in just that battle, and he was one of them, taking a bullet in the shoulder when leading his platoon on one of the many pointless slow motion suicide walks through no man's land. He'd been found in a shell hole that night by a patrol of medics, having somehow managed not to bleed to death, freeze to death, or be found by the enemy, then dragged back to his lines where he was packed off to the hospital and put back together by the surgeons. It was there that he learned that his entire company had been either killed or injured in that one assault. More than that, the majority of his battalion had gone the same way. They'd been practically wiped out. Officers and men, all were butchered as equals as they walked slowly towards the German trenches. He'd gone into a depression of sorts. Only to be pulled out of it by a young officer from the Royal Flying Corps, who'd been shot down over the trenches and broken both of his legs. Then spent his days in the next bed to Cas telling him tales of a different war, a war between knights of the skies battling one on one. He was almost romantic about it, and as Cas didn't have a battalion to return to his Brigade Commander was more than happy to sign his transfer to the Royal Flying Corps. He thought of his men, and how many of them would have been glad to turn and run when the guns started firing if it meant they got to live instead of rotting in a muddy Belgian field.

"HQ, Sir," Daisy's voice cut through Cas' daydreams and dragged him back into the moment. He turned and looked at the young Corporal standing with the field telephone in her hand. "Headquarters on the phone, Sir. The line's a bit rough."

"Yes. Yes, thank you," he said as he took the phone. "Salisbury here." Daisy watched as the conversation went on, and as Cas frowned, it finished abruptly with an "I'll see what I can do, Sir," before he put down the phone. Daisy was close enough to have heard most of what was said. "Not a word, Wilson," he warned her solemnly.

"No, Sir."

With perfect timing, the giggle of female voices filled the silence from the balcony. Cas looked to the ceiling for a moment, as if looking for answers, or redemption, then took a deep breath before calling them in.

"Is everything OK?" Harriet asked as they left the balcony.

"No," Cas replied bluntly. The smiles fell from their faces as Daisy pursed her lips in worry at what she knew was coming. "I've got a bit of a problem," Cas continued.

"Oh?" Harriet replied.

"Yes... HQ has received sketchy reports that German paratroopers have dropped to the east, and overrun one of the major French airfields."

"Does that mean they're coming here?" Harriet asked nervously

"I don't know... Not yet, at least," Cas replied, "but that's not the problem."

"Then what is?"

"Nobody has a bloody clue what's going on," he said as he frowned further. "The entire British Expeditionary Force is in chaos, and they've got no idea whether the French airfield has been overrun or not; which means they've no idea whether they can continue to reroute our aircraft there, or what's happening with the RAF units that are based there, and nobody is answering the phone."

"Why not just call the French army?" Nicole asked. "They'll know if anyone. I can even speak to them if you wish?"

"Mon Francais n'est pas le Probleme," Cas replied in a near perfect French accent, taking Nicole a little by surprise. "Unfortunately, the French chain of command is currently making their British counterparts look positively efficient by comparison, and I assure you that's quite an achievement right now! So, as no bugger has a clue what's going on, HQ want me to send a Hurricane to have a look, and I don't think I need to explain to you the predicament that puts me in."

"Will the squadron be back soon?" Harriet asked.

"They're unlikely to be back until later today, and even if they were, they'd need to refuel, rearm, be briefed, and get back into the air. If the French airfield has gone, that's valuable time lost, and every minute is a minute damaged or shot up British aeroplanes, maybe even ours, could continue to land there, and fly straight into German hands."

"I see..." Harriet replied.

"Do you?" Cas asked.

"Yes. Yes, I think I do," Harriet said with a frown.

"Is there no other squadron?" Nicole asked.

"Not that doesn't have the same problem we do," Cas said with a reluctant frown.

"Then we'll go," Harriet said with a confident smile.

"It'll only take one of you," he replied.

"If she goes, I go," Nicole said. Both girls pulled their shoulders back and nodded their heads defiantly. It's something they'd done throughout their time at school. Their professors had learned, after a while, that it was easier for all concerned to let them do things together than it was to argue. If they didn't, the girls did as they liked anyway, and no amount of punishment would change that. Cas rolled his eyes and sighed, then frowned at Daisy as she suppressed a giggle at the humour of the terrible situation.

"Very well. HQ doesn't have time for us to argue the point, fortunately. Now, you both understand that I'm asking you to do this reluctantly, and in no way should you feel pressured to comply?" Both nodded, and he walked them over to the map table. "Right, this is us, and here's the French airfield. A little over thirty minutes of flight time. You can read a map?"

"Of course" Nicole replied with disdain. "Why do you English keep asking this like we're idiots?"

"Quite..." he continued, "Anyway, you're to take off, get a bit of height and give it some throttle. Once there do a low pass, one only, then get back here. No messing about, and if there's any sign of trouble at all, at any time, you're to turn tight and drop to the ground then get back here sharpish. Got it?" Both girls nodded with excitement. "You're not to get mixed up in anything. Not wanting to dull the shine from your recent accomplishments, but you were both damned lucky with those Germans yesterday. It's a different game when they're coming after you deliberately. The Hurricane will struggle against the 109 in a fair fight. Even more so if the 109 is being driven by somebody that's been around a bit. Understood?"

"Understood!" they replied in unison.

"Right, let's get you in the sky. Chief isn't going to be happy."

"Can we leave our jackets here?" Harriet asked as they walked across the room. "It's quite warm, and I don't think we need them."

"Absolutely not!" Cas replied without breaking his stride. "Hurricanes can burn like a roman candle if they're hit in the wrong way. That jacket could be the difference between you escaping with your lily white skin intact, or being toast. You'll wear your jackets and helmets, and that's not up for debate." The girls looked at each other nervously and followed Cas.

"It's where Jen took Pops and Hugo... The airfield you're going to," Daisy whispered close in Harriet's ear as she joined them walking through the house. "She should have been there if the roads were clear."

"OK, Wilson. That'll do," Cas said before she could say any more. "Shout if they call back before take off."

"Sir..." Daisy replied dutifully. "Be careful," she whispered and squeezed Harriet's hand before leaving them to head down the stairs. Harriet stopped for a moment to look up and gave Daisy a smile and a wave.

"Get them ready to go, Chief," Cas shouted.

"Are we evacuating, Sir?"

"Not yet..." Cas replied. "Are they ready to go?"

"Sergeant Kaye?" the Chief asked as AP joined him, she had a frown on her face and her eyes were narrowed as she wiped the oil from her hands onto an old rag. "Are those two Hurricanes ready to fly?"

"As ready as they can be," AP replied. "The compass is playing up on H, but if they are flying together, it shouldn't be a problem. One between two is more than enough." Nicole raised her eyebrows at Cas in a silent 'I told you so', which he frowned at but otherwise ignored.

"It looks like I will be leading if I have the compass," Nicole said. "As it should be."

"Do you have a watch?" Cas asked as he looked at her wrist. "You'll need one if you're leading the navigating." Nicole shook her head.

"You'd better have this," Harriet replied with a roll of her eyes, as she unfastened Sully's watch and handed it over.

"Obviously," Nicole said as she took it, and fastened it around her wrist and stroking the glass in appreciation.

"Very well. Good luck to you both," Cas said warmly to the girls. "Oh, and I thought you should know. I was able to twist HQ's arm yesterday evening, and they've reluctantly formally registered you both as acting Third Officers in the ATA and sent your details over to England, so your being here is official." The girls smiled and grabbed their parachutes, then climbed aboard their steeds while AP whistled and summoned more ground crew to help. Cas looked to the sky one more time in a desperate hope that a pair of Hurricanes might turn up and stop him in his madness of sending two young girls on a combat patrol in a hostile environment. Of course, nothing came. AP leant into the cockpit and tightened Harriet's harness while one of her colleagues did the same for Nicole. "Where are you going?" she asked quietly, after checking nobody could hear her.

"The French airfield to the east. Nobody can contact them, and whoever is in charge thinks the Germans may have overrun them. We're going to have a look." Harriet replied.

"Don't take any risks!" AP said. "Use the clouds for cover, and if you get into trouble with the Luftwaffe, don't fly straight and level. Keep twisting and turning, and push it as fast as you can. This here is the boost plug, pull it if you get into trouble and you'll get a few extra miles per hour. Don't overdo it, though. It can wreck the engine." Harriet nodded. She was both excited and nervous, her stomach was spinning, and there was a tightness in her chest, right above her stomach, something she hadn't felt for a long time.

"Thank you," she muttered to AP as Cas gave the nod and the mighty Merlin engines roared into life.

"Don't break my aeroplane," AP said, then gave Harriet the faintest hint of a smile before jumping off the wing, and the pair of Hurricanes were guided out of the pen. They taxied to the grass strip runway, ran up their engines while they went through their power checks, then side by side they bounced along the grass. AP and the Chief joined Cas as he watched the Hurricanes race across the field, Nicole slightly forward and Harriet to her right. They did exactly as they were told and had their oxygen masks and helmets on and fastened up.

"I don't like it," the Chief said as they watched. "It doesn't feel right. Male or female doesn't matter, they're not combat trained pilots, and flying anywhere east or north of here is asking for trouble."

"I can assure you that you can't feel any worse than I do about this, Chief," Cas said. "I don't know how I'll live with myself sending two untrained girls into the serpent's lair."

"I know, Sir," the Chief said warmly. "I also know you wouldn't have sent them unless it was absolutely necessary. It's not a good decision, but it's the right one." He put his hand on Cas' shoulder and gave him a supportive squeeze. They were of a similar age, though the Chief was a few years older, and he'd been through the previous war the same as Cas. He'd watched more young pilots fly off never to return than he cared to remember. Though he did remember, he remembered the name and face of every pilot that had never come back to his squadron.

"They'll be OK," AP said, taking the pair of older men by surprise as they'd both momentarily forgotten she was there. They both looked at her, inviting more. "They're better pilots than half the trained combat pilots in the squadron, and maybe that's because they haven't had the training."

"How do you work that out?" Cas asked with the forced smile of sombre cheerfulness.

"They don't know what to expect, or what to be scared of. They just fly, and that may be enough to confuse any Germans they run into, at least for long enough for them to get away."

"That's a good theory, AP. Let's hope it holds up," Cas said.

"Or that it doesn't need to," the Chief added.

"Yes, quite..." Cas said with a doubtful smile. "OK, I'd better get back to Ops. The second they get back I want their aeroplanes prepped to go up again. If the Germans have overrun the French airfield, it won't be long until it's our turn. Better get on with packing the spares.

"Yes, Sir," the Chief and AP replied.

Chapter 7

Hide and Sweep

Harriet couldn't help but smile as she pushed the stick forward slightly to lift the tail into the slipstream, and her Hurricane bounced from the ground for the last time as she caught the air under her wings. Once again, she pulled back on the stick and waited for the bounce that never came, then giggled to herself as she climbed through the bumpy air and raised the undercarriage. Nicole looked over to her as they turned across the field, nodded, then wiggled her wings in a wave to Cas and the others who waved in reply as they watched.

"Does your compass work?" Nicole asked over the radio.

"I think so... Wait," Harriet replied. "What heading are we on?"

"Zero one five."

"Ah. No, mine is currently showing one thirty. Nowhere near, I'm afraid."

"That's OK. You can follow my lead. The way things should be."

"You wouldn't catch me if I had a compass!" Harriet smirked.

"We may yet see, my little Harriet."

"Don't call me that!" Harriet objected.

Nicole's giggles eventually faded as they roared across the sky, and the early summer morning brightened around them. The sun was lying quite low to the east, and long streets of cumulus clouds were lining up from the west. The girls climbed and straightened out between two neat lines of clouds, close enough to pull into them and hide if the Germans turned up. Harriet looked around regularly, following Claude's often repeated instruction to scan the horizon left to right on a repeated loop, while also following Cas' directive to check the rearview mirror, and wiggle the wings to check high and low. She spent so much time monitoring the cloud strewn sky that she'd almost forgotten what she was looking for, so when Nicole's voice came across the radio, it made her jump a little.

"I think that could be it," Nicole said excitedly.

"Where?" Harriet asked as she scanned the horizon.

"Off the nose to the right. See the large forest ahead of us?"

"Yes... But I can't. Oh, wait. Wait, yes I think I see it."

"You see the smoke?"

"I see it!" Black and grey smoke intertwined with the lower rows of fluffy white clouds dotted below. It was actually impossible to miss once Harriet had seen it. As they drew closer, Harriet could see the glowing flicker of flames from burning aircraft and vehicles.

"I don't think we need to look any closer," Nicole said.

"We should," Harriet replied. "Maybe it was just a raid."

"Harry, I'm not sure. It looks dangerous."

"Full speed across the treetops, they won't see us. We can't come this far and turn back; we need to let Cas know what's happening. Besides, he said to do one low pass. We'll go in together and surprise them, stay right on my wing tip and we'll go straight down the middle of the runway, then bank left and climb back up to the cloud line."

"If you're sure."

"Let's do it, on three, full throttle and dive. One, two…"

"Wait"

"What?"

"Do we go on three, or one, two, three, then go?"

"Nicole, let's just go, now." Harriet pushed the throttle full forward with her left hand while simultaneously pushing the stick forward with her right. The Hurricane lurched forward, dropped its nose and galloped with increasing speed towards the ground. Nicole instinctively copied and stuck slightly behind Harriet's left wing as the pair dived hard and fast towards the verdant greenery of the French countryside. Harriet could feel the sweat soaking her brow under her flying helmet as soon as the dive began to steepen, and her adrenaline started to pump. She tried to control her breathing as the pressure of the dive squeezed her head and pushed her back into her seat. The speed indicator passed three hundred miles per hour, three ten, three fifteen, three fifty. "Level now," she shouted into her mask and pulled back on the stick. The Hurricane was sluggish to respond, and it took a hard pull with both hands to make it pay attention and do as it was told. For the briefest of moments, Harriet felt sure she'd overestimated the aeroplane and her own skills, and worried that she wouldn't be able to pull out of the dive. Beads of sweat ran into her eyes as she levelled just metres from the grass, and she quickly looked to her left to see Nicole exiting the dive at the same time. She turned her head forward again, just in time to see her propeller trim the hedge marking the airfield boundary. To her surprise, the Hurricane didn't slow down once she'd levelled off, and instead started to shake and shudder as the airspeed indicator pushed on. She dipped the right wing slightly to look out, then the left; the airfield was a war zone. German paratroopers were crossing from the left to the right, and the ground behind them was dotted with parachute canopies. Some of the neatly lined up British and French aeroplanes were burning, and gunfire was being exchanged between the mix of British and French forces around the hangars, while the German paratroopers swept from the left in small groups. Near the end of the tarmac, the runway was lined with three triple engine German transport aircraft, Ju52s, taxiing slowly towards the fray, and looking like they'd just landed. A German paratrooper running along the grass stopped and looked straight at Harriet as she dipped her left wing, their eyes locked as she roared past at ground level and cleared the airfield. It felt surreal. She was flying the fastest she'd ever moved in her life, and at that moment, it felt like she'd stopped and hung in the air while he watched her pass.

"Seen enough?" Nicole asked.

"Not yet," Harriet replied. "Follow me!" She pulled back on her stick and felt her stomach tighten, and her vision darken, as the Hurricane started a very steep and swift climb. She couldn't talk, she could hardly see, and she found herself holding her breath involuntarily as she rolled to the right and on to her back, then pulled the stick into her stomach and dived back at the airfield. "One burst at those transports then into the clouds," she shouted, forcing her words out.

"Idiot!" came Nicole's reply. "Merde!"

Harriet lined up the sights with the leading transport, which was now urgently jettisoning soldiers from its rear door while still rolling, as were the two behind it. The guns roared, and the Hurricane juddered as lumps of grass leapt into the air, closely followed by sprays of smoke and blood, and then flames, as her bullets found their mark. She stopped firing and pulled up into a roll, as Nicole ripped into the second and third transports before following her. She could see the French and British waving and cheering from the hangars. It hadn't been much, but it was something. She fought the urge to turn and go again, as she knew she had to get back and let Cas know what was happening. She checked to her right, and Nicole was back on her wingtip and pointing angrily at Harriet.

"You're a fool. Why would you do that?" Nicole demanded.

"Morale."

"You know we won't have made any real difference to the outcome of that battle."

"I know..." Harriet felt her heart sink a little despite the adrenaline of the attack coursing through her veins. She knew she couldn't change the outcome, not really. There must have been hundreds of paratroopers down there. The airfield was lost, and those defending it would soon be dead or captive. She wanted to help them, or at least give them a moment of belief before the end at least, something other than the inevitability of defeat.

"But it was fun fighting back, wasn't it?" Nicole added mischievously as they roared up into the clouds.

"Immensely," Harriet smiled. "Let's go home."

"OK, happily," Nicole said. "On my mark, turn left fifty degrees. Three, two, one. Mark." They turned in unison, while still climbing into the ever deepening streets of clouds until finally they came on course and broke through to the top of the cloud cover. They skimmed the top, keeping just low enough to mix with the white haze and stay out of view of any German fighters looking for a bit of fun. Ten minutes into their return flight, Nicole broke the silence, and the tension of horizon and mirror searching. "What was that?"

"What was what?" Harriet asked as she spun her head urgently and searched the sky, scared she'd missed something.

"There. In the mirror. The sun is reflecting on something, watch." Harriet stared at the mirror for what felt like an eternity. "There, did you see it? A little below us?" Nicole asked excitedly.

"I don't think so... Wait! Yes!"

"An aeroplane?" Nicole asked.

"I think so. I can't quite make it out. If it is, it's a big one, I think." Harriet said as she strained her eyes. The glinting shape soon started streaming a trail of black smoke, and more reflections bounced around behind the first, sweeping in wide arcs towards the smoke and then away. They both focused until the picture finally formed in Harriet's mind. It was a bomber, and it was being chased. "It's one of ours," she said excitedly. "It's a bomber, one of ours."

"How do you know?"

"It's big, one of those we saw fly over the other week."

"Are you sure?"

"Almost certain."

"Almost?"

"No. I'm certain, I'm positive. It looks like they've got company, too."

"What should we do?"

"I don't know... We should get back."

"But they're smoking. We can't just leave them."

"Shall we have a go? Maybe we can scare them off if we fly aggressively?"

"OK... Let's do it. Let's help. One pass, like the airfield?"

"One pass."

"Shall we just fly at them? We'll have the sun behind us that way."

"Let's."

The girls turned and climbed, then levelled with the distant bomber, which was now smoking heavily. As they closed, they could see the two heavy German fighter planes chasing. Messerschmitt 110s. They were bigger than the 109s, with twin engines and a rear facing gunner, and they were swooping around the bomber which was pitching and rolling in ways nobody would believe a bomber could, to try and dodge the streams of bullets being hurled at it repeatedly. The two groups of aeroplanes closed with startling speed.

"I'll take the one on the left," Nicole said. "You take the right."

"OK..." Harriet replied. She swallowed hard to try and lubricate her instantly dry and tight throat; she even licked the sweat off her lips and from under her nose just to try and get some moisture into her mouth. She was terrified. She was doing everything Cas had told them not to do, but she couldn't help it. She had to help.

"Vive la France!" Nicole screamed as she closed with her target. Harriet looked out of the corner of her eye and saw Nicole's guns blazing and streams of tracer zipping across the sky. Bullets ripped across the wing of her foe, and the 110 immediately banked into a dive with Nicole chasing hard after it. The second 110 swooped up, then left, then rolled over the bomber and into a dive after Nicole. The bomber crew looked wide eyed at Harriet as she roared past them and turned into a dive after the second German. By now he was firing streams of bullets after Nicole as she rolled and dodged while firing into the back of her quarry. Suddenly, he pulled up sharply and spun, bringing Nicole up tight behind him. The second 110 followed suit but overshot, sending his bullets just off the nose of Nicole's Hurricane, but unfortunately, for him at least, pulling right across Harriet's sights. She held her breath and pushed the button, firing hard and constant, and her bullets hit the nose and the cockpit, making the cockpit flash and spark as though it had been hit by lightning. She kept her finger on the fire button, and the bullets continued down the fuselage until the 110 yawed hard right. The line of Harriet's bullets severed the tail of his aeroplane, making the nose flip up a little then start to spin violently as the tail assembly fell away. Without waiting to see what happened next, she dived and followed Nicole, getting in place as the procession swept back up towards the bomber, the 110 rolled and this time presented himself perfectly. Nicole fired, and the right engine started burning, a fire which quickly spread to the rest of the wing, engulfing it entirely by the time it passed the bomber again. Another long burst by Nicole as she chased up and past the bomber and the second engine smoked. The 110 rolled, and two crew bailed out, falling through the sky and behind the bomber as their aeroplane plummeted from the sky alongside them. Nicole rolled, and Harriet followed, then after a sweep of the sky to make sure there was no more trouble around, they lined up either side of the bomber cockpit. Harriet waved politely, and the pilot replied in kind, then pointed at the smoke spewing engine between them which had now stopped turning the propeller. He gestured as if to say they were severely damaged by swiping his finger across his neck and pointing down. Harriet checked her altimeter and noticed they were indeed losing height and slipping between the clouds.

"How far are we from home?" she asked Nicole.

"Maybe ten minutes, a little longer with some glide if they can hold on," Nicole replied.

"Are we on the right heading?"

"Close enough, I suppose."

"OK, I'll get them to follow." Harriet gestured to the pilot, keeping as close as she could. He frowned in confusion, so she pulled off her oxygen mask in the hope that he could lip read, and then he frowned more, then raised an eyebrow in surprise. "Our airfield is ten minutes away. Follow that Hurricane," she mouthed while holding up both hands and spreading her fingers, then pointing at Nicole. The pilot nodded, and she gave him a thumbs up. "Nicole, move in front and lead them home, you have the compass. I'll climb above and keep watch for any Germans following you in."

"Take care," Nicole said as she pulled in front of the bomber. Harriet pointed once again, indicating that the bomber pilot should follow Nicole. He nodded and gave her a thumbs up, she did the same then pulled back on her stick and climbed high above the pair of aeroplanes. She throttled back to slow behind them, then went back to her scanning while tracking the bomber and trying to descend at the same rate until they finally broke cloud. The bomber's wing threw up a fountain of parts as another explosion rocked the aeroplane and made it lurch to the left. The crew fought it hard and managed to level the bomber as the airfield came into view. Harriet dived to her place alongside the bomber and pointed down at the airfield. The pilot looked around, noted it, then gave the thumbs up again. Harriet nodded and smiled, then peeled away in a long sweeping circuit to check once again nothing was behind, and Nicole joined her while the bomber bounced to a rough and smoky landing. Then, when it was clear and safe, the girls lined up and brought themselves in. Harriet watched as the ground came up quickly, as it always did. Throttle back, less speed, nose up to scrub off some more speed, slowing, nose up, and bounce. She was down in one, and the engine laboured as she leant out of the cockpit into the prop blast, a brief but welcome relief from the oven like heat and torrential sweat from combat. She bounced down the grass strip, then with Nicole doing exactly the same she applied the brake, and they turned in unison, into almost the exact spots they'd left from outside the sandbag pen.

The ground crews sprang into action as Harriet cut the engine with a sigh of relief. She pulled off her flying helmet and used the tail of her recently acquired silk scarf to wipe the sweat from her face. She felt exhausted, and a little elated, but mostly exhausted. She reached up and put her flying helmet on the rearview mirror then looked down for the clasp on her harness and started to fiddle with it unsuccessfully.

"I've got it," AP said as she leant into the cockpit. The pressure of the tight harness released, and Harriet sucked in a deep breath of air before pushing against her seat and pulling herself up and out of the cockpit. AP held her arm to steady her, as her knees buckled from the adrenaline fuelled shaking that was vibrating her legs uncontrollably. She steadied herself before climbing out onto the wing while smiling at Nicole, who was waving at her excitedly while exiting her Hurricane in the same manner. "Are you OK? Are you hurt?" AP asked.

"I'm OK... I think. Thank you," Harriet replied shakily.

"What the hell have you two been up to?" Cas demanded as he appeared in front of the Hurricanes.

"The Germans are at the airfield," Harriet replied breathlessly. "Paratroopers, I think, and lots of them." Cas looked troubled as he nodded his head in acknowledgement.

"And these paratroopers were armed with heavy anti aircraft cannons too, no doubt?" he asked.

"I'm afraid I don't understand?" Harriet protested in confusion. He twirled his finger in the air as if to suggest the girls turn around, and as they did, he pointed at the tail of Nicole's Hurricane. It was half shredded. The German had clearly got some of his bullets on target before Harriet had got him. "Oh, that..." Harriet said bashfully.

"Yes, that..." Cas replied. "You can tell me about it later. I'd better let Headquarters know about the airfield. Come on." He turned and marched off towards the house, and the girls followed close behind, leaving AP and her ground crews to get to work on the battered Hurricanes.

Nicole smirked and nudged Harriet playfully with her shoulder. "I thought it was responding poorly," she whispered. Harriet smirked back at her. "But if you were anything of a friend, you'd have got him before he did that to me."

"Don't blame your poor flying on me," Harriet replied with a casual shrug. "You're just lucky I was there. Otherwise, you wouldn't be here to complain."

"Luck? You know all about luck. Jinx!"

"Enough," Cas said calmly, without turning to look at them. "And where on earth did you find that bomber?"

"About halfway between the French airfield and here, it was in trouble, so we guided it here," Harriet replied.

"Good show. They should buy you a drink for that." The tall and dominating figure of Warrant Officer Peters was walking quickly towards them. "Everything OK, Mister Peters?" Cas asked.

"Sir... The bomber," Peters replied. His face was a picture of concern.

"What's wrong with it?"

"It's not what's wrong with it. It's who's in it!" Peters replied nervously.

"Well? Are you going to make me guess?" Cas asked.

"It's loaded with officers, including an AVM…"

"Oh bloody hell, just what we need," Cas muttered.

"What is it?" Harriet asked.

"I'll tell you later. For now, get back to your aeroplanes until I come to find you. Get AP to stick the kettle on and make you a cup of tea." The girls stopped in their tracks, and Cas marched towards the bomber with Peters at his side. It was crawling with fire fighters and other ground crew, while the evacuated passengers and crew stood safely at the entrance to the house behind it. Among them was Air Vice Marshal Bristol from the Air Ministry back in England, a tall and sunken faced older officer with rows of medal ribbons on his chest and stripes on his cuffs. Beside him, among a handful of Army, RAF and Navy officers, was a civilian, somewhere in his early sixties and wearing a very smart black pinstriped suit and bowler hat.

"Flight Lieutenant Salisbury, Sir," Peters announced proudly as they approached the group. "The Squadron Adjutant."

"Sir." Cas saluted smartly.

"Salisbury..." The Air Vice Marshal stared at Cas' medals and wings for a moment. "Salisbury VC, I see. Somme, 1918?"

"Yes, Sir," Cas replied, appearing a little embarrassed.

"Your name precedes you, Mister Salisbury. I remember hearing all about you getting mixed up with that Jerry squadron. How many of them was it you knocked down that day? Fifteen, was it?"

"Thirteen, Sir"

"Thirteen... Yes, that's right. And you without a scratch."

"Not that day, Sir."

"Of course. A bloody horrible affair that was, anyway. I had a fighter squadron at the time, so we certainly shared some of the same air. Bristol's the name, Henry Bristol. AOC strategy and planning at the Air Ministry," he introduced himself and shook Cas' hand tightly and gratefully. "This is Mister Bromley from the air desk at the War Office."

"A pleasure, Sir," Cas said politely as they shook hands. "Are you all OK? Does anybody need any medical attention?" he asked as he looked around.

"Thankfully not," Bristol replied. "Damned close run thing, though. We'd been up north trying to get a handle on what the hell's going on, so we can get back to London and work out what we're going to do about it when things got a bit hot. We decided to head south, which seemed like the right idea at the time, that's until we were set about by a pair of Jerry 110s. Flight

Lieutenant Philips and his crew did all they could to shake the buggers off, of course, but they weren't having any of it."

"They got the port engine on their first run," Philips said as he stepped forward and shook Cas' hand. "It was just a matter of time after that."

"And time was running out!" Bristol continued. "Until your pilots stopped them in their tracks, that is."

"Oh?" Cas replied, trying to hide the nerves from his voice, the nerves that were climbing from the knot forming in his stomach.

"Best piece of flying I've ever seen. Those boys flew nose to nose with the Huns at full throttle without flinching, then knocked them both out of the sky like they were swatting flies. I should like to meet them both and thank them personally if you don't mind? There'll be medals, I can assure you of that. For you too, Philips, that was some tremendous flying to keep them off us and get us back after being shot up." The knot in Cas' stomach tightened.

"Yes, Sir," Cas replied. "Unfortunately, they're still with their aeroplanes, and I've not had time to debrief them just yet. Should we head inside for now? I expect you'd like to talk with Headquarters?" He waited in the hope that he'd been able to distract the AVM sufficiently.

"What's that? Oh, yes, I suppose you're right, Cas. We'd better let them know where we are, and see if we can't rustle up some transport. We must get back to London as soon as possible. Lead the way!" The group started walking, and Philips gave Cas a knowing smile before joining him in heading towards the Ops Room.

"Did you say you're the Adjutant, Salisbury?" the AVM asked.

"Yes, Sir."

"How come? A man of your knowledge and experience would be helpful at Headquarters."

"I wanted to be with a flying squadron, Sir, and Adjutant is the only post they had available. Apparently, I'm too old to be a combat pilot."

"Yes, well, I suppose the likes of you and I had our day in the last war. Though I see you haven't quite let go of the past." He pointed at the RFC wings on Cas' chest. "I thought all of us old boys had been told to wear RAF wings, and put the antiques into storage?"

"Oh, yes," Cas replied casually as he glanced down at his pilot's wings. "I'm afraid my tunic was damaged in a German raid, so I'm having to do with this old thing until I can get it repaired."

"Lucky you'd remembered to bring your old tunic with you to France, in that case." Bristol smirked knowingly.

"Quite…" Cas smiled.

Who's your CO, Salisbury?"

"Squadron Leader Barnes, Sir."

"Ah yes, of course. Is he around?"

"Not at the moment, Sir. The squadron is up escorting a raid."

"The Ardennes job?"

"Yes, Sir."

"Maximum effort, wasn't it?"

"Yes, Sir, the full squadron left over an hour ago."

"How come you had those two Hurricanes hanging around to help us out if that's the case? Not that I'm ungrateful, you understand."

"Those aeroplanes were in the process of being returned to serviceability, Sir. HQ wanted a reconnaissance of the French airfield east of here, and they're all I had. I expect they bumped into you on their way home."

"I see... And how is the French airfield?"

"Overrun, I believe."

"Bugger!"

"Yes, Sir. As far as I know, they had four squadrons there, bombers and fighters, along with a squadron of Poles and a Detached Flight of our Hurricanes." He looked over to Daisy as they entered the Ops Room. "Wilson, get HQ on the phone." She did as he asked and handed him the receiver. "Salisbury here. My reconnaissance flight has returned, and they confirm that German airborne units, paratroopers mostly, have overrun the French aerodrome. Yes. Yes, you're welcome. Also, Air Vice Marshal Bristol's party has landed at our location. Their aeroplane is a write off following enemy action, and they'll need to be recovered as soon as possible. Yes, that's right, Air Vice Marshal Bristol. One moment..." He looked at Bristol with resigned annoyance. "Sir, HQ would like to speak to you." He held out the phone.

"Bristol here!" the AVM barked into the receiver. "It's imperative that we get back to London without delay. I have Mister Bromley with me, and the PM is expecting him this afternoon. Thank you." He put the phone down and looked to Cas. "They're dispatching a relief now," he said with a frown. "Can't see why they'd need to talk to me before they'd do it, though." He shook his head in disappointment. "It's the one thing I can't stand about the RAF, too much red tape."

"I'll have Chef put some tea on while you're waiting," Cas said. He gave Peters a nod, sending him from the room.

"Thanks, Cas. I can call you Cas, can't I?" the AVM continued.

"Of course, Sir."

"When did you say your squadron is due back?"

"Should be any time, Sir," Cas replied after checking his watch.

"Well, while we're waiting, why don't you and I go and meet those young pilots that saved our bacon up there?"

"Tea should be ready shortly," Cas half protested.

"Then we'll have some shortly," the AVM replied, "but in the meantime, I'd really like to thank your young men for their efforts, and I know Mister Bromley would like to do the same." The civilian nodded enthusiastically. "I think it's good that civilians, especially Ministers of Parliament, get to meet our pilots. If nothing else, it helps when budgets and allocations are discussed in the house."

"Did you say you were heading over to see the pilots that bailed us out?" Philips asked with a casual smile. "I'd love to thank them personally if you wouldn't mind me tagging along?" he asked mischievously as he joined them. Cas nodded and smiled reluctantly.

"That's enough, Wilson," Cas said as he watched Daisy biting her lip to stop herself from smiling. "I'll be down with the aeroplanes if you need me."

"Sir," she said with a smirk.

Cas guided the small group back outside where their bomber was still smouldering and led them across the grass. He walked ahead of them, and Philips quickly joined him.

"Looking forward to this, aren't you?" Cas asked Philips under his breath.

"You're not kidding, old boy," Philips replied. "Half of me wants to make sure I wasn't seeing things, and the other half wants to see their faces when they find out."

"You're not helping."

"I'm looking forward to hearing how it came about. I won't lie."

"Well, you'll soon find out... Where are they, Sergeant Kaye?" Cas asked as they arrived at the Hurricane pen. She was standing on the wing of Harriet's Hurricane and leaning into the cockpit. Her eyes widened when she saw the entourage, then narrowed as the corners of her mouth turned up in a notable and rare smile. Other ground crews were still crawling over both aeroplanes like ants. They'd been refuelled and rearmed, and Lanky was helping one of the riggers patch the cannon shredded fabric of the tail. AP leaned back to reveal Harriet sitting in the cockpit, and Cas nodded with resignation.

"Step down here, would you, Harry," Cas said, "I've got somebody I'd like you to meet." Harriet quickly stood and was helped from the cockpit by AP, who then sat on the cockpit frame, watching and smirking while Harriet slid down the wing and met with Nicole, who entered the pen from the doorway at the rear just at the right time. Together they walked over and stood in front of the group of men.

"Yes?" Harriet asked.

"Miss Cornwall, Miss Delacourt," Cas started, after taking a deep breath. "I'd like to introduce you to Air Vice Marshal Bristol, and this is the Right Honourable Mister Peter Bromley, MP, from the War Office." He gestured to the civilian in his black pinstripe suit, and dark rimmed round glasses. Cas rolled his eyes at Philips, who was now grinning like a Cheshire Cat.

"A pleasure to meet you, Sir," Harriet replied, only just managing to stop herself bowing as she talked.

"My pleasure," Bromley replied, formally but a little quizzically. "You're attached to the Squadron?" he asked, sounding a little like a visiting house master asking about the school.

"I didn't realise we had any WAAFs this close to the front?" Bristol interrupted. "I thought you were all supposed to have been evacuated back to England when the balloon went up?"

"Oh they were certainly given that option," Cas said. "Though Squadron Leader Barnes allowed them to make their own decisions, and the WAAFs attached to our squadron all opted to stay. Which is a blessing, as they're all damned good at their jobs, and we'd be lost without them, especially the likes of Sergeant Kaye up there who's a genius mechanic." AP totally ignored his comment, not showing any change in emotion as she watched for what she knew was coming next. "These two young ladies aren't WAAFs, though," Cas continued.

"Excuse me?" Bromley asked. "I don't think I understand?"

"I'm not sure I do, either!" Bristol added. "Explain yourself, Cas."

"Well, Sir. You asked to meet the pilots who came to your rescue, and here they are. Third Officers Harriet Cornwall and Nicole Delacourt, temporarily of the Air Transport Auxiliary, and currently attached to this squadron, pending their transfer back to England. Of course."

"But... But you're girls..." Bromley muttered in mystified confusion.

"Yes, Sir," Harriet replied. "So people keep reminding us."

"Why does everybody keep saying that?" Nicole asked Harriet, totally ignoring the others. She looked down at herself, then at Harriet's chest, then face, then shrugged dismissively as if to note the obvious.

"A day for observations, it would seem," Cas added. "Anyway, girls or not, they're two of the best pilots we have, and it's thanks to them that we still have a Squadron here, and the War Office still has an Air Minister and an Air Vice Marshal, Sir."

"Yes. Yes, of course, where are my manners?" Bromley said as he straightened up and corrected himself, though he still looked a little unsure of the situation. He stepped forward and held out his hand "Indebted to you," he said as Harriet took his hand in hers and shook it as firmly as she could. Nicole followed suit, though with significantly less enthusiasm. Bristol raised an eyebrow slightly but allowed himself a slight smile before taking his turn, shaking the hands of both girls.

"You have my sincerest gratitude," Bristol said warmly. "Though you've both left me in a bit of a predicament."

"Sir?" Harriet asked.

"I was all ready to recommend you both for the DFC for coming to our aid, and taking those two Jerries down..."

"DFC?" Harriet asked innocently.

"The Distinguished Flying Cross," Nicole said. "Grandpa has one."

"Yes, thank you," Bristol continued. "Thing is, that decoration is only awarded to military personnel, as far as I know, and I'm not sure how that would fit if you're ATA girls. Besides, it changes the story a little if you're not combat trained pilots."

"Why?" Nicole demanded. "Just because we are not trained in combat, did we not still shoot down the Germans and save you both? Are we not as worthwhile?"

"I think you've misunderstood my point, my good lady." Bristol corrected her, firing her a look that made even Nicole back up a little. "Not to worry, meaning can be lost in translation, I suppose. Though you do, in fact, make my point. You're not combat trained pilots, yet you chose to put yourselves in harm's way to protect a stricken aircraft. That alone is an immeasurably courageous act. The fact that you somehow managed to shoot down both enemy aircraft in the ensuing scrap is almost unfathomable."

"It is," Nicole replied with almost no grace at all, taking his praise to prove her point, and lifting her nose in the air the way she always did when proving herself right.

"And I watched the scrap first hand!" Bristol went on. "It wasn't luck that bested those German pilots, though I dare say it played its part, what you both did was down to pure natural skill and determination."

"This is almost too fantastic to be believed," Bromley added, "I think we need to do something about this Air Vice Marshal. The PM needs to hear about it."

"I agree, Sir. He should."

"He will." Bromley smiled excitedly.

"Though I think Flight Lieutenant Salisbury and I should have a talk first, Sir," Bristol replied. "Just so I understand how they were up there in the first place..." He looked at Cas, who smiled nervously in response. Harriet felt herself blushing fiercely, but before anything else could be said they were disturbed by the familiar roar of a Merlin engine. They all turned to see a green flare go up, as a Hurricane swept around the woods in a steep turn with a trail of black smoke following it.

"If you'll excuse me, gentlemen," Cas said as he turned and left the Hurricane pen. AP and Lanky were already by his side heading for the grass runway, along with the ground crews who emerged from the tree line to await their pilots. Harriet and Nicole followed Cas, as did the others. As the Hurricane started to bounce along the grass, another two swept into sight and quickly touched down behind it. The first Hurricane slowed then turned and halted, by which time Harriet found herself running towards it at Cas' side. The engine cut and Singh extracted himself from the cockpit with the help of the ground crew, he ran down the wing and jumped to the grass, taking a moment to stretch his back and shake out his arms, before walking along the trailing edge of the wing to meet Cas. "Raj?" Cas asked almost nervously.

"It was a massacre," Singh said as he composed himself, before taking Cas' hand and shaking it firmly. He coughed heavily and bent at the waist. Cas put a hand on his shoulder in support, but he raised his arm to indicate he was OK. Another cough and he stood again. "Sorry... It's the smoke."

"Not at all, old boy," Cas reassured him. Singh turned and looked down the airfield as another Hurricane was landing and another taxiing.

"Anyone back before us?" he asked.

"You're the first."

"I see..."

"Did the bomber boys get the bridges?" Cas asked. Singh simply shook his head.

"I've never seen anything like it," Singh explained. "They must have had hundreds of ack ack guns surrounding their bridgehead, maybe more, and the sky was black with 109s and 110s, it was like flying through hell. The bombers were cut down by the squadron. We did what we could, but our fighters were outnumbered five or ten to one."

"The CO?"

"I saw him go down," Archie added as he walked over with Max. "He got two of the seven he was dancing with, but he didn't stand a chance."

"Gus got it, too," Max added, wiping the sweat from his forehead.

"Parachutes?" Cas asked, hopefully. Both shook their heads.

"It's hard to say," Max continued, offering the slightest hope. "Things were moving so fast, and there were so many of them. If you stopped to think you got shot down."

"Let's get to Ops and get some tea in you," Cas said. The pilots nodded and as a group started towards the house. Other pilots joined them as they strolled, leaving their battle weary Hurricanes in the hands of their ground crews, who were already working hard at diagnosing, assessing, and repairing their charges.

"You OK, Ed?" Archie asked Grumpy.

"Just about," Grumpy nodded. "I still don't know how I made it back," he said in his light half Yorkshire, half Welsh accent.

"I don't know how many of us did, old boy," Archie replied.

"They got Tony Clarke, and Mister Anthony," Grumpy added.

"Bloody hell."

"Tony got two before they got him, and Mister Anthony was in flames when he put down into one of the bridges. I can't be sure, but it looked like he steered it that way to try and hit the objective and take a few Germans with him."

Chapter 8

A Blue Suit

Two hours after Singh had landed, the girls were sitting with the remaining squadron pilots by the dispersal tent, where a flight of Hurricanes stood ready to respond in case of an urgent call to arms. The girls had brought tea and sandwiches for the pilots; and made sure they had everything they needed while they recovered from the morning's raid, which saw only nine squadron Hurricanes return from the fifteen that left. The squadron had paid for its commitment to trying to protect the bombers and slow the German advance. They'd lost Barnes, their squadron commander, and Flight Lieutenant Jonny Anthony, the commander of A Flight, along with others, like Gus, the excitable young pilot who'd been so gracious and welcoming to the girls, and who Nicole had developed a particular liking for. She felt his loss more than she'd expected. She was shocked more than anything, and it was only when they'd stopped fetching and carrying, and joined the pilots in sitting in the sun, that she found herself overwhelmed by feelings of loss. He was about her age, maybe a little older, and was so full of energy and life. Her grief was shared by his friends in the squadron, especially Archie and Max. Not that either of them said much about the subject.

Of the nine Hurricanes that had returned, only three were combat ready and available for standby, with the other six being in various states of damage. The ground crews were hard at work and had been since the first aeroplane touched down, and it was all hands to work to try and get the rest serviceable as soon as possible. Of the nine pilots who returned, two were injured and unable to fly. Both had taken hits in the morning's combat but had managed to drag their wrecked aeroplanes back home to safety while being injured. To add to the morning's losses there'd been no sign or word of Jen, Hugo, and Pops, who'd left for the airfield the girls had reconnoitred earlier in the day. Following the reports of the airfield being overrun all three had been posted as missing in action, probably dead or captured.

All in all, the squadron wasn't in good shape. A twin engine bomber arrived at the airfield shortly before lunch and parked in the dispersal area. It had been sent from England to collect Bristol, Bromley, and their small entourage of officers, and the crew spent a while sitting with the squadron pilots and sharing some tea while their pilot went to report in at the Ops Room. A sudden silence fell as the phone buzzed. Everyone watched as the duty orderly picked it up and answered, "Dispersal?" The air of anticipation was almost tangible as the standby pilots thought through what was coming. "A Flight, scramble!" The pilots jumped into life and grabbed their parachutes, then ran to their waiting Hurricanes. The rest of the squadron pilots stood and watched as the three Hurricanes went bouncing along the runway, only minutes after the phone had rung.

"No rest for the wicked," Archie said as they watched the trio raise their wheels and turn around the airfield before heading north, receiving their instructions as they climbed towards whichever enemy was waiting for them. The phone rang again, and everyone turned to look. "Well, unless they're going to give us rifles and bayonets, there's bugger all else we can do," Archie muttered.

"Don't say things like that too loud," Max muttered. They looked at each other with an unspoken acceptance of the reality of their situation.

"Miss Cornwall, Miss Delacourt, and Sergeant MacDonald to report to the CO."

"Don't accept a rifle," Max said as a sigh of relief passed through the group, and the three of them headed towards the house. They were met at the door by AP and Lanky, who had been summoned from their work, much to AP's irritation. They made their way to the Ops Room where Cas and Singh were waiting for them. As the senior Flight Commander, Headquarters had appointed Singh as acting CO of the squadron.

"Sergeant MacDonald, you did me a damned good turn this morning when you intercepted the German on my tail, and in return, I've done you a damned bad one," Singh said.

"Sir?" Grumpy asked with a little trepidation.

"In recognition of your superior airmanship and leadership, I've recommended that you are commissioned and promoted to the rank of Pilot Officer, and Headquarters have agreed."

"Really, Sir? Thank you, Sir!" Grumpy smiled warmly, and a sparkle appeared in his eye.

"You may curse me yet for this, Mister MacDonald," Singh said as he shook Grumpy's hand. "Congratulations; and thank you. Now get yourself back to work. Hopefully, we'll have some Hurricanes back in service shortly, and we'll need B Fight on standby as soon as they are, if you'd like to tell Mister Russel."

"Yes, Sir." The girls smiled as Grumpy left the Ops Room grinning like a Cheshire Cat, and Singh turned to the others.

"Ladies, if you'd like to follow me." He led the girls, AP, and Lanky through to his office to join the rest of the WAAFs and Section Officer Finn in standing in front of the desk and facing Air Vice Marshal Bristol.

"Is this everyone?" Bristol asked.

"Yes, Sir," Singh replied as he stood beside Bristol.

"OK, ladies." Bristol continued. "I'm Air Vice Marshal Bristol from the Air Ministry, and in my current role, it's my job to advise the Minister for Air at the War Office. Unfortunately, after a reconnaissance trip earlier today, we were intercepted by German fighters and forced down here, quite an inconvenient nuisance I'm sure you'll agree; but also a fortuitous situation which has allowed both the right honourable gentleman from the War Office and myself to see for ourselves how our squadrons are coping, and I can tell you that it's been an eye opener!" The WAAFs all stood smartly at ease while he talked, and the girls tried to follow suit while hiding at the back of the room. "Now, the reason I've called you in here is that the biggest eye opener is your presence this close to the front, not to mention your involvement in combat critical operations! Women generally aren't permitted in forward units, as you all well know, and what's happening here is something that neither Mister Bromley from the War Office nor I can ignore." Finn pulled back her shoulders and let a smug smile creep on to her usually angry looking face. She prepared herself for the 'I told you so' moment that would confirm her protestations that they all should have left when HQ instructed, and the inevitable orders to evacuate. "The reports of your commanding officer and others in your squadron, along with my own personal experiences in engaging with you, leaves me in no doubt that your contributions to the efficiency and effectiveness of your squadron have been invaluable to the war effort." The rest of the WAAFs smiled and visibly grew with pride. "It's my understanding that following instructions to evacuate all female personnel, Squadron Leader Barnes allowed you to make your own decisions, much to the irritation of Headquarters, and in response, you all decided to stay with your squadron. Despite the losses your squadron had already encountered and the knowledge of how desperate the situation was getting, you chose to put yourselves in harm's way so we could keep putting aeroplanes in the sky, and stop the Luftwaffe gaining air superiority over the battlefield. Is this correct?"

"Yes, Sir!" the WAAFs replied collectively.

"I thought as much... OK, so my first point of action is to inform you that we'll be returning to England shortly, and each of you is invited to come along with us. Now, before you decide, I want you to know that your efforts here will be recognised regardless of your choice, and your future efforts in units back in England will be equally as valuable as everything you do here in France. As such, my second point of action is to inform you that in recognition of your bravery, you've each been Mentioned in Dispatches. Mister Singh has already provided me with your service details, and HQ has been notified." There was a gasp followed by silence in the room as the gathered WAAFs accepted that they had each just received a bravery award. "These will be conferred at a later date. So, that said, we don't have any time for messing about. Anybody wanting to return should speak out now." The silence in the room continued, and Bristol looked at Singh and nodded. Singh smiled and nodded in reply. "Very well, your response is as I expected," Bristol continued. "So, if Mister Singh is happy for you to remain on his squadron, I'm happy to authorise your continued presence."

"I consider them to be intrinsically linked to the continuing successful operation of the squadron, and I'd be honoured to have them remain, Sir," Singh replied.

"That's that, then," Bristol said. "You know, ladies, there's a lot of resistance at home to women being involved in this war. Sadly, the truth is that before this thing's over, we're going to need every fit and able person we've got if we're going to win, male or female, and the sooner we realise that, the better chance we'll have of winning! Thank you, ladies, that's all." The WAAFs came to attention, and after Finn had saluted, they turned to leave.

"Section Officer Finn, Sergeant Kaye, I'd like you to stay behind," Singh said. "You two, too." He pointed to the girls. The others left and closed the door behind them. "Section Officer Finn, you'll be returning with the Air Vice Marshal's party, could you please pack your things with haste," he said calmly and without warning. She looked shocked.

"But the regulations state..." she started.

"We have the regulations covered," Singh interrupted her. "You're to report to the Air Ministry on landing. HQ have communicated your pending return, and will have your assignment waiting for you."

"But..."

"Thank you for your service to the squadron, Miss Finn," he interrupted again, and her face turned all colours. She bit her tongue and saluted before leaving without another word. The other three stood a little surprised. "Sergeant Kaye, Air Vice Marshal Bristol has approved my recommendation for your commission and promotion to Assistant Section Officer. I'm assuming you'll accept and take responsibility for the WAAF section?"

"My duties maintaining the Hurricanes, Sir?" she asked.

"Well, it's what you're good at, so it would be ridiculous to suggest you don't continue. Besides, we lost our engineering officer a few weeks ago, as you know, so you'll take on that role. You will, however, have to do your new duties alongside your mechanic work."

"Yes, Sir. I understand."

"Congratulations, AP," he said as he shook her hand. "We'll talk more later." She stood smartly to attention, saluted, then left. As she did, there was a knock at the door, and Mister Bromley joined them.

"That leaves me with the two of you..." Singh said as the girls stood facing the three men.

"I'm told that Squadron Leader Barnes commissioned you into the Air Transport Auxiliary," Bristol said, as he leaned back on the desk with his hands in his pockets. "To allow you to ferry aircraft around for him, so he could use his combat pilots to do the fighting instead of moving aeroplanes?"

"Yes..." Harriet replied. Nicole nodded in quiet agreement. Her mind was still with Gus, and she hadn't paid much attention to what had gone on.

"Unfortunately, that's no good," Bristol continued, as Harriet felt her heart sink. "It was OK as a temporary fix, but the fact is that ATA pilots just aren't allowed to be stationed in combat areas, and certainly can't be attached to front line squadrons. The organisation has a very specific mandate; and by being deliberately involved in combat operations as you were this morning, even if it was only intended as a reconnaissance flight, all sorts of uncomfortable questions are raised. We don't want to throw Flight Lieutenant Salisbury to the wolves, nor the late Squadron Leader Barnes."

"Ridiculous," Nicole responded, as she finally started to catch up. "We saved your backside. We attacked the German planes landing troops at the French airfield. She even saved your life yesterday," she rocketed at Singh while pointing at Harriet.

"Now steady on," Bristol continued. "Let me finish." Nicole bristled a little and silenced while she lifted her nose as if to invite him to continue. "I'm not suggesting for a minute that you aren't bloody good pilots, you are, and you're both incredibly brave. I'm eternally grateful to you both, as are Mister Bromley and Mister Singh. Neither am I suggesting that I'm going to cause problems for two outstanding officers. It's not my style. I'm simply saying that you can no longer be members of the ATA after this morning. At least not if you want to stay attached to the squadron?" Nicole backed away a little and frowned. "I'm assuming you do both want to stay? I did offer everyone in the room the opportunity to return to England?"

"Yes," Harriet replied without hesitation. "I want to stay as long as I can fly." Nicole quickly nodded and agreed.

"Well that's fortunate, as Mister Singh is rather short of pilots at the moment, and until we can get some replacements out to him, he's going to need all of the help he can get."

"Go on," Nicole said, still incapable of humility.

"The three of us have discussed this. We considered commissioning you to the WAAF, but as with the ATA, they have a strictly documented remit, which specifically states that WAAF officers don't fly. It's a similar state of affairs for the RAF, and we can't commission you there as women have to join the WAAF. Documented remits and rules again."

"I assume you have something in mind?" Harriet asked.

"Well, I was at a loss," Bristol continued. "It was Mister Bromley that actually came up with the suggestion after talking with Flight Lieutenant Salisbury, who it would seem has a remarkable knowledge of all things related to military flying..."

"Yes?"

"Yes... The foreign pilots act, as its unofficially known. The government passed it a while back to allow pilots from other countries to serve as combat pilots in the RAF, and unlike all of the other considerations, the act isn't so specific as to define gender. Probably because they didn't expect female pilots from other countries would turn up and volunteer to get involved in a war by flying combat missions for the RAF! Anyway, my point is that if pilots serving in a foreign air force turn up, we can use them, subject to suitable flying and medical assessment, and approval by a senior officer..."

"But we don't serve in a foreign air force," Harriet replied.

"How do we know?" Mister Bromley asked. He smiled a little, and his eyes lit up from behind his dark rimmed glasses.

"Excuse me?"

"Your accent... You're French, aren't you?" he asked Nicole.

"Of course I'm French, what else would I be?"

"Well, the French Armee de l'Air is in a frightful state at the moment, sadly. They've lost well over half of their number, pilots and aeroplanes, whole squadrons have been wiped out; and in a similar measure to the British foreign pilot's act, though less formal due to the urgent nature of things, they allowed all manner of pilots to fly for them. I've even heard of airline pilots flying bomber sorties..." He smirked a little as he continued. "It's entirely possible that one of the more ravaged squadrons, perhaps one of those wiped out or overrun so we can't corroborate your stories, allowed you to fly for them out of desperation to stem the German assault. Then, when you found yourselves as sole survivors, you offered your services here. Initially, you were taken on as ATA pilots, but on learning of your story and your combat experience AVM Bristol invoked the foreign pilots act, and commissioned you as Acting Pilot Officers in the RAF Volunteer Reserve."

"You can do that?" Harriet asked.

"We can," Bristol replied. "I'm happy to authorise it, and Mister Bromley has offered to square it with the Air Ministry, assuming you're both in agreement?"

"Yes, yes, of course," they both agreed.

"Though I'm not French..." Harriet said after a moment of reflection. "I'm English."

"Pure?" Bristol asked. Singh raised an eyebrow. "Oh, don't be like that, Mister Singh, I mean nothing offensive and you well know it. I mean is she entirely of English descent. I'm looking for a loophole." Singh smirked a little, he knew all too well but couldn't resist the opportunity. He'd experienced racism in India in many forms, and not just white British against Indian, there was also a healthy dose of deplorable bigotry going the other way, not to mention the discrimination between Indians of different areas or castes. It was something he'd grown up being very aware of, though coming from a wealthy family he'd been fortunate enough to mostly meet and socialise with those who'd managed to rise above all but the most casual racism, regardless of their own culture. There could be some bad people, but they were a minority, the rest were just uneducated. In fact, since arriving in England, he'd only ever been treated as an equal when in the RAF, if not sometimes a curiosity, especially as he refused to wear a flying helmet and only ever wore a turban. Something which had required the ground crew to fashion him a headset which clamped an earpiece and radio boom to his head when flying, so he could still use the radio.

"Well..." Harriet started. "I think my grandfather on my mother's side was from Norway. I'm pretty sure of it in fact."

"That'll do for me," Bristol said.

"I should add that it may not be permanent," Bromley continued as he nodded in agreement. "The War Office is a political animal, despite its military sphere of operations, and as AVM Bristol has already pointed out, there's a lot of resistance to women being anywhere near a war zone. There's every chance that somebody will overrule the decision, or make changes which would prevent the situation from continuing. However, in the time honoured tradition of considering it better to beg forgiveness than ask permission, if we do things this way, we can enact things now and wait until somebody notices, and deal with any protests then."

"There's a stipulation, however," Bristol added. "I may believe in equality, and that we need to make the use of people's skills regardless of their gender, but I'm not a madman. You may both be courageous and combat blooded, but you're not combat trained. We only make this happen if you agree to try your best to avoid combat at all costs, yes? That means you ferry aeroplanes, you run air tests, and you fly reconnaissance; limited risk tasks, understood?" Both girls nodded excitedly. "In that case, we'd better get ready to shove off. They're your headache now, Mister Singh. Good luck!"

"Yes, Sir. Thank you, Sir. Though if you indulge me, you may need to see them a little longer."

"Oh?"

"Your escort fighters are coming to meet you from England, and they'll pick you up at the coast. There's a reception field on the French coast, and I have two heavily damaged but airworthy Hurricanes that need to go back to England for a proper workshop overhaul. I thought I'd send these two along to keep an eye on things, and they can hand you over to the escorts from England, then drop into the reception field and bring me back some fresh replacements."

"I see..."

"It should be reasonably safe. I've talked with your pilot, and he intends to pass through relatively friendly and low risk airspace to the southwest."

"I've no concerns at all, Mister Singh. After what they did this morning, I'd be more than happy to trust them with my safety. In fact, if I had to choose an escort, I'd choose them every time."

"OK, ladies, go and see the Chief and he'll have the Hurricanes ready for you." Singh nodded towards the door.

The girls left the room, both silent and both struggling to keep the smiles from bursting out of them. As soon as they made it to the top of the stairs, they giggled a little, then quickly ran down the stairs and through the house, and the second they stepped out of the door they jumped at each other in a flying embrace and bounced up and down excitedly.

"I can't believe they're letting us stay!" Harriet gasped.

"It's the least they could do," Nicole replied happily. "We are good pilots. You heard him; they need pilots like us. We're the best, and we're too good for the Germans!"

"Leaving us?" Archie asked when they'd calmed themselves enough to walk back to the other pilots.
"We're escorting the bomber to the coast," Harriet announced with a newfound boldness and a confidence that had her walking six inches taller at least.

"Told you, Max. Give them an inch, and they'll take a mile." Archie said while rolling his eyes.

"And what do I suppose that to mean?" Nicole demanded, bordering on being playful with her scorn, though with Nicole, it was difficult for all but Harriet to know the difference between playful and deadly serious.

"He means that now we've given you girls a sniff of flying, there'll be no need for us anymore," Max said without looking up from his tatty cornered book.

"I'll be happy for the rest," Grumpy said.

"Oh, there's no rest for you, old boy," Archie chided. "Newly promoted Pilot Officers don't have time for rest." The others laughed as the girls continued walking.

"Maybe with us girls flying the Germans will give up?" Nicole responded with a smug smirk.

"I wouldn't blame them," Max said

"Of course you wouldn't," Archie teased. "You gave up a long time ago."

It was nice to see the pilots getting back to teasing and berating each other; it seemed like the natural order of things and made Harriet feel like all was well. She didn't like the quietness and solemn atmosphere of the morning; she could feel death lingering around them as they'd sat in near silence, reflecting on what had happened. They were thinking of their friends and how they'd met their end, and wondering whether their turn was to come next. Harriet and Nicole had stayed quiet and not even mentioned their role in the morning's war, in their minds it paled into insignificance, really. What was a couple of heartbeats of action compared to seeing half of your squadron killed in front of you? Instead, they simply said they'd escorted the bomber back, and nobody had said another word. The news about Jen had also hit everybody hard. She was popular in the squadron, and in the days before the madness when the pilots would find themselves drunk in the middle of nowhere, it was often Jen that would turn up in a staff car, or truck, to take them home. They'd also quickly warmed to Hugo and Pops. They were very nice men, and their English was enough for them to talk briefly about their lives. Pops was mischievous and humorous, with a love of making vodka; a skill he'd developed as a young man while learning in his family's distillery, with the intention of taking over the company one day. Hugo was equally as mischievous, but his talents lay in art, which he'd studied at university in Paris. There, he'd perfected his ability to accurately sketch whatever was in front of him in exquisite detail; a skill which had made him very popular in his short time with the squadron, as he sketched the pilots and their aeroplanes. Both had fought hard to try and hold the Germans back, and both were aces. It was generally considered a shame that such spirited and determined men didn't get a chance to die flying as their countrymen and friends had, and in all likelihood instead were shot up or captured on the ground.

Harriet put it all out of her mind as she fitted her parachute then climbed into the Hurricane she'd been assigned, and focused on remembering the Chief's briefing. Nothing above fifty per cent throttle, as the engine was shot and the cooling system was held together by string and goodwill, in his terms. Nicole's aeroplane wasn't much better, though she had the dubious pleasure of having no guns on the left side, an oil leak, and a cracked cylinder head. Both aeroplanes were flyable, just, and could barely be described as airworthy. The Chief was confident that both would reach the reception airfield without much trouble, a confidence which Harriet only shared once AP had appeared to strap her in.

"Congratulations," Harriet said as AP leant into the cockpit.

"Thanks... I didn't expect it," AP replied, still looking surprised.

"You deserve it."

"Do I? What makes you say that?"

"Because you're a genius mechanic and you inspire people around you. You look after people, and you care about those you're responsible for. That's what an officer is supposed to do, isn't it? The good ones, anyway."

"Who told you I care?" AP asked as she felt the slightest of blushes on her cheeks, something else that infuriated her.

"I know you do."

"Don't count on it... Anyway, don't break my aeroplane. Otherwise, you'll see how much I care when I kick your arse!"

"I suppose you think you can talk to me that way now that we're both officers?"

"I can talk to you that way because you're reckless and find yourself in trouble too easily, which means that every time you get back from somewhere, I have to fix something."

"I'll do my best, Assistant Section Officer Kaye," Harriet said with a sly grin, before starting the engine.

"Please do, Third Officer Cornwall."

"Pilot Officer Cornwall," Harriet corrected with an air of confident mischief.

"What?" AP shouted over the noise of the engine.

"Acting Pilot Officer Cornwall, on attachment from Norway to the RAF," Harriet smirked, and AP raised an eyebrow. "Now be a good sort and jump down off my aeroplane, would you. I have a mission to fly," she continued in the most upper class accent she could muster. AP rolled her eyes.

"It's still my aeroplane," she said before letting herself smile. "Fly safe," she added before she turned and jumped from the wing, then guided Harriet's wingtip before letting her roll away to join Nicole in forming up either side of the bomber, which was ready with both engines roaring. Bristol shook Singh's hand then climbed aboard. The door was closed, and the signal was given. The bomber went first, and once it was airborne, Harriet looked around to check the sky.

"Black Leader to Black One, let's roll," Harriet said over the radio.

"Don't be ridiculous," Nicole said in reply, before remembering they were on the same frequency as the bomber. "Black One receiving and understood," she said reluctantly before she joined Harriet in bouncing down the runway, with the last bounce lifting her into the sky.

The girls formed up either side of the bomber and joined it in a steady climb up through the light and wispy clouds. Harriet checked her revs and engine temperature; and found a happy medium where both would sit at a level which worked, then spent her time on lookout, searching the sky for anything untoward, and occasionally looking over at the crew in the bomber. It was a quiet flight, and somehow it felt a little different to everything previous. She'd flown for fun for years, and then in the last few days, she'd flown out of necessity. Now she was in the cockpit of a Hurricane over war torn France, and she was doing it as a job. She thought briefly of her mother and father, and how she didn't have a clue where they were or what they were doing, she didn't even know if they were alive, but she hoped for the best. She thought about the future, and how she'd explain to them that she was not only a professional pilot, but she was a pilot who'd flown combat missions for the RAF. She imagined how her mother would be so proud that she'd achieved her goals, and didn't just settle for life as a housewife. She even thought her dad would be proud in his own way. He often was proud, but he had difficulty expressing his emotions in a helpful way, something which had led to many of the showdowns between them, including the one about her not being a pilot. A burning smell finally pulled her from her daydreaming thoughts, and she checked the dials to see the engine temperature was rising again, so backed off the throttle a touch.

"Are you OK, Black Leader?" Nicole asked.

"I think so, Black One. The engine temperature is climbing, so I'm going to ease my throttle a bit and put the nose down to increase the airspeed and try to cool it off. We're high enough for me to lose a bit of height. Besides, I can see the coast on the horizon, so we'll meet up with the escort from England soon, I'm sure."

"You should head for the airfield; I can meet you there. I don't mind taking it from here; it's quite safe."

"That's OK. I'll just dive a little and see if it'll run cooler when I level off. Maintain your height and heading and I'll follow on behind, then we can land together once the escort picks up the package."

"OK Black Leader."

Harriet pushed the nose down and gathered speed while she pulled back on the throttle to give the engine a bit of a break. She didn't dare dive too steep as the Hurricane she was in wasn't one of AP's experimental jobs, and she ran the risk of the engine stopping altogether due to the carburettor problem. Hundreds of feet in height scrubbed off the altimeter quick enough, even without a steep dive, and as she'd hoped the engine temperature quickly cooled to within range. A few hundred feet more for good measure and she pulled back on the stick and bottomed out the dive, before starting her shallow climb back up in the direction of the bomber. As she did, her stomach squeezed, and for a moment, she thought her heart had stopped. A few thousand feet above the bomber was a row of Messerschmitt 109s formed in line astern. The first tipped its wing and started into a dive, followed by the next. Harriet pushed the throttle hard forward and pulled the plug to push the boost to maximum power. There was no time to worry about the engine. "Fighters coming down on you. Break, break, break!" she shouted into the radio as the mighty Merlin engine roared and strained with all its might to drag the Hurricane up to intercept the enemy.

"Fighters three o'clock high," the bomber pilot called and banked left into a sweeping turning dive. Nicole split right into a matching spiral as the lead German fired a burst of cannon fire, which only narrowly missed as it passed between both aircraft and zipped within inches of Harriet's cockpit. She lined up her sights and fired. He hadn't expected to see her climbing between his two targets and didn't know which way to turn until it was too late, and her bullets had rattled through his engine, seizing it and sending him past her in a plume of smoke. The second 109 was more prepared and quickly broke left, and the third to her right. By the time the fourth was in sight, he knew exactly what was going on and dived straight at her with cannons blasting. Shells ripped through her right wing, and she pulled hard right to spin and avoid the next burst, while at the same time sending another blast in the direction of the nearest 109. Already the German squadron had dispersed and was swarming in every direction like flies. Harriet banked hard left out of the spin to see a 109 pass in front of her, she jumped on his tail and chased him down as he followed his comrade in pursuing the bomber, which was turning and banking while the gunners attempted to drive the Germans away. She fired, and the 109 in front of her pulled up hard and banked left. She continued down and chased his friend, getting closer and closer until she put a neat line of bullets through his left wing, which was all the encouragement he needed to spin out and away from her field of fire, almost inviting her to bank down after him. But as he quickly began pulling back up into a climb, the unthinkable happened, the engine stuttered, forcing her to pull hard left and up to try and compensate. As she did she caught sight of Nicole knocking down a 109, then have to go straight into evasive mode to try and escape the other two forming on her tail and firing. Harriet swung hard right and level as the engine kicked in smooth again, but her cockpit hood shattered as a cannon shell ripped through the top and crashed out through the instrument panel and the bottom of the fuselage, while others ripped into her wing. She flipped upside down, then into a nose down turn as more bullets filled the sky in front of her. She was quickly running out of options. There were too many of them. As she twisted, she caught sight of a 109 charging at full speed, nose first towards the bomber. Without hesitation, she pulled up hard and put herself between the 109 and its target, then watched as in slow motion the floor of the cockpit opened up in a series of holes. Somehow the intruding cannon shells missed her, but they trashed what remained of her cockpit and her engine, which was now overheating, smoking heavily, and starting to lick with flames. She'd done what she intended, though, and by putting herself between the bomber and 109, it was enough to scare the German off track. He pulled hard right and presented his belly to the bomber's gunner, who gave him everything.

"Harry, get out!!!" Nicole screamed over the airwaves as she watched Harriet's Hurricane continue its climb in a stream of smoke and flames.

"Get out of here!" Harriet screamed back while she tried her hardest to bring the Hurricane under control. The rudder was tight, the controls were heavy, and the engine was chugging and scratching. "There's too many of them, run!" She looked down as Nicole spun and weaved with three 109s on her tail, each taking it in turns sending blasts in her direction, some of which hit home while others missed. Finally, Harriet's engine seized, and she felt the drag of the aeroplane suddenly take hold like a giant had reached up and grabbed her by the tail. She pushed the stick forward and down and managed to level out before a loud snap rattled through the fuselage and the left wing dipped, sending her into a diving spin. She stood on the right rudder with all of her strength and pulled hard right, trying to counter the stall. It eventually worked, and after another roll, the Hurricane levelled, though still in a nose down dive which was difficult to control. Harriet fought and pleaded desperately, but the controls were all but gone. She needed to do the thing she was more terrified of than anything, jump. She tried to compose herself as she pushed at her wrecked canopy, but it jammed where the metal frame had twisted having been hit by the German cannon fire, so she reached for the crowbar and rammed it in the small gap then started wrenching at it desperately, screaming as she pulled. With a loud crack, the canopy flew open. She pulled back on the stick as hard as she could to take some of the steepness from the dive and unfastened her harness. Then, with a deep breath, she reached up next to the rearview mirror and grabbed the cockpit frame and pulled herself up. She couldn't breathe as she neared the slipstream; the blast was so strong. With her foot on her seat, she was preparing to push out and escape, when a 109 slipped right in front of her heading for the bomber. Something she couldn't explain took over her, and she felt herself sit down, hold the control stick, then fire. She let loose with a stream of bullets, not letting go of the fire button until she'd emptied every bullet through her guns and ripped the 109 to shreds. She then flipped upside down and was sucked out into the sky. At first, she tumbled, with green fields, blue skies, white clouds, and smoky trails all spinning past as she rolled, while desperately breathing hard and hearing herself exhale and almost scream, she grasped at her parachute for the cord. She wished over and over she'd paid more attention to the safety instructions or practised finding it, or... she found it, grabbed it, and tugged. Nothing. Her life flashed before her eyes until she remembered AP's advice, wrapped the cord around her hand and pulled again. This time the giant grabbed her from above, pulled her backwards, and snapped her head back. Before she knew it, she was hanging from the white silk canopy billowing above her. She'd done it. She thanked God as she composed herself, then quickly reminded herself where she was and spun in her harness to see what was going on around her, finally locating the bomber. A 109 was closing on the right side as it turned slowly to the left, and behind it was Nicole's Hurricane. Not firing, but closing fast. "No... No, no, no! Nicole, no!" Harriet shouted as she saw exactly what was about to happen. The 109 kept firing, and Nicole kept chasing. Meanwhile, three more 109s were circling into position behind her. Then it happened, Nicole's propeller cut through the 109's tail, shredding it and quickly severing the entire tail empennage, and in the process shattering the propeller blades to stubs. The 109 immediately rolled into a downward spin, and Nicole's Hurricane dipped under the bomber and flipped onto its back as a trail of bullets ripped into it. The 109s swarmed after it, barrel rolling as it flipped smoothly, again and again, ploughing cannon shell after cannon shell into it as it disappeared into a thick white cloud with the 109s chasing close behind. The first 109 followed into the cloud, and then the second. Harriet's heart squeezed tight as the cloud lit up in a bright flash which showed a trail of smoke winding below. Then, before another thought could enter her mind, the most beautiful thing happened. The third 109 burst into flames and its wings folded over it as a pair of Spitfires broke through the cloud in a steep climb, their mesmerising elliptical wings almost glowing in the sunlight as they climbed. The bomber levelled, and another six Spitfires joined the fight, two more from the cloud below and four from above. They ripped the remaining 109s apart in a frenzy of bullets, making the remaining three adversaries think better of the situation, and dive for the ground and home. Four of the Spitfires gave chase while two took station on either side of the bomber, the remaining two flew a patrol circuit to check for any more problems, above and below the clouds, and in doing so flew past Harriet close enough for both pilots to give her a wave. She smiled and waved excitedly, then quickly realised how exhausted she was. She relaxed and watched them do a slow wide turn, then as they passed her a final time on their way to join the bomber and form in line astern, they commenced a victory roll before waving and leaving her to fall slowly through the sky.

As she floated, she felt the coolness of the wind blowing at the tears on her cheeks. She was crying for lots of reasons. She was crying because she'd been so scared; and because she couldn't believe she'd survived such an intense situation, but most of all because she'd just watched Nicole ram an enemy aeroplane before being shot out of the sky. She slipped into the cloud, which was an experience like nothing else she could have imagined, and enough to distract her from her tears. The tiny water droplets reflected the colours of the rainbow as they reflected the sunlight inside the cloud, as they passed by her eyes and cooled her skin, to form into enveloping wisps which tangled around her limbs while she floated weightlessly. It was almost like heaven. For the briefest moment, she wondered if maybe she'd died too. Perhaps she didn't get out of her Hurricane. Maybe this was it, she was dead, and this was what it felt like heading to heaven, or wherever. The daydream was broken as she slipped through the bottom of the cloud, and the fields below came up very quickly. Reality returned as she realised that she had no idea what to do next. She quickly looked up and around. The sky was filled with smoke and vapour trails and a few parachutes, and the ground below was littered with smoking heaps where over ten aeroplanes had returned to the ground, nose first, and sometimes in more than one piece.

As she looked more at the fast approaching ground than she did the sky, she noticed movement. Trucks on the roads and runners in the fields. Runners... Soldiers. But whose? She didn't have much time to think about it, or about what to do next. Her legs crumpled into her, and she landed on the ground with a thud that winded her, knocking the air from her lungs and rattling her head off the grass. She laid for a moment and gasped for air, then rolled and coughed before lying flat on her back again, closing her eyes, and trying to somehow force air back into her lungs with slowing deep breaths.

"English, or German, do you think?" the French soldier asked his friend, in French, as they stood over her. Harriet opened one eye to see a pair of gleaming bayonets pointing at her from the end of their rifles.

"English. English!!" she replied in her best French.

"Prove it," the soldier replied

"What uniform is it?" the second soldier added.

Harriet lifted onto her elbows and tugged at the parachute harness, then dragged it off before unfastening her flying jacket to reveal the soft blue shirt Max had given her, which was currently dark and soaked with sweat.

"There are no badges," the first soldier continued. "Besides, she's a girl, and I don't think the British let girls fly."

"Yes, I know I'm a bloody girl!" Harriet screamed in frustration. In English this time. "Everyone's telling me I'm a girl. Girls can fly aeroplanes! I just shot down two Germans. Two bloody Germans! I shot down another this morning and four yesterday! Seven Germans in two days. Seven combat bloody trained bloody Luftwaffe aces shot down by a bloody girl!" The French soldiers looked at each other in shock at her tirade as their Sergeant came over to join them, and looked down at the screaming, crying, howling mess.

"It's a girl?" he said with surprise. The other two looked at him and shrugged while nodding.

"Oh give me bloody strength," Harriet exclaimed in resignation, before collapsing flat on her back and putting her hands over her face.

"I don't think she's a pilot," the Sergeant continued. "They don't let girls fly aeroplanes." The others shrugged and nodded. "Perhaps she's a spy? Maybe she was on one of the aeroplanes, and parachuted down to infiltrate our positions?"

"Yes, take me to your bloody Headquarters, maybe they'll speak more sense than three ignorant country idiots!" Harriet shouted, reverting back to French as she climbed to her feet unaided. "I've lived here for years, it's practically home, and when I'm shot down defending the place, they think I'm a German spy!" she shouted in the face of the Sergeant. It was the angriest she'd ever been, and she could hardly contain herself. The first two soldiers jumped back with their bayoneted rifles at the ready, practically prodding her with them. She pushed one of the bayonets away, only for it to be returned to her chest with enough pressure for her to feel the point needling her flesh. She stopped, and the Sergeant tutted and waved his finger, then she was shouted at in French, repeatedly, and gestured along the field towards the road with her hands in the air.

"She's definitely a spy," the Sergeant said. "She speaks French too well to be English."

"Idiots!" she growled, again in French, as she stomped angrily through the grass. When they reached the road, they waited for their transport. Harriet was forced to keep her hands on her head, much to her annoyance. Meanwhile, the soldiers talked about spies, all the time keeping their rifles aimed at her as though she was some sort of dangerous animal. When the truck finally rolled up, she was jostled into the rear and told to sit, which she did, facing a young German pilot who sat quietly with his hands on his head. He was a handsome young man, very tall and very blonde, with chiselled features and emerald green eyes. He raised an eyebrow at the sight of her. "Don't even think of saying it," she snarled in English, as the French soldiers climbed aboard. She was told to shut up, and the French talked more about her being a spy, something confirmed, in their minds at least, by her talking to the German when she climbed aboard the truck. She thought about the battle that had just happened and wondered if the German opposite knew her part in it, and the only consolation she could think of for losing Nicole and being shot down herself was that the Spitfires arrived in time to get the bomber home. At least she'd done her job, that was the main thing. Besides, the more she thought about that, the less she thought about watching Nicole's Hurricane dive without a propeller through the clouds like a spear and out of sight.

Half an hour later they were herded from the truck and escorted at bayonet point into a tent with walls made of sandbags, and surrounded by the sights and sounds of what looked like a vast and very chaotic French army camp. The Sergeant introduced his prisoners to their officer, a young looking Captain with dark hair, who looked at Harriet with great intrigue.

"Yes, I'm a girl, I know," she said in French. She was more subdued than earlier, now the adrenaline had subsided.

"I'm not ignorant," the Captain replied. "I can see that you're a girl, but what are you doing here?"

"She's a spy," the Sergeant volunteered.

"And you're an ignorant pig botherer," she replied spitefully, making the portly Sergeant raise his rifle angrily as if to hit her with it. She pulled her shoulders back and stuck out her chest defiantly. "I dare you to!"

"What is this?" Another voice asked. "What's with the noise? It's too much noise!"

"My apologies, General," the Captain said with a roll of his eyes, as he turned to face the pale and quite elderly commander, whose left eye and pencil moustache appeared to twitch in unison as he pushed forward. He looked the German up and down and then did the same to Harriet.

"Germans! Why have you brought these pigs into my Headquarters?"

"Prisoners, Sir," the Captain replied.

"A spy, Sir!" the Sergeant added again, excitedly sucking up to his superior. "She came down by parachute not an hour ago. Girls don't fly aeroplanes, she must have been dropped during the battle to spy on us, and she would have if we hadn't captured her before she had a chance to discard her flying jacket."

"A spy?" the General repeated, his voice shocked with a whisper of terror. "A spy... A spy..." He moved closer to Harriet and looked at her over his long nose, through his tired and scared looking eyes. He pulled at the silk scarf of blue and white diamonds around her neck until the corner came away, and he inspected the golden edelweiss embroidery, "it's a German scarf..." he muttered as he looked first at the Sergeant, and then the Captain.

"She says she's English," the Sergeant said, "but speaks fluent French. What English person speaks French? They're all ignorant. Besides, the English don't have girls flying."

"Yes..." the General muttered, before turning back to Harriet. "French, you say?" he asked the Sergeant.

"Yes, Sir. Exactly what a spy would need."

"You speak French?" the General asked Harriet.

"I do, and very well thank you," Harriet replied in her best French. "Or, if you'd prefer, we can talk in Latin?" she quickly added, in Latin, instantly appreciating the hours of Latin she'd been forced to endure throughout her schooling. "But that doesn't make me a bloody Roman!" she added defiantly, and the General stood back, startled by her furious multilingual tirade.

"Spies are shot..." the General grunted as he backed away. His demeanour was that of a cornered rat. "I won't have German spies in my Headquarters! I won't have German spies here. Not here. They won't win! No, not this time, not again." He turned to his Captain, shaking with fury and looking quite disturbed. "I want her shot. Now."

"Sir... If she is a spy, and that is not yet confirmed, perhaps we should interrogate her before we..." the Captain started to reply.

"Before we what? Before we give her a chance to get away and report our position to her countrymen?" the General blustered angrily.

"But command..." the Captain protested.

"Command? Command? I am command, Captain, and you'll do well to remember it! I'm a General, and this is my brigade, I command here, and you obey. We shoot spies, Captain! Unless of course, you're disobeying my orders? In which case you can stand next to her in front of the firing squad!" Harriet started to get a little more nervous. She'd been scared of the battle. She'd been more scared of jumping out of her burning Hurricane, even if it was the only way to avoid an excruciating fiery death. She was scared, and then angry at the way the Sergeant had treated her, but now she was getting really scared, the General was clearly unhinged, and the blustering of an ignorant Sergeant was all it had taken to push him over the edge. She was starting to think she would actually be taken outside and shot. "You take her outside and shoot her, Captain. You do it now!" he screamed as if he'd read her thoughts.

"You're insane..." Harriet gasped.

"That's enough, Lieutenant," the young German Officer said in French as he stepped forward. "My apologies, General, I'm Captain Steiff of the Luftwaffe, and this young lady is a petulant but very talented pilot in my fighter squadron. We were both shot down by British Spitfires a few kilometres from here."

"What?" the General asked, bemused and immediately returning to his quiet and nervous disposition. "Fighter pilot? Nonsense."

"Alas, it is so," Steiff continued. "She may be argumentative and annoying, but she is not a spy. In fact, she wears the scarf of her home in Bavaria, as you can see." He lowered his hands and held the edelweiss scarf.

"A fighter pilot?" the General asked again.

"Yes, General, and a very good one. I do believe she fought remarkably well before she was shot down herself."

"You're a German fighter pilot?" the General asked Harriet.

"Ja..." she muttered nervously, hoping that her poor German wouldn't be tested too much, and praying his wasn't good enough to do the testing. There was an uncomfortable silence until the General burst out laughing. The French Captain and soldiers joined in, nervously, and Steiff smiled, equally as nervous.

"She's a fighter pilot!" the General turned to the Captain. "This, Francois, is why they won't win this time! They're using girls to fly their fighter planes!" he laughed and slapped his thigh, highly amused with himself, before turning back to Harriet. "You're lucky it was Spitfires you came up against, girl! Had you come up against the French Army fighters, you'd have been chased all the way back to Germany and shot out of the sky!" he continued laughing. "Get them out of here. Lock them in the barn, and we'll deal with them later." He waved his hand dismissively and walked away laughing.

His young Captain breathed a visible sigh of relief before waving the Sergeant over and whispering in his ear, "Sergeant, these are now prisoners of the French army, and they will be sent for interrogation. As such, they'll be unharmed when I send for them, do you understand?" The Sergeant nodded, and a minute later, Harriet and Steiff were marching through the chaotic French camp with their hands on their heads at the point of the

Sergeant's bayonet. He crowed triumphantly to other soldiers who he passed that he'd captured German pilots, a pomposity shared by the soldiers with him. It seemed like the whole of the French army were there to watch. Insults and jeers of all colours flew, as did the occasional rock and throat full of spit. Steiff did what he could to be chivalrous and put himself between the rocks and Harriet, and ended up bloodied, as did she from the rocks that got through. They were relieved when they were helped with a rifle butt in the back through a scrappy wooden door into a brick outbuilding no more than ten feet square. The Sergeant spat at them as they dragged themselves through the dirty straw and closed the door.

"Thanks..." Harriet said as she sat with her back against the brick wall and rubbed her bloody lip. She couldn't remember whether it was a brick or the Hurricane that had hit her in the face, then she quickly remembered it was her own knee that had struck her when her legs collapsed as the parachute dropped her to the ground.

"Don't thank me yet," Steiff replied. "Listen to them out there. I may have saved you from a bullet, only for you to join me in being lynched." She felt cold as she heard the voices of French soldiers outside demanding access to the Germans, so they could punish them for invading France.

"Thanks anyway," Harriet said. "Though it was a silly thing to do, he could have ordered you shot as a spy at the same time."

"But he didn't."

"But why would you do that?"

"Because I know you're not a spy, and you deserve better than a French firing squad."

"You do?"

"Yes. I watched you shoot down two of my friends while flying a British Hurricane. If you're a spy, the Abwehr has gone to some significant effort to develop your back story, and I don't think even they're skilled enough to pull that off."

"The Abwehr?"

"The German military intelligence..."

"I'm sorry about your friends..."

"And I'm sorry about yours. Even though they rammed the tail off my aeroplane." Harriet forced a smile and pulled her knees up to her chest. "You should sleep," he said, noting her withdrawing and looking forlorn. "Our squadron doctor fought in the last war, and he says that the body and mind are exhausted after being exposed to the extremes of combat, the best thing you can do after such trauma is sleep."

"I am tired..."

"I must ask before you do. Where did you get that scarf?"

"I was given it by a pilot I shot down, one of your countrymen."

"You shot down Major Von Rosenheim?"

"Yes, that's him. Older than you, shorter too. He's a Major I think, or a Colonel?"

"How did you come to shoot down one of our most skilled aces?"

"I don't know, really. He just kind of flew in front of me, and I fired."

"It seems that's something you're skilled at."

"Yes..."

"But he's alive? Rosenheim, I mean?"

"Yes, they sent him back to England. Him and another pilot, I can't remember his name, Hans I think?"

"I suppose you shot him down, too?"

"Sorry..."

"May I have the honour of knowing the name of Britain's most notorious fighter pilot?"

"Who?"

"You, of course."

"I'm not a notorious fighter pilot; I'm just a girl..." She caught herself. 'Just a girl.'

"You've shot down experienced pilots in combat; I think perhaps you're not 'just' anything. You're a warrior, a fighter pilot. I'm Ulrich Steiff, and it's a pleasure to meet you." He held out his hand. She nodded and smiled and shook it warmly.

"Harriet Cornwall."

"A pleasure, Miss Cornwall. Sleep, and I'll watch over you."

"Thank you..." She leant her head against his arm and felt the softness of his smoky leather jacket against her cheek, then almost instantly fell asleep.

Chapter 9

The Asylum

Harriet jumped awake, dragged from her dreams where she'd been back at school and sleeping in the dormitory, wrapped in heavy warm blankets and trying to work out where the spine chilling wail was coming from. It was a horrifying noise, somewhere between the howl of a tortured beast and a poorly played trumpet. It was loud and getting louder, so loud it almost vibrated her skin. She looked around, but it took a minute for her brain to catch up and recognise her surroundings, and realise she was still in the small brick outhouse the French had thrown her in. Ulrich, the young German pilot who'd saved her from the firing squad, was staring nervously at the patch of sky visible through the small jagged hole in the roof.

"What is it?" she asked, half dazed and shaking her head to try and dull the growing multitude of blasting trumpets.

"Irony..." he replied.

"Irony?" Harriet repeated, thinking she must have misheard, or that perhaps an English girl and a German man conversing in French was inviting an inevitable breakdown in translation. "I don't think irony has a sound."

"The noise you are hearing are the trumpets of Jericho. Sirens activated on Stuka dive bombers when they swoop for the kill... Our dive bombers." He looked at Harriet uneasily. "Or should I say German dive bombers; and the irony is that I, a German pilot, am about to be killed by my fellow German pilots; the very people who I've spent the last hour praying would find me and set me free, before that mad Frenchman has me shot for something."

"Irony indeed..." Harriet conceded. Before she could think anything else, let alone say it, the world around them erupted in a noise like nothing she'd ever experienced. They were lifted from the ground, which was vibrating violently; then thrown back down as the air thickened with dust and smoke before they were thrown up and around again. As they landed, Ulrich threw himself over Harriet, who instinctively pulled her knees to her chest and wrapped her hands around her head to dull the ear splitting sound of screeching sirens and thunderous explosions. The raid went on for what felt like an eternity as wave after wave of screaming sirens heralded explosion after explosion. Each blast seemed to get bigger and louder and closer, until the air was sucked out of the small outbuilding by a tremendous pressure wave that made Harriet think her ears and lungs would explode in unison. Seconds later, her mouth was filled with thick sharp dust, lining her throat and threatening to choke the life from her. She rolled and writhed in desperation, and dragged herself from under what felt like the weight of the world on top of her, crushing what little life she had left from her weary and terrified bones. The pressure released and she instinctively sucked in a lung full of air, then immediately convulsed into a coughing fit as the sharp grit scratched her airway, making her gasp and rub her eyes after flipping onto her back, then rolling onto her side. Her ears rang so loud she could no longer hear the sirens or the explosions, instead just feeling the vibrations shaking her through the ground. She looked around and slowly focused on the broad beams of light cutting through the haze of smoke and dust enveloping her. Two of the outhouse walls were half their previous height, the bricks and roof beams having been blown directly on top of Ulrich, who was groaning under the rubble. She rolled and pulled the bricks from him. He'd taken the weight of the collapse and shielded Harriet with his body, something he'd paid for and was now no doubt regretting. The ringing in her ears was soon joined by the screams of agony and calls for help outside; it seemed like hundreds of voices were all crying out at the same time and screaming in pain. She needed help herself, help to free Ulrich from the bricks and beams, and found herself gasping 'help' over and over through her parched mouth while she pulled at the bricks. The door, which had somehow managed to remain intact during the blast, flew open as Harriet finished shifting the rubble and managed to pull Ulrich free and onto his back. He acknowledged her, eyes wide open with fear and red from the dust and smoke, and nodded thankfully between coughs. A silhouette stood in the doorway surrounded by smoke and dust, cut out by the afternoon light behind.

"Damned Germans!" A half familiar French voice half screamed, and half growled, rising higher than any of the many calls for help. The General stepped into the outhouse. His thinning grey hair stood on end as though he'd had a frightful shock, and blood streamed down his smoke and dust streaked face from a wound above his left eye. He was the image of a madman. His clothes were ripped, and flesh scratched open, and in his hands, he held a long rifle with what seemed like an even longer bayonet attached. "I'll take at least two of you with me!" he yelled as he raised the rifle ready to strike, then plunged it forward and downward towards Ulrich's chest with frenzied ferocity. Harriet summoned every ounce of remaining strength and pushed herself in front of Ulrich, hitting the rifle out of the way as she collapsed across him and sending the bayonet into the rubble instead of her German friend's flesh. "OK," the General hissed as he pulled the rifle back. His eyes were red with smoke and dust, giving him an almost demonic appearance. "As you wish, spy. Ladies first!" He raised the rifle again, and Harriet braced herself as she waited for the bayonet to ram home. Instead, a shot rang out, and a spray of pink mist made a large halo around the General's head. He looked surprised, then instantly peaceful before he fell to his knees while mouthing something unintelligible. He looked at Harriet and tilted his head, showing a cavernous chunk missing from the rear of his skull before he fell forward with his face just short of her lap. Behind him was the young French Captain, pistol pulled and smoking.

"Come with me if you want to live," he said urgently as he reached down for Harriet's hand. She nodded and took it, and with a pull, she was on her feet. The two of them helped Ulrich to stand, which made him wince in pain. His knee had been struck hard by a falling roof beam, and he was finding it difficult to put any weight on it.

"Go" Ulrich demanded between coughs. "Leave me. Go, get her out of here," he begged the French officer.

"They'll skin you alive if we leave you here," came the reply, and with Harriet on one side and the Frenchman at the other they dragged Ulrich from the rubble of the outhouse, and out into the chaos. Harriet looked about as they staggered forward through the smoke. Flames licked all around the thick black haze, which hid their small group from the screaming, crying, and shouting going on all around them. Occasionally a soldier or a stretcher party would run past, briefly coming into sight through the smoke before disappearing back into it in confused urgency. Vehicles burned and the ground was littered with bodies, and parts of bodies, even the horses hadn't been spared. They passed the Headquarters tent they'd been grilled in when they arrived, and it was burning furiously and echoed with screams and moans. The young Frenchman led them out of the firestorm to a small copse a few hundred paces away, where he leant Ulrich by a tree before pulling branches from a hessian tarpaulin, under which lay hidden a gleaming silver Rolls Royce. Harriet's eyes widened. "Can you drive?" he asked. "Girl, can you drive?" he repeated. Harriet snapped out of her daze and nodded. "Good. Let's get him in." They bundled Ulrich into the passenger seat, then Harriet took her place behind him.

"Is it yours?" she asked.

"The General's, she drives well. Head east, and you'll find your German lines, they can't be far from here."

"You're not coming?"

"No, I have a duty here, to my soldiers. Now go before anyone sees."

"Why are you doing this?" she asked as she started the thundering engine.

"War is hell, but it shouldn't be murder," he replied. "The General had lost his mind, he'd lost it long before you arrived, he'd already murdered many of my men with his insane orders, which sent them into futile suicide missions. You may be the enemy, but you're combat pilots, and if you die, then it should be in a battle, not unarmed and bayoneted by a madman."

"Thank you... Thank you so much."

"You're welcome. Now leave. My men will be angry after the bombing, and they'll be out for blood. Go!" he tapped the car twice and flicked his hand like a long established maître d' dismissing his juniors to their tasks. Harriet smiled and revved the engine, engaged the gears, then took off bouncing across the fields until she turned into the road. She slowed and looked back to the Captain, who offered a salute before turning and heading back to his burning camp.

“Thank you," Ulrich muttered after a while, as he pushed at his knee and groaned angrily while they sped along the rural road. "For saving me back there, I mean. That mad Frenchman was going to stick me like a wild boar."

"I think we're even," Harriet replied. They smiled at each other, briefly, then she went back to glancing in her rearview mirror. The pall of black smoke from the camp could still be seen even though they were several miles away.

"You know we're heading towards the German lines," he said, dragging her attention back to the road ahead.

"Yes..."

"Why?"

"Well, you’ve hurt your leg, you can't exactly walk back to your lines, can you? Especially as you're a German pilot, in France, who I can't imagine would be welcomed with open arms by the locals…”

"It's very gracious of you to drive me, but we both know that despite our ruse and the protestations of a madman, you're not actually German. You're a British pilot, of some sort. You'll be taken prisoner."

"Do the Luftwaffe have girl pilots?"

"Actually, yes. I've met several very talented female glider pilots, and test pilots."

"Fighter pilots?"

"No..."

"Neither do the RAF, not really, except me that is, and I'm not even supposed to be here."

"I see. I didn't think there were female fighter pilots in the RAF."

"So, if nobody believes that girls are pilots, except an insane old French General, maybe your forces will let me go?"

"We should stop."

"Why?"

"So you can take off that flying jacket. That way, I can at least try and convince the army that you're a French girl who took pity on me and gave me a ride to safety." Harriet smirked and nodded, then looked in the mirror once more before pulling over to take off her jacket. Her heart skipped as she did. In the distance, skimming along at treetop height was a Hurricane. It was unmistakable. Even if she hadn't seen it, the following roar of its Merlin engine couldn't hide its pedigree. "What is it?" Ulrich asked.

"A Hurricane," she said with a big smile on her face. She looked forward again and saw a thin greying wisp of smoke spiralling into the air from the field ahead.

"We should get off the road, quick" Ulrich urged.

"What? Why?"

"Because you're driving an open top car carrying a German Officer in uniform. If the pilot is half awake, he will have noticed that, and will no doubt see us as a target of opportunity." Harriet's smile quickly disappeared from her face, and she sped up, then swung into a gap in the hedgerow. What faced her was entirely unexpected. In the field was the source of the wispy grey smoke, a half disintegrated Hurricane smouldering in the afternoon sun. She pulled the car tight against the hedgerow in an attempt to hide it in the gateway then jumped out. "Where are you going?" he asked.

"I've got to look. The pilot may need help." Harriet replied.

"If there's a pilot in that, they're dead!" Ulrich barked after her.

"I've got to try... Look, I can make it on my own from here, I'll head into the local town and make my way to safety from there. Why don't you lay low until the Hurricane has gone, then use the hand throttle and drive back to your lines? I'll be OK here."

"You're being ridiculous," he protested.

"Good luck; and thank you!" she shouted, then ran across the field towards the smouldering Hurricane. As she did, the other Hurricane, the one that had been in the distance, roared over the field. Harriet instinctively waved her hands above her head, desperately trying to get their attention in the hope that they'd recognise a British flying jacket and blue trousers and hold their fire. As the Hurricane banked around the field, dipping its right wing so the pilot could get a good view of the scene below, Harriet slowed to a walk and stared. The code on the side. It was... it couldn't be, it was Sully's Hurricane. The Hurricane she'd flown, and crash landed with a flaming engine at the airfield. She watched as it waggled its wings before circling. All the time she was walking closer to the remains of the crashed Hurricane, which as she approached, she realised the only remaining identifying mark was the tail number printed on the end of the fuselage, which with the tail appeared to have separated from the rest of the aeroplane on impact. She rubbed her gritty eyes in disbelief. It was her Hurricane. Or more accurately, the Hurricane that had been shot out from under her before she'd taken to her parachute a few hours earlier. She stopped in her tracks more than a little confused, but she was quickly rattled out of her daze as the Hurricane turned to wind, lowered its wheels, and made an approach to land. She turned back to the car and waved. Ulrich saluted then the wheels spun, and he took off out of the hedgerow and down the road, out of sight as she turned back to watch the Hurricane bounce hard, almost hard enough to catapult it back up into full flight. A few more bounces and it settled and rolled across the green and brown field, and Harriet found herself running to meet it. The canopy was already pushed back, but she couldn't make out the pilot's face, not that it was important. She screamed excitedly as she ran, not believing her luck that somebody had found her.

Her screams of joy turned to terror as bullets suddenly tore across the field, making four neat rows of earth jump into the air. The furthest row clipped the Hurricane's wing, and the nearest drew a line in the ground just a few paces ahead of Harriet as it headed straight for her. She halted in her tracks, almost comically stopping herself as though on the edge of a cliff and winding her arms backwards to stop herself falling as the dirt continued to jump while bullets ripped into the grass, and the chatter of machine guns and cannons followed. In an instant, she turned and dived flat, as a lone Messerschmitt 109 roared across the field at head height with guns and cannons blazing. The Hurricane bounced past, almost undaunted by the Messerschmitt, then swung around as the 109 climbed steeply ready to set up for another attack. As it did, its wings wobbled. Waving? To who? She wasn't going to hang around to find out. She jumped up and sprinted to the Hurricane, leapt onto the wing, and immediately dropped down as bullets whizzed past from the hedgerow at the end of the field, the thick greenery lighting up with muzzle flashes. She crawled up to the cockpit and looked in, and was startled to see AP looking back at her.

"Are you getting in or what?" AP shouted.

"What?" Harriet replied.

"Fine. Stay here then!" AP replied. Harriet didn't need telling twice, she jumped up among the flying bullets and climbed into the cockpit, sitting down firmly on AP's lap and squeezing down to dodge the bullets coming from the hedgerow as she watched the 109 bank around. "Careful!" AP winced.

"OK, how do we do this?" Harriet asked while ducking again as a bullet came close and sparked off the cockpit frame.

"Well you're a bloody terrible window, so I don't think I'll be doing the flying, do you?" AP replied. "So unless you want to switch places, I suggest you get us in the air before that 109 comes back at us." It was a tight squeeze, but Harriet quickly orientated herself as AP lowered the seat with a clunk. Throttle forward, and they were bouncing along the field.

"You'll have to do the rudder," Harriet shouted. "When I stand on your foot, you stand on the pedal."

"OK just bloody hurry up, you're heavier than you look!" Their speed increased, but the 109 was already diving back down on them, a marginally more pressing concern than the bullets which were blasting from the hedgerow and ricocheting off the airframe.

"Come on... Come on!" Harriet shouted. The 109's guns flashed again, and the ground ahead started to erupt once more. This time he was on target, and the neat strips of gunfire were ripping straight towards them. They were stuck. They weren't going fast enough yet to get off the ground, but they were going too fast to turn. If Harriet swayed even a little, they'd ground loop, spin out of control, and if they were lucky, they'd go nose first into the ground, presenting themselves as perfect targets for the shooters in the bushes. Worst case they'd flip upside down, and be trapped in the cockpit to burn alive. So it was that or keep going forward and hope the bullets hit them and kill them outright. At least that was Harriet's thinking. AP didn't have a clue what was coming, which was, in some ways, a kindness. Without warning, the 109 burst into flames and nosedived into the ground, as a pair of Hurricanes crossed in front of her. One of them shot at the 109 and knocked it right out of the sky while the other ripped the hedgerow to pieces with its eight machine guns. Harriet screamed out in a mix of elation and desperation and pulled back on the stick until they left the ground just as the 109 slipped underneath them, clearing it with the undercarriage by a hair's breadth. Harriet gulped and breathed hard as she pulled up. AP had wrapped her arms around Harriet's waist as a human harness and held her tight in place.

"Did we make it?" AP asked.

"Yeah..." Harriet replied as she checked the instruments and continued her climb at full throttle, then looked down as she crossed the hedgerow. A whole platoon of German paratroopers was shot up or taking cover; all except for half a dozen of the bravest who were still firing angrily. The pair of Hurricanes flew a tight circuit and gave the paratroopers another blast, this time both of them firing before they turned and climbed after Harriet and formed either side of her. "What are you doing here?" she asked AP.

"Being crushed by your heavy bones," came the reply.

"You know what I mean. I didn't even know you could fly!"

"You're not the only female pilot, you know," AP snapped. "I got my pilot's licence when I was seventeen. Just the bloody RAF won't let me fly because my brain doesn't swing between my legs!" Harriet felt herself laughing at AP's anger; it was a light relief from the terror she was feeling just moments earlier. "Anyway, I came to get my aeroplane back, but it looks like you wrecked it."

"Lucky you brought friends with you," Harriet said as the Hurricanes came level with them.

"I didn't..." AP replied with an air of regret. They both looked left to see the newly promoted Grumpy flying the Hurricane that had hit the hedges. He was a welcome sight. Then they looked right to see a furious looking Raj Singh waving at them to follow him. Harriet nodded and smiled, though she knew from the look on his face that there wasn't going to be much to smile about when they got back.

"He doesn't look happy," Harriet said.

"No..." came AP's muted reply. Singh flew ahead, and Harriet tucked in behind, not too close but close enough to keep up, while Grumpy flew up above as top cover.

"AP, what did you do?" Harriet asked.

"He wasn't there when I left... None of them were," AP explained. "Daisy received a message from HQ saying you'd gone down, but they'd seen a parachute, and I... Well..."

"Have you even ever flown a Hurricane before?"

"Oh piss off!" AP blustered defensively. "You hadn't even seen one until a couple of days ago. At least I've been fixing them the last few months, and know them inside out."

"Sorry... Thanks for coming for me," Harriet replied with a slight cringe.

"I wouldn't have if I'd have realised how heavy you are."

"Sorry about your aeroplane."

"It's OK... At least I got to fly in combat once before the RAF throws me out."

"Yeah..." Harriet said with a smirk, which quickly changed to a worried frown. "Wait. You don't think they'll actually do that, do you?"

"You saw Singh's face. I'll be lucky if he doesn't shoot me."

"What for? Rescuing a friend?"

"Is that what we are? Friends?"

"I'd like to think so."

"Me too... But yeah, for that. Only pilots are allowed to fly. I expect he'll have a few words about that. Not to mention the whole taking an aeroplane without permission thing." AP sighed with a genuinely forlorn expression.

They followed Singh back to the airfield, and on seeing a green flare, they touched down with a bounce and taxied to a halt. Harriet cut the engine and quickly extracted herself before helping AP out onto the wing. It didn't take a close inspection to see that the airframe was shredded, dotted with bullet and cannon holes all over; it was a wonder it had stayed in the air, let alone carried both of them to safety. They climbed down the wing and stood side by side and watched as Singh marched away from his Hurricane while Grumpy came over to join them.

"You OK?" he asked Harriet. She nodded and forced a smile, and joined him watching Singh. "What about you?" he asked AP. She shrugged, back to her quiet self. "No extra holes in either of you?"

"I don't think so," Harriet replied.

"Well, that's probably about to change," Grumpy said casually. "I dare say he's going to tear you both a new arsehole as soon as he's calmed down enough to get words out," he smirked at them both, noticing Harriet's look of worry and AP's casual resignation. "Word to the wise, from somebody who's been on the receiving end of more than a few volleys over the years. Stand smart, apologise when it's time, and don't argue. Whatever happens, at least you're both alive, and that's saying something, considering."

"Thank you, Mister MacDonald," Harriet said contritely.

"Thanks..." AP added.

"Call me Grumpy, everyone else does," he said with a warm smile. "Anyway, before the skipper gets his hands on you, I reckon 'he's' going to have words first, and that's something I certainly wouldn't want to be on the receiving end of." He pointed to Cas who was marching out of the house towards them, pulling his hat on as he did.

"Word to the wise?" Harriet asked.

"Oh no, I've got nothing for this one," Grumpy shrugged. "Nicking one of his aeroplanes while he's on the crapper is inexcusable," he smirked as he struggled to hold in a laugh.

"Mister MacDonald," Cas said as he approached.

"Sir..." Grumpy replied. "Mister Singh got a 109."

"Good. I'm sure I'll look forward to hearing about it. You're OK?"

"Yes, Sir. Germans were closer than we thought, on the ground, I mean. I didn't realise they were that far west. Further west than we are." Cas looked at him with concern and nodded.

"I see... Thank you. Best that we get the news back to Headquarters."

"Sir," Grumpy walked away towards the house and left the girls standing in front of Cas.

"He wants you in his office," Cas said after looking at them both. "Both of you."

"This is all my fault," Harriet blurted. "It's nothing to do with AP, so if it's alright with you I'll take responsibility, and she should be left to go back to work."

"Unfortunately, it's not alright with me, Miss Cornwall," Cas replied. His voice was calm, as always, but firm and chilling her to the core. "Neither is it alright with Squadron Leader Singh, nor King's regulations, so shall we?" He held out his hand in the direction of the house. AP nudged Harriet and pulled her shoulders back and lifted her head confidently. Harriet followed suit, and the pair of them marched off boldly, with Cas following behind with the slightest shake of his head. They went into Singh's office and stood smartly to attention in front of his desk, just as Grumpy had told them to, while he scribbled furiously. Cas closed the door and stood to the side of the desk without a word. They all waited in silence for what felt like an age, until Singh finally put down his pen and sat back in his seat.

"Do either of you have the first idea of what you were doing today?" he asked in apparently calm tones, with just the faintest tremble betraying his true feelings.

"I..." Harriet started. He lifted his finger to silence her, and she quickly remembered Grumpy's words to the wise.

"Let me answer that for you," Singh continued. "I believe that neither of you knew what you were doing today! If I thought for one moment that you did, I'd have you both in the back of a Lysander and on your way to England for a psychiatric evaluation!" His voice started to increase in tempo and volume. He pushed his chair back as he stood and leant on his desk, staring first at Harriet, then at AP, and then back at Harriet again. "Do you remember your orders, Miss Cornwall?"

"Sir?"

"Don't Sir me, Miss Cornwall. Do you, or do you not remember the very specific orders I gave you before allowing you to escort the bomber to the coast?" She shook nervously and squeezed her hands in a fist to try and stop herself from being so obvious. "As you're clearly struggling to think, Miss Cornwall, I'll help you by being more specific. Can you remember what I told you to do if you were engaged by enemy aircraft?"

"Drop to the deck and run, or climb and bail out," she replied.

"Drop to the deck and run or climb and bail out," he repeated. "So, you do remember my orders?"

"Yes..."

"So, you're not ignorant, which can only lead me to assume that you chose to disobey them. Unless you have another explanation for choosing to engage an entire squadron of Messerschmitt 109s?"

"They'd have shot down the bomber, Sir."

"They shot you down! Along with that other young idiot you had with you. Leaving the squadron short of combat aeroplanes, and pilots, which in turn leaves the squadron ineffective and unable to provide any useful support to the army! Which I may remind you is currently retreating across Belgium and France, and in desperate need of every scrap of support we can provide!" he thundered angrily.

"Sir, she's new to the RAF and thought she was doing the right thing," AP interrupted, redirecting Singh's furious gaze at her.

"That she may be, but how long have you been with the RAF, Miss Kaye?"

"Five years, Sir."

"Five years, and you still don't have the most basic understanding of the King's regulations!" he bellowed. "Tell me, Assistant Section Officer Kaye, where exactly in King's regulations does it permit unqualified personnel to fly aeroplanes?"

"It doesn't, Sir."

"It doesn't, Sir!" he repeated angrily. "Despite the Adjutant's attempt to cover for your stupidity by suggesting that you miraculously managed to take off while ground testing an aeroplane, I'm not convinced that such a fantastic accident would allow you to fly your aeroplane into a combat zone, to the precise location your friend is reported to have been shot down!"

"By the time I'd got the aeroplane under control I was already there, Sir. It was quite unintentional." AP explained almost casually.

"Enough!" Singh raged. "And you can wipe that look of defiance off your face. You're already on the cusp of the shortest commission in the history of the WAAF!" AP sucked air in her nostrils and did her best to bite her tongue. She'd always had a look which her mother had called 'dumb insolence', which had got her into trouble more than a few times in her life. He continued his rant. "While it may be staffed with clowns at all ranks..." He stared at them both, and glanced for the briefest of moments at Cas, who was standing silently and staring straight ahead through the tirade, "This is an Auxiliary Air Force Fighter Squadron and not a flying circus! We follow orders because if we don't, people die! It's that simple! Do you understand that most basic of requirements?"

"Yes, Sir," they both replied in unison.

"Unfortunately I have problems demanding my time that are much more pressing than dealing with immature, ignorant, and plain bloody stupid junior officers! Such as being stuck in a war zone with an ever nearing front line while having hardly any pilots, and even fewer serviceable aeroplanes with which to fight!" he continued. "Which means that you will both, for the time being, consider all possible means of being both invisible and indispensable while I decide what to do with you! " He took a breath. "Kaye, that bag of bolts you just flew needs work, and you don't sleep until it's ready to fight. Cornwall, you still have a Hurricane to collect. Cas, get them out of my sight." He turned his back to them and looked out of the window. Cas nodded to them both and led them out of the door, closing it quietly behind him and waving his finger in the air gesturing them to follow him. They passed the adjoining Ops Room, and Harriet gave Daisy a nervous smile as they did. She gave her a wink then quickly stood to attention as Singh's voice boomed down the corridor. "Corporal Wilson, have you managed to get Headquarters on the phone yet? If we're to stay in the fight, I want my bloody replacement pilots today!" They continued down the stairs and into the Mess room, where a slender yet curvaceous bottle of brandy and a scattering of glasses sat on a silver tray at the head of the table. Cas sat at the head and gestured Harriet and AP to join him, which they did, sitting either side while he poured three brandies. By the time they were comfortable, the drinks were standing in front of them, and they were both looking a little confused. They'd just been in front of Singh for a deafening rocketing, and neither was expecting a brandy afterwards.

"First time having to take to your parachute, and first time flying a Hurricane in the combat zone," Cas said as he lifted his brandy. "And you both lived to tell the tale... I suspect you've both earned a drink today. Cheers." The girls looked at each other. Harriet raised an eyebrow, and AP smirked, then they lifted their drinks and clinked glasses with each other and with Cas, then the three of them downed the brandy. Harriet's eyes bulged, and her throat burned. AP did a better job of masking the shock and managed to keep her standard emotionless expression, though her eyes watered just a little. Cas refilled the glasses then sat back in his chair and looked at the girls thoughtfully.

"You know, when this squadron first formed it was an anomaly in the Auxiliary Air Force, and still is in many ways." He sipped at his brandy this time, encouraging the girls to do the same. "Many auxiliary squadrons had been formed by men of standing, men who then recruited through friends and acquaintances of similar caste, so to speak. Some recruited exclusively from Cambridge, Oxford, or the University Air Squadrons, others through the old boy network. Lords, lawyers, businessmen and the like, even a few millionaire playboys here and there for good measure, in fact, Lord Trenchard himself stated that he intended the Auxiliary Air Force to be the 'Royal Yacht' of the RAF, the elite. Those who joined weren't bad sorts of course, not by a long way, all keen to be pilots and do their bit, and many good men and outstanding pilots among them. In fact, the first pilot to fly over Everest was an auxiliary. Unfortunately, those recruiting methods excluded a significant number of gifted, talented, and keen, yet unconnected people from flying. Those of perhaps more modest means, who couldn't afford the lifestyle, or even to fly. Then this squadron was formed with the backing of an anonymous financier, somebody with connections in the most exclusive of circles, or so rumour has it anyway. A person who wanted an auxiliary squadron for all, regardless of their background, and was prepared to fund it. Even the squadron motto serves to remind us of our equality in the grand scheme of things, 'Pulvis et umbra sumus'."

"We are but shadows and dust?" Harriet said. "Horace?"

"Yes," Cas replied. "You know your Latin. An interpretation of Horace's meaning may be that we are but shadows on the pages of history, and when we die, which we all must, we return to the dust from whence we came, indistinguishable regardless of titles, wealth, power, race, or gender." Harriet found herself smiling at the notion of equality and how it sat at the heart of the squadron. It made her feel truly at home, and it made her feel like she wanted to be part of the squadron more than anything else. "Of course, we picked up chaps like Russel who you met last night, and whose fine silk shirt your friend has been wearing," Cas continued. "He chose this squadron despite the best attempts to lure him elsewhere because of his name and title. There's also Maxwell, our American friend, who gave up a very lucrative position in his family's timber company to cross the border into Canada, buy false papers, then make his way to Britain to fly for the RAF. Then there are people like Mister MacDonald, who you've also met. He was a Corporal in the army before leaving to become a policeman, having grown disillusioned with service life; not to forget Sergeant Douglas, a farmhand before he turned up on our doorstep. I certainly doubt that either would have been a fighter pilot in many of the other squadrons nor would many of the others of less connected backgrounds. Then, of course, there are the ground crews and the female flight mechanics..." He fixed his eyes on AP. "Female flight mechanics so desperate to work with aeroplanes that her parents sent her to live and work on a farm near an aerodrome many miles from home, so she could volunteer and learn while working. Female flight mechanics who had no advancement in the regular service due to the fact that they were female, and more than a little stubborn. Not to mention downright insubordinate at times; but were rescued by Squadron Leader Barnes from being thrown out of the WAAF in disgrace for punching an officer, however much he may have deserved it. Barnes having recognised her near genius skill with engines and recruited her for this squadron. A squadron that gave her everything she wanted, including promotion to be the first female squadron engineering officer in the entire Royal Air Force, let alone in the elite of fighter command." AP blushed, and for the first time let herself look remorseful and vulnerable in front of others; sentiments she was feeling very deeply as Cas continued. "Mister Barnes was a good man with an eye for talent," Cas continued as he turned back to Harriet. He was still talking in his warm fatherly way and sipping at his brandy. "He saw that you're one hell of a pilot, and gave you an opportunity you'd have nowhere else in the armed forces, of that I can assure you." It was now Harriet's turn to feel remorseful. "If you'd have landed anywhere else when you flew Sully's Hurricane home you'd have been thanked, put in a car, and sent off to who cares where. No matter how many Germans you'd shot down, you are, as you're well aware, female, and you'd have been treated as such. You'd certainly not be commissioned into the ATA and allowed to stay on station. Not even in England, not even in peacetime."

"I know..." Harriet said quietly. "I'm sorry I disobeyed orders, that wasn't even on my mind, I just wanted to try and protect those people on the bomber. The Germans would have massacred them."

"I'm sorry, too," AP added. "Disobeying orders wasn't on my mind, I did what I did deliberately and with full knowledge of the repercussions. There were no pilots, and there was no hope. Harriet's a good pilot, an amazing pilot in fact, and we need people like her. When I heard she'd been shot down, I just wanted to help her, to get her back to safety. I was desperate. I know I should've come to you, but I know you have rules to follow, and the RAF would've hung you if you'd let me go. I thought it better just to do it and hope for the best. I mean, I didn't want to get anyone else in trouble."

"Repercussions..." Cas repeated while sipping his brandy. Not changing the pitch of his voice in the slightest. "The consequences of our actions; intended or otherwise..." Both girls sipped their brandy slowly, fully intending to fill the moment, so they didn't have to speak. Cas sat forward and put his elbows on the table. "Repercussions... That's what we're talking about here, isn't it?" he smiled warmly. "You know, there are many who would like to see this squadron break. There was a great deal of reluctance at all levels to its open to all policy, and there still is! We were given the oldest aeroplanes, the lowest standard of equipment, and the slowest support. Those in power could make the squadron exist, but that didn't mean it couldn't be frustrated in its efforts at every opportunity by those who disliked the whole idea. It's why we're based here out on a limb with no other squadrons nearby, and why we're given the hardest of missions. We didn't even get our own air defence until this morning, and even then, it's a company of machine gunners thrown together from a decimated battalion who barely escaped the slaughter of the German advance." Cas swirled his brandy. "Can you believe that they haven't sent us any replacement pilots since the show started, as other squadrons have priority? We had nineteen pilots when we arrived in France. As of now, we have eight, including you." He pointed at Harriet, then sipped his brandy before continuing. "I don't suppose you happen to know our squadron heraldry? Our badge, in other terms?" Harriet shrugged, then shook her heads. "Of course not, you haven't been here for five minutes... The squadron heraldry is a Wild Goose in flight. We were named the Wild Geese after the many thousands that circle over the East Riding of Yorkshire in the late autumn, ahead of their flight south. It's where the squadron was formed," he sighed and looked the girls in the eyes for a moment. "Yet the comedians in the RAF call us the black sheep because nobody really wants us. Old men, silly girls, and misfits. I can guarantee you, ladies, that if news of female flight mechanics flying Hurricanes; or female pilots disobeying orders in combat gets back to the wrong people in the Air Ministry, or parliament, or wherever else that wants to be rid of us, the squadron will be finished quicker than the Luftwaffe can do for what's left of us!" Both girls blushed, and Harriet clenched her muscles to try and fight the stabbing feeling in her stomach, and the accompanying the nausea that was sweeping over her. Cas fixed AP in his stare. "I know that your father taught you mechanics from an early age, and I know your family almost bankrupted themselves giving you flying lessons, some of which were with the legendary Amy Johnson unless I'm mistaken?" AP nodded. "And I know that what you did when you took that Hurricane was nothing less than heroic. Bloody stupid, but mostly heroic, and I'm in awe of the courage it took to do what you did, everyone on the squadron is, and we're all very proud of you." He shifted his stare to Harriet, as AP fought hard to keep the tears from her eyes. "You've only been with us five minutes, and already the squadron considers you one of our own. You have a higher number of combat victories than most in the RAF, let alone the squadron! Choosing to deliberately engage in combat with twelve battle hardened and experienced 109s instead of turning and running, is probably the bravest action I've heard of thus far in this war. Though I can't help think a hint of Kaye's unthinking stubbornness and stupidity may have rubbed off on you in the short time you've known each other..." He paused for a moment, letting the silence bring home his point as both of his charges squirmed uncomfortably in their seats. "You saved lives, that's without doubt," he said, breaking the silence that had felt like hours to Harriet, who was now tearing herself apart inside. She was desperately distraught that she'd let people down, the very people who'd been so welcoming to her and allowed her to live her life's ambition. "The AVM said as much when he sent a message personally to let us know you'd been shot down defending him."

Both girls blushed more than ever, and Harriet's stomach spun so much she thought she was going to be sick over the table. "However, you both need to give some consideration to your actions. Consequences, and all that. Mister Singh is the first non white squadron commander in the entire Royal Air Force, auxiliary or otherwise, something I'd like to think that you both appreciate the significance of, and how the very thought of it will put some noses well out of place." Both girls nodded. "I can assure you, ladies, that if we're to win this war, the RAF is going to need every old man, woman, and misfit they can lay their hands on from all corners of the world, to both support and fly its aeroplanes. We need to be showing that black sheep can fight every bit as hard as everyone else if that's to happen. We can't give them anything to beat us with."

"How do we make it right?" Harriet asked.

"You do your jobs to the highest standards," Cas replied calmly. "Don't worry about anything else, Mister Singh has been on to Headquarters and squared everything so that we won't hear much more about it."

"I see..."

"You know, he was distraught when he landed from patrol to find out you'd taken off ten minutes earlier, AP. He and Grumpy went on after you without refuelling or rearming, desperate to watch over you and get you back safely."

"They did that," AP said quietly.

"Yes... He cares a great deal for this squadron, all of the squadron, even its newest members. It was he who asked for the AVM to let you stay on the squadron as a pilot," he said to Harriet. "And it was he who got that bloody snapdragon of a woman, Finn, sent back to England!" AP smirked, despite trying her best to fight it from her face. "Oh, it's OK, we're all officers here," Cas said with a wink which signalled the storm was settling. "It's not a secret that she treated the WAAFs like servants. We're all equally as happy to see the back of her." Harriet joined in with the smirking as her stomach eased. "Anyway, Harry," he continued, "I've got a job for you. One of the Lysanders got back while you were out scaring the Germans, and you're scheduled to go for a ride in it to collect a new Hurricane. It'll be a tight squeeze. Hopefully, the brandy makes the trip more tolerable." She nodded and smiled, then finished her drink before standing to leave. "Oh, Harry."

"Sir?"

"The last we heard from Headquarters the AVM had personally put you forward for the DFC, seconded by the Minister from the War Office, so it's pretty much in the bag. Though the line's down and we haven't been able to let them know you're alive as yet, so the medal is still posthumous I'm afraid. Well done all the same."

"Thank you..." she replied with a raised eyebrow.

"A woman never got a DFC before," AP half gasped as she finished her drink.

"They haven't," Cas replied, as the three of them left the Mess room and headed outside. "Mister Singh has recommended you for the DFC, too, AP."

"What for?" she asked with a confused frown.

"For risking your life to rescue a downed pilot. We kept it simple and glossed over the whole stealing an aeroplane thing. We just said that you were there, not necessarily doing the flying," came the dry reply as AP's mouth fell open a little. "It's not often we see you lost for words; we should decorate you more often..." He smirked and patted her on the shoulder. "Well done, old girl, it's thoroughly deserved. Just maybe next time don't do anything quite so dangerous, or against the rules." She hardly smiled, just nodded formally. "Harry, there's a very important package at the dispatch tent when you arrive at the airfield. You're to collect it for me before returning, and make absolutely sure that it gets back here in one piece, got it?"

"Got it."

"Good luck," AP said. They shook hands, and Harriet headed off towards the Lysander while Cas and AP stood and watched.

"Come on, Harry. We haven't got all day!" Max said from the bottom of the steps of the Lysander.

"Max? You're coming too?"

"Only if he sits outside with the riffraff," Archie shouted from the rear cockpit. "Hurry up, anyway, let's get this over with!" Harriet smiled as she climbed the ladder and looked inside. The seat had been ripped out, and a wooden board had been laid across the floor so more than one could squeeze in. Archie helped her in, and they both sat on their parachutes, then Max climbed aboard, squeezed down, and closed the canopy before reaching through and tapping the pilot on the shoulder.

"All aboard, Foggy," he shouted, then jammed himself tight between the bulkhead and Harriet, and not a minute later they were bouncing uncomfortably along the grass. It was noisy, so the conversation was difficult but manageable at a shout.

"You'd think they'd provide a silk cushion for a DFC," Archie said while he grabbed and steadied Harriet as they lifted into the air.

"Can't believe she's riding coach with us commoners," Max added.

"I don't even know what you're talking about," Harriet replied.

"You're a DFC now, Harry. King's Commission and a DFC in one day, not a bad result," Archie said warmly.

"I heard she knocked down another two 109s, too," Max added.

"Well, I've had worse days," Archie said somewhat dismissively.

"I've still no idea what you're saying," Harriet replied, a little irritably. It was nice to be distracted by them, and she enjoyed their comedy routines which seemed to flow so naturally. It stopped her thinking about Nicole so much, though it was difficult not to, but she was so exhausted that she found herself biting easily.

"Distinguished Flying Cross. They don't hand them out for free," Max said, sensing the time had come to stop the teasing.

"Singh told us earlier," Archie added. "The AVM said you'd both gone down fighting off a squadron of Huns who were intent on shooting him down." She forced a smile and relaxed into Max, letting the big American support her. Her mind wandered back to the battle. It had been over in minutes, maybe less, and the last thing she remembered of Nicole was watching her ram the German which was attacking the bomber. They bounced about in the air as the pilot threw the Lysander around at treetop height, staying low to avoid the enemy and hopefully stay out of trouble. It'd be a high price for the squadron to pay if a stray 109 found them. The Lysander was unarmed, slow, and loaded with four very high value pilots. Fortunately, there wasn't much to worry about, the pilot was beyond talented and had flown Lysanders since he'd qualified. The Germans had tried to shoot him down many times already, but he'd earned the name 'Foggy' on the squadron as it was said that trying to catch him was like trying to hold on to fog. He was also one of only two survivors of his entire Lysander squadron, the rest of which had been lost in combat in the last week, many in a failed suicide mission thought up by command which had the Lysanders fly a bombing raid against German ground troops.

The journey ended without incident, and once the engine had shut down, the trio extracted themselves one at a time and climbed down the ladder to the ground. Archie threw down the parachutes, including one that had been packed for Harriet as her last was still in a field somewhere. They hadn't been able to wear them in the Lysander due to space constraints, so they'd been used as seat cushions, and their owners just hoped they didn't have to find a way of putting them on and jumping if they were attacked. They'd joked that Foggy had flown so low that they wouldn't have time for the parachutes to deploy anyway, which was more accurate than any of them were really prepared to admit.

It was early evening, and the airfield was a hive of activity with aeroplanes coming and going, and others parked in very neat lines. As they walked in the direction of the dispersal tent, Harriet was distracted by the sight of a fantastic beast, a Spitfire, an azure blue Spitfire. It was the most beautiful thing she'd ever seen. She walked over slowly with her mouth open in amazement; and watched as a young woman ran down the wing, jumped off, then walked over to the neatly stacked parachute, flying jacket, and map bag which had been left a few paces from where Harriet had come to a stop.

"Pretty, isn't she?" the young woman asked, breaking Harriet's Spitfire induced daze. She blinked and came back to reality, then focused on the young woman standing before her in shirt sleeves, Mae West, and a smart hat which looked pitch black in the half light of early evening, but for the gold buttons and badge half glowing, half glinting, and catching Harriet's eye.

"Yes... It's a Spitfire."

"I know..." came the reply. "I'm about to fly it home to England."

"What?" Harriet asked, realising she was still half dazed by being so close to a Spitfire, despite having been close enough to touch one in her combat earlier. This was different, though, she could actually appreciate its beautiful lines now it was standing in front of her. She looked again at the young woman and screwed her eyes to focus. "But you're a girl..." she muttered, then instantly felt consumed by regret the second the words left her mouth.

"Well that explains the awkward blushes in the men's toilets," came the quick and witty reply, delivered softly and quietly, but most definitely confidently. The pilot couldn't have been more than five feet tall, maybe a little more, but not by much. She had short blonde hair swept back under her hat and big dark blue eyes.

"I am so sorry..." Harriet proclaimed.

"It's OK. I'm used to it," the pilot replied as she picked up her jacket.

"I just... I mean, I was told there were no other female pilots here in France."

"There's not supposed to be, not really anyway. I'm supposed to be with the rest of my ATA flight on a nice little airfield on the south coast of England; but there was an urgent call for pilots to bring Hurricanes across to resupply the fighter squadrons, and they needed aeroplanes more urgently than they needed to follow the rules about women flying to France. I was there, I was willing, and my boss said OK..."

"That's incredible."

"Not as incredible as getting to fly that home!" She pointed at the Spitfire. "It's a photographic reconnaissance Spitfire, that's why it's blue, for camouflage."

"What are they like to fly?"

"I'll let you know soon..." she smirked.

"You've never flown one?"

"I've read the notes... Anyway, to return the compliment, you're also a girl..."

"Yes, yes, I am," Harriet blushed.

"So what are you doing here in France, you don't look like ATA?"

"I've come to collect one of the Hurricanes you brought over. They're needed back at the squadron."

"Don't mock me."

"What do you mean?"

"I mean, what are you really doing here?"

"Come on, Harry. It'll be dark soon, and we need to get these Hurricanes back," Archie shouted.

"Come to collect a Hurricane," Harriet replied with a smile.

“How on earth did you get them to allow that?”

“Well, you’ve got to reach for the stars…”

"Indeed you do...” the young blonde pilot said with a smile and a nod of acceptance. “Anyway, I have the pilot's notes if you'd like to read them before you fly it?" she offered with humility and a hint of disbelief.

"Oh, that's OK, I've flown a few before," Harriet said with a smug smile.

"I bet..." the pilot replied before offering her hand. "Abigail Columba" She introduced herself. "Abby to my friends."

"Nice to meet you, Abby," Harriet replied as she shook hands. "Harriet Cornwall. Or Harry to everyone."

"It's a pleasure, Harry."

"I have to go. We need to get back before it's dark."

"Me too. Safe flying, Harry."

"And you, Abby," Harriet replied. They smiled for a moment as Harriet thought how much she’d like to continue their conversation if she had the time. She was intrigued by the young blonde pilot and wanted to know how she’d come to be flying aeroplanes. Finally, she waved, then turned and ran off after the others as they approached the group of pilots standing outside of the dispersal tent.

"Which one of you is Cornwall?" the Flight Lieutenant asked. He had smart dark hair, pushed back and held down with wax, and an equally smart waxed moustache.

"I am," Harriet replied.

"I'm told you're expecting a package?"

"Yes, I'm to collect it from the dispersal tent."

"Well, I'm Ardilles, the dispersal Officer, and that's the dispersal tent. Better get in there and collect it before you push off." He had half a smirk on his face as he nodded to the tent door.

"We ain't got all night, Harry," Max said as he slapped her on the back and gestured towards the tent. She nodded and walked into the tent, looking for a package on the table; but sitting on a cot in the corner was something she wasn't expecting.

"Nicole?" she gasped; her eyes were wide as though she'd seen a ghost. Something she was convinced of as her brain fought to make sense of the scene before her.

"Harry?" Nicole replied, prompting Harriet to run across the tent as Nicole jumped from the cot. They hugged tight and danced in a circle with excitement. "You're alive…" Nicole gasped excitedly.

"So are you!" Harriet replied.

"Yes! I was able to glide and force land. I was picked up by the army and brought here."

"I'm so happy to see you! I thought you were dead! I saw you ram that German then dive down through the clouds."

"I saw you on fire!"

"I jumped. The French army picked me up and were going to shoot me for being a German spy!"

"What? The idiots! How did you get away?"

"When you two are ready," Ardilles said as he poked his head into the tent. "Those Hurricanes aren't going to fly themselves..." The girls laughed and ran from the tent. "Strange thing, war," Ardilles muttered as they joined the group. "You don't see a woman for ages, then three of them fly onto your airfield at once." He turned to the three pilots stood by the tent, each next to a neat pile of personal equipment. "Well, you three. Best get your stuff together."

"Who are they?" Max asked.

"Your replacements, old boy. They came in a while ago, with a message from the Air Ministry that they're to go straight to you."

"I see... You boys got any combat experience?" he asked in his deep American accent. The three of them shook their heads.

"Not yet, but if you point us in the direction of the Hun, we'll soon be knocking them down," one of them replied in a confident bluster.

"Combat experience isn't that important," his friend added with an almost identical upper class accent. "We're fresh and ready to help you chaps out of the muddle you've got yourselves in."

"Oh, is that right, and who are you?" Max asked with a frown.

"Pilot Officer Cameron," the second to speak replied, "and this is Pilot Officer Johnson. Both of Eton and Oxford."

"Eton and Oxford, you say? I see... I guess we're lucky to have you gentlemen on our side."

"Certainly are, Yank," Johnson blustered confidently. "Anyway, it's good to see the Americans arrived early to this war."

"What's that, now?" Max asked.

"Oh, come on, Yank, only pulling your leg! Right, are we ready for off?"

"What about you?" Max asked the third pilot, who stood quietly apart from the others.

"Pilot Officer Bevan," he replied with a strong New Zealand accent. "Of Shit Creek and the School of Hard Knocks!" Max smirked and nodded.

"Combat experience?"

"Got punched square in the nose by a WAAF in a bar back in London, if that counts?"

"That'll do for me, Bevan," Max looked at the New Zealand flash embroidered onto the shoulder of Bevan's uniform. "Kiwi?"

"Yeah... Me and my mate volunteered last year. He went to Army Cooperation. I only just finished training on fighters."

"OK, well, grab your gear. We want to get home before dark." He turned to Harriet and Nicole, who were muttering quietly and excitedly between themselves. "You girls ready?"

"Of course," Nicole replied firmly, almost insulted that she had to be asked. "I've been waiting here long enough, and I don't like it!" Max smirked, and the group started to stroll towards the line of Hurricanes Ardilles had pointed them to.

"What, the girls are coming with us?" Cameron asked as he looked over his shoulder at Harriet and Nicole, who both stared daggers at him.

"More a case of you going with them," Max replied. "They were members of our squadron long before you."

"It looks like you girls missed your bus," Johnson said with a deep laugh while pointing at Foggy's Lysander which was already droning into the sky.

"Then they'll have to fly Hurricanes, won't they?" Archie barked uncharacteristically, without even turning to look at the young pilots. "Think you're up to that, ladies?"

"We'll do our best," Harriet replied dutifully, pinching Nicole's arm in the process, and stopping her from letting go with a tirade of insults and abuse.

"Nothing to worry about then, good show."

"WAAFS Flying Hurricanes? It's unheard of," Cameron said with disgust. "It's not allowed. Anyway, the RAF forbids it. WAAFS are none flying."

"Lucky they're not WAAFS in that case, isn't it?" Archie continued. "Though there are WAAFS where you're heading, and I'd be very careful about telling them what they can or can't do if I were you. Those that did so in the past have lived to regret it, mostly."

"ATA flyers then?" Johnson added. "I'd heard they'd let girls join. Either way, I'm not sure I approve of silly little girls flying Hurricanes. It's preposterous!" The group stopped as they reached the first Hurricane and came together. Max stepped forward and stopped almost nose to nose with Johnson.

"Listen here, sunshine," his deep voice snarled. "If you boys can fly half as good as these silly little girls, you'll still be lucky to make it to the end of tomorrow before some German knocks you clean out of the sky." The pair of pilots looked a little spooked by Max's sudden change in temperament and the imposing darkness that came with the changing of his mood. At six feet two inches, he was a formidable and towering presence. "Miss Delacourt, formerly of the French Army Air Force, before being commissioned into the Royal Air Force Volunteer Reserve, has four kills to her name, three Messerschmitt 109s and a 110. Two of which she rammed out of the sky after running out of ammunition." The pair looked at Nicole, who in turn looked at them with cutting disdain. "Miss Cornwall was commissioned to the Volunteer Reserve from the Norwegian Army Air Service and is an ace with seven confirmed kills. All fighters. Four of which were 109s which she took on alone, and won." Harriet felt herself blush, but stood confidently with her shoulders back, and head held high and stared down the cowering pair. "Now that's clarified the picture for you boys, we need to get on. The CO is expecting us back at the squadron before nightfall, so unless you've got anything useful to say for yourselves, get to your aeroplanes and get ready to take off." He stared at Cameron first, and then Johnson, both of whom shook their heads. "No, I didn't think so... What about you, Kiwi?" he asked as he looked at Bevan.

"Hey, don't lump me in with those upper class wankers," Kiwi replied, looking surprised that he'd even been questioned.

"No problems with girls flying Hurricanes?"

"I told you about my experiences with women in uniform," Kiwi pointed to his slightly flattened nose as he talked. "I reckon any woman armed with a Hurricane and a good argument would be bloody lethal in a scrap, and I'd rather be on the same team if it's all the same to them?" He looked hopefully at the girls. Harriet smiled and nodded.

"We'll see," Nicole said as she turned her nose to the air dismissively.

"OK, let's get this show on the road," Max said. "Wheels up in five. You three form up behind us, and we'll lead you home. Girls, hang back a few hundred yards and watch our backs for rogue Germans."

"Oh, Kiwi?" Archie said as the group split to head off to their own aeroplanes.

"Sir?"

"Not all of the upper classes are wankers..." Kiwi looked a little uncomfortable as Archie's upper class tones danced lightly across the evening air. "At least not all of the time." He gave a playful wink after he'd left Kiwi swinging in discomfort for long enough. "See you in the Mess. Stay close."

While the ground crew started the Hurricane, Harriet stood on the wing and tightened her parachute straps, determined to keep everything snug and in place should she need to step out of another aeroplane mid flight for the second time in a day. She was a little nervous. It was only a few hours since her escape from the flames of the burning Hurricane had left her hurtling through the clouds, towards an unknown fate on the ground. As she prepared herself, the blue Spitfire passed as it taxied to the end of the runway. Abby waved at her and gave a bright smile which lit up the darkening skies. Harriet waved back excitedly. She watched as the tremendous machine rolled to the end of the runway and commenced pre take off power checks, before gliding effortlessly into the sky with the familiar roaring Merlin dragging the aeroplane and pilot back to the safety of England. Ten minutes later, and it was Harriet's turn. The others took off first, leaving Harriet and Nicole to follow a few hundred yards behind as ordered, and together all seven aeroplanes climbed into the colourful evening sky and headed in the opposite direction to the Spitfire. No safety on the English coast waited for them, just their airfield, firmly in the centre of harm's way.

Chapter 10

The Visitor

The flight back to the airfield was uneventful, other than the most beautiful sky filled with copper and purple, turning blood red as the night swept westwards while the Hurricanes circled to land. A green flare welcomed them, and burning torches lit a path in the last of the crimson daylight, and as quickly as they were lit, they were doused again by the waiting airmen as Harriet's tail passed each of them. She followed the ground crew torch which appeared in front of her and taxied to her usual pen, where she wheeled around and cut the engine.

"You made it back, then," AP said as she jumped onto the wing, and reached into the cockpit to offer Harriet a hand to get out, pulling her free in one smooth move.

"It looks that way. Sorry..." Harriet replied with a smirk as she released the straps of her parachute.

"Just don't break any more of my aeroplanes now you're back, or the Germans will be awarding you the Iron Cross for the number of Hurricanes you're putting out of service."

"What's an iron cross?"

"Never mind..." AP rolled her eyes in mock disappointment. "The boss is waiting for you in the Mess. They've put supper on for you all as you missed dinner. Cocoa and biscuits, I think."

"Thanks, are you coming?"

"No, I want to get this thing checked over and ready for whatever tomorrow brings. Who are the other three stragglers you've picked up?"

"The who?"

"Well we were expecting four of you, and seven came back..."

"Oh, right. Replacements sent by the AVM, apparently."

"What are they like?"

"There's a New Zealander, Kiwi. He seems pleasant enough."

"The other two?"

"I'll let you make your own decisions," Harriet smirked as she walked off the back of the wing and jumped down to the ground.

"Great... Welcome back."

"See you later," Harriet shouted as she joined Nicole, and arm in arm they headed over to the mansion house across the increasingly darkening fields. Max, Archie, and the new arrivals were talking with Cas and Singh, and a tray of cocoa was sitting on the table with a plate of dried fruit biscuits big enough to be mistaken for scones.

"Ah, ladies. You made it back, OK?" Singh asked, in much more settled, and much warmer tones than those Harriet had heard in their last conversation.

"Yes, Sir," they replied in unison.

"Good," he said with a half smile. "Have yourselves some cocoa and a biscuit. Chef made them fresh this evening." The girls dumped their kit and grabbed a mug and biscuit each before joining the group. "I was just welcoming our guests." He gestured at the replacements. "It's good to have you back with us, Miss Delacourt. I was happy to hear you'd been picked up safe."

"Thank you, I'm happy to be back," Nicole said courteously.

"You've both had quite the day. You should probably get some sleep after you've finished your cocoa and biscuits." They both smiled and made a start on their evening treat.

"I see you brought the package back safe," Cas said as he joined them and stood by Harriet, leaving Singh and the others to brief the new arrivals. He pulled a silver flask from his pocket and unscrewed the lid, then poured a large tot of brandy into each of their mugs. "A nightcap," he said with a warm smile.

"You could have told me she was alive," Harriet replied, before gulping the cocoa, which with the brandy made her eyes open wide.

"I thought you'd enjoy finding out for yourself," he smirked. "Besides, the way the war's going at the moment, I couldn't be sure she'd still be there when you arrived, or if you'd arrive at all if you take my meaning."

"Is there any news from the front?"

"Nothing. Our telephone lines are down, unfortunately; we sent a party into the local town to find out why, but unsurprisingly they've not yet returned. The whole town is chaotic, to say the least, they've had a whole army of refugees passing through since mid afternoon, we've had to post sentries to keep them off the airfield and out of our stores."

"I see... So, what will we do if we can't get orders from Headquarters?"

"The CO is sending Foggy up to HQ tonight to check in, and let them know our comms are down. Not to worry, I'm sure they'll give him any routine orders, probably the regular patrol lines. How's the cocoa?"

"Good," Harriet smiled.

"Better with French brandy," Nicole added.

"Everything's better with French brandy. Everyone knows that." Cas winked, which brought a rare smile from Nicole. "You know, the boss is right, the two of you should probably push off and get some sleep, you've more than earned it today. Besides, there'll be nothing much happening here tonight. The replacements will need briefing and settling in, and that's about it."

"Was there any news about Jenny and those other pilots?" Harriet asked.

"Sadly not. If they weren't at the airfield when it was overrun, they wouldn't have been far away. Most likely in the bag."

"What bag?" Nicole asked with a frown.

"Sorry, please excuse my anglicisms, it means taken prisoner."

"Oh..."

"Don't worry. They'll probably be having it better than many at the moment. At least they'll have a roof over their heads and meals every day, and won't have some silly bugger trying to shoot them out of the sky every other minute." His attempts to settle their concerns were warm and genuine, but all three of them knew that the chances of being taken prisoner were slim and that there was every chance that their friends were dead. Even if they'd been taken prisoner their lives weren't going to be easy by any stretch.

"Lucky them!" Harriet said, breaking the forced and uncomfortable silence. "When I was taken prisoner by the French army earlier today, I was thrown into an old outhouse and left to rot. That's until a mad General decided he wanted to bayonet me for being a spy. Hopefully, the Germans are a little more hospitable!"

"A spy?" Cas asked in disbelief.

"Because girls don't fly fighter planes, and I spoke what they considered to be perfect French. They dreamed up a story that I was parachuted in to spy on them and report back on their movements."

"That explains everything," Nicole said.

"What explains what?" Harriet asked.

"If they thought your French was perfect, they were clearly drunk and weren't thinking straight, so it's perfectly understandable that in their inebriated state they would jump to the conclusion that you're a spy."

"Hilarious..." Harriet rolled her eyes as Cas chuckled. Before she could respond any further, the door opened, and one of the sentries walked in.

"Mister Singh, Sir," he said with an edge of worry in his voice.

"Yes, what is it, Corporal?"

"Dispatch rider, Sir." He gestured to the door, and a green and brown clad soldier entered the room. Helmet strap swinging and scarf over their face like a highwayman, the creature half staggered into the room wrapped in a waterproof motorcycle jacket, army trousers, and buckled black leather motorcycle boots. Another step and they stumbled, and were caught quickly by the sentry and helped to the table, while the rest of the room gathered around as they pulled off their helmet and dropped it to the floor, releasing her tousled light brown hair. The young woman pulled away the scarf, taking a breath through gritted teeth while looking around the room and grasping her thigh. Cas dropped to one knee and moved her hand to show a bloody and dirty rag tied six inches above the knee of her left leg.

"Archie, get the doc," Cas ordered. Archie quickly left the room in search of the squadron medical officer, Flight Lieutenant Reynoldston. "It's OK, let me have a look," he said softly and lifted the rider's hand. She nodded and sucked in breath while Cas looked at the wound. He prodded a little then put her hand back over the wound. "Somebody been shooting at you?" She nodded and bit her lip. "Yes, it looks like it too. Not to worry, our doctor will be here shortly." He looked up at Singh and nodded. "I've seen worse."

"What brings you here, young lady?" Singh asked.

"Sister," the young woman replied.

"Sister? I'm afraid I don't understand?" Singh looked around the gathered faces for guidance.

"Sister Coleman, Queen Alexandra's Imperial Military Nursing Service," the young woman replied.

"Oh, I see. A nurse?"

"A nurse..." Coleman replied between gasps. Cas pulled his hip flask and handed it to her, then looked a little surprised as she took a very long deep swig before letting out a sigh. "I was sent to find you."

"Find us?" Cas asked with a raised eyebrow. At that, the door opened, and the squadron medical officer entered carrying his bag, with Archie at his side.

"Ah, Simon," Cas said. "It looks like our friend here has had a bit of a scrape with a German machine gun?" The Sister nodded in agreement.

"Well, let's get you on the table," Simon said calmly as he stepped forward. Harriet put her parachute pack down as a pillow as Max swept the young Sister up onto the table. Simon cut the rag dressing away then cut her trousers with a hefty pair of scissors to reveal a crudely stitched bloody wound. "Your own handiwork?" he asked. She nodded, and he smiled back at her. "Well you certainly helped stem the bleeding, that's the main thing, but I'm probably going to have to open it up again and have a look."

"You'll probably need to," she replied. "I think there's a foreign body still in there, I can feel it."

"OK, well this is as good a place as any. I'll give you something for the pain, and then we can get on with it. Archie, would you send for my orderly, I'm going to need help. The rest of you gents can clear out and give the Sister her dignity. Though if you ladies want to stay, it can't hurt to have the support?" he asked as he looked to Harriet and Nicole, both of whom nodded.

"Wait," Coleman said.

"I'd rather not," Simon replied. She bit her lip then lifted onto her elbows and looked at Singh. "My field hospital is heading west tonight with the brigade they're supporting."

"Go on..." Singh encouraged intently.

"The entire division is retreating, heading for the ports on the coast. Anyway, the hospital is trying to move at night and get to a wooded area protected by anti aircraft artillery, but due to the traffic and refugees on the road it's expected they won't make it until a few hours after sunrise."

"I see..."

"I was sent to ask for air cover at dawn. Your Headquarters was packing up and in the middle of evacuating after a bombing raid when I got there, and I was told to come and find you here. The officer, Group Captain somebody, gave me orders for you," she reached into her jacket and pulled out a flat leather satchel which she handed to Singh.

"Cas, I want all pilots assembled in the Ops Room in five minutes," Singh said after reading the orders. Cas nodded and left, then Singh turned back to Coleman. "OK, my squadron will cover your move the best we can," he said warmly. "Ladies, upstairs," he said to the girls. "I'm going to need every pilot I've got for this."

"Thank you," Coleman half whispered, then pulled herself upright and tried to get off the table, only stopped by Simon who held her shoulders.

"Woah, steady young lady. Where do you think you're going?"

"I have to tell the hospital you'll cover them."

"I don't think so," Simon said kindly, but firmly. "You had to stitch up your own leg to get this far. If I don't look at it, clean it up, and get out whatever's in there, you'll have an infection by breakfast and be in your grave by dinner. Though as a nursing Sister, I suspect you know all of this already." Coleman nodded.

"Tell me, Sister," Singh said with undoubted authority. "Has your hospital already started its move?"

"Yes," she nodded. "They were moving at last light. The idea is to travel at night to avoid enemy bombers."

"A most sensible idea. I'm assuming that whatever happens, they'll be heading down the same road at the same speed while heading to the same destination?" She nodded again. "Then, in that case, it doesn't matter whether you get back to them or not. They'll know you got through when they see our Hurricanes watching over them."

"I have patients to care for," she protested.

"You can't care for patients if you're dead," Simon said firmly. "Now lay back and let's get this leg fixed. You're now a guest of the Royal Air Force.

"And as such following my orders," Singh said. "Which means you're to rest and recover. We'll look after you and watch over your hospital, I promise. Put her in Finn's quarters, Simon. I'm sure Cornwall and Delacourt won't mind the company."

"Not at all," Nicole quickly replied. "We were both going to nurse school anyway. We'll look after her."

"Thank you. Now let's go to the Ops Room." They all left together, and Coleman lay back as Simon's orderly joined them and they went about fixing her up. Soon everyone was gathered in the Ops Room that needed to be there. AP joined them and sat on the floor between Harriet and Nicole.

"What's happening?" she asked.

"Mission for tomorrow," Harriet replied.

"OK everyone, listen up," Cas said, silencing the room and drawing everyone's attention to Singh.

"We've been assigned a high priority mission for tomorrow." Singh started. "We have a brigade moving west along this road." He pointed his stick at the large map board behind him. "They're heading towards the Channel ports, and they have a German armoured division hot on their heels. They're expecting to reach an air defence perimeter here sometime in the morning." He tapped the board again. "Where anti aircraft guns are in place to cover their movement, along with support from fighter squadrons flying from southern England. Unfortunately, the volume of military traffic combined with refugees means that they're moving much slower than anticipated, so they'll be vulnerable to air attacks between sunrise and about nine in the morning. Everything else the RAF has in France is already tasked, so it's down to us to try and cover the withdrawal. Also, for your information, the brigade field hospital is evacuating along the same road, moving many of our wounded towards hospital ships docked at the coast. We must do all we can to cover them."

"What the plan, boss?" Max asked.

"Simple... We'll set up a patrol line along the main evacuation road. The full squadron will be wheels up just before first light, split into two flights of four. I'll lead, and Miss Cornwall and Miss Delacourt will fly overwatch. That's eleven aeroplanes. I want to be over the far end of the road by sunrise so we can get a better picture of the situation on the ground, then we'll patrol in squadron strength and deter or intercept any German aircraft intent on causing problems. I'll coordinate, and on my command Flight Commanders will conduct their flights accordingly. If nothing much is happening, we'll return and refuel in flight order, so we always have one flight over the road while the others refuel. If we get into a fight, it's best efforts; and as soon as your ammunition is spent, or your fuel is critical, you're to head back here for replenishment. Chief, AP, your crews are going to have to be on the ball and ready for a quick turnaround!" Both nodded without hesitation. "Once you're rearmed and refuelled, you're to wait until there's at least a section of two aeroplanes to return. I don't want anyone heading out solo, there are too many Germans around for that, and I don't want to lose anyone, you're far too valuable a commodity. Any questions?"

"What time do we end our patrols?" Archie asked.

"I'll advise when we know more in the morning. Initially, I'd say we should be able to break and review the situation between ten and lunch. The plan is for the withdrawing troops, and the hospital, to reach the air perimeter by nine, but it won't hurt for us to plan for delays due to congestion on the road. Hope for the best and plan for the worst. Anything else?" The room was silent. "OK, sunrise will be around six and first light an hour before that, so I'll have Chef prepare breakfast for four, with wheels up at four thirty. Flight Commanders will brief with me at four fifteen. Goodnight, everyone. I recommend you get what sleep you can, dismissed." The room burst into life and quickly emptied as the pilots left for their beds, leaving Harriet and Nicole with Singh.

"What does overwatch mean, and why aren't we flying with the others?" Harriet asked, a little disappointed.

"I'm happy you asked," Singh replied. "It's quite simple, really. You are two of the best pilots I've ever had the pleasure to command; however, neither of you are trained in formation flying or group tactics. If you fly with the flights, there's every chance you'll crash into another aeroplane without even knowing until it's too late, and that's not a commentary on your flying ability, it's simply a case of training. However, what I do need is two pairs of young and observant eyes about two thousand feet above the squadron watching for fighters. You see, if we encounter bombers, and I'm sure we will at some point, they're almost always escorted by fighters; which are usually positioned conveniently above their bombers so they can drop down on any attackers with the combat advantage of height and speed. Basically, you're my early warning insurance. If we see a flight of bombers, I'll take the squadron in to attack. You're to stay above and let us know if and when the fighters start to come down on us so we can break and be ready for them, that way they don't get to surprise us. Get this right, and you'll save lives. Oh, and try to resist the urge to take them on yourselves, we need this to be a team effort, OK?" Both girls nodded, and Singh left with a bold final statement, "I'm relying on you both to watch over us."

"You know, many of those at the top in the RAF didn't learn that much about tactics from the last war. Despite many of them being pilots," Cas said as he replaced Singh, and stood looking at the girls with a frown.

"Oh?" Harriet replied

"Yes. They still insist on us using formations and tactics which just don't work when fighting the Germans. The new boys you brought back will be trained that way, old school, which is going to make tomorrow a challenge, as the squadron agreed back when the war started that we'd mix things up a bit and take Jerry on at his own game. Anyway, that's for the boss to deal with. You two, however, can fly any way you like, and if you'd take some advice from an old man, I can tell you what we learned the hard way, and what the Germans have been doing from the Somme to Spain."

"Please do," Harriet nodded keenly.

"It's simple. You fly as a pair, one left and one right, and you watch your arcs inwards, so the pilot on the right is looking left and behind, and the pilot on the left is looking right. That way you're not focusing on trying to keep in formation as you're staring straight at your partner, so you know exactly where they are and how close you are to them. You're also looking past them at the same time and watching for the enemy, and it makes it impossible for them to jump you unexpectedly. It's been tried, and it works, give it a go tomorrow." The girls thanked him and said goodnight, then left and returned to their room above the old stables, where they freshened up with the bucket of warm water that had been left for them before climbing into bed. Both were so tired from the day's events that they were out as soon as their heads hit their pillows. Neither of them so much as flinched when the young Sister was brought to the room by Simon and his orderly, and deposited in what had been Finn's bed. She could have been screaming out in pain all night, and they wouldn't have flinched. Fortunately, it wasn't a problem. Coleman slept through, equally exhausted after her experience riding for help and her unplanned surgeries, and she was still fast asleep when Daisy came to wake the girls for breakfast. They washed and dressed silently, and joined the rest of the squadron for bread, butter, and jam, before heading out to check their aeroplanes over and get ready for the morning ahead.

"I don't have a good feeling about this," AP said as she helped strap Harriet into her Hurricane.

"She'll be fine," Lanky said as she closed the final gun bay, after checking the ammunition was loaded and ready to go. "It's any German she bumps into that should be worried."

"Indeed they should," AP agreed. "Make sure Nicole's ammunition is OK, and that she knows the guns are sighted for two hundred feet the same as Harry's, will you?"

"Sure," Lanky said with a smile, before dancing off to the next Hurricane.

"Remember what I told you," AP continued in hushed tones to Harriet. "If you get into trouble, run. You're not trained for this, and I'd rather you got out of France safely."

"I have a job to do," Harriet replied.

"Yes, and it's called overwatch," AP argued. "Look, I'm not getting into this with you, just make sure you come back in one piece."

"I will. I promise. Thank you for caring."

"I care about my aeroplane. Not even a scratch, remember?"

"I remember..."

"Good luck!" AP quickly turned and left without another word or even a smile. Harriet busied herself with her cockpit checks, looking at the mint green glow of the dials in the darkness of the early morning. She was comfortable with what she now considered to be her Hurricane, with its carburettor modification. She didn't mind in the slightest that her Hurricane had seen better days, she was just happy to be flying.

The engine rumbled and coughed, then the now familiar cloud of blue smoke enveloped the cockpit and accentuated the flashes of fire from the exhaust ports; before the blast of the propeller pushed the smoke to the rear and brought wisps of warmed air from the exhausts into the fringes of the cockpit. The whole aeroplane vibrated comfortably. After checking the magnetos and running through her cockpit drills, Harriet followed AP's instructions and taxied out to follow Nicole into position at the end of the runway, tucking neatly behind the other nine aeroplanes which were formed up in flights behind Singh.

"Goose Squadron will take off by flights," Singh said over the radio. "I'll lead, followed by A Flight, then B Flight, climb to ten thousand feet. Black Section to follow on once we're clear and climb to twelve thousand feet on overwatch. Keep your eyes open and your mouths closed unless there's something to report." Harriet felt a flutter of excitement in her tummy. It was the first time she truly felt part of the squadron, even if she and Nicole were to follow behind. She looked across, and Nicole waved excitedly, obviously feeling the same about the very poignant moment. Another check of her instruments and she sat ready to go. The distant sky was a dark silvery blue, and the blackness of the ground was only punctured by the purple, blue flickers sparking from the exhaust ports of the collected squadron. "OK, Goose Squadron, let's go," Singh said calmly yet forcefully, and a second later the air vibrated as each pilot throttled forward and brought their engines up to take off power. Singh bounced down the grass runway with A Flight, and B Flight following obediently behind. Harriet gave Nicole a nod, and they followed along. Already the black silhouettes of the squadron ahead were climbing into the sky with their undercarriages folding neatly out of sight, to leave them looking sleek and streamlined. As always, Harriet waited for the big bounce which would lift her into the air, but this time it didn't come. Instead, the Hurricane simply lifted like a feather on the breeze. She was getting the hang of its handling, apparently. She raised the undercarriage and checked her position, then checked the glowing dials and needles of her instruments to make sure all was OK. Once satisfied, she joined Nicole in a climb to sit high above the rest of the squadron, and about half a mile back, as instructed. They had a full view of the sleek black silhouettes which had now fanned out into Singh's instructed formation, which was very similar to the formation used by the Luftwaffe who'd attacked the bomber, just as Cas had said. Cas had seen how effective the Germans had been in structuring their flights in two pairs of two, and how that formation was significantly superior to the British 'Vic' formation, which the upper echelons of the RAF continued to insist was used by all fighter squadrons, despite its apparent failings. It was an impressive sight to see, nine Hurricanes flying in orderly formation. Watching it had Harriet understanding exactly why Singh had decided to keep her and Nicole out of the way, they'd had no training in formation flying, and she knew herself that being that close to so many other aeroplanes would end in disaster. She smiled as she looked over to Nicole, who was a good hundred feet away from her wingtip, and even then, it was taking effort to keep that distance, keep on track, and make sure they didn't converge and get dangerously close. Having them fly with the squadron would have been suicide, or murder, depending on where one was sitting.

The flight was smooth in the cool morning air as the squadron sped towards the ever brightening horizon, keen to get into position and be ready to intercept any German bombers intent on mischief. Thirty minutes into the flight Singh's voice cut through the hum of the engines; and distracted Harriet from straining her eyes as she searched the horizon for signs of the Luftwaffe, making her jump a little in the process. "The main road is coming up on our twelve, keep your eyes open." Harriet squinted and searched, then the tip of the sun crested the horizon over to her right and shone a long golden beam which bathed the road in light and revealed the most unexpected scene below.

"Bloody hell..." Archie said over the radio in a tone of genuine surprise.

"Would you look at that," Max added.

"Alright, that's enough!" Singh quickly interjected. "Keep your eyes open and let's follow the road east."

The sight causing so much alarm had already made an impression on Harriet. She had to physically shake her head to break herself away from staring and focus on keeping her eyes open for Germans. The road was alive. Military trucks and columns of slowly marching soldiers were tightly mixed with civilian cars, carts, livestock, and thousands upon thousands of refugees. It was chaos, and so tightly packed that nothing was moving very quickly at all. From her position above Harriet could see a blockage in the west, smoking and burning vehicles which were forcing the living snake of a road to divert through the fields either side before returning on track and continuing their journey west. She could also see red crosses to the east. The hospital maybe, but surrounded by other military personnel, trucks, and even tanks, all of which were further surrounded by refugees. As she swept the horizon, a massive plume of orange and gold flame caught her eye, she quickly spun her head and watched as a second plume leapt into the still dark blue western sky. She tipped her wing and strained her eyes, as she did the sunlight glinted in the sky above the smoke and flames. Enemy aircraft!

"German bombers at three o'clock!" Harriet called into her radio. "Maybe five thousand feet, it's a swarm of them!" She banked to get a better view and could see the black dots filling the sky, dropping down in ones and twos in steep dives towards the road, and releasing their deadly cargo. Already it looked like the road was burning.

"Stukas!" Grumpy's voice barked over the radio.

"Swarms of the bastards!" Archie added.

"OK Goose Squadron, let's go," Singh said. "A Flight form on my right, B Flight on my left, we've got the cover of darkness on our backs so we can surprise them if we're lucky. Black Section, keep your eyes open for fighters." The squadron formed and banked, and screamed towards the Stukas at full throttle. Harriet felt nervous, excited, scared, and every other emotion as she and Nicole followed behind and kept their height. The Hurricanes hit with tremendous force, cutting through the assembled Stukas like a scythe and sending several flaming German bombers crashing to the ground in the first pass. Battle had been joined, and it was like nothing Harriet had seen before. The neatly formed squadron splintered as they passed through the Stukas, each chasing their own target, and soon the air was full of smoke trails and tracer bullets, and the airwaves filled with voices calling out positions, warning each other, and shouting excitedly as they claimed kills. Harriet and Nicole kept their height above the battle, which was quickly descending closer to the ground as the Stuka pilots dived for speed in an attempt to escape the fury of the Hurricanes. It was a was a mesmerising sight, which Harriet was only distracted from when the black shadow of a twin engine Messerschmitt 110 fighter dived from above and passed just a few hundred feet ahead of her as it headed for the fight below.

"Fighters coming down!" she shouted. "Goose Squadron, fighters coming down!" She looked around as a line of fighters followed from the darkness above. Keeping her course, she fired as the next shadow approached in a dive and watched as her stream of glowing bullets ripped through the cockpit and the left engine of the 110, immediately sending it into an uncontrolled flaming spiral. She pulled back on her stick and dragged the nose of the Hurricane upwards, just as another 110 passed in front of her. She flipped the Hurricane over and went straight into a dive, quickly catching the tail of the 110 and receiving a spray of bullets from the rear gunner, which formed into a widely spun cone of light that seemed to veer away from her, then somehow curve through the air and rip through her left wing. She steadied herself, relieved that AP's modification had held strong and the carburettor hadn't failed, then lined up her sights as she came within one hundred feet of the fighter. She pushed the fire button and heard the familiar ripping of rough canvas that was the sound of her eight machine guns rattling. Her bullets hit home in the narrow fuselage just ahead of the twin tail, with such devastating impact that the fuselage spilt, and the tail came loose. It appeared to flap in the wind before it snapped off entirely and the 110 joined her last victim in spinning out of control as it headed for the ground. She pulled up as a line of bullets streamed past the left side of her cockpit so close that she could see them glowing as they passed. She pulled her stick hard to the right and spun as the bullets coned around her, reaching out toward her like long ghostly fingers. She looked in the mirror as her sight started to dim from the g forces pulling on her from the sudden climb and spin and was able to make out another 110 on her tail, its guns flashing as it blasted at her furiously. She pulled back on her stick and flipped the Hurricane into a dive; quickly leaving the 110 behind and out of position. Her sight dimmed so much that she blacked out as her aeroplane dived towards the ground out of control.

Meanwhile, Nicole was having her own battles. Having followed Harriet down into the fight, she chased her 110 right through the melee as the pilot, who'd been much more awake than either of Harriet's adversaries, was weaving and turning past Stukas and over Hurricanes to get away. All the time the gunner fired wispy fingers of tracer bullets in Nicole's direction. Fortunately, the twisting and turning made it difficult for the gunner to find his target, and Nicole was able to avoid his fire while all the time letting off bursts here and there. Finally, the 110's left engine erupted in flames and chunks of debris flew off the wing. Seconds later the crew took to their parachutes and Nicole watched the 110 crash to the ground not far from the road, before pulling back on her stick and heading back to the fight.

As Harriet stumbled back to consciousness, she saw the ground ahead of her, less than a thousand feet ahead of her, and she quickly pulled the stick hard into her stomach, summoning every ounce of strength while screaming at the Hurricane to pull up. Something it did very slowly. While praying that the Hurricane would level in time to stop her burrowing nose first into the ground and disintegrating into a million pieces, Harriet noticed a trio of aeroplanes pass in front of her at treetop height. A Hurricane swinging, swerving and rolling in every direction as two 110s closed on it with lines of bullets streaming from their guns. Harriet instinctively rolled to her right and got the wind beneath her wings, then lifted from her dive just as the 110s drifted in front of her. She hit the fire button and held it tight while still levelling and banking, and with determination, she raked both aircraft with every last bullet she had. The 110 to the right immediately nosedived into a copse of trees and exploded as it ripped into the ground. The second pulled up sharply with a stream of white smoke coming from the right engine and quickly dropped to the ground and headed east in a desperate escape. Harriet was dripping with sweat and gasping for air as she pulled alongside the other Hurricane, which was now steadying, and nodded at an equally exhausted looking Kiwi. He waved and nodded, and then his voice came over the radio.

"Cheers," he said.

"Got any ammunition left?" she asked.

"A bit I reckon, why?"

"Look over to your right, over the road at two o'clock." A 110 was following the length of the road and strafing it indiscriminately with its cannons, shooting soldiers, tanks, trucks, and refugees alike. "Fancy having a go at him? I'll watch your back."

"Damn right I do, let's go!" He swung right and headed for the 110. Harriet took up station behind him to protect his tail from attack while he went in for the kill. She was out of ammunition, but the Germans didn't know that. Anyone diving from above would likely go for her first as the furthest back, and she could lead them away so Kiwi could knock the 110 down unmolested. She kept her eyes in her mirror when she wasn't spinning her head and watching all around her while swinging left and right to check for Germans. Kiwi closed on the 110 and hit it right along the fuselage from the rear left quarter. The 110 immediately rolled to its right and pulled away, in doing so, showing its belly so he could empty his guns into it. The 110 never recovered from the roll, and instead just kept turning and banking until the right wing caught the ground, and the aircraft spun and explored in a ball of flames. Kiwi and Harriet followed overhead in a sweeping turn and watched its demise.

"Ammunition gone?" Harriet asked.

"Yeah..."

"OK let's head back for a refuel and rearm. Follow me."

Harriet led the way at full throttle, and in just over twenty minutes, they were in a circuit over the airfield. It was still only just sunrise, and the squadron had already been outnumbered at least three to one in the bloodiest fight Harriet had thought imaginable. She was soaked in sweat, tired, thirsty, and thankful to be heading back towards her home field in one piece. After instructing Kiwi to land, she circled the airfield to watch for German raiders and noticed a twin engine aircraft skim over the hedges ahead just of her. It was difficult to make out properly in its camouflage paint, and being so close to the ground; but it was heading straight towards Kiwi's Hurricane, which was already bouncing along the grass. She immediately remembered her first arrival at the airfield when a flight of Messerschmitt 109s had followed Singh's section home and shot them up on landing. Was it happening again? Had a 110 followed them? How the hell was she going to deal with them without any ammunition? She thought of Nicole's ramming, it was the only option, but she was so low that there was no way she'd have the time or height to glide to the ground, she'd surely go straight down with the 110. She didn't have to think twice; it would have to be ramming. As she banked to take up position and bring the 110 into range, she noticed the camouflage again. It was British camouflage, and it had the RAF roundels on its wings, and on closer inspection, it didn't even look like a 110. She throttled back and swung away while she thought of what to do. The aircraft then lowered its landing gear and positioned for landing. Harriet breathed a sigh of relief then followed it down and landed behind it, leaving it to head for the spot in front of the tents near the mansion while she taxied to her pen, spun, and cut her engine.

"Are you OK?" AP asked as she reached into the cockpit and unfastened Harriet's harness.

"I think so..." Harriet replied as she pulled off her flying helmet and hung it on the mirror, before climbing to her feet.

"I'm not sure the same can be said for my aeroplane!" AP said as she handed Harriet a canteen of water, which she swiftly drained before pouring more over her head to cool herself down. She looked around at the swarm of ground crew all over her aeroplane. Gun bays were open and

Lanky was already directing a team of armourers in checking and rearming the guns, while others were checking the airframe and a bowser quickly approached.

"Will it be OK?" Harriet asked as she looked at the holes where chunks had been blown off the wings and fuselage by enemy fire.

"I'll let you know," AP replied as she led Harriet off the wing and onto the ground.

"Let me know quickly. We're going to need to get back in the fight as soon as possible."

"How bad is it?"

"A nightmare. We were outnumbered three to one at least, fighters and Stukas, and the road is so packed it looks like the whole British army is on it. The Germans won't leave a target like that alone for long."

"OK, I'll get to work. Best get over to the dispersal tent and let Cas know what's going on." Harriet nodded and offered the water canteen back to AP.

"Keep a hold of it for now," she said with a shake of her head. "Bring it back in about ten minutes, and I should be able to tell you what condition it's in. I'll do my best to get it airworthy."

"Are there no other aeroplanes I can take?"

"Nothing serviceable."

"What about that one over there?" She pointed to a Hurricane a few hundred feet away. "What's wrong with that one?"

"The guns weren't firing, according to its pilot."

"There's nothing wrong with those guns!" Lanky shouted down from the wing with irritation. "They weren't even fired in the first place; the red tape was still where I left it, and I've tested them myself. They work absolutely fine!"

"So, I can take it?" Harriet asked

"No..." AP replied. "No lone flying, remember? You'd have to wait for somebody to go with anyway, and you need a drink and to check in with Cas. Do that first, and we'll see what we can do." Harriet nodded reluctantly then headed over towards the dispersal tent. She wiped the sweat from her eyes with her blue and white diamond silk scarf as Kiwi joined her and walked at her side.

"I reckon I owe you a drink," he said.

"What for?"

"Getting rid of those Huns back there. I thought I was a goner for sure."

"Don't mention it... Just remember not to fly straight and level for more than five seconds in the combat zone."

"Yeah... I got that. I knocked a Stuka down and was so full of myself I didn't check my tail. The first I knew those bastards were there was when they tried to shoot my wings off."

"Bet you won't do it again."

"You'd win that bet."

"Well, did you get one?" Cas asked as he stepped out of the tent.

"Three 110s," Harriet said.

"Three?" Cas asked

"I saw one," Kiwi replied. "In my rearview mirror, after she shot it off my tail."

"Did you get any?" Cas asked him.

"One Stuka and one 110."

"Not bad for your first scrap. Anyway, we've still no communications with anywhere outside of here, so what's it like? What's happening?" Harriet and Kiwi recounted their story of the jammed road and the heavy fighting to Cas, who looked disturbed, despite his best efforts to hide it. Another Hurricane joined the circuit overhead as they talked.

"If you don't mind, I'd like to get back to the road?" Harriet said.

"Me too," Kiwi said. "Sir."

"I think the situation has changed a little from the pre flight brief," Cas replied. "If the Germans know the road is that busy, they're not going to leave it alone, and they're not going to attack in ones or twos either."

"All the more reason to get us back up there," Harriet argued.

"For you to be shot down? I don't think so... That won't do anybody any good. The rest of the squadron will be back shortly, and then we'll get everybody together and go up in force. We can do more good that way."

"But...". Another two Hurricanes returned, and Harriet groaned with frustration. "Fine... Anyway, which idiots were flying that thing? I almost shot it down while trying to land!" she barked as she pointed at the Blenheim which was parked along the airfield.

"This idiot." said Hugo, as he, Jenny, Pops, and a couple of French ground crew approached the dispersal tent.

"Jenny, you're safe!" Harriet said with a smile.

"Aye..." she replied in her north eastern accent. "We spent last night in a ditch hiding from the Germans who overran the airfield," she explained.

"We borrowed the Blenheim this morning while they were sleeping," Pops explained.

"Welcome back," Cas said as they shook hands. "We were worried we wouldn't see you again."

"I think perhaps we'll stay with your squadron this time if you don't mind?" Hugo said with a smile.

"Happy to have you," Cas replied as they shook hands. "I'm sure we'll discuss what comes next when Squadron Leader Singh returns, but for now I think you all need to head inside and get yourself something to eat and rest up a bit." They nodded as Grumpy and Archie joined them, with Johnson tagging along behind, still with his confident swagger but without the edge of the previous day.

"Well? Cas asked.

"Two Stukas," Grumpy replied.

"One," Archie added. "and I saw that new lad Cameron go down," he continued. "Poor bugger didn't even see it coming, got too close to a Stuka's rear gunner." He looked at Johnson, "Looks like you made it, though."

"Ah, yes," Johnson said. "Got one, then had a bit of a problem with the old guns so headed back," Harriet stared at him while he talked, and he didn't even flinch. More Hurricanes returned, but not many. All in all, of the eleven that had taken off, nine had returned. One of which was as written off as its pilot, leaving eight. Singh had returned, fortunately, as had Max and Nicole, and after about thirty minutes they were all heading off to their aeroplanes ready for the next patrol. Hugo and Pops had even volunteered to take the Blenheim up with the squadron, which Singh had agreed to after it had been given a quick check over. The two French ground crew volunteered to operate the guns, which with some discussion was also agreed. Harriet walked close to Johnson and whispered quiet enough that she could be sure only he would hear her.

"If you run from a fight like that again, I'll shoot you down myself."

"What? How dare you! I'll have you know..." he started to bluster.

"Your guns weren't even fired before you returned... You forgot to at least fire them off a few times before you landed to rip the fabric, you're as ignorant as you are stupid."

"Now look here." he protested loudly as he stopped and turned to face her. She nudged her shoulder against his and walked straight past.

"Coward," she muttered, then jumped onto the wing of her rearmed, refuelled, and patched up Hurricane. Five minutes later, she was in the air again. The Blenheim had been sent to fifteen thousand feet to look for fighters, Harriet and Nicole at twelve thousand to respond to any fighters coming down, and the rest of the squadron flew side by side in three sections of two. Still an impressive sight, but not as impressive as the last time. They found the road, which was easier in daylight, mainly due to the plumes of black smoke winding into the blue sky from almost every mile as it stretched into the distance. The Germans had been busy and still were. As the squadron approached the road, they could see a swarm of Stukas were busy hitting at a row of tanks. Once again, the squadron attacked, and once again a chaotic series of one on one battles formed. Harriet, Nicole, and the Blenheim stayed on station waiting for the inevitable arrival of the fighters while the rest of the squadron did their work. All except one. Harriet noticed a Hurricane at treetop height heading home as quickly as the mighty Merlin could drag it. "Bastard..." she muttered while contemplating following through on her threat and shooting him down herself. She couldn't, obviously, and wouldn't, the squadron could do without a cowardly pilot, but they needed the Hurricane. She wouldn't need to shoot him down, though, as heading towards Johnson at the same height and speed, and closing very quickly was a squadron of Messerschmitt 109s. Twelve of them in six pairs of two, lined up side by side as they closed on their unwitting prey.

"Fighters three o'clock low," Hugo called from the Blenheim, as it dived past Harriet and Nicole, heading for the fighters.

"Fighters, three o'clock. Coming in fast," Harriet repeated as she flipped her Hurricane and dived after Nicole, who was already chasing the Blenheim. She hadn't heard a response to the first warning, so wanted to repeat just to be sure everyone heard over the ongoing chatter.

"Roger Black Leader," Singh replied. "Goose Squadron, keep your eyes open and watch for fighters!" Harriet smiled and sweated, as her Hurricane screamed into battle. Before they even got close the German squadron were on Johnson, he didn't stand a chance. The lead 109's cannons ripped through the engine and cockpit, puncturing the coolant and fuel tanks and starting a raging fire. Seconds later his Hurricane was a ball of flames bouncing into the ground in front of the unflinching 109s. The Blenheim hit the lead 109 as it pulled out of its dive, with the gunners spraying his wingmen with bullets as they passed through the formation. The first 109 trailed black smoke and crash landed while the rest of the squadron splintered and started turning in every direction to get around onto the Blenheim. Nicole took them by surprise, shooting one down just as he lined up with the slow moving Blenheim, and Harriet ran a line of bullets through the tail of another which was coming at the Blenheim from the left, making the aircraft shudder as the pilot struggled to maintain control at speed. Another burst and what remained of the tail was almost gone. The 109 yawed to the left and to his absolute credit the pilot pulled up the nose as he dipped under the Blenheim, scrubbed off his speed, then managed a belly landing in a field. Harriet followed him down just to be sure, then pulled the stick back hard as a stream of bullets trimmed the tip off her wing, making her wobble and have to fight to keep from flipping into a spin. More bullets hit, and her right wing was like a sieve. She pulled the stick back and left and pointed her Hurricane straight up, and the 109 followed. As she saw the flash of gunfire in her mirror, she centred the stick and felt the damage to the right wing drag the aeroplane around in a corkscrew as the bullets flickered past the cockpit, not touching the Hurricane. She pulled hard left to stop the spin just as she stalled and flipped left and backwards so she was immediately faced with the fast approaching 109 which couldn't have been more than 400ft behind her. She let out a burst as it flew past, almost crashing into her and having to turn wildly to avoid her. Her bullets hit but didn't do any real damage, but she must have scared him as he carried on in the direction he was heading, staying low and fast as he skipped over the hedges. Her Hurricane was becoming increasingly difficult to control, so she checked her mirror then climbed in the direction of home, determined to get enough height to be able to jump if she needed to. She couldn't see Nicole or the Blenheim, but there was nothing she could do to help them even if they needed it. Her instinct was that it was best not to know and instead focus on getting herself home. The engine felt OK and kept her in the sky, but it was a constant sweat to keep the wings level. She could see the right wing was a mess at best, and she wasn't quite sure how she was staying level at all, but she didn't want to question God and bring his attention to the matter, so she put her efforts into fighting the stick and pedals until her muscles and bones ached. Her efforts paid off, and the manor house came into view after what she considered to be the longest flight of her life. She didn't have time to circuit, not that she expected the aeroplane would let her anyway, so she lowered the landing gear, which dropped with a reassuring clunk, then lined up, reduced her speed, and bounced uncomfortably to the ground. It took every effort to stop the Hurricane swinging hard to the right, which it was instinctively desperate to do on this occasion until finally, she was as close to her pen and the running ground crews as she could get. She let the nose swing before putting on the brakes and cutting the engine with a sigh of relief.

"What the hell have you done to my aeroplane?" AP demanded as she looked into the cockpit. Harriet simply shook her head in reply and pushed her sweat drenched flying helmet onto the rearview mirror before slumping into her seat. "Come on," AP said, reducing her tone when she saw Harriet's absolute exhaustion. She reached down and unclipped the harness then helped Harriet out and down to the ground. "I don't know how you got it back," she said as she turned Harriet to look at the right wing. "The control surfaces are wrecked; you should have spun into the ground."

"I think it got me back," Harriet said before dropping to the ground and lying on her back, gasping deep breaths while looking up at the blue sky above.

"Seriously, Harry, are you OK?" AP asked as she dropped to one knee.

"I will be," came the reply. "I just need to lie down a minute." AP handed her the canteen again, and she poured it over her face, keeping her eyes closed while she fought to calm herself and cool down.

"Was it bad?" AP asked after a while.

"I don't even know..." Harriet replied as she opened her eyes and looked up at the young engineering officer. "The squadron went in on a swarm of

Stukas that were hitting some tanks. Then the fighters arrived, and I can hardly remember what happened next. I got one. I know that much, and then I was surrounded by them. I had to run."

"You did the right thing. I'm still amazed you made it back with that wing the way it is. You certainly couldn't fight."

"Thanks..."

"Seriously, you're OK? You're not injured?" Harriet shook her head and forced a smile. "OK, well I need to go and see if there's anything we can do to fix it. Either way, it won't be ready for the rest of the day at least, so you may as well get some rest." Harriet nodded and didn't offer any resistance. As much as she wanted to do her part, she knew that she was exhausted, and she knew that her last trip was cutting things fine when it came to flying and fighting with sheer luck. She sat up and took a drink from the canteen as she felt her heart start to slow. Cas was on his way over, stopping only briefly to watch as another chugging and spluttering Hurricane approached.

"OK?" he asked.

"Better than my Hurricane," Harriet replied with a half smile.

"Bloody hell, the wing's almost off!" he exclaimed when he saw it.

"I know... AP brought that to my attention."

"You're lucky you got back at all."

"She brought that to my attention, too."

"I thought she might... How are things at the road?"

"It's been a massacre from what I could see. It looks like traffic has thinned out or gone into hiding, the Germans were attacking the tanks at the rear when we arrived."

"I see. Any sign of the field hospital?" She shook her head. "Of course not. Probably made it to their hideaway."

"Honestly, they could've been in front of my nose, and I wouldn't have noticed. It was like the whole road was burning. There were dead people and animals everywhere, and wrecked vehicles beyond recognition, apart from the tanks."

"Sounds frightful."

"Quite..."

"Well, I don't expect you'll be flying that anytime soon." He gestured over to the Hurricane. Harriet shrugged in response. "May as well take a break, get yourself some sleep."

"What about the rest of the squadron? What will they do?"

"In the absence of orders to the contrary, we shall keep going back, while we're still able to." They both watched as Singh climbed from his Hurricane, and another three buzzed over the field into the circuit. "Well, that's five of you," Cas said. "There's hope yet for more."

"Johnson won't be coming back."

"Oh?"

"He ran straight into a squadron of Hun fighters."

"I see... You saw him go down?"

"He went down alright," she said with a distinct happiness, having seen him run from a fight for the second time in a morning and leave his comrades in trouble.

"OK... Well, that'll be another letter to write," Cas said with a frown. Harriet instantly felt bad for him, and for how she was feeling. All she'd seen was a cowardly pilot, she hadn't thought of what his loss would mean to others, to Cas who had to write to his parents, to his parents who had no idea of their son's cowardice, and were no doubt proud of his volunteering to play a part in the war as a fighter pilot. "That's two out of three replacements dead in less than twenty four hours. I hope Bevan makes it back."

"Sorry, I didn't mean to sound pleased that Johnson didn't make it," Harriet said remorsefully.

"Don't worry, Harry. I know all about Johnson. He'd have got good men killed, and women." He gave her a wink. "Still, not nice for his family."

"No..." They watched as another pair of Hurricanes arrived. Cas pulled Harriet to her feet, and they walked over to the dispersal tent to meet the others. Other than Johnson, there was only one missing. Nicole. Harriet couldn't help but stare at the empty sky while the others talked and reported their actions. All together they'd accounted for five Stukas and four 109s, not a bad tally for an under strength and highly stretched squadron. Singh sent for drinks and food to be brought out from the kitchens while the remaining serviceable aeroplanes were rearmed and refuelled for their third sortie of the morning. Singh's own Hurricane was grounded by a hit to the engine, which was going to take some repairing, so he'd ordered Sergeant Evans to rest so he could take his aeroplane instead and still lead the squadron from the front. As they discussed the plan for going up again and flying as two flights of three, a lone Hurricane roared overhead. The canopy was open, and trails of golden hair fluttered from under the pilot's helmet. Nicole. A cheer went up as she rounded the airfield and landed, and Harriet ran and met her, jumping onto her wing as soon as she came to a halt. The engine cut and Nicole quickly jumped onto her seat.

"Where the hell have you been?" Harriet demanded angrily.

"Did you miss me?" Nicole replied playfully.

"Stop it. It's not funny! I was worried!"

"So, you did miss me... How sweet!" She jumped down and beckoned Harriet to follow her. "Did you get any?"

"One..."

"Ah, two for me."

"That doesn't explain where you've been! Everyone else has been back fifteen minutes!"

"Keeping watch," Nicole replied as they joined the others. "Mister Singh, the Blenheim has crashed thirty miles north west," she reported. "I stayed with them and chased away some Germans. They seemed alive when I left, though." Singh frowned at the news.

"You remember where they crashed?" he asked.

"Of course."

"OK, show me on the map... Cas, have Foggy get the Lysander ready. Everyone else wheels up in fifteen minutes. We'll cover Foggy while he picks them up if they're still there, and once he's clear, we'll head back to the road. Chief, I want you to get as much fuel and ammunition on the aeroplanes as you can." The Chief nodded and left quickly while the pilots went about their business, preparing for the next flight. Harriet and Nicole turned to leave too. Harriet's mind filled with bothering AP enough to let her take up her battered Hurricane. "Where do you think you're going?" Singh asked.

"To get my aeroplane ready to fly, of course," Nicole responded dismissively.

"To see if AP has my Hurricane airworthy yet," Harriet added.

"I don't think so," he replied firmly. "Your aeroplane won't be ready until tomorrow at the earliest, you and I both know that. You'll stay here and help Cas."

"But..." Harriet started to protest. Singh gave her a look which could only be interpreted as a dare for her to challenge his authority. She bit her tongue as her shoulders slumped. "Yes, Sir."

"Perhaps if you were a better pilot, you wouldn't let Germans fill your aeroplane with holes." Nicole teased mercilessly as a huge smile spread across her face, and she turned to leave again.

"Not so quickly, Miss Delacourt," Singh said, stopping her in her tracks. "You both stay."

"What? Why?" she demanded. "My aeroplane is serviceable."

"Because you fly together or not at all, that's what you said, isn't it?" he asked with a raised eyebrow. "Anyway, we'll be patrolling in formation, so you'll stay here and prepare for our afternoon patrols."

"Ridiculous," she blustered.

"Excuse me?"

"I'm a good pilot!"

"And good pilots need rest. Besides, your Hurricane needs fuel and ammunition. Now let us all pretend that you're graciously accepting of my orders, and would welcome the opportunity to rest from combat while you help Cas with his ground duties; which are equally as essential to the successful operation of our squadron..." She pursed her lips angrily. She knew she didn't have any chance of winning the argument.

"Come on," Harriet said as she put her arm around Nicole's shoulders. "Let's see if we can find a cup of tea. I'm parched after that last flight." Harriet had spent many years helping Nicole walk away from an argument while perfecting her calming tones.

"I am thirsty..." Nicole muttered. "Though you English and your tea frustrate me. Why can you not have coffee like everyone else, or even wine, perhaps?" she ranted. It was Nicole's way. Once she knew she couldn't win an argument she'd quickly find something else to become unnecessarily annoyed about, it helped her climb down without backing down. Harriet knew it and worked with it. Singh smiled to himself then shook his head and headed for the dispersal tent to talk with Cas while the girls made for the kitchen and picked up a couple of drinks.

"Excuse me, Ma'am," one of the airmen in the Mess interrupted. At his second time of asking the girls stopped their conversation about the morning's fighting and looked around for somebody, then quickly realised they were the only people he could be talking to. Harriet looked at him, then pointed to her chest.

"Are you talking to me?" she asked.

"Yes, Ma'am," he answered nervously. Harriet raised an eyebrow in surprise and Nicole giggled silently while nudging her friend with her elbow.

"Yes, Ma'am, he is," she teased.

"Oh... Yes?" Harriet asked as she pulled her shoulders back confidently while feeling the familiar tingle of a blush on her cheek.

"If it's not rude of me to ask, Ma'am, I wondered if you were heading towards the lady officer's quarters?"

"Why do you ask?"

"Well, one of the WAAFs was supposed to come to take a cup of tea and some bread and jam to that young nurse who arrived last night."

"Oh..."

"You see, Ma'am, there's no sign of the WAAF yet, and the young nurse's tea will get cold. I'd take it myself, but I didn't want to disturb her in case she's not decent if you get my meaning? So, I was wondering, Ma'am, if you wouldn't mind..."

"Not at all," Harriet said with a smile. She was handed the tray, and Nicole led her through the house. They passed out of the back door, and across the courtyard to their quarters. Up the stairs and they entered the room to find the Sister laid in the bed previously used by Finn. "Hello," Harriet said as she headed towards the bed.

"I'll leave you to it, I'm going to freshen up," Nicole said as she headed to the bathroom with the buckets of hot water she'd picked up from the kitchen. "Don't let your water get cold!" Harriet nodded and smiled then turned to Coleman, the nurse who was shuffling to sit up in her bed.

"How are you?" Harriet asked as she handed over the mug of tea.

"OK, thank you," came the polite reply. She took the mug and sipped at the tea. "I appreciate you bringing me this."

"My pleasure... How's your leg? The last I saw the doc was patching you up."

"Oh, it'll be fine," she frowned as she tried to bend her leg under the coarse RAF blanket that she had pulled over her.

"Sore?"

"A little... The bullet lodged in my thigh, but fortunately, it was nothing more than a flesh wound. No serious damage."

"Fortunately."

"Quite."

"How did it happen, if you don't mind me asking?"

"I was sent to find the brigade Headquarters in the hope that they'd be able to get a message through to your squadron asking for help. Unfortunately, the Germans had got there before me, and I arrived in the middle of a pitched battle, I only just got away. It was getting dark, and I found myself riding through a forest full of Germans. They let me ride through their positions at first, I suppose they thought I was one of theirs, then somebody got close, and the shooting started. They got me, but I was able to shoot my way out and keep riding."

"Wow... That's pretty incredible. You're lucky to be alive." Coleman forced a smile and nodded. Her eyes watered a little too. "Sorry, did I say something?"

"No," Coleman shook her head. "I just... My hospital. I haven't heard a thing, and I worry whether they made it to safety. I have so many friends there, and so many patients."

"The road was busy, much busier than I'd imagined, with lots of soldiers and civilians," Harriet said as she sat on the bed. "I didn't see signs of many British units left out there when I left if that helps, and certainly nothing with red crosses painted on it? So maybe they got to the British lines safely." Coleman nodded and smiled again, then continued with her tea.

"Wait, you were at the road?" she asked with a frown.

"Yes, not an hour ago. We just got back."

"How were you on the road?"

"Well, technically I was over the road. We were there keeping the Germans at bay, so to speak. Just as you asked when you got here last night." Harriet smiled warmly and passed Coleman the bread, which she took and placed on her lap while staring at Harriet.

"You were flying?"

"Yes, a Hurricane."

"But you're a girl..."

"So are you," Harriet replied, resisting the urge to roll her eyes. "It didn't stop you getting into a gunfight with the Germans on the front line, did it?"

"I suppose..." Coleman said with a half smile. "Though I didn't think the RAF let girls fly?"

"I didn't think that army nurses rode motorbikes through German infantry positions while shooting machine guns."

"Touché"

"I'm Harriet Cornwall."

"Willow. Willow Coleman"

"Nice to meet you, Willow. Enjoy your bread and tea. You need to keep your strength up. Hopefully tonight we can get you out of here."

"Thanks..."

"Is there anything else you need?"

"Well, there is one thing..."

"Name it."

"I'm so bored stuck in this stuffy room. The windows are too high to be able to see out of, and I slept all night and all morning... I wondered if you could help me outside for some air?"

"Let me freshen up, and I'll see what we can do," Harriet gave a wink then stood and left to join Nicole in the bathroom while Willow carried on with her food and drink.

"How is she?" Nicole asked. She stood in her underwear and washed herself in front of the old mirror, balanced on the chest of drawers. Her shirt and jacket were hanging over the bath, and her trousers were rolled down to the tops of her boots.

"She rode her motorbike through a forest while firing her machine gun at German infantry and lived to tell the tale," Harriet said as she threw down her kit and started unfastening her shirt.

"Brave girl."

"Yes." She threw her shirt by Nicole's, dropped her trousers, then stood next to Nicole. "Move over."

"You can't wait?"

"Should I?"

"I've already started using the water. It isn't clean."

"I've practically lived with you for seven years. I think I'm safe." Nicole shrugged and moved over, and then handed Harriet the soap and a face cloth. They stood side by side and washed, then threw the water and filled the bowl with fresh water before dipping their heads and scrubbing the sweat and dirt from their hair before towelling dry. The Merlin engines had roared and faded while they washed, heralding the squadron's departure. "Why are we here?" Harriet asked as she looked at herself in the mirror. She looked tired, especially in her eyes, and older, much older than only a few days ago.

"Where else would we be?" Nicole replied.

"I don't know... Home?"

"Where is that? Where are our families?"

"I... I don't know... What's going to happen, Nicole? What will happen to our families and our homes?" She turned to face her friend.

"All I hope is that what we do here gives the army time to reorganise and fight back," Nicole replied. "Then they can push the Germans back into Germany, and we can go home and find our families. That's all I can hope. I have nothing else."

"That's it," Harriet said with a smile, taking Nicole by the hands. "That's what we'll do. We'll keep fighting until we kick the Germans out, then we'll go and find your grandparents."

"You know, if you asked Singh, he would send you back to England. You could go home. Maybe your family is there waiting for you?"

"You are my family."

"No... I mean your mother and father."

"And I mean you're my family. You and your grandparents have taken care of me since I arrived in France. I'm staying with you, and I'm fighting. You watch, another few days and the army will have regrouped and started to push back. Another week and we'll be able to go together to find your grandparents."

"You're kind to me, Harriet. I can be so spiky and angry, and you always love me. I'm blessed to have met you."

"Don't be silly. It's me who's blessed." They smiled and hugged then dressed and returned to the bedroom where Willow was sitting uncomfortably on the edge of her bed, having pulled on her uniform, ready to go outside. Her uniform consisted of a grey shirt and dirty army trousers, which were ripped and bloody where she'd been shot, and tucked into her black motorcycle boots. She held her dark green motorcycle jacket ready to go. Harriet and Nicole helped her into an oval high back wicker chair. Between them, they carried her down the stairs, clumsily, and out into the courtyard where they composed themselves, stopped their giggling, and carried her out to the edge of the runway and set her down a little distance from the dispersal tent, which Cas was leaving as they arrived.

"Ah, there you both are," he said as he walked over and looked down at Willow. "And how's our guest?"

"Fine, Sir. Thank you."

"Oh, call me Cas. No need for that Sir business when the troops aren't around. How's the leg?"

"It hurts, but I think it'll be fine."

"Lucky you're a nurse, and were able to close the wound so you could keep riding."

"Yes... It didn't feel lucky at the time."

"You closed your own wound?" Harriet asked.

"I had to, or I'd have lost too much blood," Willow replied, matter of fact.

"Well it's good you're improving. Good to get out in the fresh air, too, I'd imagine?" Cas said with a smile.

"Oh, yes, absolutely. I was so bored in that room, though I'm very grateful for the bed."

"I don't blame you; I'd be bored too. Hopefully, that won't be for much longer, though, we're planning to get you a ride back to England tonight, all being well."

"A ride to England? How?" Willow asked excitedly.

"Our Lysander communications aeroplane will take you."

"Wow... I've never flown before."

"What should we do?" Harriet asked. "The CO said we should help you?"

"You both know your way around an aeroplane, don't you?"

"Yes," they both replied.

"Good. Get yourselves over to AP and see if you can help her bring your Hurricane back to life. Take our young friend here with you if you like? Got to be more fun than sitting here. I'll let the doc know where she is." The girls nodded and picked up the chair again before heading over to the Hurricane pen, where AP was directing ground crews in their tasks.

"What do you want?" AP asked as she saw them. She was frowning a little as she looked briefly at Willow.

"Cas sent us to see if you need any help," Harriet replied.

"As far as this aeroplane is concerned, I think you already helped more than enough when you added all of the extra ventilation holes the designers had clearly overlooked..."

"I can't help it if Germans keep shooting at me."

"Maybe you should be a better pilot," Nicole replied, almost predictably. "My aeroplane is fine; they never get me."

"I seem to remember you having to crash land your Hurricane not so long ago..." Harriet replied while rolling her eyes.

"I had to crash land because I rammed a German out of the sky when I ran out of ammunition, to stop them shooting at you."

"Oh, so you're now trying to say that your crash was deliberate?" Harriet continued, teasing and needling Nicole with a mischievous smirk. "I thought it was just bad flying that led you to collide with that other aeroplane."

"You're an idiot!" Nicole frowned.

"Now, now. Let's turn that frown upside down," Harriet continued.

"Hey, children, when you've finished!" AP shouted, stopping their argument in its tracks. They both looked at her. "We've got work to do. If you want to bicker, go sit out on the grass somewhere out of my earshot."

"That's no way to thank us for offering our help," Nicole replied with disgust, raising her nose in the air.

"Charming," Harriet added with the same mock disgust.

"Go away!" AP said sternly without looking up from the cockpit. The girls smirked at each other then turned to lift Willow's chair again. She put her hand up to stop them, then held out both of her hands.

"Help me walk. It's only a few paces." They looked at each other, nodded, then pulled her from the chair. There were a few gasps and groans. Then with her arms around their shoulders, Willow limped out of the Hurricane pen to a sunny spot on the grass a few paces away. The three of them sat, then laid back and looked up at the clouds. "So, you've both been in combat?" Willow asked.

"Some of us more successfully than others," Nicole replied.

"Remind me, Nicole," Harriet said. "How many Germans have you shot down?"

"That means nothing!"

"Some would argue it means success."

"Some who have been fortunate enough to have more opportunities may argue that."

"What's it like?" Willow asked, ignoring their bickering. "Flying I mean, in a Hurricane?"

"Incredible," Nicole replied, quite simply.

"Like no other feeling," Harriet added. "You can see forever. I swear yesterday we were so high that I could see England."

"It sounds amazing."

"You'll see for yourself later when you're flown home in the Lysander."

"If you are lucky, it'll be a beautiful sunset. You'll remember it forever."

"I look forward to it... Is that it up there?" She pointed to the dark cross of an aeroplane which flew into view from behind the woods. It was high, and silent, at least for the first few seconds, until the light drone of its engine followed on the wind.

"I don't think so..." Harriet said as she squinted her eyes in the sunlight and tried to make the aeroplane out as it weaved in and out of the high clouds while flying a large circle over the airfield.

"It's too high to be in the circuit," Nicole said. "But why else would he be flying circles?"

"I don't know... Maybe he's lost, or looking for something?" All three jumped as one of the army's heavy machine guns erupted into life from its sandbagged position close to the tree line. A stream of glowing tracer bullets wound into the sky towards the aeroplane. A second gun joined in and started firing from the balcony of the manor house. "It's a German!" Harriet gasped as she saw the outline of a cross on the fuselage became clear.

"I think he wants you," Willow said as a phone rang not too far away.

"How can you possibly think that?" Harriet replied, not moving her eyes from the aeroplane droning above. "He's far too high even to recognise me."

"I mean him!" Harriet and Nicole followed Willow's pointing finger in the direction of Cas, who was standing outside the dispersal tent waving his arms and gesturing at the German aeroplane. At that moment, the familiar sound of a Merlin engine roaring into life filled the air, and the three girls turned to look towards the Hurricane pen. AP was running towards them and soon stood over them.

"Nicole, Cas says that if you're not too busy, would you mind getting off your arse and shooting down that German reconnaissance aeroplane before he tells the whole German air force where we are?" Nicole stared at AP while nodding and looking both surprised and a little perplexed. "Come on. We've got her started for you!" AP held out her hand and pulled Nicole to her feet. Harriet was already standing excitedly.

"What about me? Is my Hurricane ready?" she asked.

"No..." AP replied bluntly. Nicole quickly grabbed Harriet and hugged her, then turned and ran, with AP at her side.

"When?" Harriet shouted in frustration.

"Maybe later," came the still blunt reply. Harriet stood frustrated, kicking at the ground nervously as adrenaline flowed through her body with nowhere to go. She was desperate to do something, but there was nothing she could do other than watch as the pitch of the Merlin engine changed, and Nicole's Hurricane edged out of the pen. Nicole hadn't even put on her flying helmet she was in such a hurry, and her golden hair fluttered in streams as the backdraft from the propeller hit the cockpit. She quickly waved at the girls as she passed, watching just long enough to smile at Harriet as she waved forlornly to her friend. A turn and a mighty roar and Nicole bounced along the grass before lifting into the air and turning in to a steep climb.

"Will she be OK?" Willow asked

"Yes... She's a fearless pilot," Harriet replied. "It's him I feel sorry for." She nodded in the direction of the reconnaissance aeroplane, which was turning east and beating a hasty retreat as the Hurricane roared up in pursuit. Both were moving at speed and quickly disappeared out of sight behind the thick woods behind the Hurricane pens. "I'm just disappointed I can't help."

"If what you say is true, I don't think she'll need any."

"Yeah... Doesn't stop me wanting to be with her, though."

"Be with her or beat her to the kill?" Cas asked as he joined them, having walked over from the dispersal tent. Harriet scowled at him. "Oh, come now, Harry, don't be like that."

"I'm more irritated that my aeroplane isn't fixed. I want to fly."

"Don't we all, old girl. Don't we all..."

"Every pilot in the squadron is flying now, except me. I'm left here shaking with energy and thinking a thousand thoughts."

“And me...” he said with a shrug.

“You’re too old to fly,” Harriet replied, instantly catching what she’d said and how she’d said it. “I mean… I don’t mean. I mean you said you didn’t fly because the RAF said you were too old to… Oh, God.”

“Harsh…” Cas said, looking wounded.

“Sorry… I won’t speak ever again.”

"Chin up, chum," he said with a mischievous smile as he put his hand warmly on Harriet's shoulder, making her shudder nervously but instantly feel safe, though from what she couldn't work out. "I'm sure she'll be back soon. That Storch, the German reconnaissance aeroplane, can fly a little over a hundred miles per hour at best. The Hurricane can fly more than three times faster than that. Even the best pilot won't stand a chance, not against her." They both stared up into the empty sky hopefully. "I'll bet you a packet of cigarettes she's shot him down and back on the ground before the rest of the squadron get back."

"I don't have a packet of cigarettes," Harriet replied with a frown.

"Nothing much to lose then, is there?" he smirked. She frowned at his logic but thought better of saying anything, in case she embarrassed herself again. She could argue fiercely with Nicole, but she had a respect for her seniors, she always had, and even if they made her angry, she always swallowed the fury and kept her mouth closed. Though Cas hadn't made her angry, she quite liked him really. He was almost like a father figure to her; he cared about her and kept her safe. She immediately thought of her own father. He was a very different type of man, and she didn't doubt that he cared about her, but he wasn't what anyone could mistake to be warm. He worked hard and made sure his family wanted for nothing, materialistically at least, but work and business were everything, it's where he'd spent most of her life. She found herself smiling at Cas while she thought. He was OK, and if they'd met under different circumstances she'd liked to have listened to his flying stories while they drank tea, though in different circumstances would they even have met? And if they did, would they even have anything to talk about? Her thoughts were disturbed by the sound of distant engines.

"That sounds like more than one engine..." Harriet said.

"So it does..." Cas replied

"Which means I win..." she said mischievously. She stood with her hand held out.

"Do you even smoke?" he said with a frown, as he pulled a pack of cigarettes from his pocket and slapped them into her hand.

"No," she replied mischievously.

"Then why do you want the cigarettes?"

"Because I won."

"Though we haven't actually seen the aeroplanes, yet..." he said as he kept a grip of the packet when she tried to pull it away.

"There's more than one engine, so more than one aeroplane. I won!"

"Yes..." he said as he let go of the packet.

"Ha!" she said with a giggle. She stared at the packet with a smile on her face. She didn't know what on earth she was going to do with the cigarettes inside, but she was satisfied that she'd won. She looked up at Cas, but he wasn't smiling, or even looking at her. His brow was furrowed as he searched the sky. "What is it?" Harriet asked. "Cas?"

"They're not Merlins," he said.

"What do you mean?"

"The engines. Listen... They're not Rolls Royce Merlins," he said. Harriet listened as the distant buzz of multiple engines droned closer and became more distinguishable. She hadn't been around Hurricanes long, but it had been long enough to recognise the inimitable sound of a Rolls Royce Merlin, and what she was hearing wasn't that.

"Then who?" she asked, then stopped as she saw a line of black dots passing between the clouds to the south of the airfield. "Look, there..." The line was heading north, and then the lead aeroplane dipped its nose like it had driven off the edge of a cliff, and dived downwards. As it did, a siren sounded high above, a siren that grew in intensity as the second and then third of the little dots followed into a dive.

"Stukas..." Cas gasped. "Stukas! Take cover!" His gasp turned to a yell, and he instinctively reached down and swept Willow up into his arms. "Don't just stand there!" he shouted at Harriet, who was staring wide eyed at the screeching, howling German dive bombers as they screamed towards the ground. She flinched as Willow reached out and grabbed her, then quickly joined Cas as they ran towards the sandbagged Hurricane pen.

The sky erupted as every gun the army had rattled lines of hot red tracer bullets towards the incoming aeroplanes, making glowing spiralling cones as the bullets curved around the fuselages, getting so close but somehow dancing all around without striking home. They rounded the sandbagged wall to see Lanky extending the bipod legs of her Bren gun and resting them on the top row of sandbags while Matthews, one of the airmen, laid out full magazines for her. Cas sat Willow against the sandbagged wall then turned to join Harriet, who was already standing by Lanky and watching as the first Stuka came close. A pair of bombs released from underneath, and tumbled in the direction of the line of Hurricane pens to their left. As the Stuka pulled up, Lanky emptied an entire magazine at it, catching its tail before it levelled out and shot across the airfield, heading north and quickly out of sight. The bombs erupted and turned the sky red with fire and black smoke, shaking the ground and sending a spray of earth and shrapnel in every direction. Cas grabbed Harriet and pulled her down below the parapet as the others all ducked in unison, and the sandbag wall shook with a thousand vibrations as it was peppered with flying debris. Lanky immediately jumped up and changed magazines, then fired again as the second Stuka screamed in and released its payload. This time she didn't miss. The Stuka pulled up and showed its belly, and received a full magazine of bullets in the engine. It immediately streamed white smoke, which was quickly joined by a lick of yellow flame and a cough of thick black smoke; before it flipped onto its back and nosedived into the ground right in front of the dispersal tent, with an explosion to match that of the bombs it had jettisoned which had hit one of the pens further up the field. The smoke cleared to show the third aeroplane pulling up and jettisoning its load, as the rear gunner sprayed Harriet's pen with machinegun fire. They all squeezed themselves close into the bottom of the sandbagged wall as bullets ricocheted off Harriet's Hurricane. She watched them spark and dance as Cas pushed himself against her to keep her safe. He twitched and let out a snarl between his teeth. She pushed and rolled from under him and laid him down, clutching at his upper left arm, which was red with blood. One of the airmen quickly appeared with a medical bag, which Willow took from him and promptly got to work dressing Cas' arm. Lanky was already up shooting again, with Matthews changing the magazines for her, while AP was still under the engine cowling of the Hurricane, wrenching at something furiously. Willow looked up at Harriet, her steel blue eyes were wide with fear and questioning, silently demanding to know how they were going to escape as the sky turned black with countless Stukas, either diving or awaiting their turn. Harriet looked around, desperately looking for answers of her own. She was scared, very scared, and she knew that any second a Stuka could get its bombs on target and flatten the very pen she was standing in. Above the noise of guns and bombs, Harriet's attention was drawn upwards to a buzzing roar. She looked up to see a Stuka trailing black smoke and heading straight down with no hope of pulling up, and a Hurricane not far behind, a stream of tracer reaching out from its wings and seemingly tying the two aeroplanes together with a glowing thread. Nicole! She pulled up to show the pair of 109s not that far behind her, firing in hot pursuit as they dived on the lone Hurricane; which was already climbing and spinning, and riddling the cockpit of the next diving Stuka with bullets, making it spin out of control as it headed to the ground.

"Will it fly?" Harriet screamed at AP

"What?" AP shouted in reply.

"Will it fly?"

"Yes... Yes, it'll fly."

"What the hell are you doing?" Cas shouted as he watched Harriet grab the parachute from the wingtip and run around the wing.

"I've got to get up there and help her fight," Harriet shouted as she ran.

"Don't be stupid! They'll shoot you down before you even get off the ground!"

"I've got to try." She threw her parachute into the cockpit, jumped in, and as AP gave her a wave before screwing down the engine cowling, she started the engine, filling the pen with blue smoke before the prop wash cleared it all to the rear.

"Lanky, get on," AP shouted as she reached into the cockpit and started pulling at Harriet's harness, their arms weaving around each other as Harriet checked her instruments and checked her power. "No time to mess about, taxi straight and I'll guide you", she screamed at Harriet who nodded wide eyed as Lanky jumped up on the wing with her Bren gun. Matthews threw up a couple of magazines which she caught and stuffed into her shirt, and then he ran to the wingtip. Harris was by the other, and as Harriet let off the brakes, they guided the aeroplane safely forward. Harriet looked at Cas as he sat beside Willow, who was holding his dressing in place.

"Good luck," he said quietly, leaving her to lip read his words, which she did with a nod, then threw open the throttle a little more as they passed the sandbagged walls and headed into the firestorm of the open field. AP screamed directions, left and right, to guide Harriet through the rapidly appearing craters in the smoke covered grass, while Lanky took shots at passing Stukas hurrying northwards after dropping their bombs.

"Lanky! One o'clock low!" AP yelled above the furious explosions and barking machine guns. Lanky looked up at her and followed her pointing finger towards the pair of 109s speeding towards them at ground level from the west. The ground jumped up in neat lines as bullets trailed along the grass towards the Hurricane. Lanky pushed on a full magazine, held the Bren gun at her hip, and blazed away at the lead 109, clearly taking the pilot by surprise as he wasn't expecting return fire from the side of a Hurricane. Her bullets found their mark and rattled around the nose cone of the 109, making it wiggle until a propeller blade shook loose and spun out to the side and straight through the cockpit of the second 109, dousing the inside with blood and sending it nose first into the ground.

"Now, go straight and get out of here!" AP yelled. Harriet opened the throttle as AP grabbed Lanky and they both jumped from the wing as the Hurricane picked up the pace. They rolled and held each other tight, keeping their heads down as the 109 Lanky had shot at bounced off the grass only a few feet behind them, then kangarooed back into the air before returning to the ground at speed and digging its nose into the ground and grinding to a halt. A huge ball of fire expanded somewhere behind, but Harriet couldn't think on it, she was bouncing at full speed while bombs erupted around her, she had to get up into the fight. One more bounce and she was in the air, climbing rapidly, she pulled up the landing gear and switched her guns to fire just as a Stuka passed in front of her, so close that it obscured everything. She fired a burst, and its left wing broke loose before it disappeared out of sight and she climbed into the battle on full boost. She searched the sky, weaving and turning through the mass of aeroplanes that were swarming like flies until she caught sight of Nicole's Hurricane as it barrel rolled through the sky to avoid the streams of bullets reaching out at her from the pair of pursuing 109s. Harriet set course through the melee of Stukas, rolling and pitching until she got to exactly where she wanted to be. Nicole had started another roll to the right, and the pursuing 109s had obligingly followed. They showed Harriet their bellies as they passed, they were so focused on knocking Nicole out of the sky that they didn't see the second Hurricane closing on them, and didn't have time to avoid the stream of bullets she let them have. The first 109 burst into flames as Harriet's bullets rattled the engine and split the main fuel lines, it simply continued its long arcing roll and crashed into the trees below. The other narrowly escaped her fire, pulled his stick back, and turned his roll into a wide turn which Harriet followed. Nicole had been watching in her mirror, and as soon as the second 109 was off her tail, she completed her roll and pulled a tight left turn onto a collision course with the 109 which only seconds ago was about to kill her. She fired, and the 109 pointed straight up while trailing smoke. The girls rolled their Hurricanes to avoid hitting each other, then joined together as the pilot of the stricken 109 floated towards the ground below his parachute. Harriet pointed to her helmet, and Nicole looked, then searched, then pulled it on. She hadn't bothered with it in the excitement of chasing the Storch.

"What are you doing here?" Nicole asked over the radio.

"Charming!" Harriet replied. "Saving you by the looks of it!"

"Nonsense! I had them both just where I wanted them!"

"Whatever! Anyway, what now? Do you have ammunition left?"

"A little, I think."

"OK, let's go get some more Stukas before those 109s up there get us. There's at least twenty of them circling, and we may even scare them off."

"OK, follow me."

"What?!" Nicole banked left then flicked over and dived, Harriet followed, and the pair dived down at a string of Stukas below them. They'd already started their steep dives towards the wrecked airfield below when Nicole tagged on behind the second in line and blasted it, sending it into a spiral and overtaking the second. She lined up and fired but got nothing but silence. Her guns were empty. Harriet dipped as Nicole pulled up, switching places just in time for Harriet to let the lead Stuka have the last of her ammunition. It shuddered and shook as she sent it straight into the ground, before both of the girls pulled up together and swooped around as the rest of the stream of Stukas broke up and flew in every direction to escape their fury. "I'm out of ammunition."

"Me too. What do we do now?"

"Fly like we're still in the fight," Harriet shouted. By this time the 109s were screaming down in sections of four making their way through the scattering Stukas in a staggered line. The girls pulled their noses around to face the 109s. "Fly through them and scatter them, then down to the deck and run." Harriet swallowed hard, her mouth and throat were dry, yet her clothes were soaked with sweat, as was her face as it ran in streams from under her flying helmet and stung her eyes. She was more scared than she'd ever been as the violet nosed 109s closed on them. She had no idea what she was doing or how it would end, but she was pretty sure that this would be the end.

"We should ram them," Nicole said. "Take two with us at least."

"Yes..." Harriet said almost instinctively, hearing the word come from her mouth but not entirely sure how. She didn't disagree with her instinct, though. "Let's!" The pair flew at the 109s full throttle, the two groups of aeroplanes closing on each other with a combined speed of close to seven hundred miles per hour.

"Tally ho, Goose Squadron. Let's get to work," Singh's distinctive voice came over the radio. Harriet looked to the left and saw the squadron stretched out in line abreast heading for the 109s. The girls pulled hard right to pull the Germans into a game of chase, which they couldn't resist, and led them low over the airfield where they were followed by the rest of the squadron who picked them off at ease. The girls rolled over the woods and started a wide circle around the airfield to search for more Germans, but they were heading away, running in every direction eager to escape the unexpected slaughter. "OK Goose Squadron, that's enough" Singh instructed. "Green Section get up to angels 20 and stand station for a while, make sure they don't come back. Everyone else, pancake. Black Section, get yourselves in first and be careful to watch for the potholes." A pair of Hurricanes broke off and started a turning climb while the girls brought themselves around to line up for a landing. One at a time they dropped to the ground and landed at the far edge of the airfield, then followed the perimeter tightly to avoid the potholes. Their propellers blew the thick black smoke into twirling streams as they passed the house, which was part rubble and part burning, and came to a stop at the very edge of the airfield, unable to find a way through the smoke and devastation to get back to the pens. Hurricane after Hurricane followed, and then came the Lysander. They all parked in a staggered line and shut down their engines, then one by one the pilots extracted themselves and came together to survey the burning hell before them. "What happened?" Singh asked solemnly as the girls joined them.

"They came out of nowhere," Harriet replied. "Cas sent Nicole up to chase away a reconnaissance aeroplane, and before we knew it, we were being bombed by Stukas."

"I chased him until I saw the Stukas," Nicole added. "I climbed so I could attack them from above, but the 109s were up there, and they chased me down. Then this idiot took off in the middle of a battle and somehow managed to get off the ground." She nudged Harriet.

"You both did well... We'll talk about it later." Singh said with a smile. "For now, we need to get refuelled and rearmed and think about moving the squadron to the reserve field. Now, where's Cas?"

"He was shot," Harriet said, remembering the moments before she jumped into the Hurricane, and feeling her heart squeeze tight as she remembered. What happened to him? To the others? She looked at Singh with fear in her eyes and a sickness deep in her stomach, and she instantly felt cold and dizzy.

"Max, go and get the bowser, I want us refuelled and ready to go in twenty minutes," Singh said as he recognised her discomfort. "Archie, go with these two and look for Cas. The rest of you come with me to the HQ, let's see what we can salvage."

"Come on, you two," Archie said. "You're in the RAF, remember? Stand still too long, and some bugger will paint you." He stood between them and put his hands on their shoulders, giving them a friendly push and running with them through the smoke in the direction of the Hurricane pens. They skirted crater after smoking crater until out of the smoke a blackened, yet familiar face stepped forward.

"Where's my aeroplane?" AP asked sternly. "If you've lost another one, I'll..."

"You're OK!" Harriet said, cutting AP off mid rant with a hug that clearly made her uncomfortable.

"Of course I'm OK, now where's my aeroplane?" AP demanded, shrugging off the hug and quickly dismissing any emotion.

"Over there, with the others. We couldn't get any closer," Harriet pointed to where they'd landed. "Where is everyone? How's Cas?"

"They're in the woods, they're fine, he's fine."

"The CO wants them refuelled and rearmed as soon as possible," Archie said.

AP nodded then turned and looked behind her. "Chief, they're all up here. We need to refuel and rearm quickly."

"Alright, you heard her," the Chief bellowed from the smoke shrouded woods. "You Erks get some life in you, or you'll have me to answer to, and get that bowser moving!" Shadows quickly moved forward, some running, and soon airmen were passing, carrying tools and ammunition boxes before disappearing back into the burning smoke. AP followed after them just as a pair of airmen came through the smoke with Willow slung between them, and Cas walking by their side. His bandaged arm was tucked in his jacket, and his hat, bent and crumpled, slouched to one side.

"Are you hurt bad?" Harriet asked nervously.

"What, this?" He looked at the bloody bandage. "It's nothing more than a scratch."

"Didn't realise there was a war going on down here?" Archie said. "Dangerous place, a chap could get shot."

"Yes, quite..." Cas laughed. "The CO?"

"Over at the house, it looks like it's been in the wars too, shall we?" Cas nodded, and the small group walked out of the smoke towards the manor house, which had been badly bombed and was a hive of activity as airmen scrambled through rubble and doused fires with shovel loads of dirt. A medical post had been set up in the courtyard by the Simon, and he and his orderlies were busy patching up injured personnel. Daisy was one of them. Her blue uniform was pale with dust, and her face streaked black with smoke. The doctor was cleaning a gash down the side of her cheek and jaw which had bled dark red blood into her dirty blonde hair. Already at the back of the courtyard, there was a row of bodies covered in white sheets held down with rubble. Willow was set down with the other casualties, and the others joined Singh and his officers and pilots.

"Cas, you're OK?" Singh asked, noting the injury.

"Yes, I'll be fine."

"Better let the doc have a look at that."

"When he's finished with the more serious stuff, maybe," Cas shrugged. "Did the rescue go OK?"

"Yes, we got them back fine. There's a lot of activity to the east, though."

"Oh?"

"Yes, long columns of refugees heading in this direction, thousands of them, maybe more. I don't expect the Germans to be far behind them."

"I see..."

"We should probably get ready to withdraw to our emergency airfield."

"Yes, Sir. I've had Mister Peters working on the planning. We'll need to assess the impact of the raid, but we should be able to move with minimum delay."

"OK, I want an advance party sent out as soon as possible. I want fuel and ammunition there before the aeroplanes land, just in case things get a bit hot, and we should get some of the army up there, too."

"I'll see to it." Cas turned and wandered off.

"Pilots, I want you by your aeroplanes. Get two up to patrol as soon as they're replenished, so we can get green section in to refuel and rearm. We need to stay sharp and keep a patrol up until we can clear the way for the Hurricanes to be put in pens and be safer from another raid. We also need to be ready to scramble at a moment's notice, and we're too bunched up at the moment, we could be wiped out too easily." He looked at Harriet and Nicole. "The two of you have done more than enough today. You'll stand down and help Cas."

"But we have aeroplanes to fly!" Nicole argued.

"Our friends can cover for you for the rest of the day." He gestured to Pops and Hugo.

"Ridiculous!" Nicole argued. "We are good pilots."

"Yes, you are, and to remain good pilots, you need rest! Now get yourselves a drink and relax a while, then report to Cas later this afternoon."

"Sorry about that," Evan, the army officer, said as he arrived. "We fired everything we've got, but we only have machine guns, no heavy stuff, so we maybe weren't as scary as we'd hope to be. Managed to knock a couple down, though!"

"We appreciate your efforts, Captain, at least you gave them something to think about," Singh replied as they shook hands. "While you're here, we're moving to a new house, and I'd like you to prepare a third of your men to move out to our fallback airfield with our advance party. The rest will need to stay here until the main body of the squadron moves later."

"I'll get them ready right away," Evan said before quickly leaving, as the girls headed towards the ruins of the house. The cooks had already set up by the old barn and had hot tea and rock cakes ready for the working airmen. The girls grabbed a couple of cups each, and walked over to Daisy who was sitting in the shade of a tree with Willow.

"You two OK?" Daisy asked as she took a cup of tea.

"Yeah..." Harriet replied as she joined them sitting on the grass.

"We've been grounded," Nicole grumped as she threw down her helmet and jacket.

"Grounded?"

"Rested," Harriet corrected.

"Grounded so that men can fly," Nicole continued.

"What happened to you?" Harriet asked Daisy, choosing to ignore her friend's complaining.

"The bloody house fell down with me in it, that's what happened!" Daisy replied. "One minute I'm trying to get through on the radio to

Headquarters, the next the floor has gone, and I'm sitting in the Officer's Mess with half the roof on my head. What about you two? How did you get on? I saw you knocked a few down."

"Yeah... Not enough to stop them wrecking the airfield," Harriet sighed.

"Enough to stop them finishing the job, though. Would've been worse if you hadn't got among them," Daisy said with a reassuring smile. Harriet nodded, then smiled and sipped at her tea as she looked around at the disaster surrounding them.

Chapter 11

Moving

Not long after sitting down, both girls dozed off, curled up next to each other and sleeping through the haste and hustle around them. Hurricanes came and went on patrol, and the airfield was repaired as well as it could be, while an advance party was sent on its way to make sure the reserve airfield was ready to be operational. The Squadron Warrant Officer had dispatched a couple of teams to do the prep work in securing the site and making it ready, and now the fuel, ammunition, half the kitchens, and the air defence were on their way to join them. Foggy had flown ahead to give instructions and return when the airfield was ready for the Hurricanes. Though that wouldn't be for a while, it would take a good few hours for the convoy to move along the French roads.

Harriet's eyes opened wide as a shot fired in the distance, and then another. She sat up and looked around in the late afternoon sun. The others were all still asleep, so she stood and stretched her aching muscles, then limped slowly with a deep soreness over towards the dispersal tent, which had now become the command tent in the absence of the building. Cas was standing outside, smoking a cigarette and looking in the direction of the trees. A pair of armed airmen were arguing with a group of French civilians who'd arrived in a couple of black cars with mattresses and bags strapped to the roof. The civilians were reluctantly backing away from the pile of stores they'd been seeking to loot.

"What's happening?" Harriet asked.

"Refugees," Cas replied. "French civilians. We've had cars turning up all afternoon trying to steal our food or fuel."

"You're shooting them?" Harriet asked in horror.

"Above them... For now," he said with a smile. "Though if they don't back off, we'll have to think again. We need all we've got."

"I see… When will we be moving?"

"Not for a while yet. The convoy is making slow progress due to the number of fleeing civilians on the road. They'll be lucky to get there before nightfall."

"We'll be here all night?"

"Maybe."

"OK... Is there anything you need me to do? The CO said we're to help you instead of flying."

"You know why, don't you?" Cas asked warmly.

"Rest." She shrugged.

"Well, Yes, but something a little more important, too."

"Oh?"

"Yes, of course. The CO cares about you both a great deal, and he respects you both without comparison, but he also knows that things are heating up. We're likely to get into more fights with greater numbers, and things are likely to step up a notch or two; and as much as he wants to keep his squadron flying, he doesn't want to risk either of you unnecessarily."

"But we want to fight."

"And fight you do. What you did today was nothing less than miraculous, and miracles take a lot of energy, which is why you've slept under that tree most of the afternoon. Anyway, why the rush to get yourself killed?"

"What do you mean?" Harriet asked with a frown.

"Combat gets the best of us sooner or later, and you've got to remember that while you're a remarkable combat pilot, a natural in fact, you've had absolutely no formal training. That rather shortens your odds up there, you know?" Harriet frowned a little more and nodded. "Now, if we can get you through this and back to England so you can be trained properly, you'll be virtually unstoppable, and when we regroup to give Jerry a bloody nose, you'll do even more damage than you do now. They'll be terrified of you, and rightly so."

"But I still want to fly."

"All of the good pilots do, my girl, but the best pilots know when to stay on the ground and let somebody else do the flying. For a while, at least." She rummaged in her pocket and pulled out the crumpled pack of cigarettes, then handed them to Cas. "What's this?" he asked.

"I don't even smoke." She said with a shrug.

"But you won them, fair and square."

"And you won this debate," she said. He smiled, then politely put them in his pocket.

"Look, there's not much happening, and it'll likely be dusk soon, why don't you get some more sleep? We'll wake you if anything changes." She nodded and turned away.

"Thank you, Cas..." He winked, then went back to watching the darkening early evening skies. She saw the cook and got four plates of chicken stew and some half stale bread which she took to the others. She kicked them all gently and handed them the food, and the four of them sat together in the silence and enjoyed their meal. Not long after finishing their food, they all drifted back to sleep.

Once again, they were woken by rifle fire, this time Harriet shivered in the cool night air.

"What is it?" Nicole asked quietly.

"Looters," Harriet replied. Nicole snuggled against her as they both pulled their flying jackets closed to keep out the cold. Willow and Daisy were warm under the blankets that one of the airmen had brought over, and still sound asleep.

"What is there left to loot?" Nicole asked as she closed her eyes again.

"Food? Fuel?"

"Let them take it... I just want to sleep." Nicole sighed. Harriet smiled and followed her friend's lead in going back to sleep. There was no reason to stay awake, and there was nothing that needed doing. After the bombing, Daisy had been scared of sleeping in a building, understandably. So they'd all decided to stay together outside under the tree, instead of using one of the outbuildings. It was cool, but not cold, and they were comfortable in the soft grass, so all that needed to be done was to sleep. Through the night they woke, sometimes to the sound of shots, or the noise of engines and work; and in the early hours the squadron doctor, Simon, collected Willow and Daisy to put them on a truck that was leaving for the reserve airfield with the other wounded.

Harriet stirred sometime around dawn, she was awake and uncomfortably stiff, so in the dimness of near twilight, she extracted herself from Nicole then walked through the dew soaked grass and looked out across the airfield. A silver light was rising in the west heralding the arrival of sunrise sometime in the next hour, and a dense mist hugged the ground up to knee height. She watched in the stillness, the Hurricanes were lined up at the end of the airfield, and the silhouettes of pilots moved around them, while ground crews worked under tarpaulins to finish repairs and prepare their charges for flight. They had worked all night to make sure that when the time came, the squadron would still be in the fight. As her tired mind started to wake, Harriet began to think about what would happen next. The last few days had been like nothing she'd imagined in her wildest fantasies, and she couldn't begin to imagine what else would come, or what could come. What could be more than she'd experienced? More flying? More fighting? Whatever happened, she'd either die, or she'd live to see the British and French regroup and push back. Or for them to be defeated and for her to become a prisoner. Though whether the Germans were even taking prisoners these days was something many of the airmen questioned in their daily rumours. The more she thought about it, the more she felt that she didn't really care. Though the more she thought about it, the more she thought that dying in the air would be the better of all outcomes. She was just eighteen years old, and whatever she did in her life after this would be less. How could it not be? How could anything feel like flying a fighter at over three hundred miles per hour with eight machine guns blazing while fighting against a smart, skilled, and cunning enemy who was trying to kill you, and who at any second could do just that? The adrenaline of living life on the edge of everything and nothing would be impossible to replicate, or to better. Maybe going out in a blaze of glory would be the only real way to go, like Barnes had, twisting and turning and battling with every fibre of his being, like others in the squadron before him and after. Better than dying of old age. She walked as she thought, enjoying the silence that came just before first light. The pilots would be briefed soon so they could prepare for their day, whatever it may bring, and the squadron would be moving to the new airfield, hopefully. They were supposed to have left the previous day, but the advance party was so delayed that nothing had happened until the early hours of the morning when the bulk of the squadron had finally departed and left a rear party behind to take care of any remaining business. She walked along the airfield and enjoyed the solitude as the silver light grew a little stronger in the eastern sky, though it was still mostly a deep inky blue. Dawn wasn't far away. She was distracted from her daydreams first by Nicole who appeared beside her looking cold and tired, and then by Cas who emerged from the command tent and lit a cigarette.

"Ah, there you are," he said quietly. "Get enough sleep?"

"Some," Harriet replied.

"There were lots of engines in the night. They were noisy," Nicole added as she hugged herself to warm up.

"Yes, Foggy flew in at about two to tell us the advance party had reached the reserve field and would be ready for us by dawn, so most of the squadron was dispatched to join them. There's just a few of us left behind to look after the Hurricanes until they push off, which shouldn't be much longer."

"What will we do?" Harriet asked.

"You'll travel with me in the staff car. The vehicles are out on the road, ready to go, and as soon as the Hurricanes are off, we'll load the power trolleys and the remains of our stores, and the army of course, then get moving."

"Is there anything we can do now?"

"AP is over in the corner of the airfield preparing to destroy the lame ducks. You can take her a cup of tea if you like, and let her know to burn them as soon as the squadron has taken off. There are some cups in the command tent, get yourselves some tea and biscuits, too. Unfortunately, the cooks and food went with the main convoy in the night, so it's all we have I'm afraid."

"Why will you burn ducks?" Nicole asked. "Can we not just eat them for breakfast?" Harriet rolled her eyes and smirked.

"Sorry, old girl," Cas said. "Forgot myself for a moment. A figure of speech to describe the pair of Hurricanes we've not been able to get airworthy. AP and her team have been stripping them for parts all night, so they're no more than shells now I suppose. Anyway, we can't risk them falling into German hands, so we need to burn them."

"A truly British, and truly stupid phrase."

"Quite..."

"Is there nothing we can do to save them?" Harriet asked. "Nicole and I can fly them, maybe?"

"Sadly not. Both AP and the Chief looked them over, and they were beyond flying. One has a twisted wing spar, and the other's fuselage is half severed. Even if they got off the ground, they'd come straight down again."

"I see... That's such a shame."

"You don't need to tell me. We've managed to get eight airworthy, largely with the help of donated parts from the lame ducks, which is better than I'd hoped, but I'd still have preferred ten. Anyway, nothing we can do about it. Better get on, the squadron will be taking off in about ten minutes, and I'll want the rest of us on the road before the sun's up." The girls grabbed mugs of tea from the tent and filled their pockets with biscuits. They headed over to the silhouetted Hurricanes in the far corner of the airfield by the edge of the woods, silently passing the pilots gathering by their aeroplanes, some of whom already sounded quite boisterous, especially Archie and Max. They walked until they found the lame ducks and looked around for AP.

"What do you want?" AP asked from the cockpit of one of the Hurricanes.

"We brought you a message from Cas," Harriet replied. "You're to burn the lame ducks after the squadron has taken off. He wants to be on the road before the sun's up." As if waiting for her to finish her sentence the familiar cough of distant Merlin engines spluttering into life filled the air, and soon they were being pushed to full power as the pilots went through their pre flight tests. Then, one by one, they lined up on the stretch of grass, newly flattened by the airmen after the previous day's bombing, then took off into the deep dark blue sky with blue and purple flames flickering from their exhausts as they revved and sped. Each turned west in a climbing turn after taking off, until finally the last droned out of sight. "We brought you tea, too," Harriet continued after being distracted by the departing Hurricanes.

"Thanks, I'll be down in a second."

"What are you doing?"

"Just having one last sit in her," came the reply. The girls climbed the wing and stood beside the cockpit, and Nicole handed the tea to AP which she sipped gratefully while staring out of the windscreen.

"It's silly they won't let you fly," Harriet said. AP looked up and forced a smile. Her heart yearned for flight. She'd loved every second of flying to rescue Harriet, despite the danger and despite the mission, she just enjoyed flying the machine she'd worked hard to keep flying for so long. She'd have flown to collect a pint of milk from the farm if they'd let her.

"It's OK..." she replied after some thought.

"No, it isn't. They let us fly. They should let you fly."

"They still need somebody to fix the aeroplanes you break," she smiled, relieving the tension in the air. "Besides, I'm an officer now; that's something. I'll have opportunities in the future, and I'll get to fly one day, in my own aeroplane that I buy from my officer's pay." A droning sound stopped their conversation and had them straining their eyes as they searched the dark sky. It didn't sound like anything else. It wasn't the Hurricanes, and it wasn't Stukas or Hun fighters. It seemed deeper and more cumbersome. Yet still distant.

"Bombers?" Harriet asked.

"Maybe," AP replied as she stood in the cockpit as if to get higher and see more.

"Look," Nicole said as Harriet and AP searched the skies above them for signs of aircraft. They looked at her, then followed her gaze to the long black shapes silently approaching the airfield from the south. Swooping low like they were coming in for a landing, but how? There was no sound, no engines. They couldn't be aeroplanes. Could they?

"Hurricane with an engine failure?" Harriet asked.

"No..." AP said. "They're too big... Besides, there's more than one of them. Two Hurricanes and two engine failures at the same time is almost unheard of." The first of the long tubes with exceptionally long wings hit the ground some distance away. It slid with a scrape as it bounced across the uneven airfield, before burying its nose in a bomb crater and coming to a sudden halt, flipping its tail into the air then slamming back down again. The girls watched in shock, then as the dust cleared and another aircraft scraped along the ground, this time closer and avoiding the craters as it slowed, they were able to see the white outlined black crosses on the long grey hull. Germans. "Oh, God! Assault gliders..." AP gasped. "We need to leave," she said urgently as she jumped from the cockpit. "Get down, and I'll burn it." They climbed from the wing and ran a few paces, then turned as AP pulled the matches from her pocket to light the fuel she'd poured over the airframe. They paused as another engine buzzed above, and drew their attention to the line of dots dropping from a trio of passing aeroplanes. "Paratroopers. We're going to be overrun!" She quickly sparked the match and lit the rag, then threw it at the Hurricane she'd been sitting in, which immediately burst into flames that quickly spread to the next Hurricane. The three of them then promptly ran into the woods as the massive inferno they'd started lit up the airfield. The flames silhouetted the twenty or more

German paratroopers who'd dismounted from the first few assault gliders and were advancing slowly on the squadron command tent and the ruined manor house.

A machine gun immediately burst into life from the rubble around the house, and the German paratroopers started running, crawling, and returning fire. The light showed more gliders, some already scraping to a halt and others coming in to land, while the black dots above had expanded into slowly descending parachutes. The squadron position came alive with rifle fire and the rattle of the machine guns. Silhouettes of airmen staggered towards the house from where the Hurricanes had been parked, laden with equipment and starter trolleys. They were unnoticed and unhindered by the assaulting Germans, who were now being supported by machine gun fire from positions on the top of their gliders. The girls, hidden in the woods, found themselves cut off from Cas and the rest of the squadron as one of the gliders stopped almost parallel to them, leaving them unable to do a thing. Suddenly they heard a noise behind them. Remembering the pistol that she'd been given after shooting the German Major from the sky, Harriet pulled it, cocked it, and held it out in front of her as she stood ahead of the other two. Through the shafts of silver light from the east, she made out the silhouettes creeping through the woods, bodies wearing the familiar British battle bowler helmet. Her heart was in her mouth as Evan stepped forward into her sights. He raised his hands to signal her not to shoot, then walked forward.

"It's OK, we're on your side," Evan whispered. She nodded and lowered the pistol.

"Paratroopers," Harriet whispered back.

"Yes, we saw them. We're going to counterattack their rear and try link up with your chaps over at the house. You girls should probably come along with us." Harriet nodded again. "Stay low and do as we say." His men set up some of their heavy anti aircraft machine guns at the edge of the woods, and then, when he dropped his arm, the trees came alive with fire. Rifles, machine guns, and pistols, everything fired at once and sent hot lead in the direction of the German paratroopers, who now they were being hit from behind were in a state of confusion. Some even started to run towards the woods for safety, but were quickly cut down in the ambush. Slowly, those still fighting started moving back to the rear gliders at the south of the airfield, though still firing and fighting as they headed to regroup. "OK, let's go!" Evan shouted. "Put a perimeter around our friends!" He grabbed the girls and pulled them upwards, then pushed them out behind his soldiers who were already sprinting across the open runway. Evan ran beside them, firing his revolver at the retreating Germans, and other soldiers joined him in forming a protective circle around the girls as they ran. Some were hit by return fire and fell. Their comrades grabbed some of the fallen and dragged them along, and others were left. The ground spat up dirt all around them until they jumped into the rubble of the manor house, where airmen were returning fire on the Germans. Evan's soldiers quickly set up their heavy machine guns and returned fire, while Evan guided the girls through the dust and confusion to find Cas.

"Where the hell have you been?" he asked.

"Burning the Hurricanes," AP replied sternly.

"Best get these three and the rest of your blue jobs out of here," Evan said as he shook hands with Cas.

"Well, we're ready," Cas replied. “We've got a truck for your chaps. We’re just out the back waiting in the lane, but I have a feeling they'll overrun us and knock us off as soon as we start to move."

"Not if we have anything to do with it," Evan replied.

"What do you mean?"

"I mean it's the army's job to close with the enemy on the ground, not the RAF’s. You get your lot together, and we'll hold them off as long as we can."

"There are hundreds of them. You'll be overrun. You'll be killed," Cas protested.

"Then I'll be killed doing my job," Evan replied confidently. "Look, if we're going to stand any chance of fighting back in this war, we need air superiority, we need the RAF. Otherwise, they'll roll us all the way to the coast and kick us into the sea. Get yourselves out of here and keep flying, keep fighting."

"Take care of yourself, Evan," Cas said as they shook hands.

"You know, Cas, I think this is why we escaped when the Germans broke through in the north. So that we can be here for this!" Evan said, almost excitedly.

"I think you're right."

"Do something for me, would you?"

"If I can?"

"Give this to my parents." He handed over a neatly folded and perfectly white envelope. "Tell them I did what I thought was the right thing. Won't you?"

"I promise," Cas put the letter in his pocket, then turned to watch the airmen who were still bouncing supplies and starter trollies toward the rubble, then to the airmen around him who had been using their rifles to repel the advancing paratroopers. "OK, lads, let's give our boys some cover while the army gets set up!" He stepped forward and snapped his revolver open to reload it, just as a group of paratroopers rose from the fog covered long grass to the right and started firing. A young airman was hit in the chest by a burst of automatic fire which knocked him flat, while his friend was hit in the legs. Bullets danced all around Cas and sent spouts of dirt leaping into the air as he stood unmoved and calm, and slowly and calmly loaded each round into its chamber. Harriet ran forward instinctively and stepped in front of Cas while raising her pistol in front of her, she squeezed the trigger and fired two shots at the leading paratrooper, the first aimed and the second in shock at the noise and power of the first. They hit him square in the chest and knocked him flat. She fired again. AP threw the wounded airman's rifle to Nicole and took another for herself, and they both joined the fray. Cas finished reloading and snapped his revolver closed, then took careful aim and fired a couple of shots at an advancing paratrooper, dropping him into the grass, before an army machine gun opened fire and finished off the rest. Already the airmen were pulling their wounded comrades and injured soldiers to safety, while others dragged the trolleys and equipment through the rubble and out to the waiting trucks.

"Better get yourselves out of here," Evan shouted from the machine gun that had saved them. "They're getting closer!" Cas nodded and saluted, then grabbed at Harriet.

"Come on, through the gate and to the car," he ordered, and as a group they ran. A German paratrooper appeared from the darkness above as they passed through the gate, his submachine gun at the ready as he hung from his parachute. Harriet shrieked in fear and surprise as he touched the ground, then raised her pistol and fired a single bullet before it jammed. The paratrooper shuddered and staggered backwards a little as her bullet hit him, then raised his machine gun to aim again. Cas threw himself forward, and hit him in a hard rugby tackle, knocking him flat before he could fire, then wrestled with him on the ground before using the grip of his revolver to bludgeon the paratrooper's face repeatedly, silencing him. He spun his pistol and fired two shots into another paratrooper already running at them from the dark. AP looted the paratrooper's weapon, and the girls helped Cas to his feet, then together they made off to the waiting car. Cas jumped into the front, and the girls piled into the rear. Harriet looked out of the window at the silver blue sky behind them where paratroopers hung in the air, suspended by the canopies of their parachutes, some firing as they descended into the army's position. She knew they would be able to see from their vantage points that a convoy was hastily leaving the battle, and it made her nervous to think as soon as they touched the ground, they'd tell their friends. If they were able to break through Evan's small force of soldiers, they could be down the road and following them in no time. Her heart was pounding, and her body was flowing with adrenaline from facing the paratrooper. She found it difficult to stop trembling as she clasped the grip of the pistol tight in her hand.

"You should probably put that down before you shoot the driver of the truck behind us," AP said. Harriet turned and looked at her, then Nicole put her hand on Harriet's and steadied her.

"It's OK..." Nicole whispered. Harriet nodded and lowered the pistol to her lap; while Nicole put an arm around her and pulled her close.

"Are you all OK?" Cas asked as he cleaned his revolver with a rag and reloaded.

"Yes..." AP replied. "Are you?"

"Yes... Bloody unsporting of them to turn up like that, don't you think?" he added with an air of humorous disgust.

"I didn't get to finish my tea!" AP said, adding to the light hearted nature of the conversation.

"Well, hopefully, the cooks are set up when we get to the reserve field, and we can have brunch."

Albert Grieves, one of the airmen who'd brought the girls hot bathing water on the day they arrived, was driving. He looked in the mirror and gave Harriet a warm smile, then focused on following the vehicle in front. At Nicole's insistence, AP joined the girls on the back seat and sat between them so they could keep her warm with their flying jackets, both of which were huge anyway, so when they were taken off and laid together, they covered all three girls like huge fleece blankets. The car fell silent, and the girls fell asleep, snuggled together, while Cas held his revolver ready just in case. He looked at them sleeping and thanked God they got out. He was flippant with his humour, but he knew it had been a close thing. He also knew that Evan and his soldiers had paid for the escape with their blood.

The drive became less anxious as the hours passed. The roads weren't too bad at first, but as the sun rose in the sky, the refugees became more numerous. By mid morning, and only five miles from the reserve field, they were crawling along at walking pace and surrounded by civilians carrying belongings, pulling carts, and dragging livestock along with them. Men, women, and children, young and old, everyone was there. French soldiers were mixed among them in ones and twos, their helmets and tunics slung on their backpacks in the unusual warmth of late spring, and hardly looking like soldiers at all, except for their cropped hair and their shoulder slung rifles. Few of the soldiers smiled as the small RAF convoy brushed slowly past them. The soldiers were dirty and disillusioned and not particularly happy to see the British military, who many didn't trust for a whole host of reasons. Matters came to an uncomfortable head when Grieves honked at a group of soldiers limping slowly along the middle of the road, refusing to move and let the convoy pass. The soldiers turned and surrounded the car, silently pushing their unshaven faces against the windows and sneering at the occupants.

"What do you want, Anglais?" a burly grey haired soldier demanded through the half open driver's window.

"For you to shift!" Grieves replied gruffly.

"Eh?" Came the reply, accompanied by a scowl of confusion.

"Shift. Move, off the road so we can get through!"

"Off the road? This road?" the French soldier asked in surprise, stepping back slightly and waving his hand around him.

"Yeah, that road, now be a good lad and get out of the way."

"This is a French road," came the reply, as the soldier returned to the window with a sneer.

"And this is a British car that'll run you over if you don't get off it."

"That's enough, Grieves," Cas said, unable to hold his tongue any longer.

"You are the officer?" the soldier demanded of Cas. Meanwhile, the others were sneering more and making lewd comments to the girls in the rear of the car.

"Yes, I'm the officer. Now be a good chap and let us pass, will you? We have a war to fight."

"Your war, Anglais, not ours. You should go home and leave us in peace."

"Well if you'd be good enough to let us pass, we'd be happy to go home."

"Perhaps you should pay to use our French roads, and pay for the damage your war has done to France."

"Quite out of the question," Cas replied casually. "We don't have any money."

"Then maybe you'll pay with something else." He put his head through the window and leered at the girls.

"Oh, I don't think so," Cas said, in his perfect French. Something which surprised the French soldier, but not as much as Cas reaching across Grieves with his revolver and pushing it tight against the French soldier's forehead. "Now, let my convoy pass unmolested, and I'll resist the urge to resurface your beautiful French road with your brains," he said calmly. The soldier's surprise at Cas' flawless French turned to terror. Unfortunately, instead of taking the intended warning, his comrades decided to pull their rifles and aim at the surrounded car, as a large group of civilians and other French soldiers started to form around them. Before anything else could be said or done, the back door flew open, and Nicole jumped out in a furious storm.

"You filthy cowards!" she raged, taking them all by surprise. "You can pull your rifles on a car of girls, yet you run from the Germans. You make me ashamed to be French!" she blustered in a way only a native Frenchwoman could.

"You're French?" one of the soldiers muttered.

"Yes, I'm French, but right now I wish I wasn't! I've spent my days fighting alongside the British, and French, and Polish, and even Indians, New Zealanders, and Americans, to try and stop the Germans from invading our country, and I've watched many of them die in the act. Yet here you are, running with your tails between your legs, only brave enough to threaten those not expecting it and make nasty comments to young girls. You disgust me, and you should be ashamed of yourselves!" she raged on.

"What else would you have us do?" a young French soldier asked in reply. "The entire army is running."

"Stand and fight!" Nicole blustered angrily. "Look around you, look at the old people, the women, the children," the soldiers looked around at the gathering crowd. "Are they not deserving of your protection? Of your lives? You are soldiers of France. Is it not your duty to stand and fight to give these people a chance at escape, to save their lives, whatever the odds you face?"

"And who are you to lecture us?" the same soldier asked. "Are you not running like the rest?"

"Yes... Yes, I am running... I'm running to the nearest airfield so I can get back in the air and keep fighting the Germans. You see, I'm a pilot, and I fly with the British Royal Air Force, with the other people in this car and convoy. Yesterday alone I shot down two German fighters and two bombers! That's four fewer aeroplanes to attack our cities and our people; and I'll go on fighting until we either win or I am dead, because I love my country and my people, and they're deserving of my best. Vive la France!"

"Vive la France!" a woman called from the crowd.

"Vive la France!" Was repeated by the crowd, again and again. The soldier stepped forward and pulled his bulky colleague from the window of the car, and the others joined him at the side of the road.

"Come on," said the young soldier to his colleagues. "We have Germans to fight!" The crowd cheered loudly. "We stand and fight right here. Not one German will pass until our people are safe!" More soldiers pushed their way through the crowd and joined in the jubilation. The young soldier stood in front of Nicole. "Thank you for reminding me of what's important, bonne chance." He held out his hand, which she took and shook.

"We'll keep fighting, for France," Nicole said.

"For France," he replied while holding the car door open for her, before closing it firmly and waving them off. The crowds parted, and the convoy moved unhindered through cheers and waves of the newly roused civilians.

"Well, that could have gone worse," Cas said as he gave Nicole a wink.

"They made me angry," Nicole said, still raging, shaking more than she'd ever care to admit. Returning the favour from earlier, Harriet took her shaking hands and held them. "They're idiots, swaggering and waving their rifles around like they're Napoleon's Old Guard! They're nothing more than scared children. They needed telling."

"And you had to be the one to tell them, right?" Harriet asked.

"Well somebody had to, and your French is so bad they'd have shot you for being an imposter if you'd tried."

"Here we go," Harriet said while rolling her eyes. "Can't we just be nice?"

"What do you mean? I am being nice."

"Are the two of you always like this?" AP asked.

Their conversation was drowned out by the familiar rumble of a Rolls Royce Merlin engine, which was soon followed by a shadow which passed low over the convoy as it followed the road, leaving a trail of grey black smoke behind it.

"That's a big Hurricane..." Nicole said.

"That's because it's not a Hurricane," AP replied as she looked out of the window. "It's a Fairey Battle, a light bomber; and by the looks and sound of it, it's lucky to be flying." They followed the trail of smoke until they reached an old wooden gate with flaking white paint, which was guarded by a couple of airmen sentries who stepped out from the trees with their rifles at the ready as the convoy turned in.

"Morning, lads," Cas said as one of the sentries approached his window. "We've found the right place, then?"

"Yes, Sir. We've been expecting you. Follow the track down to the farmhouse, and you'll find directions to the squadron there."

The small convoy followed the dusty track to the old farmhouse, where they were met by a Corporal who sent them along a track to a wooded area sitting between a pair of fields that were tall with spring wheat. They were guided into a clearing and into parking spots covered with camouflage nets where the engines were stopped, and the occupants could get out and stretch their legs. Mister Peters, the Squadron Warrant Officer, appeared as if from nowhere to greet the weary travellers.

"Good to see you, Sir," he said to Cas. "We were worried you wouldn't make it."

"Thank you, Mister Peters. Unfortunately, the traffic was rather heavy. It slowed us down somewhat... Where's the CO?"

"He's up with the squadron, Sir. They're flying bomber escort with a couple of the other squadrons for the day. We were told to expect them back this evening."

"I see... Does that mean we have radio contact with HQ?"

"Sadly not, Sir. There's an army brigade at the next village, and their signals section has contact with their divisional Headquarters, which in turn have a link to our HQ. They've allocated us a dispatch rider who's been up and down with messages. It's not perfect, but better than nothing."

"Well, that's something, at least."

"We've also had a stores delivery, Sir. Fresh bread and rations arrived a short while ago. The chef is putting a bit of a meal together for tonight, and will have sandwiches ready for lunch."

"Defences?"

"The army that came with us have set up positions along the runway under Sergeant Oliver's command, and we've posted our own sentries. Nothing much is doing at the moment with the aeroplanes away, though, so I've stood the squadron down to catch up on a bit of rest while they can."

"Good show, Mister Peters. I'd better have a look around."

"Begging your pardon Ma'am's," Peters said to the girls. "The WAAFs have headed down to the stream to freshen up if you'd like to join them? Sentries are posted far enough away not to be a bother, and to make sure you're not interrupted by anyone else. We even have some spare soap bags that came up with the rations." The three looked at each other, their eyes sparkling a little. "If you'd like I can have chef prepare sandwiches for you all, and you could have your lunch down there?"

"May as well," Cas said, "You've had a busy morning, and I dare say things will pick up again when the squadron returns. Make the most of the opportunity." He gave them a wink and a nod of reassurance.

"What about that Fairey Battle we saw heading this way?" AP asked. "It looked in a bad way. It'll need working on if it landed here?"

"It did, Ma'am" Peters confirmed. "Chief already has a team assigned to it, and it should be out of here this afternoon."

"Looks like it's the stream or nothing," Cas said. AP shrugged, and the group walked to the supply tent where they were given soap bags and towels, before being shown to the Mess tent where they were given a box of sandwiches and flasks of tea. Cas set them off, and an airman showed them through the woods and past a pair of vast wheat fields, separated by a grass strip wide enough for aeroplanes to land. They caught sight of the Battle sitting under a camouflage net which had been thrown over a pen cut into the long crops, and it was almost perfectly camouflaged. A sentry stood beside a hedgerow at the end of the track, and as they approached, he pointed them down a trail to a copse of trees about half a mile away. They walked in the warmth of the sun until they heard the sound of giggling and laughing coming from a luscious green clearing littered with trees and crossed by a wide blue stream, though the dominating feature was the Gloster Gladiator biplane parked up in the clearing and looking very sorry for itself.

"Well look who it is," Daisy said as she saw the trio walk from the hedgerow into the clearing. "I thought you'd got lost." She walked over to them slowly, leaving the others who were laying out towels and clothes on the banks of the stream. She had a mischievous smile on her bruised and scarred face. She was wearing only her blue shirt and underwear, which had Harriet feeling a little flustered. She'd always been the same. Even though there had been plenty of nudity throughout her time at school, her reserved English blood always had her lost for where to look when somebody wasn't wearing much. "I was just going in for a swim if you fancy joining me?" Lanky, Jen, and Suzy were all pulling off their boots ready for a dip, and Willow was sitting on the bank of the stream in her grey army blouse, swinging her legs in the water. "Assuming Officers are allowed to swim with us commoners, of course?" Daisy added mischievously.

"Well, I don't know," AP replied without changing her expression. "I haven't had my inoculations..." She stared Daisy in the eyes, and the pair of them were locked in a standoff. Each was waiting for the other to break until finally, AP smirked. "As long as we have different areas of the stream, I suppose we'll be fine. The cleanest water for the officers, naturally, you riffraff can bathe downstream." They both laughed and walked together to where the others had laid out their towels.

"We don't have any bathing costumes," Harriet said innocently.

"We don't need them," Nicole replied in her usual dismissive tone. Harriet looked at her and raised an eyebrow.

"What? But surely you don't..."

"Every time we fly, I sweat my own body weight," Nicole replied. "My hair is a mess, I'm filthy, and I stink; and believe me you're not much better." She pulled off her jacket and walked to the edge of the stream and started stripping.

"Don't worry, we're all friends here," Daisy said to Harriet with a wink. Harriet shrugged nervously, though she still felt her cheeks burning as she looked around, then joined Nicole in removing her clothes. Nicole was a long way ahead and already stepping out of her trousers, which she'd dropped around her flying boots. Harriet blushed some more as she started to strip, but Nicole was fearless, as always. Her shirt and underwear came off, and she took off into a graceful short run before diving into the stream headfirst. She finally surfacing with a gasp before floating on her back and grinning happily.

"Harry, it's beautiful. Come in!" she called happily.

"Don't be shy," Daisy said. "The 'erks won't see us down here. Mister Peters put them on the threat of death if they come within a half mile. Besides, we ain't got anything that ain't normal." She looked down at herself as she dropped her shirt and bra. Harriet's eyes widened in surprise at how well endowed Daisy was, something that hadn't escaped Daisy, who gave a mischievous wink. "Well, maybe some of us are less normal than others, I suppose." She smiled then quickly stepped out of her pants and followed Nicole's example and dived headfirst into the deep waters of the stream, her pale white body clearly visible as it slipped through the crystal clear water. AP was the next in, followed closely by the others, leaving Harriet standing in her shirt and underwear, being called by the entire group and encouraged to join them. Finally, she took a deep breath, shed her clothes, then dived headfirst.

"Oh God, that's cold!" she gasped as she surfaced. Nicole splashed her and giggled, which resulted in a retaliation that soon expanded to involve everyone. They giggled and laughed as though they were friends swimming together back home in England. Rank was forgotten, jobs were forgotten, and the war was forgotten. It was the perfect late spring day. After the fun they bathed, Willow threw them the soap bags, and each was able to scrub away the war from their weary bodies and soap their hair clean. Willow managed to stand in the shallows and bathe herself, then with the help of the others, she stripped and waded into the cool deep water before lifting her legs and letting herself float weightlessly and clean her wound, which was healing quite well. Eventually, one by one, they climbed from the water, towelled dry and wrapped in their shirts and underwear before sitting together in a large circle to enjoy the tea and sandwiches brought from the Mess tent. They talked about getting back home to their lives, the general consensus was that the war wouldn't last the summer; and they talked of committing to meet in late August so they could swim together again. Harriet felt herself smiling and relaxing like she'd found a group of true friends who'd just accepted her for who she was, and she liked it. After a statement about the lily white skinned English, Nicole threw off her shirt and laid back on her flying jacket to enjoy the sun. After some giggles and retorts, the others followed suit, and Harriet soon found herself folding her jacket into a comfortable pillow, pulling off her shirt, then laying back and feeling the sun's rays on her skin. She stared at the sky and watched as the fluffy white clouds floated by on the light southerly wind. She had so many thoughts drifting through her mind. Thoughts about the war, her family, and even about Evan and his soldiers; and whether any of them made it out alive. As she relaxed, the thoughts, as constant as they were, began drifting just out of reach, taking second place to the soothing warmth of the afternoon. Before closing her eyes and drifting off into a doze, she thought of the young woman she'd met only a couple of days ago, Abby Columba. Did she manage to get the Spitfire home to safety? There would never be a way of finding out, but Harriet hoped so. For some reason, their meeting had made her smile, like it was meant to be. Maybe it was the young woman's confidence in handling a Spitfire having never flown one before, or perhaps it was just her pleasant demeanour. Harriet hoped she got the Spitfire home. Those were her last thoughts before slipping into a deep sleep, accompanied only by the birds in the trees and the sweet smell of the lush green grass they were laid on.

A heavy rumble finally brought Harriet out of her sleep, Instantly she thought of the bombing raid the previous day and sat bolt upright. The others had done the same, and all looked around bleary eyed, searching for black smoke or any other sign of a bomb explosion. There were no bombs to be seen, but another rumble focused them on the heavy black clouds that had blocked out the sun and dropped the temperature a few degrees.

"A spring storm," Nicole said. "They happen here when we have such warm weather so early in the year. We should get to shelter."

"Listen," AP said. "Engines. Merlins!" The group looked around.

"There," Harriet said as she pointed at the four Hurricanes skipping the treetops ahead of the storm clouds in the south. In seconds they passed overhead in a Vic formation, with the last in the flight churning out a stream of black smoke. A green flare went up over by the airfield, and the formation banked in a circuit turn, then formed line astern with the smoker in the lead.

"They're not ours," AP said.

"Bet the perverts had a good look," Daisy said as they passed, but not making any attempt to cover herself.

"We should get back," AP said. "They look like they've been in a scrap. Come on." She stood and started to get dressed, her emotionless frown replacing the smiling and laughing of only a short while before. The rest of the girls reluctantly made themselves presentable, then with Willow held up between them they prepared to make their way to the hedgerow and back to the woods. They talked happily as they went, about the future, about their hopes and what they looked forward to. It was the most relaxed Harriet had ever seen AP, who talked at length about saving for a DE Havilland Gypsy Moth, an aeroplane of her own, and getting a job as a transport pilot. Lanky wanted to be a dancer in West End shows. She was tall and lean, and exactly what most would expect of a dancer, and she'd trained in dance right through school; it was a passion second only to firing guns. Something she professed to enjoying far more than she should, and she took particular pride in having shot down a Stuka and a Messerschmitt 109 from the ground. She had more kills than some pilots. Daisy wanted to start her own business. She loved the idea of being her own boss, and couldn't imagine having to answer to anyone else after her time in the WAAF. Willow wanted to be a motorcyclist, of all things. She loved sport and fitness and enjoyed the challenge of racing motorbikes competitively. She'd ridden a motorcycle since she was young, and saw racing them professionally to be the most logical next step. They arrived at the runway as the last of the Hurricanes was being pushed back into a camouflage netted pen. Simon, the squadron doctor, was kneeling by the pilot of the smoking Hurricane as a pair of orderlies helped him onto a stretcher. He was bloody and blackened with smoke but appeared to be able to communicate. The field was busy with a fuel bowser and ground crews tending the aeroplanes. AP, Harriet, and Nicole walked over to Cas, who'd just arrived as two of the pilots joined him.

"We weren't expecting visitors..." Cas said with a frown.

"No..." the South African pilot replied. He was drenched in sweat and looking a little shell shocked. "Sorry, Sir. Pilot Officer Van Darné. This is Pilot Officer Murphy," he introduced the young officer to his right.

"Lovely day for it," Murphy added in a strong Irish accent while smoothing his ruffled hair. "Sorry to drop in uninvited."

"Sergeant Lock," Van Darné introduced the final pilot to join them. He was an older man with dark hair and eyes. He was distracted and frowning, and pulling at a red silk scarf he had wrapped around his left hand.

"Sir," he mumbled.

"Everything OK?" Cas asked.

"Blasted 109 got me in that last turn," he grunted. "Cannon shell came right through the instrument panel, and a great dirty shard of metal ripped my hand open."

"Simon," Cas shouted over his shoulder, while he offered the pilots a cigarette each, which were gratefully received. "Have a look at this chap, will you?" Simon joined them while his orderlies lifted the stretcher and headed off.

"What have we here?" he asked as he took Lock's hand. Lock winced while Simon opened the scarf, looked around the wound, then wrapped it up again tightly. "Oh dear, that's a bit of a mess, isn't it? Come on, let's get you to the clinic." Simon winked at Cas, then led Lock after the orderlies.

"Get yourselves into a bit of a scrape, did you?" Cas asked.

"You could say that," Van Darnè replied. "We were on our way to the transit field, but when we arrived there was a bloody great air raid going on. The skipper pulled us south to avoid it and look for somewhere to land. We ended up chasing our tails for a while as we watched the fuel tanks get low, then we ran into a swarm of 109s, thirty of them at least."

"Sure we didn't stand a chance," Murphy added. "Came out of the sun and just fell on us they did, we didn't even know they were there until the skipper blew up. Must have hit the fuel tank."

"It was a blood bath," Van Darnè continued. "We were lucky to get away."

"Did you get any?" Cas asked.

"I was lucky to get away with my life," Murphy said as Van Darnè shook his head. "Lockie got one, though." He pointed after Sergeant Lock. "Sharpie maybe got one, I didn't see properly, but a pair of them got him. I'm surprised he got this far."

"I see..." Cas said. "So you lost your CO? Anyone else?"

"Twelve of us set off from England..." Van Darnè replied solemnly.

"Well, we'd better get word to Headquarters. What squadron did you say you are?"

"We're not..."

"Oh?"

"We were assembled from training units last night. Flight Lieutenant Hamley led us over, and we were supposed to be deployed as replacements for front line squadrons."

"You came straight from a training school?" Cas asked in surprise.

"Yes, Sir. We all did. Except for Mister Hamley, he came from one of the squadrons up north."

"OK... Did you bring any kit with you?" Both nodded, "Well, best you grab it, and we'll go get a cup of tea," they nodded and turned. "AP, go look at Lock's Hurricane, will you? See if it's airworthy?"

"I'll go now."

"What about us?" Harriet asked.

"Back to the tents," he said as he looked at the rest of the girls. "All of you back to the squadron." Thunder rumbled again in the distance, and they all looked up at the distant wall of black thunder clouds slowly edging towards them from the south.

Chapter 12

New Faces

"How did you know to find us here?" Cas asked the new arrivals as they walked back towards the woods.

"Luck of the Irish," Van Darnè replied, receiving an inquisitive eyebrow raise from Cas in reply. "Honestly, we were flying around lost when we saw the army positions around the village to the north. We were about ready to land there and ask for directions when Murph swore he saw an aeroplane. We did a circuit and saw the Gladiator down by the stream, and what looked like friendly forces..."

"Told you they saw us," Daisy said quietly to Harriet with a roll of the eyes. Harriet blushed a little in silent reply.

"Anyway," Van Darnè continued. "We saw the RAF personnel and what looked like a landing strip as we passed over the field. The green flares went up, and that was it, we were in."

"Lucky indeed," Cas said. "We only arrived here today ourselves."

"From England?" Murphy asked.

"From here in France. Our airfield was overrun by German paratroopers this morning. This is our reserve field."

"Bloody hell... They're that close?"

"Apparently," Cas forced a smile of resignation. "Keep your possessions close and don't go wandering off while you're here, one never knows when a German may drop in unannounced." He looked over his shoulder at Daisy. "Would you try and rustle up a couple of tin hats for these chaps?"

"I'll see what I can do, Sir," she said with a smirk.

"Tin hats?" Van Darnè asked.

"Yes. The Luftwaffe has a habit of attacking our airfields when they find them, and it can get a little boisterous down here on the ground." The new arrivals looked at each other nervously as they passed through the woods. "Everything OK, Simon?" Cas asked as the doctor slammed closed the back door of the ambulance and gave it a loud slap, which set it off slowly rumbling along the track that ran through the woods.

"I thought it best to send them both off to the brigade medical post," Simon replied. "The lad from the smoking Hurricane is a little worse off than I thought and needs more help than I can give him. The other chap's hand is almost split in two, sliced to the wrist. Their surgeons should be able to help, though, and get them both evacuated back to England. They're no good here."

"Will they be OK?" Van Darnè asked.

"The chap with the buggered hand, Lock is it?"

"Yes..."

"He'll live, though he may not be flying again any time soon. Your other friend, though, well I'm afraid that's out of our hands, so to speak. Still, he's fighting, so fingers crossed."

"Thank you, Simon," Cas said with a hard smile. Their conversation was halted by a motorbike dispatch rider arriving in the clearing. "Quick service..." Cas muttered. "Can I help?" he shouted over the engine noise as the soldier came to a halt in front of them.

"Are you the commanding officer?" the soldier asked.

"No, I'm the Adjutant, but I'm afraid that's the best you're going to get at the moment. Why do you ask?"

"I'm from brigade Headquarters, Sir."

"I'd gathered as much. How can I help?"

"Message from Headquarters, Sir." He opened his satchel and pulled out a file, which he handed to Cas.

"Thank you... Was there anything else?"

"The Brigadier said I'm to wait for a reply, Sir."

"I'd better get reading then, hadn't I?" He opened the file and read. "It would seem that your Brigadier would like us to go and look for the Germans..." His face turned to a frown as he looked at the dispatch rider.

"Yes, Sir," the Sergeant replied. "The French have reported German armour about thirty miles north west of our position. The brigadier asked if you'd be able to send up a plane to have a look. We need to know what we're facing, and how long we've got."

"Aeroplane," Cas replied after a moment of thought.

"Sir?"

"Always an aeroplane, Sergeant, never a plane..."

"Yes, Sir." The Sergeant looked bemused.

"Well, the squadron is up north at the moment flying bomber escort."

"Sir." The Sergeant looked a little more dejected and a little more concerned. "You see, Sir, it's just that we're an infantry brigade. If the Germans are sending tanks this way, we're going to have to request support from division if we're going to stop them, and it'll take a while to get here."

"Don't worry, Sergeant, you can rely on the RAF."

"Sir?

"Tell your Brigadier I'll put a flight up right away and find out what Jerry's up to."

"Yes, Sir." The Sergeant smiled. "Thank you, Sir."

"Oh, and Sergeant. Let our Headquarters know that the Hurricane replacements arrived from England, and if they don't mind, we'll keep both of them, Van Darnè and Murphy, for the time being."

"Yes, Sir," the Sergeant replied with a smile, which soon melted from his face as Cas continued.

"Two more arrived injured and ineffective, sent for evacuation to England. Speak to your surgeon, he'll have their names; and the other eight are posted missing, including Flight Lieutenant Hamley." The Sergeant nodded solemnly as the realisation hit him that ten valuable pilots and fighters had been lost. "Thank you, Sergeant. We'll get word to your Headquarters as soon as we're back." He nodded then forced a smile and left as Cas turned to the others. "Right, it looks like we've got some work to do. Van Darnè, Murphy, in what condition are those Hurricanes you landed?"

"With fuel and ammunition, mine's ready to go," Murphy replied.

"Mine too," Van Darnè added. "We're ready to go as soon as you give the word."

"Go? You two have just arrived from a training unit, and you aren't going anywhere just yet. Harry, Nicole, you're up. Playtime is over."

"Playtime? What?" Nicole frowned.

"Never mind," he continued with a smirk. "Get yourselves up and have a look around. Head north west and see if you can find any Germans, you heard the man, but don't hang around! Look but don't touch, I'd rather the RAF doesn't lose any more pilots today."

"What is he talking about?" Nicole asked Harriet.

"I think he means don't get into any unnecessary fights," Harriet shrugged.

"I think he means don't get into 'any' fights," Cas said. "unnecessary or otherwise, and don't stay up there longer than you need to, either. That storm front isn't far away, and you don't want to be flying around in that mess."

"You English talk nonsense," Nicole said as she rolled her eyes and put on her flying jacket, while Harriet smirked.

"But Sir, they're..." Van Darnè started, with a look of surprise on his face.

"I'd stop there," Cas said as he raised a finger "if I were you…"

"Sir..."

"No risks!" Cas called after the girls as they headed back through the trees towards the Hurricanes.

"No unnecessary risks. Got it!" Harriet shouted mischievously.

"I mean it!"

"I know!"

"Don't tease him," Nicole said

"You taught me," Harriet replied with a smirk.

"I don't know what you mean..." They smirked and giggled their way to the airstrip, where they found the Chief.

"Chief... Cas is sending us up, are the two that just came in ready to go?" Harriet asked.

"Yes Ma'am, pretty much. They're fuelled and armed, and we've checked them both over. Going far?"

"Just up the road, shouldn't be too long."

"Be careful, Ma'am, that storm's almost on us."

"We'll be back before it hits," Harriet replied confidently.

He nodded and winked, and the girls hugged before heading to their respective Hurricanes and starting their pre flight checks. With a thumbs up and a shout of 'clear prop,' the mighty Merlin engine coughed a couple of times as the propeller struggled sluggishly to life. Then with a throaty roar, the air filled with the familiar blue smoke of life and a flame shot from each of the exhaust port in turn, flickering as the cloud of smoke was blown back past the cockpit. Harriet scanned the instruments and tested the controls, and when she was sure that everything was as it should be, she was about ready to go. Before opening the throttle for her final power check, a voice boomed around the cockpit, shattering the noise of the engine.

"Where are you going?" AP demanded. She'd heard the Hurricanes starting and come to investigate, and when the Chief told her who was making the noise, she climbed up the wing and stuck her head into Harriet's cockpit almost instinctively.

"To look for the Germans," Harriet replied.

"But I haven't checked this aeroplane over yet."

"It'll be fine."

"You don't know that!"

"Chief has checked it."

"But I haven't!" AP became more insistent.

"AP, it'll be fine. We won't be long." The engine pitch coming from the next pen changed, and the crops started to sway as Nicole began to taxi ready for take off. "Look, we don't have time for this," Harriet continued. "I have to go."

"It's just..." AP continued with evident frustration.

"Get down. I have to go!" Harriet repeated more firmly. Feeling very nervous, scared even that Nicole would take off without her and she wouldn't be able to do the job she'd been given.

"Fine!" AP retaliated. "Just remember I haven't modified this one, so be careful in a dive or inverted!"

"Yes!" Harriet barked and gave the signal for the chocks to be removed, then pushed the throttle forward, making the Hurricane jerk a little as it started to roll. AP frowned while Harriet kept her eyes straight ahead, deliberately refusing to acknowledge AP was still there. She reluctantly jumped down and watched as Harriet guided her Hurricane out onto the grass strip between the wheat fields and bounced along the uneven ground as she weaved after Nicole. Finally, she swung alongside her, and they went through their final checks.

"Black Leader to Black two, are you ready?" Nicole asked over the radio.

"I'm usually Black Leader," Harriet replied.

"Not today." Nicole laughed.

"Whatever," Harriet replied, still feeling a little flustered about what had happened with AP.

"OK, in that case, let's go!" The girls revved, and Harriet waited a couple of seconds to let Nicole take the lead, then let off the brakes and followed, to the left and slightly behind. The ground crews watched as the Hurricanes roared and bounced along the field. Harriet gulped in the cool petrol tinged air as it whipped past the open cockpit, then pulled back on the stick as she felt the wheels start to lift. Undercarriage up, check temperatures and pressures, all looking good. She pulled the oxygen mask over her face and clipped it in place as she followed Nicole in a low circuit of the airfield. "Climb to angels one zero," Nicole instructed as they came onto a north easterly course, and passed over the British brigade positions in the town and countryside west of their airfield. Some soldiers looked up and waved, and Harriet gave her wings a brief waggle in reply. The girls flew in their side by side formation, as Cas had drummed into them. It was Cas who'd advised Barnes on the formations when he joined the squadron, and who demonstrated their effectiveness. Barnes was convinced to ignore RAF standing orders and adopt Cas' pairs formations right from the start, and Singh was happy to do the same when he took over. They climbed quickly to ten thousand feet, remaining vigilant, but finding to their surprise that they were quite alone. The sky was a peaceful silver blue all around, except for the south, which in contrast was a wall of towering black storm clouds so dark it looked like night.

"Smoke," Harriet said. "On the ground, about one o'clock." She squinted as she looked into the distance. Wispy spirals of black smoke were weaving into the sky along a staggered line running south to north on the horizon. Flames flickered as they got closer, then the battlefield opened up below them. Tanks, French and German, were smoking and burning, as were wrecked buildings and what seemed like entire streets, while infantry engaged each other in the town and surrounding woods. "I think we found the Germans…" They got closer and closer to the town, and the closer they got, the more desperate the fighting appeared, even from the height they were at.

"Yes..." Nicole said. "It looks... Horrible…"

"It's about to get worse, look! One o'clock, about five thousand feet and heading for the town!" A squadron of twelve Stukas were formed in a column of fours. "What should we do?"

"What else can we do? Those are French soldiers down there. Besides, if they break and run, there's nothing else between them and our airfield; and look at that to the east." About twenty miles out of the town was a long column of German troops, tanks, and supplies. "We have to do something."

"OK, but we need to be sensible." Harriet insisted. "There's only two of us. I say we dive on them and try to scare them enough to break them up and send them home. If we get a couple, even better."

"OK, we can do that."

"No messing about. In and out, then treetop height and home."

"Yes... I'm ready."

"Me too. If I take the leading flight of four and you take the rear, it may confuse them and make them think that a much bigger force is attacking them."

"Good idea..." Nicole's voice sounded nervous. "Black Section, Tally ho!" She pushed the nose of her Hurricane down into a dive, not too steep, as they were still some distance from the Stukas, but steep enough to fall on them just as they reached the town. Harriet followed suit and lined up with the second aeroplane from the left of the leading four. Her pulse raced, and her heart pounded in her ears, as her Hurricane shook from the pure speed of the dive. She briefly looked over to Nicole, they were well spaced and around the same height with the same angle of dive, and rapidly closing on the oblivious Germans who hadn't yet seen them.

Pulling her head forward against the g forces, she lined her gunsights just ahead of the nose of the lead Stuka. Closer and closer until the Stuka filled her gunsight and filled her windscreen, she held her breath then pushed the fire button and watched as bits flew off the nose of the Stuka, right in front of the cockpit, and then bits of the cockpit flew off, and the pilot shook as her bullets hit him. He slumped left, and the Stuka flipped in the same direction, clipping the right wing of the Stuka flying alongside as it drifted, flipped, and dived. Chunks flew from the second Stuka's wing, and it immediately spiralled, narrowly missing colliding with Harriet, who to avoid him flipped her Hurricane over on its back and pulled back on the stick to dive down out of harm's way. She narrowly missed the now spiralling Stuka and took a burst of fire from the rear gunner, who bravely stayed in place and focused enough to have a go at her and leave a row of bullet holes in her right wing. Her engine stuttered, and she lost all power as she twisted in an uncontrolled and unpowered nose down dive towards the town below; following the smoking Stuka she'd just shot down, which the gunner was in the process of jumping from. He slipped from his cockpit and tumbled through the air towards an increasingly scared Harriet. She pulled at the controls with all of her might and spun around him as he passed so close, he could briefly stare at her. Sweat was now pouring into her eyes and burning as she gasped and screamed while trying to control the aeroplane. She looked around the cockpit. She had a few thousand feet at the most, and she needed to jump. She fumbled with the canopy and slid it open. Her mind flashed through a thousand conversations, and to the last that she'd had with AP, maybe she knew there was something wrong with the Hurricane? Maybe she knew the engine would fail, and maybe she should have been allowed to give it a once over before flying? Maybe she knew it would fail? Of course, she knew it would fail! "You bloody idiot!" Harriet shouted as she remembered AP's warning that she hadn't modified the carburettor, and to be careful in the dive or if inverted. "The bloody carburettor!" She stamped hard on the rudder bar and pushed the stick hard over. The Hurricane went from a tight spin to a wide circle, and then control came back as she lessened the angle of the dive and the engine restarted. She pulled off her oxygen mask and desperately sucked in the air as more and more control came back, the circles widened and became less angry, and she pulled level just above the rooftops to the cheers and waves of the French soldiers below. She pulled up and rolled the Hurricane before levelling out and gathering speed while trying hard to slow her heart rate, and breathing, an attempt made in vain as the flash of tracer zipped behind her right wing. She spun her head to see a pair of 109s diving on her. What was she thinking? It was the worst she'd behaved since she'd started flying Hurricanes, she'd forgotten her lessons about the carburettor, ignored her ground crew and friend, and now she'd flown straight and level in combat for more than a few seconds. It was like she was trying to get herself killed. She pulled the stick hard left and entered a tight turn which the 109s followed, but being so fast they couldn't turn as tight as the Hurricane, and in a couple of turns Harriet was able to get the tail of one in her sights and give him a blast, cutting his rudder and making him wobble. She then broke away and pulled up quickly, climbing away from them and seeing the chaos above. The Stukas were scattered, what was left of them; and the fighters were swarming, mostly in confusion, apart from the one screaming down in flames as Nicole's guns battered it. Harriet headed towards her and put a stream of bullets past a 109 diving in to have a go at her, forcing the pilot to panic and pull away, leaving enough space for Harriet to get on Nicole's wing. As she watched him pull away, she saw the darkness enveloping them all, it was like night. The storm clouds had arrived, and large spots of rain splattered on her windscreen as a huge crack of thunder rumbled above the noise of the engine and boomed around them; they were in a storm.

"Where did they come from?" Nicole asked as she saw Harriet pull level.

"I don't know," Harriet replied, "and I don't want to hang around and find out. Shall we go home before the storm gets us?"

"I think so."

The girls formed in their pair and hit full throttle as they sped west at treetop height, almost ripping off the roof of a farmhouse they passed; both spinning their heads like they were spinning tops as they looked out for more Germans. It appeared, though, that they were safe.

"Did you get one?" Harriet asked over the radio.

"No. I got two. A Stuka and a 109, what about you?" Nicole replied, excitedly.

"Two Stukas…"

"I think we spoiled their party," Nicole said, her voice was relaxing a little, and the tension easing.

"Yeah..." Harriet didn't mention her incident with the carburettor. She was feeling quite stupid, but more than that, she was feeling quite shaken. They weaved their way across the countryside as the air filled with turbulence and bounced them uncomfortably while the rain intensified. Harriet slid her cockpit closed as the visibility dropped and they found themselves navigating field to field, not able to see much ahead and nothing above; their flight suddenly became very dangerous.

"Harry, I can't see where we are going," Nicole said after a while.

"It's OK..." Harriet replied as she strained her eyes. "Can you remember any hills from our flight out?"

"I don't think so..."

"OK, well that's one thing we don't need to worry about. If we keep flying south east, we should find the airfield eventually. We've just got to stay above the treetops."

"Yes... I keep losing height, though. I don't know if I can do this."

"You can. We can. We've just knocked four German aeroplanes out of the sky all by ourselves. We can certainly get ourselves home through a bit of rain!"

"Yes, you're right, we can do this."

"I'll take the lead, just sit behind me and follow everything I do. I'll get us home."

"OK, you lead," Nicole said nervously. She pulled back and sat behind Harriet, who strained her eyes and worked her way through the filthy weather, insistent she'd get them home; desperate to, in fact, to help resolve the nagging fears of doubt and upset she was feeling after her mistakes. Minutes dragged slowly, and they talked constantly, checking on each other and keeping each other awake as they both struggled to focus. "Maybe we should just land somewhere?" Nicole asked nervously as the clock went long past when they should have landed.

"OK, we're going to have to..." Harriet conceded as she searched desperately for somewhere safe to put down. She was being shaken by increasingly turbulent air, as the oppressive gloom of solid rain closed tighter and tighter around them. The cloud lowered with each minute that passed, and the ground was almost entirely obscured by a combination of thick cloud and sheets of torrential rain. Water was streaming down the cockpit walls, and starting to condense in the window. It became almost impossible to see out, leaving Harriet with no option but to drag the canopy open and risk a soaking.

"I can't see the ground," Nicole said nervously.

"I know..." Harriet replied, feeling just as nervous but doing her best to try and at least sound confident. For her own sake as well as Nicole's. Her heart almost burst from her chest, as a row of trees came out of the murk. Every nerve twitched as she pulled back hard on the control column, hitting herself hard in the stomach with it as she fought to drag the Hurricane into a climb steep enough to avoid the trees while shouting to Nicole to do the same.

"Look!" Nicole replied.

"Trees, I know!"

"No, there. One o'clock, look." Harriet glanced over to see a glowing green ball climbing into the sky from beyond the trees. It flew on a graceful trajectory, not like a bullet or a shell, it was a flare. She felt a surge of excitement run through her body as she scoured the ground where the flare had come from, then saw another, and then a succession of orange balls started to glow in a neat line. It was the ground, and what looked like a runway. She couldn't be sure which airfield it was, but she didn't have any other options.

"OK, follow me in and be careful. Watch for the ground!" Harriet instructed as she flew a circuit while keeping one of the lights firmly in her eye and scrubbing off as much speed as she dared. She levelled off and dropped through the hammering rain, leaning and looking out of the cockpit to keep the orange balls of light in sight until the ground rushed up to meet her just as she came level with the first light, which was nothing more than a flickering of flames jumping from a tin can. She hit hard with a bounce that lifted her back into the air; but she responded quickly and closed the throttle, dropping the Hurricane into the wet grass which pulled at the wheels and made the landing slip by quicker than usual. Worrying that Nicole would run right into the back of her, she quickly opened the throttle again and taxied along the burning runway lights until an airman appeared and waved for her to follow to her pen. She was home, and she was safe. Nicole followed without incident, and almost simultaneously they cut their engines, leaving only the sound of heavy rain and the creaking of the airframe. Harriet pulled off her helmet and mask and threw them onto the rearview mirror then closed her eyes, slumped in her seat, and lifted her face towards the sky; and just for one moment thought of nothing other than how good it felt to be on the ground and feeling the rain on her skin.

"You OK, Ma'am?" the Chief asked as he looked down into the cockpit. She opened her eyes and squinted through the rain to see his worried looking face staring down at her.

"Yes... Yes, I think so," she smiled as she fumbled at her harness, before pulling herself to her feet and with the Chief's guidance stepping out onto the wing.

"That was a close thing if you don't mind me saying?" he continued.

"What do you mean?"

"I mean the army was all ready to shoot down the circling aeroplanes, convinced you were Germans looking to bomb us. It was only young AP that stopped them, convinced that the engines were Merlins, she was."

"Oh..."

"Yes. I've been working with Merlins as long as she as, longer in fact, and even I couldn't tell. Not in this weather. She was insistent, though, and she convinced the Adjutant to let her fire flares to show you where we were, and give our position away."

"I need to thank her, where is she?" Harriet looked around.

"Busy working," came the reply. "She's working on one of the other Hurricanes and wants to get it flying before last light." Harriet frowned and felt her shoulders slump in disappointment that AP hadn't been there to greet her, as she usually was. "Anyway, Ma'am, I know the Adjutant is keen to hear from you in the command tent. I'll let AP know you're looking for her."

"Thank you, Chief..."

"Were you hit?" he asked as she jumped off the wing.

"What?" she asked as she turned back to look at him.

"The aeroplane, Ma'am. Did you take any hits? Is there anything I need to look at urgently?"

"Oh... No... No, I don't think so. Unless you can get AP to modify the carburettor, it almost killed me."

"Yes, Ma'am..." He frowned and shook his head as Harriet turned to meet Nicole, then putting their arms around each other they walked through the rain towards the woods and the command tent.

"I decided, I don't like flying in the rain," Nicole said. Harriet smiled in reply. "I saw you got two of those Stukas, and I was surprised."

"Surprised I got two?" Harriet frowned.

"Surprised by how you flew. So aggressive, and your dive was so steep. It's not like you."

"No..."

"Maybe now with the new aggression, you'll be as good as me at flying," Nicole said mischievously. Harriet smiled again, not really able to find the words to explain that what had happened was mostly luck after her engine had cut out and she'd nearly nosedived straight into the ground. She knew what she'd done, and she knew why it had happened, but it had still shaken her.

"We both know I'll never be better than you, Nicole," Harriet said with mock resignation.

"At last you admit it."

"Yes..." They walked arm in arm through the woods. Cas was at the entrance of the tent waiting for them, standing with his hands on his hips, and half smiling.

"Well?" he asked as they joined him in the tent.

"We found the Germans," Harriet replied.

"Show me." He stepped aside, and guided her to the map spread on the table behind him. "We're here." He tapped his pencil on a wooded area by a farm. Harriet studied the map for a moment and followed the long main road that ran to the north west, and the intersecting junction at the town.

"Here," she said. "German tanks and infantry, with supplies and whatever else blocking the road maybe ten or fifteen miles behind."

"I see... How fast were they moving, and in which direction?"

"They weren't. The French army was holding them on the perimeter of the town. There weren't many of them, though, maybe half a dozen tanks and a handful of artillery guns that I could see. As soon as the German reinforcements get there, I can't see them lasting long."

"At least we gave them some time," Nicole added. Harriet felt her eyes rolling as she heard the words and already felt Cas' brow creasing.

"And how exactly did you do that?" Cas asked.

"We stumbled on a squadron of Stukas forming up to attack their positions," Harriet said, thinking it was better to take control of the facts before Nicole said something that would get them both in trouble. More trouble that is.

"And you had no option but to get involved, I suppose?"

"We were above them..."

"I see."

"We had the advantage and we... Well... I thought that with our speed and height, we could surprise them and maybe break up their attack and then run for safety. They're Stukas, and we're faster."

"You are... Unusual that they'd be out without a fighter escort, though, but go on, how did it work out for you?"

"We knocked a few down, and we broke up the attack. The others turned and ran." Harriet said as confidently as she could, keen to move the conversation on.

"Well done," Cas shrugged. "Despite disobeying orders, which we'll talk about later, you bought the army a little more time and took a few dive bombers out of the war, so I suppose we should be thankful."

"I also killed a Messerschmitt 109," Nicole added. Harriet shook her head and stared furiously at Nicole. "What?" she asked, casually. "It's important we record these things accurately."

"You mean it increases your score!" Harriet hissed.

"So they did have fighter cover," Cas asked. "I thought it unusual they hadn't. So, tell me, where were their fighters while you were attacking the bombers?"

"I don't know," Nicole answered with a traditionally French shrug. "Probably somewhere above us, as they attacked from above while we were diving through the bombers."

"You didn't see them before the attack?"

"Of course not, do you think we're stupid?"

"As it happens, yes, yes, I do. We will talk about this later, but for now, get to your tent and get yourselves dried off," he barked, clearly frustrated. "I'll need to go visit the brigade Headquarters and give them this information. We won't be doing much flying until this filth lifts, so get some rest. Both of you."

"Have you seen AP?" Harriet asked.

"Yes, I have," he replied as he pulled on his flying jacket. "She's busy repairing a Hurricane that we desperately need, so don't go disturbing her. She's good like that. She understands the need for good discipline and to follows orders." Harriet felt her stomach squeeze, and her cheeks burn with embarrassment. "Anyway, the mood she's in at the moment she's probably best left to it. It's my experience to give her a wide berth when she feels this way out." He pulled on his hat and left the tent. "Rest, we'll talk later!" He climbed into the black squadron staff car, the car they'd escaped the overrun airfield in, which had just arrived outside with Jen at the wheel. She smiled at the girls then drove off.

"I think we're in trouble," Harriet said as she watched Cas leave.

"From who?" Nicole asked, totally oblivious to what was happening.

"From him... From AP..."

"You English are so temperamental. Everyone always seems to be in a mood," Nicole said as she stood beside Harriet.

"I suppose..."

"And you. Since I've known you, you always worry so much about what others think."

"I don't like to disappoint people."

"The French soldiers facing the Germans at that town won't be disappointed. They'll be happy we stopped them being bombed. So will all of those civilians we saw on the road."

"I suppose..."

"The only people who have any right to be disappointed are the crews of the German aeroplanes we shot down. Disappointed in their poor flying. The idiots."

"Yeah..."

"Don't think too much. We should eat and then get some sleep."

"I'm not hungry..."

"Don't be stupid. I'm starving."

"Really... I'll be fine. You go ahead."

"I'll see you in the tent."

They hugged, and Nicole left, marching head down through the rain and heading for the Mess tent. Harriet looked out, pulled the collar of her flying jacket up and fastened the zip, then stepped out into the rain. She wandered slowly, consumed with thoughts of what had happened, and the persistent thoughts of why AP and Cas were so disappointed with her. She walked along the track until she found herself staring at the old Gloster Gladiator by the river they'd swum in earlier. Before she knew it, she was pulling the canopy closed and closing her eyes as she snuggled the best she could into the seat. The solitude was exactly what she wanted. She pulled the sheepskin collar of her jacket tighter around her neck then listened to the rain bouncing off the frame. It was almost therapeutic, relaxing enough that she quickly felt herself fighting to stay awake, a battle she soon lost.

Chapter 13

Friends

"What are you doing in this old bucket?" AP asked as she looked down at Harriet, who despite being dragged rather rudely from her sleep by AP pulling open the canopy of the Gladiator she'd been sleeping in, was still struggling to open her eyes. She pulled her fluffy warm collar closer around her face and tried to bury herself in her jacket.

"Trying to sleep!" Harriet replied coldly.

"You'll get a stiff neck sleeping in there."

"I don't care."

"Oh, do grow up." AP frowned and rolled her eyes.

"Leave me alone."

"I can't."

"Why?"

"Because I want to talk to you."

"You didn't earlier."

"I had work to do... Look, I'm going to sit out here anyway, so if you want to talk you can swallow your pride and come and sit with me. If not, enjoy your stiff neck." She climbed onto the upper wing and sat with her legs hanging over the leading edge, while looking out over the grass as the late afternoon sun evaporated the downpour that had stopped after some hours of turbulent storms, leaving a crystal clear blue sky smudged with lines of steam from the ground and a beautiful vibrant rainbow. Harriet sighed; she was irritated with herself, and more than that she was angry. She huffed then rolled and dragged herself to her feet, instantly regretting sleeping in the cramped cockpit as her legs ached with stiffness. She groaned, then climbed up onto the wing and slumped down beside AP with a grunt, still not making any eye contact and feeling her cheeks burn with embarrassment. "Sore?" AP asked with a mischievous stare as she watched Harriet sit.

"No..."

"OK..." The girls sat side by side in silence. "I'm sorry," AP said, finally breaking the tension.

"What?" Harriet replied, a little taken aback. "What have you got to be sorry for?"

"Being a bitch."

"I..." Harriet struggled to find anything useful to say while staring at AP, who slowly turned from staring at the rainbow to look Harriet in the eyes, making her blush instantly.

"You can't deny it; I have been since you got here."

"You saved my life..." Harriet muttered. "You stole an aeroplane and rescued me from the Germans, and risked your life and career in the process."

"Doesn't mean I haven't been a bitch to you, too. I can do both simultaneously..."

"I..."

"Don't argue."

"OK..."

"The thing is, I'm a bitch to you because I think that you're the most amazing person I've ever met."

"What? Don't be stupid!" Harriet's blush was now burning fiercely.

"Shut up and listen, this is hard enough as it is..." AP scolded. "Do you know what it meant to me to see a girl climb from the Hurricane which had just shot down four Messerschmitt 109s? It was incredible. It was like watching a dream, my dream, coming true right in front of my face, but you were playing my part! The armed forces have never let a woman fly, not at all, not even communication flights, and there 'you' were, flying a Hurricane and shooting down Germans." Harriet was speechless. Stunned into silence by AP's abnormal, for her at least, openness. "Honestly, I was as jealous as hell. I was in awe of you, but I hated you." Harriet's stomach spun and sunk all at the same time. "I always wanted to fly, ever since I was a little girl. My dad's an engineer, ever since leaving school, and after years making engines for cars, he ended up working at the aeroplane factory across the river from where we lived. Anyway, the Auxiliary Air Force were based there, and he volunteered. He used to take me on family days, and then I'd go with him on weekends. I learned all about engines and aeroplanes, but as much as I loved helping him fix them, I always wanted to fly them." She drifted off for a moment as she thought back to her childhood. "As I got older, some of the pilots would take me flying with them. It was all against the rules, of course, but that didn't stop them, it was all a bit of harmless fun. They even let me fly a few times..."

"It sounds amazing..."

"It was. It was amazing!" AP smiled, and her eyes lit up. It was the first time Harriet had seen her smile properly, and her face glowed. "Mum was so annoyed with him when she first found out. She said it was dangerous and that he was an idiot for risking my life, but she always supported me and told me I could be whatever I wanted to be, and they found the money from somewhere to pay for me to have proper lessons. I loved it, and one day when I'd been flying, Amy Johnson landed at the aerodrome. All of the pilots flocked around her, she was the darling of the skies, but after a few minutes she came and talked to me, and before I knew it, she was giving me a flying lesson. A woman teaching a girl to fly at an RAF airfield, it was unheard of. She taught me to loop and roll. It was the best."

"Then what happened?" Harriet was transfixed by the story.

"I qualified as a pilot," AP beamed, her eyes sparkled, then slowly dimmed. "Then the RAF told me I couldn't fly for them because girls don't fly..."

"I'm sorry..."

"Me too... Nobody would give me a job as a pilot, so I practised with old engines at the airfield until the Women's Auxiliary Air Force advertised for mechanics. It was that or get married to some lad from the factory and have kids, and I wasn't having that; so, I thought that if they wouldn't let me fly them, at least I could fix them and be around them." Her smile was now less of a glow, more forced, tinged with disappointment.

"But the Air Transport Auxiliary let girls fly," Harriet said with a frown. "I met one just the other day. She'd flown one of our Hurricanes over and was taking a Spitfire back to England. She was only young, too. My age, I think. Why didn't you join them?"

"Because they didn't take girls at the time... They didn't even exist."

"You could leave the WAAF and apply? You could go and be a pilot, they'd take you with all of your knowledge, and you flew that Hurricane like a natural, you even landed first time out!"

"If only," AP forced a smile. "There's a war on if you hadn't noticed, the WAAF won't be letting me go anywhere for a while."

"Surely they'd let you transfer, especially now you're an officer."

"Sadly not... The only way out is if I was kicked out, which would mean the ATA wouldn't even entertain me anyway, or by getting pregnant, and I've absolutely no intention of that!"

"But what will you do?"

"I'll fix Hurricanes and keep our pilots flying against the Germans, so we can keep fighting as long as we can... Anyway, my point is that you've done it, Harry, you've done what I couldn't, you've done what no other woman could. You've not only flown fighters, but you've also flown them in combat, and the RAF has let you. You're the one, Harry; you're the one that's going to change things."

"Change things, change what? I don't understand?"

"Harry, I was jealous, I hated you for doing what I never could, but that changed when I got to know you. You're quiet, and you're polite, you're funny, you can fix an engine with your eyes closed, and you're so intelligent you make my head spin..." Harriet was back to blushing intensely. "But more than that, you're an incredibly gifted pilot. You're not trained in combat, yet you go up time and again without a second thought, and every time you do, you do something ridiculously brave and put yourself in harm's way. You're the best of us, Harry. I service your aeroplane and try to tell you how to keep safe because you've got to get through this, you've got to live. You've got to get through the war and get back to England so the Air Ministry can see what girls can do. A female fighter ace with over ten kills to her name. You'll be impossible to ignore."

"Ignore? I don't understand. I just fly and do my bit, that's all."

"It's more than that, Harry, you're more than that. The RAF still don't get it, not at the moment. They're in a new kind of war, but they're still flying with old tactics, which any idiot can do; and their only worry is how many aeroplanes they've got. There's a bigger problem coming if this war goes on, I promise you, and that's a lack of pilots."

"Pilots?"

"You can have all the aeroplanes you want, but if you don't have the pilots, they're nothing but expensive lawn ornaments. It takes the RAF between one and two years to train a fighter pilot, and they're going to need as many as they can get, regardless of what they've got between their legs!" Harriet let out a stifled giggle, making AP smile with her innocence.

"Some pilot I am... I forgot about the carburettor on my last flight, even after you warned me. I nearly crashed."

"Don't be stupid."

"I am stupid. I almost killed myself because I was too focused on flying to listen to you."

"You've been flying Hurricanes for five minutes, Harry. The RAF hasn't even trained you. You haven't been through the formal conversion to Hurricanes. You haven't even been rated on them. You're not even a trained combat pilot. You got a quick briefing from an injured pilot, an hour around the circuit with Singh, and a few bits and pieces from Cas and me."

"So?"

"So you were so focused on what was ahead of you that you forgot something. If you'd been trained properly you'd maybe have felt less pressured or less stressed, and been able to hear me, and if you'd been trained you'd have had long enough on type to know about the carburettor, and you'd have trained and practised to counter the problems, and wouldn't have even had to think about it anyway. Don't be so hard on yourself." Harriet forced a smile and blushed as she recognised the sense in the words she was hearing.

"Thanks..."

"Don't mention it."

"I mean it. You've saved my life more than once. I owe you."

"Just stay alive. I meant what I said; you're the best of us, Harry. What you're doing is for all of us."

"OK, you can stop now," Harriet blurted with a smile. Before either of them could say another word, they were disturbed by the roar of Merlins. They looked up to see a Hurricane speeding towards them, with others following.

"Singh..." AP said as she saw the letters on the side. "The squadron's back. Come on, I'm going to have work to do." The girls stood as Singh passed overhead.

"Only five..." Harriet said as they watched the Hurricanes pass and stretch into a line ready to land.

"How many did we have when we left last night?"

"Seven"

"Oh..."

"Come on." They jumped down and walked towards the trees and the squadron airfield.

"How did you know?" Harriet asked as they walked.

"Know what?"

"That it was Nicole and me flying in the rain earlier when you put the flares up."

"Which other idiots would be flying around in that type of weather? Even the birds were walking!"

Harriet smirked to herself. AP was back to her usual blunt and harsh self; things were back to normal. They walked with no more words until they reached the grass strip and watched the first Hurricane land and be pushed into a pen in the wheat field. The next followed, and the next. Cas was there waiting and watching as ground crews rushed into action.

"There you are..." he said as Harriet and AP joined him.

"There's only five," AP said.

"Yes..." he replied solemnly. "How are the Hurricanes that came in earlier?"

"They'll fly," AP replied. "It took a bit of work but the second two are OK, the crews have worked hard on them."

"Good work, AP. Thank the ground crews for me."

"I already have."

He smiled at her and gave her a wink then turned to Harriet. "And where did you get to?"

"I found her having a snooze by the river," AP said.

"I see... Well, let somebody know where you're going next time. There's no telling when the Germans could turn up. You were there this morning. You saw what happened; we can't afford to lose you, not now."

"Sorry..." Harriet's smile faded again, and her heart sank.

"Don't be sorry, be smart. Pilots are hard to come by." Singh walked over to join them; he looked tired. "We need pilots more than ever."

"Cas," Singh said. "Who do those four Hurricanes belong to?"

"Reinforcements that came in earlier. They got shot up, two of the pilots have been evacuated for surgery, and the other two are resting up." Cas explained.

"Two are better than none," Singh said as Archie joined them.

"How were things with you?" Cas asked.

"Tiring... They had us up five times. We'd meet bombers from England at the coast and escort them in, take them back out, refuel, rearm, then back up ready for the next wave."

"Losses?"

"Two... Including Mister Maxwell." Harriet's stomach squeezed tight as she heard the news.

"I see. I'll inform Headquarters."

"Is there much I need to know here?" Singh asked as they started to walk as a group towards the trees.

"The army has put in a telephone line connecting us to their brigade Headquarters."

"That's something."

"Yes... Their Brigadier put in a request for a reconnaissance flight earlier. Apparently, the Germans are heading this way."

"Oh? Do we need to put somebody up now?"

"Not for now. I sent Cornwall and Delacourt up."

"And?" Singh asked as he turned to look at Harriet.

"There's a German column about thirty miles away, but the French are holding them." Cas continued.

"Air cover?"

"Stukas," Harriet said shyly.

"They got a pair each, and Delacourt bagged a 109 too," Cas added.

"Really? Good show, Harry."

"Thank you, Sir."

"OK, well, AP I want all aeroplanes refuelled, rearmed, and ready to fly as soon as possible. I want us ready."

"Sir." She turned from the group and left.

"How many is that now, Harry?" Archie asked. His voice was flat, and he wasn't his usual mischievous and boisterous self.

"Twelve, I think. I really don't know; I don't really count anymore."

"Yes... It can get a bit like that, can't it?" he conceded.

"Yeah... How about you?"

"Two more today... Between us, we'll have them licked if we keep going like this, Harry. You and me." He gave her a wink and a smile, which simultaneously warmed her while showing how cold and empty he felt.

"I'm sorry about Max..."

"Thanks, Harry. Me too! He sold his life dear, though, got a brace of the buggers before they got him. His engine started smoking as he dived into a cloud, and that's the last we saw of him."

"Sir, the army is here for you," Daisy said as she ran out to meet the group.

"I'll be there in a minute," Singh replied. "Archie, make sure everyone gets a drink and something to eat. We've got an hour or so of daylight left, and I want to be ready if we're needed. Oh, and the two new boys, make them at home, if we're not called up to fight, I want them drilled ready." Singh and Cas wandered over to the command tent where a couple of army officers were waiting for them. They shook hands and went inside while Harriet, Archie, and the assembling pilots headed for the Mess tent where they met with Nicole, Van Darnè, and Murphy, who were sitting at a table talking over a cup of tea.

"They the new boys?" Archie asked.

"Van Darnè, and Murphy," Harriet replied. "They arrived earlier."

Both jumped to their feet when they saw Archie enter the tent. His dark sandy hair was tousled, and his face black with sweat and smoke, and his welcoming smile was noticeably absent.

"Dolph Van Darnè," he introduced himself with a handshake.

"Elliot Murphy, Murph to most," his Irish friend followed.

"How much combat experience do you have?" Archie asked.

"Just today," Dolph replied.

"Which squadron did you come from?"

"The training unit," Murph added.

"I see..." Archie grunted. "Well, you're in the thick of it now. Finish your tea, and we'll see about getting you up for some proper training."

"Yes, Sir"

"Less of the Sir. Come on, Harry, let's have a drink." The returning pilots grabbed a tea from the urn and helped themselves to the hard biscuits Chef had made earlier in the afternoon. Kiwi sat the other side of Harriet, who was sipping her tea and trying to think of what to say. One of the nicest people she'd met, a man who'd been so welcoming to her when she arrived, and Archie's closest friend was now gone; along with Gus, the excitable young man they'd met on their first night. The squadron had certainly thinned out a bit since then; and been through a lot.

"How was it?" she asked Kiwi, choosing to open what she hoped would be the most comfortable conversation.

"Bloody ridiculous," he replied as he swept his hair from his face. "Every time I got one of the bastards off my tail, another one jumped on. Straight up, I'm knackered."

"Did you get one?"

"Oh, he got one alright," Grumpy added from across the table. "Got so caught up in it he nearly got himself shot out of the sky, but he got one."

"Yeah, thanks for getting him off me."

"You'll learn, Kiwi," Grumpy said with a wink, "You'll learn. Either that or you'll end up with a few extra holes in you."

"Probably preferable to the rocket he's going to catch for the extra holes in his Hurricane," Archie added, much to the amusement of the others. "I'd rather not come back at all, than bring a wreck back to AP."

"Steady on," Kiwi protested. "It's not a wreck; it still flies straight."

"Aye," Grumpy replied "and that's the problem. Fly straight and level in the combat zone for more than a couple of seconds and they'll get you."

"Alright, alright, fair play. Lesson learned. At least I got one…"

"You did," Archie replied, "that's something at least. Remind me again, Harry, how many have you shot down?"

"Oh, I don't know..." Harriet said with a blush, quickly shrinking and trying to remove herself from the spotlight.

"Twelve," Nicole added. "Five more than me, but only because I let her have the easy ones."

"You've shot down twelve Germans?" Dolph asked in amazement. Harriet shrugged and sipped her tea.

"She's lucky," Nicole continued, back to her usual self. The joking and laughing continued, and soon the low that had filled the tent was lifted. Pilots laughed and joked together as though they'd had a day at the races. Each of them knew their losses, and each knew how close their own end was, but for that moment they were able to laugh and be happy and forget what was going on around them; right until Harriet noticed Cas standing silently at the tent door. He was watching them with a sadness in his eyes. He looked like he was at a funeral, watching from a distance as an old friend was lowered into the ground. Harriet's stomach knotted as she watched him. Finally, he noticed he was being watched, about the same time as the others saw he was there and one by one fell silent until they were all staring at him.

"Everything OK, Cas?" Archie asked.

"The CO asked that you'd all come outside," he replied quietly, before bracing himself and straightening up. "When you're ready." He turned and left, and the murmuring pilots pulled themselves upright and headed outside. The rest of the squadron were gathering, too, mechanics, storemen, armourers, drivers, and Sergeant Oliver from the army detachment, along with a couple of Corporals. There was a general hubbub of conversation as everyone waited for the last to arrive, AP and the Chief.

"Anyone missing?" Cas asked, silencing the gathering.

"Only the sentries, Sir," Warrant Officer Peters replied.

"Ladies and gentlemen," Cas called, signalling a quietening of the mutterings going around the clearing, "The CO has an important announcement."

"My chocolate ration says they've agreed to an armistice, and the whole thing's off." Arthur, the supply Officer said.

"I'll take your chocolate off you, old boy," Archie replied without turning. Singh wore a heavy frown as he stepped forward, more than his usual stern glare.

"I've just been briefed on the war as it currently stands," Singh started, "and I'm afraid the news isn't good." Archie held his hand over his shoulder, and a small bar of chocolate was placed in it silently. "In fact, that's something of an understatement..." Harriet felt her stomach knot as she tried to imagine what would be coming next.

"Christ, it can't get any worse..." Grumpy muttered.

"Want to bet your chocolate ration?" Archie replied.

"As of approximately one hour ago, a general retreat to the port of Dunkirk has been ordered by the commander of the British Expeditionary Force," Singh announced with a firm forcefulness, and a ripple of gasps spread through the gathered squadron personnel.

"Bloody hell..." Archie said out loud.

"Our squadron has been tasked with covering the withdrawal of the British and French forces that will be passing through this area, and stopping

German bombers from breaching the defensive perimeter and getting through to the ships at the coast."

"Ships?" Archie asked. "Reinforcements?"

"Quite the opposite, I'm afraid," Singh replied. "I'll hand over to Major MacDowell, the intelligence officer for the 96th Infantry Brigade, and he can give you a better idea of the plans." He gestured to the tall Major of stocky build with broad shoulders. He looked at the assembled squadron with his piercing green eyes. His face was dirty and weathered, but he couldn't have been more than thirty.

"Thank you, Squadron Leader," he started. He was very well spoken, with just the lightest of Scottish accents. "As has already been mentioned, the General Staff received orders from London this afternoon to initiate a general retreat to the coast, where what remains of the British Expeditionary Force will be evacuated home to England." Another gasp rippled around the gathering. "Some units have started to embark on Royal Navy transports, but the Germans are already throwing their bombers forward. The Navy is taking significant losses; which is entirely unacceptable, as they're going to need every ship they've got if they're going to get us all out. However, if we're going to get anybody out at all, we've got to stop the German divisions which are hitting from the north and east; and now from the south after they humbugged us entirely when they broke through the French line and made a run for the coast; cutting us off from the rest of France. That's where we come in. The General Staff have drawn a defensive line with the Channel as the base; and the French army is going to hold it for as long as they can, with support from several British units, like mine, the 96th Infantry Brigade. We're about thirty miles inside the south east tip of the defensive perimeter, which is currently being held by a depleted French division, the commander of which sends his personal thanks to you by the way. Apparently, the intervention of your Hurricanes today broke up a German attack and gave the French enough time to get more men and armour forward under the cover of the storm. Anyway, I digress. We've been tasked with holding this sector at all costs, as there's a major rail hub and military stores complex behind our lines. This railhead must stay open to allow withdrawing forces to transit through quickly, and allow the distribution of the stores to the units that need them to hold the defensive line. This is where you chaps come in... We have an anti aircraft battery attached to the brigade, and there's another at the rail depot, but as you'll know well enough, that's not going to be enough to stop a determined attack. We know the importance of the depot, which means that the Germans will know, and I expect they'll be heading this way shortly. Any help you can offer in breaking up bombing raids will give us a bit of breathing room, either by turning them back or splitting them into less concentrated groups that'll do less damage... So there you have it, are there any questions?"

"How long are you expected to hold?" Archie asked

"Indefinitely," came the stark reply.

"So how long are you expecting to hold?" he asked, rephrasing the question.

"A very different question... It depends on the French division ahead of us. Once they break; and assuming we receive no further reinforcements, perhaps forty eight hours after our first ground engagement."

"And then?"

"I'm afraid there is no 'and then'. Once we become ineffective, individual units will try and make it to Dunkirk."

"What about fuel and ammunition?" Archie asked. "We don't have enough of either for sustained air operations."

"The Royal Army Service Corps are going to supply you with fuel and ammunition from the depot, and you'll have all you need. That goes for food, too. Was there anything else?" People looked around, and in the absence of any more questions, MacDowell stood back, leaving Singh to talk.

"So now you know," Singh said out loud. "I want the full squadron up in thirty minutes, and we'll get a patrol done over the French positions before last light. Before we leave, does anyone have any questions about what the Major has just briefed us on?" Everyone shook their heads and a light mumble carried around the group again. "Good, get to work, we've got a tough few days ahead of us. Cornwall, Delacourt, I'll see you both in the command tent if you don't mind. Everybody else dismissed."

Harriet's heart sunk further; she knew another telling off was coming.

"Go on, Harry. Stand straight and smile, that's the way," Archie said as he slapped her on the shoulder, before walking away and leaving the two girls standing together.

"Oh, I wish I could just be left alone to fly," Harriet said with a sigh.

"I think I don't like the military life," Nicole said. "Do this, do that. Especially you English... So many rules."

Harriet shrugged, and the girls walked to the tent where Singh was talking to the Major and another officer.

"Ah, there you are," Singh said. "Major MacDowell, Captain Rouge, these are Pilot Officers Cornwall and Delacourt. Ladies, Major MacDowell you've already been introduced to. The Captain is the brigade's French liaison officer," Rouge nodded politely and smiled. "Gentlemen, these are the pilots who broke up the German bombing earlier."

"But they're..." Rouge started.

"Yes," Singh said, stopping him in his tracks. "They are indeed such very talented combat pilots. Miss Delacourt, in fact, is one of your countrywomen who joined us from the French Army Air Force.

"My pleasure," Rouge said as he stood smartly, "and my thanks on behalf of the French division. I've been asked to let you know that the General has sent a signal to your Headquarters regarding the action earlier today. He commends your flying skills and courage."

"Merci," Nicole said, almost flirtatiously. "It's our duty."

"OK, you'd better get ready for the flight briefing. I'll do it by the runway," Singh said. The girls nodded politely and then left.

"This war gets more and more confusing," Nicole said as they walked side by side towards the Mess tent, where they each had a drink of water before walking down to the airfield.

Harriet met with AP, who was waiting for her with a smile. Together they checked around her Hurricane, which AP revealed to have been freshly painted with a large H. Something which made Harriet smile so much her cheeks hurt.

"H for Harry," AP said. The smile lifted Harriet even further, and she felt much brighter than the morning, picked up by her lengthy conversation with AP and the congratulations from Singh and the French Officer, she felt normal again, mostly. Though Cas' irritation with her was still playing on her mind for reasons that she couldn't begin to identify, but she was right enough to listen to AP's every word and pay attention to suggestions and advice. That done they joined the others for Singh's briefing.

"We'll fly a route along the main highway," Singh said. "I'll lead A Flight, Archie, you'll lead B Flight. Harry, you and Nicole will fly as C Flight, you'll fly above us and to the rear, as usual, and watch out for bandits trying to get the jump on us."

Ten minutes later and they were in the air, climbing hard and chasing the squadron to take their places in overwatch, protecting them from any prowling Germans hanging around in the orange and blue evening sky, ready to drop down on them. The roads, as expected, were packed full of refugees, but other than a small unit of French tanks and trucks there wasn't much military activity to report. It was even quiet over the town that the girls had flown over earlier when they engaged the Germans. There were waves from the ground, but all seemed peaceful. As they crossed the front and nudged into German territory, Harriet found herself mesmerised by a glowing orange red football which seemed to hang in the sky ahead of her. Another appeared behind it, and another, they were so pretty in the now dark pink and blue sky. She caught herself smiling, then instantly terrified as one of the glowing orange balls exploded underneath her and shook the aeroplane, turning the sky black with smoke and shocking her into action. As realisation dawned that they were over the German positions and attracting increasingly accurate anti aircraft fire, she immediately became hyper vigilant. Singh had her and Nicole climb and watch their backs while he led the rest of the squadron in an attack on the German positions. Fuel and ammunition stores erupted as the Hurricanes strafed them again and again, weaving in and out of the flak rising to meet them. Finally, the ammunition ran out, and the sky darkened, and Singh ordered the squadron to reform and head home, where they were rearmed and refuelled before nightfall. A rota was posted for duty pilots through the night, meaning two were always on standby to intercept enemy raiders. Every pilot was absolutely exhausted from a hard day of flying and fighting, except for Harriet, who laid on her bed staring at the roof of the tent overthinking everything, especially what had happened to her family and Nicole's grandparents. Finally, she couldn't stand it any longer so grabbed her jacket before heading out into the night, to wander down the trail and past the sentries until she was back at the old Gladiator. She climbed on the top wing again, where she sat and looked at the brightening moon as it filled the inky blue sky and lit up the thousands of stars above. She lost herself in them, staring and gazing, and emptying her head of all thoughts for what felt like an eternity. She felt tears run down her cheeks as the pressures and tensions of recent days finally found a way out.

"I thought you'd be here," Cas said from the shadows. Harriet jumped as she was dragged back to reality and looked around in the darkness to see his silhouette walking from the wooded track behind her.

"What do you want?" she asked abrumptly, as she quickly rubbed the damp tears from her cheeks.

"You..." he replied.

"Why? What have I done now?"

"Done? Nothing. At least nothing I know of?" He climbed up the aeroplane and sat beside her on the wing. His cobalt blue eyes looked into hers in the silver light of the moon, and she quickly looked away. "You've been crying... Harry, are you OK?" he asked. His voice was softer than usual, comforting even, and it made Harriet tremble nervously.

"If you don't want anything, you could just go away!" she snapped, feeling like she was going to explode with embarrassment.

"No... No, I don't think so. If you're upset, I want to know about it, and I want to help."

"You can't help. There are no wise words from air force manuals that are going to help, I can assure you of that! So you may as well say what you've come to say, then leave me alone."

"I don't think I can do that."

"Because you're the Adjutant, and responsible for your pilots?"

"Because for some stupid reason, I care about you deeply, and it concerns me that you're so unhappy." She turned and faced him; intrigued but scowling.

"What?"

"I've noticed since we were overrun by the Germans this morning just how tense you've been, and honestly I'm worried for you."

"Worried? You've done nothing but tell me off all day!"

"Tell you off? What? Don't be so ridiculous!"

"I'm not being ridiculous! You've been in a foul mood, more so since Nicole and I got involved with those Germans earlier; and before you say it, I know you ordered us not to attack, but what were we to do? Let them go? Let them bomb those French soldiers? We had a chance to stop them, or at least break them up. I don't care what you say. We did the right thing!"

"Finished?"

"Finished!"

"OK, well, my turn, I suppose... First, I may have been in a foul mood, but it certainly wasn't with you, and isn't with you. In fact, you couldn't be further from the truth. Second, yes, you did do the right thing when you attacked those Germans earlier."

"Wait. What?"

"You did the right thing. From the report Nicole gave me, I'd probably have done the same myself. You were in a perfect position, they hadn't seen you, and from what the French say, you were able to break up the attack and give them a fighting chance at holding off the German assault. You not only did the right thing, but you also did it very well. At least that's probably what the air force manuals would say..." She felt herself blushing more. "And as for the mood..."

"Yes?"

"What we say now stays between us, right?"

"Of course."

"Well, in that case, my mood has been due to my absolute ferocious annoyance at one person, and one person only... Me!"

"You? What? What on earth have you done to be annoyed at yourself? You've pretty much run the squadron, and it's your leadership that got us here now and kept us in the fight."

"I've also almost got you killed more times than I'm comfortable with..."

"I don't understand?"

"I should have put you on the first transport to England as soon as you arrived."

"But..."

"Instead, I found a way of letting the squadron keep you, and I have done since... There were plenty of opportunities to send you home to England. Barnes suggested it, Finn demanded it, and the AVM offered it. Each time I found a way to keep you around. I even used my knowledge of those air force manuals that you hate so much to get you commissioned into the RAF Reserve."

"But you needed pilots, why wouldn't you do that?"

"Yes... Yes, we do need pilots, especially good ones like you. Alas, while that may have been my reasoning, it wasn't entirely selfless."

"I really don't understand."

"Honestly, and I'll deny this if you ever tell a soul, I quite enjoy having you around," he said nervously. Harriet felt her face burning with a blush. "You make me feel... I don't know. You make me feel young, I suppose."

"I'm happy you kept me around," Harriet said without thinking, and instantly felt herself blush even more, if that was possible.

"Well that's the problem, isn't it?" he replied. "Every time I send you up, I feel sick, and I have my heart in my mouth until you return! You're not a combat trained pilot, yet I send you into harm's way again and again. That's just not right..."

"But I can do it."

"Yes, you can, you're a natural, but that doesn't mean there isn't risk. I flew in the last war, remember? I've seen plenty of talented pilots lose their luck, and their lives."

"You made it through..."

"I'm not talented. I got through on ignorance and dumb luck, nothing more."

"You won medals."

"Only because almost everyone else that deserved them had already got themselves killed... As I said, I was lucky."

"I'll be careful."

"It's not just the flying, Harry. I wish it were. I know you're a good pilot, probably the best I've ever seen, but this morning changed things. You stood in front of me when I was reloading my revolver, and shot that German paratrooper. He could have killed you, so many of them could, and I couldn't protect you from them all. I suppose that focused my mind a little on how bloody silly the situation is getting."

"I'm sorry..."

"What? What do you have to be sorry for?"

"I didn't understand. I thought you were angry at me for some reason. I didn't realise you just wanted to protect me."

"Well, now you do..." He forced a smile. "You know, Harry, Barnes was a good friend, as was that damned idiot Sully who got you into all this in the first place. They were good friends, but I could take what happened to them, and to the others that we've lost. They're professional fighter pilots, it's their job, but if anything were to happen to you..."

"I'll be OK," she said as she put her hand on his. He looked at her in the moonlight. She was no longer crying or scowling; she had a warm smile on her face.

"You can't know that."

"I can. I will be OK, I promise."

"Funny how you've just done that."

"What?"

"Put me at ease when we're stuck in the middle of the most ridiculous of situations. A most ridiculous situation mostly of my making."

"Our making... I could have gone home at any time."

"Either way, things are about to get a whole lot worse, and I haven't the first idea what to do about it."

"Keep doing what you always do. Be the leader that we all know we need."

"And what about you?"

"I'll be careful. I promise. We'll get through this."

"I hope you're right."

"I am. You'll see." She smiled then leant her head on his shoulder and stared into the moon as its reflection shimmered in the river ahead of them, bathing them in an ice white silvery light. She smiled to herself. She smiled for lots of reasons, but most of all she smiled because it felt nice to be cared about. They sat in a peaceful silence for what felt like forever, and a million miles from the war, but the silence wasn't to last. Merlins roared into life over at the airfield, and minutes later a pair of Hurricanes scrambled into the night sky. They flew a circuit, with their exhaust stubs spluttering flames into the darkness as they headed into the moonlight, flying side by side and heading into the distant night.

"I'd better go," Cas said as he grabbed his hat.

"I'll come."

"No... It's a beautiful night out here. Enjoy it, but get some sleep when you can, tomorrow's going to be hectic." He looked down for a moment, then lifted his sleeve and unfastened his watch, before handing it to Harriet.

"What's this?" she asked as he put the watch in her hand.

"You gave yours to Nicole."

"I know. She needed it at the time. I don't really need it now, though, as we're always together. Besides, it wasn't even mine to start with. Sully lent me it so I could find my way to the squadron."

"Things are a lot different from then," he half smiled. "You're a fighter pilot now, a proper one, and the way things are going, there's every chance that you could end up being separated from the other pilots. If that happens, you'll need a watch to help you calculate your position, fuel, and flying time, amongst other things."

"But it's yours..." Harriet protested as she tried to hand it back to him. "You're the squadron Adjutant, and you practically run the show, you need a watch more than anyone."

"Oh, don't worry about that. I have my old pocket watch." He held her hand and closed it around the watch, stopping her from letting it go. "It's not like I need a pilot's wristwatch these days, anyway," he smiled. "You need it much more than I do."

"But..." Harriet said as she tried to think of her next argument to refuse the gift. "I'd hate to damage it. Cas, you can't just give me your watch, it's not right!"

"That's what you're worried about?" he laughed. "I can easily resolve that. I'll loan it to you, not give it. You can return it to me in once piece when we get back to England, and we can get you one of your own issued from the stores. How about that?" Harriet felt a smile on her face, she couldn't help herself, and she quickly found herself nodding in agreement. "Good, that's it settled." He let go of her hands, slowly, then took the watch and put it on her wrist. The numbers glowed softly in the darkness and lit up the pale white face, which Harriet had thought so beautifully unique when she'd seen it in their many previous conversations. From a distance, it looked like many of the other Swiss made pilot watches, except for when the light caught the face in a certain way, and it shimmered with a pearlescent hue of purples, pinks, and turquoises. "It's an Omega, and it keeps time flawlessly. I bought it in Geneva, you know," he said as he gazed at the watch, "I remember it like yesterday... An unexpected twist of fate took me to Switzerland a year or so ago, where I'd been told there was a boutique which had the most unique collection of bespoke watches, produced by some of the finest of all Swiss watchmakers. I walked all around Lake Geneva trying to find the place, and finally found it just as it was about to close. The owner was moving the watch from the window display as I arrived, and I was captivated the moment I saw it. I had to have it, of course."

"It's beautiful..." Harriet said as she looked at the watch in the moonlight. "I promise I'll look after it, and I'll give it back to you in the same condition."

“I don’t doubt that,” he smiled. “Goodnight, Harry."

"Goodnight, Cas. Thanks for checking on me," she replied. He smiled and jumped off the wing, then headed off into the trees. Harriet found herself smiling again as she watched him leave. She'd felt torn apart by everything that was happening around her, but one conversation had made it all OK. An idea popped into her head, and she went into the cockpit and pulled the headrest off the seat. She sat it on the wing, zipped her flying jacket up around her neck, then laid down and stared at the watch for a while, smiling as she did, then looked into the moon until slowly her eyes closed.

When Harriet woke the next morning, she was surrounded by a low violet tinged mist which hid the ground. The sky was still dark, with just the slightest hint of silver which illuminated the fog. It was beautiful, and as she woke, she felt like she was in another world, a peaceful world, somewhere away from the war. She thought of the conversations she’d had with AP and Cas, and how safe she'd felt as she'd talked, and how for the first time since it had all kicked off, she started to think that maybe she should be much more careful, maybe getting home was important after all. She smiled to herself as she climbed from the Gladiator and walked through the wet grass towards the woods and the squadron HQ. The sentries gave her a cheery ‘good morning’, as did Chef, uncharacteristically, as she took some tea and biscuits in the Mess tent, joining Kiwi who was already awake.

"Morning," he said casually. "You wide awake too?"

"Yeah..."

"Seriously, is there anything as uncomfortable as those camp beds?"

"Didn't sleep?"

"Nah... Probably all the excitement from yesterday. You look relaxed enough, how do you do it?"

"Do what?"

"Sleep so well after going through a fight? You were up a couple of times yesterday, one of them you were outnumbered maybe twelve to one. The others were talking about it. Yet you still knocked a couple down and went up again, and flew through a storm, and still, you look like you slept like a bloody baby."

"I was told that after the body's gone through a traumatic experience, it just wants to sleep, so I let it..." Harriet shrugged.

"Fair enough... Mind if I ask you something else?"

"Sure"

"How the hell am I supposed to shoot the bastards down?"

"What?" Harriet asked with a laugh.

"I got one yesterday, but that was pure luck. The fellas said you've got twelve and you're the best shot in the squadron, so I wondered if you could tell me what the hell I'm doing wrong?" Harriet giggled again, partly of embarrassment and partly at the sincere irritation and confusion on his face as he asked. "What? It isn't that much of a bloody silly question, is it?"

"No... No, I'm sorry, it isn't. You just look so... Angry about it."

"Angry? I'm bloody furious. I emptied my guns and got one, just."

"Better than them getting you..."

"Yeah, I reckon. I just want to pull my weight on the squadron, you know?"

"I know... Look, I don't know if I'm doing it right, I just know I've got lucky so far."

"Whatever you've got, I'll try it…"

"Get close," she said, and he leant over the table and listened intently. "Not to me, you idiot, to them!" He blushed as he adjusted himself in his seat. "Get close enough for them to fill your windscreen, then let them have it."

"Get close, that's it?"

"Well you can't miss them that way, can you?"

"I suppose not..."

"Oh, and try to hit the fighters from above or below. The front is dangerous, and the back has too narrow a profile."

"OK... Well, I can only try."

"Just make sure you don't fly straight and level for more than a few seconds, and always keep looking around. Try to find something smooth like a silk scarf or something, it's easier on your neck than your shirt and tie when you're looking around."

Over the next thirty minutes, the rest of the pilots joined them. They had eggs and bacon with mugs of tea, then sat through their pre flight briefing. Dawn patrol and take off at first light. It was Harriet's first experience of taking off in the ground fog. It was beautiful. She was mesmerised by the glow as the sun's rays electrified the fog and lit up the landscape. They climbed high, and the girls climbed even higher, keeping their usual station above the squadron and keeping them safe from predators.

"Black one to Goose Leader. Bombers at twelve o'clock!" Nicole called out. "Angels twenty." Harriet scoured the sky and finally picked out the swarm of tiny black dots heading towards the town in the distance.

"Received, Black One. Goose Squadron, form pairs line abreast on my mark. Three, two, one, mark." Harriet watched as the squadron fanned out into a loose line of pairs either side of Singh. "OK, Goose Squadron, we're going to hit them head on. Work in your pairs and watch your tails. Black Section, watch for the fighter cover. Tally ho!" The squadron closed quickly on the German bombers. They were long, slender, twin engine Junkers 88s, ten of them in all. They held their course despite not being able to miss the sight of the closing Hurricanes, and white streaks of tracer leapt out from the noses of the bombers as their gunners opened fire. It went unreturned by the Hurricanes until they were close, then all hell broke loose. Immediately the bombers broke formation. A couple went down with Hurricanes following them, the others weaved and turned as they tried desperately to stop a Hurricane from getting on their tail. Harriet strained her eyes, searching for the fighter cover, then there it was. Six twin engine 110s flying in pairs and diving out of the sky, heading for the battle below.

"Fighters, fighters, fighters," Harriet yelled. "Diving on you now."

"Watch out for fighters, everyone," Singh called.

"Black Section, Tally ho!" Harriet yelled, then dropped her left wing and flipped over into a dive, lining her sights with the last 110 of the six. "I've got the one closest to us, at the back," she called.

"OK, got it," Nicole replied. "I'll go for his friend next to him."

Harriet aimed as she pushed the throttle forward and dived hard. The rear gunner saw her, and a swirl of white tracer reached up like long ghostly fingers to grab at her. At first, they were in a wide arc, but somehow quickly tightened into a narrow cone which spun around the fuselage of her Hurricane and missed everything. She pulled left as the carburettor failed once again and the engine cut, instantly slowing her dive, and the left engine and cockpit of the 110 filled her windscreen. She pushed the fire button and watched as the engine spluttered and coughed out smoke and fire. As she rolled and kicked the rudder bar while correcting her spin, she saw the 110s left wing snap right off, sending the fuselage into a slow yawing spin. Nicole's had already pulled out of his dive before she could fire, but in doing so kindly showed her his long flat profile, which she courteously filled with bullets that passed straight through the cockpit and killed the crew outright. The rest of the Hurricanes joined the fight, and the sky was a mess of aeroplanes, all fighting to get into position or get away. More Germans went down, and one by one the others sped towards the deck and ran, followed by the Hurricanes as they gave chase, nudging in front of each other to get a shot until one German after another crashed into the ground. It was a total slaughter. As Harriet and Nicole came back together and climbed, an image of horror met Harriet's eyes. The rising sun was filled with black specks. A wave of twenty fighters or more 109s were speeding west. It had been a trap. Most of the squadron would be low on ammunition after taking on the first wave, and now they were charging headfirst at enemy fighters who were coming out of the sun at a low level.

"Goose Squadron! Bandits twenty plus, twelve o'clock. Closing fast." Harriet called. "Break now. Break, break, break!"

"Goose Squadron, break and home, watch for bandits, stay low," Singh echoed, and immediately the squadron split and wheeled away, all except one which was sticking on a smoking 110, still firing. Harriet watched as she banked into a tight turn as the Hurricane closed and knocked the 110 down into the fog, where it lit up with a fiery orange explosion. The Hurricane pulled up and banked, as it did a 109 fired from a distance and the Hurricane immediately started spewing white smoke as it climbed in a fast spiral. Flames flickered briefly. The sky quickly filled with orange balls of fire, flak, French flak this time, they'd watched the battle and held their fire until the Hurricanes were clear, and now they were putting up a wall of fire to keep the 109s from pursuing, at least temporarily. They curved back and climbed while taking a wider sweep to avoid the town. Harriet watched as the damaged Hurricane dropped into the fog. It didn't come back out of it. The girls hit full throttle and followed the squadron home, keeping overwatch while they landed, then coming in themselves. Harriet breathed a sigh of relief as she touched down and taxied to her pen, where she cut the engine and put her sweat soaked helmet on the mirror once again. AP smiled as she looked down at her and unfastened her harness.

"You brought it back in one piece for once, that's an improvement," she said. Harriet smiled as she took AP's hand and stood on her seat. "Are you OK?"

"Yes... I think. It was a trap. They led us in with some bombers, and then as we engaged and emptied our ammunition, they launched a wave of fighters at us. Somebody went down. I don't know who it was."

"At least you're OK."

"Yeah..." She climbed out of the cockpit and ran down the wing to meet with Nicole. "Are you OK?"

"Yes... I didn't like that fight. It's like they were waiting for us." Nicole said nervously.

"Well done spotting those fighters," Singh said as the pilots grouped. "Anyone missing?"

"Murphy, Sir," Dolph replied.

"Did anyone see what happened?"

"A 109 got him" Harriet reported. "It didn't look like he heard your order to break, so kept chasing the 110. He got it, but he stayed too long. I saw him go down this side of the town."

"OK... is everyone's radio working?" Everyone nodded and reported positive. "Good. We need to be awake up there. The Germans obviously set a trap for us, and we almost fell for it. Unfortunately, we have to go straight back up, but this time we'll fly higher and hold our attack until we know their game." As he finished talking the thud of artillery sounded. He looked up in the direction of the explosions. "Scramble!" he shouted. "Get one up!" Everyone sprinted to their aeroplanes. AP saw Harriet running at full speed and quickly slipped into the cockpit and started the engine, then stepped out as she stepped in and fastened her harness.

"We've only been able to reload two guns," Lanky shouted.

"I'll go with what I've got, fasten up and get clear!"

"Be careful! Climb fast and turn into them, if you put your back to them, they'll knock you down, and remember you've got hardly any ammunition, make it count."

"Get out of here, hide somewhere safe!" Harriet replied, then quickly hit the throttle and pulled onto the grass strip. There wasn't time to taxi, so she straightened up and fully opened the throttle. Soon she was bouncing down the grass strip ahead of the others, and then the bump that lifted her came. She raised her undercarriage and instantly started a turn east to face whatever was coming, which happened to be a Messerschmitt 109 with its guns blazing. Cannon shells ripped through her starboard wing as her enemy charged her without flinching. A sustained blast let loose as she held the gun button down and listened to the fierce ripping sound that signalled her guns were responding as they should. Long white streaks of tracer reached forward to the 109's cockpit, making it sparkle with golden sparks as bullets ricocheted around the inside of the airframe. The side window sprayed with blood, and the pilot slumped and pushed the nose down, as Harriet pulled up to narrowly avoid a collision. Harriet pulled hard on her stick and climbed steeply while the 109 dived into the ground. She twisted and turned as more 109s dived and curved to attack the hapless Hurricanes. The last off the ground was Singh, she could see him spinning his head as his wheels lifted, but a 109 was already closing on him, speeding below treetop height and probably unseen. Harriet pushed her stick hard left and pulled into a dive. She had no time to get into position behind the German, and she was only going to have one shot. She slipped her rudder and pulled her nose left, closed one eye and lined her sights then opened fire and emptied her guns some distance ahead of the 109, which flew straight into the bullets and immediately pulled up with thick black smoke spluttering from his engine. Harriet continued down and waved at Singh as she shot past him. The eastern sky erupted with fire as the brigade anti aircraft battery intercepted a high flying German bomber formation heading east. Sergeant Oliver's soldiers were also engaging the fighters with machine guns, having been caught as much by surprise as everyone else. Their heavy machine guns converged on one as it flew a low pass machine gunning the Headquarters; it spiralled out of control, pulling up first before losing all height and looping into the ground. Harriet watched as the squadron got itself together and turned the battle on the remaining four 109s, which soon became three, and then two. Leaving the remaining two speeding at full throttle in the direction of home, pursued by a pair of Hurricanes.

"Does anyone have ammunition left?" Singh asked over the radio.

"I think so," Archie replied.

"A bit, I reckon," Kiwi added.

"OK, you two form on me, let's see if we can have a go at those bombers. Everyone else, pancake, refuel and rearm."

Harriet looked around to make sure things were clear, then pulled back on the throttle to scrub off some speed as she circuited the area and came in for a bumpy landing. Her hands shook with adrenaline as she taxied into position and was quickly pushed to her pen where ground crews were waiting with ammunition, while one of the fuel bowsers arrived to top up the tanks.

"Are you OK?" AP asked as she reached into the cockpit. Harriet held her hand and squeezed lightly while nodding and smiling.

"Yes... It's OK. I'll stay fastened in case they come back."

"Are you sure?" Harriet nodded again, and AP smiled and held her hand, feeling it shaking and doing what she could to calm her.

"Is everyone OK down here?" Harriet asked after steadying her breathing.

"I don't know... They got the second fuel bowser and the crew, and shot up some of the other vehicles."

"I'm sorry... I couldn't get up any quicker."

"Don't you dare be sorry, you got up as fast as possible and flew like an absolute demon. You did incredibly well, given the circumstances."

"I'm sorry all the same."

"Thank you." AP was handed a tin cup of water by one of the mechanics, which she passed to Harriet who drank it gladly. Two other Hurricanes landed as she waited, Nicole and Dolph. Harriet sent AP with word for them to stay in their seats until refuelled and rearmed, which they did. Grumpy arrived back after his chase, and after what felt like an entire day, Singh and his flight returned too. As soon as they'd refuelled and rearmed, the squadron was in the air again flying another patrol.

There were no Germans on this occasion, just a black smudge stretching into the sky from the many fires in the French held town below. The squadron arrived at what appeared to be a lull in the action, though the German anti aircraft guns had moved much closer to the town and made sure the Hurricanes kept a distance with a curtain of flak. Singh led his flight on a quick strafing run designed as much to buoy up the French defenders as it was to irritate the Germans, both of which were achieved. After a few passes, Singh took the squadron up high and circled a while. As soon as they were sure that the Germans weren't sending anyone to intercept, he ordered them home, where they were refuelled while the pilots ate sandwiches and drank tea in the tent that had been set up in the trees at the end of the runway. The afternoon patrol was much of the same. A terrific anti aircraft barrage kept the Hurricanes a little further from the town this time, which was now under a renewed full on attack from German assault troops. A small convoy had been spotted on the road west, and a low level pass by Grumpy and Dolph confirmed it to be French trucks and guns escaping the onslaught. Before returning for more fuel the squadron spotted a scattering of 110s flying very high above the battle, but they didn't come down, and as Singh suspected they'd be hanging around to protect a bombing attack on the town the squadron stayed low. Nothing came of it, though, and both sides eventually retired. The thunder of artillery in the late afternoon started the next patrol, and the squadron went up to intercept a German reconnaissance aeroplane, which Singh knocked down quickly before another patrol towards the town showed German tanks working around to the rear of the French defences. There wasn't much the squadron could do. Another handful of strafing runs while dodging flak was the best they could offer, leaving the pilots frustrated and the French on their own. The squadron returned and touched down to eat and drink before preparing for the evening patrols. As they entered the HQ area, which they now lovingly called tent town, they saw a long line of French trucks out on the track. Cas greeted them with a young French officer in tow.

"Any luck?" Cas asked, and Singh shook his head in disappointment. "Oh well, at least one of us has some good news. This is Captain Reynard of the French anti aircraft artillery; he's come to join us."

"Captain," Singh shook the Frenchman's hand. "How can we help?"

"I think we are the ones who can help, Squadron Leader," he replied with a small smile. "My General sent us to defend your airfield."

"That's very kind of him."

"Yes... He's with what remains of our division in the town you've been flying over. He dispatched us this afternoon as he believes we'll be more help here. Your Brigadier agrees, which is why we're with you now."

"I'm certainly happy to see you, Captain, we could use a little protection. We had some nasty visitors this morning who almost caught us on the ground."

"We'll station ourselves around your position, and we'll do our best for you."

"I don't doubt it, Captain. Thank you again. Please tell your men they're welcome here if they need supplies." The Captain nodded politely. "Strange your General should release you from the fight at such a critical time?"

"Not really... The town is finished," Reynard replied with a forlorn hopelessness. "He will hold it as long as he can, maybe until the morning. If we'd stayed, we'd have been overrun with the rest. At least this way we can fight a little longer, and the General was very grateful to the Hurricanes who helped us before the storm. Stopping the air raid allowed us to evacuate our wounded and many civilians under cover of the storm, so it's the least we can do to be here."

"It's been our pleasure, Captain. Get your men in place, and I'll have Chef make food and tea." The Captain gave a short and smart bow then left.

Chapter 14

Relentless

It had been a long night. Harriet had passed out on her cot shortly after eating, absolutely exhausted from the day's almost continuous patrols. She and Nicole had been stood down while the rest of the squadron made one last sweep towards the town at sunset, to give what remained of the French division a helping hand against the last light assault that the Germans had launched. The squadron broke up yet another bombing raid, knocking down two Stukas and a 110, then finished off their ammunition by strafing the advancing ground troops before heading home and landing just as darkness was enveloping the airfield. It was a relief to everyone that they hadn't lost any more aeroplanes, though they'd arguably lost something more valuable. Singh had been shot up by a pair of 109s, and while his Hurricane was still just about airworthy, he wasn't. A German cannon shell had ripped through his cockpit and shattered his instrument panel, sending slivers of metal and glass into his thigh. He could walk, just about, but flying was out of the question for the time being, and despite his protests Simon had him transported right away to the brigade casualty clearing station. Both Harriet and Nicole had slept through the lot, and Nicole continued to sleep when Harriet was shaken awake by the sound of artillery, and the constant rumble of bombs. Having pulled on her flying boots and jacket, she wandered down to the airstrip where she found AP and the mechanics working diligently on the Hurricanes, and making sure they were in the best condition they could be for the following morning. Harriet helped with her own Hurricane the best she could, and when she'd finished, she sat with AP and Lanky on the wing and watched as the distant skyline burned in the blackness of night. It was the depot, or so they assumed. It was that direction, anyway, and they couldn't think of much else that would burn as hard or bright. It was while they were talking that AP told Harriet about Singh. Everyone was low about it as Singh was a much respected leader, and an experienced combat pilot, something they were running short of. Fortunately, they still had Cas, who as the senior officer in the squadron was now in command, for the time being anyway. A low fog rolled across the fields as the skies lightened, there weren't many clouds to be seen in the deep purple and gold sky which suggested it was going to be good day, a clear day, and the type of day that would see the squadron in the air at least as much as the previous day. AP and Harriet arrived in the Mess tent just as the other pilots were arriving in a half comatose state to help themselves to a mug of tea. Cas entered the tent as they ate breakfast in relative silence, ready to give his first morning brief as Commanding Officer.

"Ladies, gentlemen..." he said firmly, demanding attention as representatives from the army and French air defence unit arrived, along with the rest of the squadron senior ranks. "As most probably know by now, Squadron Leader Singh was wounded in our last patrol yesterday; and after assessment by the squadron medical officer, he was evacuated to the brigade casualty clearing station for surgery. Headquarters are aware, and they've asked me to look after the squadron until a new commanding officer can be assigned."

"Is there any word on how he is?" Archie asked.

"I'm reliably informed that the surgery to remove the shrapnel was successful; and that Mister Singh is currently sleeping it off..." Cas replied with a slight smile. "While we're on the subject of pilots, I'd like to welcome Mister Murphy back." He nodded, and the assembled group looked at Murph, who was looking a little blackened and wide eyed, but happy.

"Thank you, Sir," Murph replied a little sheepishly.

"Good job on getting your aeroplane down in one piece, despite the damage," Cas continued. "We need you both." Murph smiled while Archie ruffled his hair playfully and a few of the others cheered. "OK, that's enough of that," Cas calmed them, before continuing with his brief. "As you'll all have heard during the night, the Germans have been at the depot and railhead with their bombers under cover of darkness. Brigade Headquarters haven't confirmed details as yet, but their hitting those targets would suggest that the main German force in this area has broken through the French lines and is heading our way. As such, our aeroplanes will be flying similar patrols to yesterday, and our orders remain unchanged in instructing us to protect the town and railhead from German bombers; and assist the local army units by conducting ground attack missions as and when possible. Does anyone have any questions?"

"What time are we up?" Archie asked.

"Fifteen minutes... I want the squadron up and patrolling a line from the French held front to the depot before first light. You'll lead the patrol, Archie. No unnecessary risks, but the bombers must be engaged as a priority, understand?"

"Sir..."

"OK, that's about everything for now. The weather is expected to be clear, and we'll have breakfast waiting for you after the patrol."

"Come on, then," Archie said as he stood.

"Not you two," Cas said to Harriet and Nicole as the pilots started muttering as they stood and made their way to the tent door. Nicole rolled her eyes, and the pair of them wandered over to him as he waved his finger to summon them.

"Why not us two?" Nicole demanded.

"Because I want the two of you up right away to watch over the airfield."

"Oh..." Nicole replied.

"You're so tetchy," Harriet said to her with a smirk.

"Tetchy? What?"

"Tetchy... Short fused, irritable..."

"You're one to talk."

"I think that's enough," Cas said, stopping the bickering before it could take hold. "Get up high and watch for raiders. If the squadron is going to do its job properly, we need to get the Hurricanes in and out of the airfield to rearm and refuel without being harassed by Jerry." The girls nodded in acceptance of the task ahead of them. "Unless you're having difficulties, I want you to stay up until the squadron are all safely down, then come in yourselves. Understood?" They nodded again. "Harry, you'll lead."

"Always her," Nicole said with a roll of the eyes.

"Maybe you, when you learn to temper that aggression and focus it," Cas said with a wink and a smile. Nicole shrugged and let out a groan, something she did very well when she could see sense in what she was being told but didn't want to agree with it overtly. "Perhaps we'll let Harry do the leading so that you can focus your energy on the fighting?" he suggested warmly, giving Nicole the dignified exit he knew she needed.

"It makes sense to use our skills. After all, I am the better fighter," Nicole said while raising her nose in the air slightly. It was Harriet's turn to roll her eyes.

"Well, off you go. The squadron will be wheels up in just over ten minutes. If you're to be in a position to cover them, you'll need to be up in five."

"Come on, leader," Nicole said as she turned and walked. Harriet and Cas held a smile for a moment. She'd grown since their conversation, and she felt taller and more confident knowing she was respected. "Or should I go on my own?" Nicole added impatiently from the tent door. "Not that it would be a bad thing to go by myself, I could put all of my efforts into shooting down Germans instead of looking after you."

"See you soon..." Harriet said to Cas with a smile.

"Yes..." he replied as she turned and left. "Be careful! Both of you!" he bellowed after giving his head a shake. Harriet ran to catch up with Nicole, and the two of them walked quickly through the darkness towards the Hurricanes.

"You and he are friends again," Nicole said.

"We were always friends," Harriet replied.

"Until he told you off, you didn't like that."

"He was right to tell me off..."

"What?"

"You heard, and you know what I mean. He has responsibilities, and so do we these days. We're not girls anymore. We're fighter pilots. We have duties and people depend on us to do them properly."

"You've changed."

"You haven't."

"I think maybe you like the old man."

"What?"

"You like him."

"He's nice to us, and he's looked after us both since we arrived."

"I know... And you know that's not what I mean."

"I don't know what you're talking about."

"Oh, but you do, my little English friend. You do."

"Shut up."

"Ah... If it weren't so dark, I'd think you were blushing a little."

"Can't we just be nice?"

"I'm always nice," Nicole said nonchalantly as they arrived at Harriet's Hurricane, where AP was waiting for her.

"Well get your nice self into your cockpit, and let's get up there."

"Yes, Ma'am," Nicole giggled as she walked off to find her crew.

"Ready?" AP asked.

"Yes, I think so."

"Good. The aeroplane is OK and ready to go, and we modified the carburettor last night so it should stop the engine cutting in a dive; if we've got it right."

"I'm sure it'll be fine," Harriet smiled as they climbed on the wing and into the cockpit, where AP helped strap her in before the engine was started and jets of gold and blue flames shot out of the Merlin exhausts, lighting up the dawn darkness and making AP's face glow as she looked down into the cockpit. Harriet quickly ran through her checks and gave AP a thumbs up, which was returned with a smile.

"Bring my aeroplane back in one piece!" AP shouted with a smile. Harriet shrugged and winked at AP, who jumped from the wing, leaving Harriet to taxi out into position. One last power check and she released the brakes. There was just enough silver dawn light for her to make out the edges of the grass track and see her runway stretch ahead to the horizon, and it was all she needed. The Hurricane bounced, and the silhouettes of bodies and aeroplanes swept past as she gathered speed before feeling the familiar dip in her stomach as she pulled back on the stick and climbed into the sky. She lifted her wheels and flew a circuit while watching Nicole take off, then after forming their pair they did another circuit before starting a steep, wide, and winding climb, keeping the airfield at the tip of the right wing as they circled and climbed. Harriet scanned the horizon as well as keeping her eyes on the airfield and Nicole, checking for Germans and anything else that could cause them a problem. It got colder as they climbed, and she pulled the sheepskin collar of her flying jacket tight around her neck and face. Harriet was freezing when she levelled out at twenty thousand feet and entered a wide circuit. The cold was welcome, though, it kept her awake and sharp as she tried to stop herself focusing too much on the purple and blue light in the east, which was slowly expanding upwards and mixing with the silver and gold colours that followed. It was going to be a beautiful sunrise, and she felt blessed to be able to watch it from such a vantage point. The squadron took off below them, all safely, and were able to form up before climbing to the west, in the direction of the burning depot which Harriet had been watching as they climbed, it seemed like the whole town was glowing red in the blackness of the predawn sky. She tried not to think about it too much. Instead, she focused on the east, looking for the black dots of approaching German fighters. The squadron disappeared into the darkness, only occasionally showing itself in the red glow before slipping back into blackness as they climbed. As the sun finally breached the eastern horizon, a wave of light slowly expanded westward and chased the darkness in a long seamless line. It looked like a heavy blanket was being pulled off the world to show the countryside below; and racing along its leading edge were a gathering of black dots, only distinguishable by the diamond shape they were arranged in. Harriet counted twenty four dots in total, eight in the lower diamond and sixteen above; it was a bomber force covered by fighters, and they were heading straight for the airfield.

"Black Section to Goose Leader. Enemy bombers and fighters, twenty plus. Ten miles out at angels one zero."

"Roger, Black Section, hold position and watch for their little friends," Archie replied. Harriet and Nicole continued their circuits, all the time keeping their eyes fixed on the Germans, who kept rigid in their approach. The few minutes they watched seemed like a lifetime, and the Germans seemed to be flying faster than light. Harriet became more and more nervous that the squadron wouldn't intercept them, then as she tipped her wing ready to dive down and do the job herself, she saw the row of Hurricanes pass about five thousand feet under them, charging towards the Germans. As they came level they tipped, flipped, and dived in line astern, Archie leading them down into the fighters below and ripping into them, catching them napping and immediately splintering the fighter cover and sending the 110s in every direction as the Hurricanes chased. "OK Black Section, if things are clear up there you can come down and see if you can break up the bombers. Watch for the rear gunners," he ordered.

"Roger, Goose Leader," Harriet replied. She had a quick scan of the horizon to make sure no other fighters were watching them, and once satisfied, she gave Nicole the nod. "Black Section coming down!" She flipped her Hurricane on its back and pulled into a steep dive in the direction of the bombers. Nicole followed, and they screamed down together. It took all of Harriet's strength to keep the Hurricane under control as the full airframe started to shake, and she breathed a sigh of relief that AP's adaptation had held and the engine hadn't spluttered. She closed one eye and lined up the sight a few fingers in front of the nose of the leading bomber, and pushed the fire button. A long stream of white tracer reached out and converged on the cockpit. Immediately the nose slumped forward, and the bomber headed down in a steep dive, leaving a pair of dark dots to slip out of the hatch and into their parachutes, which filled and hung in the cool morning air. Nicole hit the next bomber in the engine, making it smoke immediately and forcing it to pitch to the right, sending the bombers behind it in all directions as they fought to avoid colliding with it. Nicole followed it as it turned east and dropped to the deck in a bid to escape, while Harriet looped to her left and scrubbed off some of her diving speed, then turned again and came back around to the right to sight her guns on the side of the nearest bomber. She fired as she got so close her windscreen was full of nothing but wing. Its engine spewed white smoke, and her bullets rattled along the airframe. She pulled up and over the bomber as tracer flew at her from every direction. She needed no more encouragement to flip upside down and pull into another dive below the bombers so their gunners couldn't get her in their sights. She pulled up and hit the next bomber all along the belly before turning hard right and diving to the ground, followed by trails of tracer from the five bombers which were still pressing towards the airfield. As she weaved and swung to avoid the gunner's fire, she felt sweat dripping down her neck. Minutes earlier she'd been shivering at twenty thousand feet, and now she was heading for the treetops and sweating buckets. She started to bank around and climb, ready to go at the bombers again, but as she did, she realised the sky around the bombers was filling with small black clouds.

"Get out of there, Black Section," Archie barked. "Back up on station, and we'll chase." Harriet pulled up hard and climbed with full power, to her right and below she saw Nicole at ground level circling a crashed bomber. On receipt of Archie's order, she waggled her wings and climbed to join Harriet high above the field of battle. Harriet smirked a little as she saw the bombers battered by the French anti aircraft fire. Two were knocked down in quick succession, and the rest turned, dropped, and ran for home; only to be met by Archie and the rest of the squadron, who between them knocked another two down, leaving the last to limp into the east with the remaining fighters. The raid had been broken. The squadron returned and landed with all present and accounted for. Once Archie had touched down, he called the girls down too, and they quickly circled and descended, Nicole first and Harriet following, bouncing along the grass strip to where AP was waiting. She was pushed rapidly into her bay by the waiting crew, who instantly went about refuelling and rearming. AP greeted her with a smile and gave her a hand climbing out of the cockpit.

"Good flying..." AP said with a smirk.

"You saw?"

"I saw... We all did. You scared the life out of those bombers."

"I couldn't have done it without you."

"Me?"

"Yes, you. You worked all night to modify the carburettor on our Hurricanes so that I could dive like that; so that one was for you."

"Thank you..." AP said with a slight blush, not sure what to do with herself for once. "Anyway, better get to Cas. He wants to see us all again." They both jumped from the wing, Harriet threw her parachute over the tip and unzipped her jacket while getting ready to join Nicole and the rest of the pilots, who were waiting for her while the ground crews busied themselves frantically.

"Do you know what he wants?" Harriet asked AP.

"No... Some army types turned up to talk with him while you were busy upstairs. When they left, he ordered us to get the aeroplanes ready to go right away as soon as you were down, so we'd better get a move on." She smiled, and they walked over to join the others, who were all in high spirits, having had a great success for no losses. Nobody had even been shot up particularly badly. There were a few extra holes in airframes but nothing serious, not compared to the Germans who had clearly been spooked when the squadron took them by surprise, and then by the anti aircraft guns. The consensus was that the Germans must have felt they'd walked into a trap, hence their turning tail and running without much of a fight. Especially the fighters, who'd left the bombers to their fate almost immediately.

"Any time today," Cas shouted from the Mess tent as the pilots walked into the woods. There was a buzz of activity around the camp, and airmen seemed to be running in every direction carrying heavy loads and looking generally busy.

"Bit of a flap on is there, skipper?" Archie asked casually.

"You'll find out if you ever get yourselves into the tent," came Cas' cutting reply. The pilots filed in and joined the other squadron officers and seniors, Sergeant Oliver, and the French anti aircraft Captain. The pilots grabbed a mug of tea each as they entered the tent, and bread and cheese was handed to them by one of the cooks. Cas made his way to the front after making sure everyone had their breakfast, then quietened the murmuring gossip with a clearing of his throat. "If I can have your attention..." The group stared at him in silence. Harriet felt a sickening knot in her stomach as she looked at him, something wasn't right, his eyes were full of unhappiness. Was it Singh? Had he died after the surgery? Her guessing was soon stopped in its tracks. "Unfortunately, as many of you may already have worked out, the supply depot to our rear was walloped by German bombers last night, to the extent that command deems most of the supplies stored there as lost. The army is working as we speak to recover whatever's left, but by all accounts, the bombing was pretty devastating." Most nodded in reluctant acceptance of what they'd already thought to be true. "Now, the smarter of you will have already worked out that this is going to have a significant impact on the fuel and ammunition we'd been promised! Not to mention the food, spares, and other stores essential to our continuing battle, but that concern has been superseded by something much worse." Harriet felt her throat dry and had to sip at her tea, something which seemed to make the most furious noise in the now absolutely silent tent. "Through the night a German armoured division swung around our southern flank and is currently engaging the defences at Calais, all but cutting us off out here in the south eastern corner of the defences. There's a thin corridor from here to the rail depot, and for now, the trains are still able to get through in the direction of Dunkirk. However, as hard as they're fighting, the French army can't guarantee how long this will remain the case. The Germans are sending thousands of troops along the path cut by their armoured division, which is soon likely to swing north and cut us off entirely, along with the army types down the road. Once that happens, we'll effectively be in the bag, if we're lucky..."

"Bloody hell," Archie muttered.

"I think that pretty much sums it up, Archie," Cas said with a forced smile. "Anyway, the silver lining is that the Air Ministry has decided in their wisdom that Spitfires flying from bases in Kent are going to cover the withdrawal, and our squadron has been ordered back to England." An excited murmuring filled the tent for a moment. "The majority of the squadron will be evacuating to the rail depot in the next hour, along with much of the army brigade; where a troop train will take them all as far as Dunkirk, and they can jump on a ship back to England. However, before our aeroplanes can head back, we're ordered to fly cover for the trains and give everyone a sporting chance of getting away."

"How long for?" Archie asked

"Until the last train is away. It's scheduled to leave this afternoon, so we'll probably have four or five hours of work ahead of us before we scarper across the Channel."

"I'm assuming there's a plan for fuel and ammunition?" Archie continued. "I know we're particularly low on bullets, and maybe have enough for one good scrap?"

"There is... A small team have volunteered to stay behind to refuel and rearm; and do basic repairs to patch us up and keep us flying, under the protection of Sergeant Oliver and his men. The French anti aircraft gunners are also going to stay behind and cover us from air attacks." The pilots looked around a little nervously. "Once we're done with the trains, assuming this location hasn't been overrun, we'll refuel and rearm, and then we're to fly to Dunkirk and conduct a sunset patrol over the perimeter, and keep the bombers away from the beaches, and more crucially away from the navy, before we head to England." Another mutter went around the gathered pilots and officers, some whispering about heading home, but most asking who'd volunteered to stay behind. "As for the ammunition situation," Cas continued, silencing everyone again. "Our army friends have promised to have a delivery here most urgently."

"What about the rear party?" Archie asked.

"They'll make a run for it as soon as we're clear..." Everyone felt uncomfortable at those words. Not least Cas.

“It’s OK, we’ll get them out,” Sergeant Oliver said confidently, his moustache still looking pristine despite all they’d been through.

“Thank you, Sergeant, and good luck,” Cas said with a warm smile. "Well, that's it. Finish your breakfast, and I suggest you get as much as you can, as I can't guarantee when you'll next eat something. Then you can pack your kit and stand by your aeroplanes. I'll let you know when we're ready to fly."

"We?" Archie asked.

"Yes..." Cas replied. "I'll be taking Mister Singh's Hurricane. The way things seem to be going, I'm assuming we're going to need every aeroplane we've got when we get back to England. Now, if there are no other questions, I suggest you get packing. Only take what's essential, there'll be no space for baggage on the train, so you'll need to take your personal items with you in your aeroplanes. The rear party will burn everything else." He looked around the tent, taking a moment to look each of them in the eyes. "OK, let's get on with it." The pilots burst into conversation, mostly about how bad things had got for them to be evacuated back to England. "Come with me, you two," Cas said to the girls as he left, waving his finger in the air behind him. Harriet and Nicole looked at each other, then followed him out of the tent. He lit a cigarette as he walked a safe distance into the trees then turned to face them. "How are you both?" he asked warmly.

"Archie called us down to attack the bombers," Harriet replied. She’d been nervous and worried they were in trouble for something, again.

"What?" Cas asked with a frown. "Oh, that. Yes, and you both did very well. Damned good flying."

"You're welcome," Nicole said dismissively, while Harriet frowned right back at him, not sure where to go next.

"Look, I wanted to talk to you both about what I said in there, about us evacuating."

"Yes?" Harriet replied.

"It's likely to be dangerous, very dangerous, in fact. Patrolling the rail depot is one thing, but patrolling Dunkirk is quite another..."

"I'm not sure where you're going with this," Harriet said.

"The Germans are throwing everything they've got at the coast, the intelligence officer confirmed as much when I spoke to him earlier, and we'll be heading into it to plug a gap until darkness gives the ships and beaches a little more cover, it could get messy."

"We've been in worse," Nicole replied.

"No, no, you haven't," Cas replied. "We'll be heading into an area of concentrated military activity, which is quite different to intercepting small scale local patrols and raids. It's the front line."

"So, what should we do?" Harriet asked.

"Let me send you to England now," he replied, almost nervously.

"No," they replied in unison.

"Look, you've both done something incredible here with the squadron, but I really think it's time you got yourselves home."

"To what?" Nicole asked

"Excuse me?"

"Home to what?"

"I..."

"Our home is that way!" She pointed to the northeast. "Our families were there, our friends, our school, everyone and everything we know was overrun by the Germans minutes after we arrived in your squadron. We are at home."

"I'm sorry... I didn't mean to offend, quite the opposite in fact," Cas said with a pained smile. "I respect you both immensely, we all do, and I simply wanted to offer you the opportunity to get to England. Something I can't guarantee if you fly the Dunkirk patrol, and frankly I rather like you both and think you've earned the right to stay alive a little longer. The RAF is going to need people like you in whatever comes next, as will the entire country."

"Do we have a choice?" Harriet asked.

"You're commissioned officers in the Royal Air Force Volunteer Reserve, and I could order you both to England..."

"If we're officers in the RAF then surely our place is with our squadron?"

"Surely, you're right..." he replied after a few moments with a smile of resignation. "I'm afraid there won't be any unnecessary combat," he continued, referring to his previous demands that the girls stayed out of trouble. "I expect our sweep over Dunkirk to be difficult, to say the least, so remember what I've taught you! Once the shooting starts, you're never to fly straight and level for more than five seconds. Use your mirrors, and use the clouds; not just to hide, but to change direction and make yourself an unpredictable nuisance of a target, or make a menace of yourself if you get the opportunity. As soon as you're out of ammunition, you head west to England." Both girls nodded. "You've seen the maps, and you know where you're heading, don't you?" They nodded again. "Good, then we'd better get ready to take off. Oh, and there's one other thing."

"Yes?" Harriet asked.

"If you're in trouble and can't get home, point your aeroplane out over the water and take to your parachute over our lines. Don't mess about, understood?" They nodded.

"You don't need to worry," Nicole said with a mischievous smile. "There isn't a German alive who can beat us."

"You know, I'm starting to believe that," Cas replied with a slight laugh. "I get so worried about sending you both up there to fight, that I sometimes forget how terrifyingly dangerous you both are to German aeroplanes, and maybe it's the Germans who mix with you I should worry for."

"Exactly!"

"Well, don't do anything silly and I'm sure your winning streak will continue. Right, let's go."

The three walked through the woods and joined the other pilots at the grass strip. As they did, an army ambulance bounced along the track towards them.

"Bloody hell, they're keen," Archie said as he looked at the ambulance. "You'd at least think they'd wait until we've been shot up before they come to us."

"Maybe they've heard about the young Kiwi's flying?" Grumpy added, making a rarely heard humorous quip; something quite unusual for the man who'd been nicknamed grumpy since arriving in the squadron as a Sergeant pilot.

"Maybe it's you they've come for, old boy," Archie said to Grumpy. "Seems you've found your sense of humour and the resident head shrinker has sent for you as he worries you've had a turn..."

The ambulance slowed to a halt, and the passenger door flew open. After a few moments, Singh extracted himself, back in uniform and leg heavily bandaged and strapped. He waved the driver off then limped over to the pilots.

"How is everyone?" he asked Cas

"Good, Sir... We're just about to commence patrols. I must say it's good to see you, how's the leg?"

"Better," Singh replied, lying blatantly. "The surgeon was able to remove most of the shrapnel, but it's going to take a few days until I can use it fully and get back to flying."

"I see... Begging your pardon, Sir, but shouldn't you be in bed resting your leg?"

"Don't be ridiculous. My place is with my squadron!" He let a rare smile spread across his face. "Don't worry, Cas, I'm not here to steal your moment, you'll still be leading the squadron in the air." Cas raised an eyebrow in response. "The army is currently packing up and heading west, the same direction as our squadron, so it made sense to come back and make myself useful with administrative duties, then travel back with Simon in his ambulance."

"Well, it's good to see you up and about so soon," Cas replied.

"Thank you... Now if I may, I'd like to say a few words to you all," the pilots quietened and looked at him. He cleared his throat as he looked around at the tired eyes watching him in anticipation, then started his speech. "It's been the single greatest honour of my life to command this squadron, and to fly with such a determined, committed and naturally talented group of pilots." He took a swig of water from the canteen handed to him by Cas. "We've lost many of our number since the hostilities started here in France. Many old faces and old friends have been posted missing, evacuated injured, or killed in combat, men who have left large flying boots to be filled, and while those men will forever be a part of our squadron's story and never be forgotten, it fills me with pride to know that their boots have been filled by some of the brightest and best pilots that the world has produced. Whether you're British, Irish, South African, Polish, New Zealander, French, or Norwegian; young or old, new or veteran, male or female. You've all fought bravely to do your duty, and in doing so, you've given this squadron the honour of being the most successful fighter squadron in France. Hold your heads high and be proud of all you've achieved here, and know that while we may have lost the battle, we've not yet lost the war. We'll go back to England, we'll re equip, we'll retrain, and we'll come back stronger than ever before. We cannot lose, you cannot lose, you are, quite simply, the best." Archie started an applause which was soon joined by the others.

"Three cheers for the skipper!" Archie called out and rapidly followed with a rowdy "hip, hip, hooray," three times before a humbled Singh waved his hand to quieten them.

"Today, you'll be led by the most decorated, talented, and skilled pilot in our squadron," Singh continued. "Flight Lieutenant Salisbury, VC." There were smiles and even polite applause at the news. "The squadron may have had several different commanding officers since we arrived in France, but it's always had the same leader in Cas. Do as you're told, and I'll see you in England. Now get to your aeroplanes!"

"Cas. Cas. Cas!" The pilots cheered as they hoisted Cas to their shoulders and carried him off to his aeroplane, then quickly dispersed to their own, each excited and full of vigour after Singh's rousing speech. Harriet grabbed her parachute from the wing of her Hurricane. The engine was already running, and Lanky was waiting to fasten her into her cockpit.

"Where's AP?" Harriet asked as she strapped in, a little disappointed that her friend wasn't there to say goodbye before heading home.

"I don't know," Lanky replied. "She went off somewhere with the Chief and a few of the Flight Sergeants."

"Oh..."

"I can tell her you said goodbye if you want?" Lanky offered, sensing Harriet's disappointment.

"Please do... Just let her know I'll be waiting for her in England."

"I will. Take care, Ma'am."

"You too, Lanky. Safe journey." Lanky jumped from the wing and Harriet went through her checks, then at Lanky's signal, she taxied out into the field, and waited while the rest of the squadron formed up ready for take off.

"Goose Leader to Goose Squadron," Cas said over the radio. "On my signal take off in pairs and climb to angels one five. Archie, you lead B Flight, I'll lead A. Black Section, climb to angels two zero and sit on overwatch. Keep us safe."

"Black Leader, understood," Harriet replied.

"OK, let's go," Cas said as he led the way, and the squadron followed until the girls were left with empty grass ahead of them. Harriet gave Nicole a nod, and they hit their throttles and bounced along the grass and up into the air, climbing quickly after the squadron. They took up their position and followed the squadron to the rail depot where they watched the long train being steadily loaded, then swept along to the south where they could see the French and Germans locked in battle around a wooded area. Cas kept the squadron high and out of the action, preferring to watch for German aeroplanes, which eventually turned up in the form of a pair of Junkers 88 twin engine dive bombers. Cas had the rest of the squadron watch for their escorts, then led A Flight down into a head on attack. He descended on the bombers at high speed, firing as he closed to spitting distance and killing the crew outright, before pulling hard on his stick and climbing straight up vertically. Meanwhile, the rest of his section scattered to get into position to take on the second bomber, unnecessarily it turned out as Kiwi had hit its cockpit and port engine. It was already coughing black smoke and banking hard left. The bank continued, and the bomber slowly rolled onto its back before heading down to the ground. Cas took his flight back up to the squadron, and they continued their patrol. More German aeroplanes passed far to the north, obviously heading elsewhere and travelling high and fast, making it difficult for the squadron to give effective chase; so instead Cas had them hold the line, before returning to the train station, passing the squadron on the way who waved from their trucks as the Hurricanes passed overhead.

"Skipper, nine o'clock," Archie said over the radio. "Must be something bothering the army." The sky was filling with fluffy black balls of cloud as the anti aircraft guns went into action.

"There they are," Harriet called. "Just above the ack ack. Stukas." Flying between the anti aircraft fire, swinging in and out of it but not climbing to avoid it, either stupidly or bravely, were eight Stukas heading in the direction of the train station.

"Right, Goose Squadron, let's have a crack at them," Cas ordered. "A Flight, form line abreast on me, we'll hit them on the nose. Archie, take B Flight and grab them by the tail. Black Section, keep your eyes open for the fighters. Tally ho!" Cas' flight quickly formed as he'd instructed, then followed as he flipped to port and started a dive at the lead Stuka. B Flight formed up the same way, and Archie led them straight and level above Cas before leading a dive at the rear of the formation. The ack ack didn't stop as the squadron hit the Stukas, diving in and through the explosions and knocking two down on the first pass, Cas again claiming first blood and Archie taking one from the rear. The rest quickly broke up with Stukas flying in every direction, as Nicole saw four pairs of Messerschmitt 109s heading into the fight out of the sun, and pointed them out to Harriet.

"Goose Squadron, fighters approaching from the east," Harriet called. "Black Section, tally ho!" She pushed the throttle forward and started a dive. Lining her sights with the leading 109 and opened fire just seconds before she passed it, narrowly missing its wing, but sending it spiralling down after her bullets had crashed through the top of the cockpit and killed the pilot outright. The 109s instantly scattered in every direction, and by the time Harriet had pulled out of her high speed and very steep dive, the battle was nowhere to be seen. She searched the sky to see the fighters and remaining Stukas hedgehopping east and quickly followed, opening her throttle full as she lined up on a Stuka straggling at the rear. She fired as she closed and watched as her bullets cut along the Stukas right wing, then a stream of tracer flew at her as the rear gunner got her in his sights. She slipped wide to avoid the tracer bullets, then pulled hard left and out of the gunner's field of fire before she came back in a sweeping curve to put bullets into the Stuka's engine, making it cough black smoke. She passed and watched as it put down safely in a field. A truckload of soldiers was already disembarking and running to greet the German crew. She smiled and gave the solders a waggle of her wings in reply to their waving. The rest of the Germans were already gone, flying full throttle out of trouble. Cas called the squadron back home for fuel and ammunition, so she pulled her cockpit open and pulled off her oxygen mask and enjoyed waving at the troops on the road. Soon she saw familiar vehicles, RAF vehicles. It was the squadron. She watched and saw Singh standing from the door of the ambulance and waving, so she quickly pulled up into a victory roll as she flew past. Soon they were gone, and she was approaching the airfield. She was the first back, so after a quick circuit during which she saw the others starting their approach she landed and was immediately approached by the fuel bowser. AP appeared on her wing as the airman started refuelling her Hurricane.

"What are you doing here?" Harriet asked.

"Is the aeroplane OK?" Came the simple and almost expected reply, as a team of airmen quickly started checking her guns.

"What?"

"The aeroplane, is it OK? Have you taken any hits? Is it handling alright?" AP demanded.

"What? Yes, yes, it's OK, never better," Harriet replied with a frown. "AP, what are you doing here? You're supposed to be heading home."

"My job, the same as you're doing yours," she replied as she handed Harriet a canteen of water.

"And why are you carrying that?" Harriet pointed to the pistol holster on AP's hip.

"You know why. Drink quickly!" AP urged. Harriet nodded and did as she was told, then handed back the canteen. "OK, stay put. Stand by to take off if the Germans appear, we only have enough bullets for two of your guns, for now. We'll rearm the others as soon as the rest of the ammunition arrives." She jumped from the wing and shouted instructions to airmen before running off to the next Hurricane. Harriet watched as she left, while the airmen finished off her refuel and reload. The bowser was done first, and it quickly moved off, then the gun bays were secured, and she was left alone until Cas called them up for another patrol, and the same routine was followed again. Everyone was there, which was good news. Not a bad result for the scrap they'd had! They patrolled for over an hour, but this time the Germans stayed away, and soon they were back on the ground to be refuelled before heading off again to patrol the railway lines and roads, which had apparently had some attention in their absence, before returning to the airfield once again having not found the Luftwaffe. They were all quickly refuelled, while biscuits and water were delivered for the pilots.

They were soon taken up again, after a break to stretch their legs and relieve their bladders. It was late afternoon, and the last train had finally left the station, evacuating hundreds of British personnel, if not more, and leaving a mountain of abandoned equipment by the station. A long snake of trucks followed, carrying those that couldn't fit on the train, and making the more perilous journey to the coast by road, surrounded by and enveloped in an endless procession of civilians. Already smoke from the burning equipment and supplies that had been left behind was starting to obscure the ground, as it mixed with the smoke still rising from the bomb ravaged town and train station; but the squadron kept watch until the convoy of trucks was well on its way, before they headed back towards the airfield. On their way, they engaged four unescorted bombers heading for the train station, three of which were knocked down, before the last dropped to the deck and ran for home. Harriet and Nicole gave chase for a few miles, and both emptied the last of their short supply of bullets into him, making the right engine stream black smoke; but neither had the ammunition to finish it off, so all they could do was fly aggressively enough to scare the pilot and make sure he would think twice about turning back and trying to put his bombs on the train station, or escaping convoy. Finally, they broke off the chase and returned to the airfield where the others were waiting for them, gathered in a small group by the trees at the end of the runway.

"Are you OK?" AP asked as she reached into Harriet's cockpit and unfastened her harness.

"Yeah…" Harriet replied. She was sweaty and tired; the intense concentration and constant stress of the day's combat were starting to take their toll on her. "We had to chase the last bomber away and shout at him. We didn't have a bullet between us."

"You're not alone," AP replied uncomfortably. "Come on. You'd better get out and stretch your legs while we refuel you, and wait for the ammunition to arrive." She handed Harriet a canteen of water while helping her step out of the cockpit.

"You mean the supplies haven't arrived yet?"

"Not yet... Right, anything I need to look at on your Hurricane?"

"No... Not that I can think of." Harriet smiled, then met with Nicole, and together they walked over to join the other pilots.

"Did you get him?" Cas asked.

"No," Harriet replied. "Nicole knocked his right engine out, but neither of us had the ammunition for anything else."

"That'll have ruined his day, at least. I can't see him coming back from that for a while. Well done."

"I'd have finished him if I'd had the ammunition," Nicole said unhappily, as she forced a smile and shrugged. She was irritated that she'd had to let the bomber go.

"I don't doubt it," Cas replied. "Unfortunately, we're all in the same boat for the time being. That last scrap expended the last of our ammunition, so as of now we're ineffective."

"What does that mean for us?" Harriet asked.

"It means that that if the army resupply doesn't get here soon, we're going to have to head straight back to England and forego the rest of our work here, and our sunset patrol over Dunkirk. Leaving the army and navy without air cover, and at the mercy of the Luftwaffe." He looked around at the exhausted pilots. "OK, you may as well get comfortable," he said with a hint of resignation mixed with irritation.

The pilots sat in the grass and waited; and waited. None had much to say, and most just took advantage of the respite to catch their breath and prepare themselves for whatever was to come next. Cas paced impatiently, marching up and down, smoking and looking up at the sky, appearing desperate to be up there. Harriet watched him and felt a need to do something to reassure him in some way, but she had no idea what she could say or do; she was as impatient as he was, as they all were, nobody was comfortable sitting and waiting, and feeling useless. The buzz of an engine made everyone flinch in unison, and had them looking in the direction of the squadron HQ, hoping to see an ammunition truck bouncing down the track and out of the woods. There was an air of disappointment when an army motorcycle appeared instead, though it was being ridden erratically and urgently, which was enough to hold the interest of the pilots, who stood as it came close.

"Flight Lieutenant Salisbury?" the army dispatch rider asked breathlessly, as he removed the scarf from over his mouth.

"Yes?" Cas asked.

"Major Adams sends his regards, Sir, and suggests that you get your blue arses out of here. His words, Sir."

"Oh?" Cas asked.

"The Germans are just a few miles down the road, Sir. We're holding them for now, but we've been strafed by fighters a couple of times, and the Major is expecting the main assault to come in shortly. Once that happens, it's unlikely we'll be able to stop them."

"AP, is there any ammunition at all?" Cas asked as AP joined them.

"None," she replied.

"What about the rifle and machine gun ammunition? Isn't there enough to rearm a couple of Hurricanes at least?"

"Maybe, but we'd have to belt the ammunition, and that would take time; and even if we could do it, we'd use up pretty much everything we have."

"I see..." He nodded solemnly. "As desperate as things are, I'm not about to make the lot of you and the rear party any worse by taking the only thing you have to defend yourselves. I've already put you in a bad enough position as it is. No, we'll do the sensible thing." He shook his head with annoyance. "OK, everyone, to your aeroplanes. Let's get out of here and back to England." The pilots quickly prepared themselves to leave. "Good luck, AP, thank you for staying behind and keeping us flying. Now, get your party to the coast as quickly as you can, no hanging around!" He shook AP's hand while looking across the airfield. "Where's Sergeant Oliver?"

"I think we're too late…" Harriet said, as she stepped forward and pointed down the runway to the cloud of dust racing towards them from the adjoining fields. Cas looked at her, and then at the cloud, it looked like an entire army was charging at them.

"Oh God," he said quietly. "Arm yourselves!" He pulled his revolver and checked the bullets, as did everyone else who had a weapon, including Harriet who still had bullets in the Walther the Major had given her. The small group stood ready to face whatever was racing towards them. "Don't fire until I give the order," Cas instructed. "I don't want a bloodbath unless it can't be helped!" Harriet felt her heart pounding as she raised her pistol and aimed at the dust. Her mouth dried, and her eyes watered. It was more terrifying than anything that had gone before, in the air or on the ground. She looked to her right where Nicole was standing nervously, unarmed but refusing to hide, so Harriet took a pace to her right and stepped half in front of her friend. To her left, Cas and AP stood with their revolvers drawn and ready. As she looked forward again and prepared to take a shot at whatever came out of the cloud, she noticed the thunderous noise accompanying it, and something didn't sound right. It wasn't men running, and it wasn't trucks or tanks, it was… Horses! The dust cloud reached the edge of the grass runway and spat out a column of charging horses, mounted by khaki clad soldiers and leading a train of heavily laden and fast galloping mules.

"Who are they?" Harriet asked, then she saw a familiar moustache riding near the head of the charge. "It's Sergeant Oliver…" she gasped.

"So it is…" Cas said. "So it is! And that's a mule train he's riding with!" he laughed as the horses slowed their approach.

"Found you something, Sir," Sergeant Oliver shouted as they halted. The Indian officer riding next to him jumped down from his horse and quickly approached.

"Captain Khan, Royal Indian Army Service Corps, Sir," he said as he stood smartly in front of Cas. "My apologies for the delay, we had to fight our way through a German position, but we have your ammunition."

"My God, Captain, are we pleased to see you!" Cas replied. "AP, let's get those Hurricanes ready to fly!" She stepped forward, and Khan instructed his Sergeant to follow her instructions. Soon the mules were being led to the Hurricanes, where their charges quickly unloaded their precious cargo and handed it to the waiting ground crew. "You've saved lives today, Khan," Cas said as he offered his hand, which Khan shook while Sergeant Oliver dismounted and walked over to join them. "What are your orders from here?"

"The coast, if we can," Khan replied. "We were heading there when we heard that you needed ammunition. The roads are blocked, mostly, and the truck bringing your ammunition had run into a ditch; so I decided to try with our mules, as we could travel over fields and through woods, unlike motor vehicles. Your Sergeant found us at the airfield perimeter and led us in." He nodded to Oliver in acknowledgement.

"I'm indebted to you, Khan. You should probably head off as soon as you're unloaded, the Germans are only a few miles away, and I expect they'll be here before long."

"You won't need to tell me twice," Khan replied. "I lost a few good men fighting our way in here, and I don't intend on hanging around and losing any more. What about your people? They can't all fly out?"

"No, they can't," Cas said remorsefully. "The aeroplanes have been ordered back to England to help the defences there. The rear party are going to make a run for the coast as soon as we leave."

"They'll get there faster on horseback," Khan said.

"I don't know how we're going to be able to repay you for today, Mister Khan," Cas nodded and smiled.

"I'll get your people to the coast. I hope they won't mind a bumpy ride."

"I'm quite sure they'll take that any day, better than being overrun by the Germans."

"We've got enough ammunition to fill all guns for two sorties," AP said as she returned.

"Good," Cas said with a slow nod. "AP, Mister Khan has agreed to take your party out on horseback, but before that, I'm going to give you the best chance of getting away that we can."

"How?"

"We'll fly a sortie over the advancing German lines and try to slow them down a bit. It'll only be a quick one. I want your teams ready to refuel and rearm as fast as possible as soon as we're back, then we'll be off to Dunkirk, and hopefully, you won't be too far behind."

"I'll have everybody ready."

"Can my men be of help?" Khan asked.

"Happy to have them," AP replied.

"I want a pistol," Nicole said, as she and Harriet made their way back to their Hurricanes.

"I think the eight machine guns on your Hurricane are enough, don't you?" Harriet replied, teasing a little.

"You know what I mean. I didn't enjoy the feeling of being helpless back there."

"Were you scared?' Harriet continued to tease, knowing full well that she herself had been absolutely terrified.

"Not at all. I just didn't like having to wait until you'd been shot so I could take your pistol, and use it properly," Nicole hit back, amusing herself in the process.

"You're horrible."

"But you love me."

"God alone knows why."

"Because I'm beautiful and wonderful, and the most talented fighter pilot you've ever met."

"Of course," Harriet said as they arrived at Nicole's Hurricane. "Make sure this beautiful, wonderful, talented fighter pilot gets back to England in one piece." She hugged Nicole.

"I'll be there waiting for you," Nicole replied. "Be careful." She kissed Harriet on her cheeks, then skipped off to get ready to fly, while Harriet smiled to herself as she continued on her way to meet AP, who was waiting by the wing of her Hurricane.

"She's all set for you," AP said. "Fully fuelled, and all guns fully armed."

"Nothing I need to worry about?"

"Only that if you manage to get any more holes in your airframe, I'll have to reclassify it as a net officially."

"I'll do my best," Harriet laughed as she climbed up the wing, and eased into the cockpit.

"You'd better. You've been through too much to do something silly now," AP said quietly as she helped strap Harriet in. "I mean it. You're a couple of hours away from being home and safe."

"I promise… AP, are you going to be OK?"

"Why wouldn't I be?"

"Because the Germans are on the doorstep, and you have to get through a war zone to escape them!"

"Thanks for the reminder..." She winked at Harriet, who immediately rolled her eyes in frustration.

"You know what I mean."

"I do, and I'll be fine. Trust me; we're not hanging about. As soon as you've been in for your last stop, I'll be on the fastest horse they've got!"

"Take care of yourself."

"Shut up. You just keep your mind on what you're supposed to be doing up there." Harriet nodded, then from nowhere AP leant into the cockpit and hugged her, something she'd never done. "It's been nice getting to know you, Harry," she whispered, then disappeared and jumped from the wing, leaving Harriet with nervous butterflies in her stomach that she couldn't control.

"OK, let's go," Cas said over the radio, and Harriet started her engine. The exhaust stubs flickered with fire once more, and the familiar blue cloud of smoke hung in the air just long enough to be tasted, before being blasted away by the roaring propeller. She went through her checks, then with a wave from AP she rolled out onto the grass, turned, then quickly bounced along the runway following the others. Cas led the squadron into a low circuit while everybody took position, then took them east towards the smoky horizon, and almost immediately they sighted a squadron of Stukas heading for the British position at the crossroads not ten miles away. The Hurricanes didn't have time to climb, but they didn't need to. The Stukas were already starting their dives. "Right, let's break this little lot up before they get started. Pick your targets, get in and get out, and watch out for fighters! Tally ho!" He led from the front and knocked down the leading Stuka with a short burst, sending it spiralling down in a dive it would never come out of. Harriet followed him in and hit the next, sending it spinning, then she pulled up hard to look for fighters. Bullets flew all around, and the sky was filled with the long white snakes of gunfire and black smudges of engine smoke, as the Hurricanes ripped into the Stukas and sent what remained of them running east. Tracer came up from the ground as the Hurricanes gave chase, and passed over the German infantry below. "OK, let them go," Cas instructed. "Put the remainder of your ammunition into the infantry, and watch out for their return fire!" Harriet didn't need telling twice. She flipped her Hurricane onto its back, then pulled back on the stick and dived down, lining her sights on a long hedgerow which was blinking with gunfire. She levelled off just above treetop height and fired, strafing the hedgerow and sending leaves, branches, and dirt in the air, and cutting through the hiding German infantry. As she completed her sweep, she watched as Nicole dived down from the opposite direction, ready to go over the same hedgerow. She smiled at the look of determination on Nicole's face as she knocked down the line of soldiers now running from the hedgerow, desperately trying to escape her attack. It was a forlorn hope, her bullets danced across the field, and the soldiers fell. Meanwhile, Harriet was sweeping around to the east, and her eyes were on a long line of trucks rolling up the road and moving at speed. She levelled and hit the first, making it burst into flames, then pulled up as another pair of Hurricanes hit the convoy from the side. They slipped and shot up the trucks before passing over, while Harriet swung around for another attack, this time heading back to the front line and targeting what looked like a heavy machine gun position, one of the few still bravely taking shots at the attacking Hurricanes. She opened fire and emptied what remained of her ammunition into the gun, killing and scattering the infantry surrounding it, and putting it out of action. Her guns were empty, and her job was done. A quick look around showed no sign of enemy fighters, so she sped over the friendly lines and gave a waggle of her wings to the British and French infantry below, who replied with cheers and waves. Not fifteen minutes after taking off, she was bouncing back towards her pen and being waved into position, followed by the other Hurricanes of the squadron.

"Keep yourselves strapped in; we're not stopping," Cas instructed over the radio. Harriet waited for the fuel bowser while airmen assisted by Khan's soldiers rearmed her guns. Finally, the bowser made its way to her, and the airmen started the refuelling.

"Everything OK?" AP asked as she appeared on Harriet's wing, carrying water once again.

"Yeah... You'd better hurry up, though, the Germans aren't far away," Harriet replied.

"That's OK. We're not hanging about. You're the last one needing fuel, and as soon as you're done, we'll be getting off."

"Good. The roads don't look too bad towards the town, and you should be able to move quite quickly."

"Don't worry about us. We'll be fine."

"You never did tell me why you stayed."

"Somebody had to stay and make sure you kept flying."

"But why you?"

"We drew straws. The Chief, me, and the senior Flight Sergeants, to decide who was going to stay and run the rear party."

"And you won..."

"I cut the straws."

"You cheated."

"My place is with the aeroplanes. I made sure I was able to do my job; that's all." The fuel truck pulled away and left them. "All done, are you ready?"

"I think so... "

"Good. Remember everything you've learned here, and if you run into trouble, don't be a hero!"

"Shut up."

"I mean it. When I get to England, I want to see..."

"Your aeroplane in one piece?" Harriet said with a smirk, cutting her off mid sentence.

"I want to see my friend in one piece."

"Shut up!" Harriet repeated, feeling a blush burn her cheeks.

"I mean it. Don't mess about, things could get serious over the coast, and you don't want to put down in the sea, you'll be lucky to be picked up. Do what you have to and then run, understand?"

"Don't worry about me."

"I do worry about you."

"Well don't. You're the one that has to get to the coast, so worry about yourself. Don't hang around."

"Why? Will you miss me?"

"I'll miss you nagging me."

"OK Goose Squadron, let's get out of here," Cas said over the radio.

"I have to go..." Harriet said.

"I know... Look after yourself, Harry. See you in England." AP said with a rare smile.

"Wait!" Harriet said as AP made to leave. "Thank you. Thank you for everything."

"Just get my aeroplane back safe," AP said with a smile and a wink before jumping from the wing. Harriet shouted 'clear' then started her engine, filling the air with blue smoke as the propeller kicked around before sparking into life and clearing the air. Pre flight checks were quickly done, and she looked around before rolling forward and taking her place at the rear of the squadron alongside Nicole. At Cas' command the Hurricanes left in ones and twos, then finally it was her turn. She let off the brakes and rolled forward, giving AP a wave and a smile before lifting from French soil for the final time, and following the squadron towards the coast, and England.

Chapter 15

Endings

It wasn't a long flight to Dunkirk. Cas had chosen to lead the squadron to the coast, before turning north and following the line between sea and land towards the thick black column of cloud which was climbing and swirling up from Dunkirk like a giant whirlwind, darkening the sky from many miles away. His logic was simple, it was early evening, and the sun was low in the southwestern sky, for once giving them an advantage over any Germans in the air. They'd flown over snaking lines of civilians and soldiers, and over battles between tanks and infantry as they approached the southernmost defences of the Dunkirk pocket. It was chaos, even from such a height, and between periods of intensely spinning her head in search of enemy aircraft, Harriet managed to glance down every now and then. She couldn't comprehend the unfolding disaster. Barrage balloons were tethered over the many ships in the distance, bobbing about among the clouds stretching across the orange and blue sky of early evening. As they got closer to the town, more trails of smoke could be seen spiralling into the sky, maybe hundreds of them. But none were as big as the enormous black plume coming from the oil depot at the docks. The unrelenting barrage of the Luftwaffe was wreaking utter devastation on the town and beaches. Harriet felt her mouth drying at the sight. Cas had been right. She wasn't prepared for this; she wasn't prepared for any of it. She hadn't even imagined anything like it. As they crossed the defensive lines, she was able to see the beaches, which seemed to be shimmering and rippling in fascinating long lines which took more of her attention than it should. Her eyes opened wide as she realised that the wind on the sand wasn't causing the ripples, the ripples were men, thousands of them, moving and twitching while standing in lines for the ships at the docks. She was horrified. How could so many men be in one place? How badly had the army been broken, that this was what they were reduced to? Closer still and she was able to see smouldering and submerged wrecks of ships sunk close to the harbour. The Hurricanes flew a patrol over the length of the long beaches, all of which seemed to be covered in soldiers; some were coming and going, some standing and waiting. They banked east, then headed inland to the perimeter, where they were able to see the battle raging with their own eyes. French and British soldiers striving to hold their positions against a sprawling mass of

German men and equipment which had formed a solid wall around the town. It was then that a realisation hit Harriet like a punch in the stomach. With a solid ring of Germans practically surrounding the town, how were AP and her rear party going to get through to be evacuated? She felt sick at the thought. They'd be prisoners at best. At worst they'd be killed when they arrived at the German perimeter if not before, assuming they hadn't been overrun before they had the chance to escape. They continued their patrol along the perimeter, all the time searching for German aircraft as they followed Cas' lead back to the south of the town where they turned out over the sea again, and into the lowering sun. They then turned and started another patrol loop, this time going further up the coast before turning back in. On the next circuit, they passed directly over a large Royal Navy cruiser, which was sitting flanked by a pair of destroyers in the deeper water further out to sea. It was being served by a stream of smaller tender craft carrying small groups of soldiers to the safety of the mighty steel beast. The sailors waved at the Hurricanes, and Cas gave them a wing waggle in return. On Cas' orders, the squadron flew a wide circuit out to sea and searched for submarines or surface craft intent on causing the cruiser problems. For a moment Harriet glanced west, the orange sun was lighting up the coastline, England was almost within reach. She let herself smile for a moment; it wouldn't be long until Cas pulled them off in that direction. Home, or whatever home was, or would be. At least it would be safe, for the time being at least. She snapped herself out of her empty daydream of what England would actually be like, mostly because she couldn't even imagine up enough to fill in the gaps; she'd lived in France almost as long as she'd lived in England, and she'd been gone so long that she'd forgotten what it was like.

"Looks like the Germans are all at home having dinner," Cas said after their large sweep of the sea finished. "We'll take one more pass along the beaches, then head home. Well done, everybody, we made it." Harriet felt herself smiling, she instinctively turned and waved at Nicole, who was flying close by her side and got an excited wave in return.

"My God..." Archie said over the radio, sending a nervous twitch deep into Harriet's stomach and a cold chill down her spine. She instantly spun her head, looking all around. "Three o'clock, skipper, angels ten, coming in fast!" Harriet followed the instructions and watched as line after line of black specks came out of a distant bank of heavy cloud, which glowed with the orange and gold reflections of the sinking sun. Small puffs of black anti aircraft fire scattered around the specks but didn't appear to deter them from driving forward. "Heinkels, thirty or more!"

"A Flight on my starboard side, B Flight to port, form line abreast and follow my lead," Cas ordered. The squadron spread out in loose pairs along a line either side of Cas' wings, just as he'd ordered, with Nicole and Harriet out on the far left of the squadron. "We've got to keep those bombers away from the ships," he continued. "There's too many for us to hope to take them all down, but we can try and break them up by punching them square on the nose. Pick one each and give them everything you've got through that greenhouse of a cockpit. God willing you'll knock the pilot or the controls out and scatter the pack. They'll likely dive when we hit so climb over them, but watch for the rear gunner, get underneath them as quick as you can and have another go. As soon as your ammunition is spent, get yourself out of here and head home."

"Skipper, fighters above them," Archie said.

"I see them... Watch out for them, but it's the bombers we want. We must protect the Navy at all costs. Otherwise, the army will be stranded on the beaches, and the game's over." The nine Hurricanes charged forward, stretched out in a long staggered line as Cas masterfully manoeuvred them into a position where they could approach the bombers almost undetected, with the large low sun to their backs hiding them from the strained eyes of the German crews. The Hurricanes passed over the cruiser and raced for the crowded beaches, crossing them just as the bombers passed over the town. "OK Goose Squadron, here we go. Tally ho!" The two formations of aeroplanes were closing at a combined speed of over six hundred miles per hour, and the Germans still hadn't seen the Hurricanes even though they were directly ahead. "Now!" Cas said calmly, and the entire squadron opened fire. Streams of long, white, lance like tracers reached out and stabbed into the glass cockpits of the leading bombers. Harriet had eyed her target carefully, fixing it in her sights. When the time came, she carefully pressed the fire button and watched as the cockpit glittered with sparks as her bullets ricocheted off the metalwork inside. A slight skid left, and then right with the tiniest amount of pressure on her rudder bar and the cockpit was thoroughly sprayed, but not before the front gunner had started to reply with a stream of bullets which whipped around the fuselage of her Hurricane. She held firm and gave another burst, more in response to the gunner than of necessity, because her first squirt of bullets had done the job and the bomber lurched downwards as she pulled back on the stick and climbed over it. The rear gunner took a shot at her, but his bullets were wide of the mark as his aircraft was dragged into a diving spin and Harriet flipped her Hurricane onto its back and pulled the stick into her stomach, giving her an inverted shot at the next bomber in line and spraying its right wing and engine before dragging into a sharp dive. As she flipped, she saw Nicole to her left. Her bomber was smoking, and the wing was burning. Its starboard engine had failed, but Nicole had also taken hits, and a thin smudge of oily black smoke was trailing from her engine; drawing a dark line in the sky as she pulled wide of the many streams of tracer bullets that were crisscrossing all around her. Harriet spun her head as she banked and pulled out of her dive, checking her tail and every direction around her; then looked over to Nicole again just in time to watch her bank in a steep turn and head back towards the bombers. Her focus was on the bomber she'd already shot up, which was pulling to the right of the formation and starting a slow turn, clearly intent on heading for home, something Nicole wasn't about to let happen. She quickly closed and launched another attack into the front quarter of the bomber and shot up the fuselage. Harriet got back on her own job, pulling back on her stick again and lining up with the light blue belly of the bomber almost directly ahead. She waited until she was as close as she dared get, and when the bomber filled her windscreen, she fired along the underside of the fuselage. Unexpectedly, the bomber exploded into a giant cloud of black smoke, and orange and blue flames, as her bullets somehow detonated the bombs in the belly of the beast. There was nothing Harriet could do except fly through the turbulent storm which shook and buffeted her Hurricane and flipped it on its side before throwing it on its back and sending it through the sky. Harriet fought to control her aeroplane, then was blinded briefly by a bolt of golden orange light from below. She looked down at the source, and found a large stretch of the cockpit floor was missing, ripped away by a chunk of exploding bomber which miraculously took just the floor and not the controls just inside it, letting in a beam of sunlight which filtered through her smoky and dusty cockpit. She also noticed a smoking gash in the right forearm of her flying jacket and felt an uncomfortable burning on her flesh. She stabilised and checked her instruments, then levelled out while she got her bearings. Her eye was drawn by sudden movement and she watched in shock as her starboard wing, already sieved by the exploding bomber, was ripped open in a nice neat zipper line as tracer rounds cut from the tip towards the cockpit.

"Harry, flip right!" Nicole shouted over the radio. Instinctively, Harriet did as she was told. She stood on the rudder bar while slamming her stick over to the right, and her Hurricane skidded and tipped, and a flaming 109 fell past her as tracer bullets lanced into it from Nicole's smoking Hurricane which was chasing close behind. Behind her were another two 109s, firing and blasting as she spun and rolled while diving after her target, refusing to give it up while at the same time making herself a hard target. Another flip and Harriet dived down after Nicole. The air was now full of anti aircraft fire as well as aeroplanes, and a massive explosion shook Harriet and rocked her just as she fired at the closest of the two 109s, clipping its tail and making it shudder. At the same time, the 109 nearest to Nicole hit home, and a blast of fire coughed from her engine, enveloping her and her pursuers in a cloud of black smoke.

"Nicole!" Harriet yelled. The 109s banked to the right as Nicole's Hurricane spun downwards leaving a trail of fire and smoke behind. "Nicole, get out! Get out!" There was no reply, and the Hurricane just wound into a steeper and steeper dive until she passed into a cloud and out of sight. "Nicole!!" Despair and desperation took over Harriet's body and mind, paralysing her completely. She couldn't think. She couldn't act. Nicole was gone. Her best friend, her sister, was dead and gone in an instant; after looking after her one last time by saving her from a diving 109.

"Look out, Harry!" Cas shouted over the radio. She snapped out of her daze and looked up into her rearview mirror, a swarm of 109s were charging up on her tail. The two closest fired, showing flashes of orange as their guns chattered and streamers of white as the bullets and cannon shells passed either side of Harriet's Hurricane. She flipped upside down and pulled back, dropping into a steep dive. A quick look over her shoulder and she counted five 109s banking and diving to follow her. As the last entered the dive, she hit the throttle and pulled up tight enough for her vision to start to go black from the g forces, leaving just the narrowest cone of light ahead of her. As the climb straightened, her vision eased a little, and she was able to see, however briefly, the battle she was in the middle of. The bombers had scattered. Some were heading to the ground and others for home, while fighters weaved and rolled around the sky among the black explosions of relentless anti aircraft fire. The 109s had stuck to her and were still firing. Their bullets hit her left wing, and she instantly rolled, narrowly missing a bomber before diving as hard as she dared, watching the needle pass the numbers on the speed indicator then leave them in its wake. Bullets continued to zip past her and hit the fuselage. She rolled and twisted, aware of the speed and not wanting to rip off her wings, but the Germans weren't budging, the five of them jostled for position on her tail trying to get the killer shot that would no doubt come soon enough and send her into the ground. Sweat stung her eyes, and her goggles started to mist, she could hardly breathe as the force threw her into her straps, which squeezed her lungs tight. She heard her own words repeating over and over, 'God help me!' As she felt thuds against her back as cannon shells hit the seat's armour plating. "The smoke, Harry. The smoke!" Cas shouted. She looked around and locked her eyes on the thick column of smoke spewing from the burning oil tanks. As she approached the ground she started pulling on her control stick to fight the stiff controls out of the dive, which she did close enough to the ground to see the soldiers laid on their backs in the sand dunes and firing their rifles at the pursuing 109s, or four of the five, anyway. One hadn't pulled up in time, or had maybe taken hits from the soldiers below and lost control, but for whatever reason it nosedived into the waves crashing against the shore. Harriet rolled again as more gunfire ripped into her wing, then levelled as she approached the giant pillar of black smoke. A line of bullets hit her wing and engine cowling, sparking off the right side exhaust stubs and making them cough grey smoke. The pillar couldn't come soon enough, and as she was swallowed up by the black smoke which plunged her into virtual darkness, she pulled the stick back into her stomach until she was flying straight up, rolling slightly to keep straight and stop herself from coming out of the other side. The mint glow of her gauges saw the speed dropping quickly as the oil temperature raised. The hit to her engine had done damage, holing the radiator maybe, or the oil tank. The engine started to run roughly as she climbed harder and harder. The bullets had stopped, and all she could see in her rearview mirror was smoke. Her speed scrubbed off as the smoke lightened a little, she could just about see out of the column, and there weren't so many aeroplanes about, but still some, 109s circling and bombers running. She couldn't just break the cover of the smoke, and her engine was grinding and starting to sound rough. Then it happened. Her speed had hit critical, and she felt the Hurricane start to stall. She'd done this before, not in a Hurricane, but it couldn't be that different. She waited, held her nerve, and when the wing stalled and dipped, she kicked the rudder bar hard and slung the tail over the top of the aeroplane in a near perfect stall turn, which made the entire airframe creak agonisingly. As the nose pointed into the darkness of the smoke column, she straightened up and headed straight down. The engine rattled, and she throttled back to try and preserve it a little, as gravity did the work of taking her down. She peered out of the smoke to get her bearings and rolled accordingly, planning to exit the smoke column at a few thousand feet and head straight out to sea and home, hoping her engine would hold. She dived through the smoke and took the time to control her breathing and check her instruments. The oil temperature was holding, it was much higher than it should be, but it was holding. Of bigger concern was the fuel consumption. She'd used much more than she'd expected, and her quick calculations had her just about reaching England, as long as she didn't have to get into any more fights and there wasn't a strong westerly wind. The altimeter was quickly unwinding, and the time was coming. She took a deep breath, then gently pulled back on the stick and left the column of smoke. As she did, she almost collided with a Hurricane charging straight at her, winding and slipping with a 109 hot on its tail; firing and blasting furiously. It flipped and rolled, and Harriet fired. Her bullets hit home, and the 109 burst into flames as it passed underneath her. She continued downwards and looked in her rearview mirror, the Hurricane was climbing away, and a parachute was floating above the spiralling 109. As she headed out over the beach she immediately saw the lumbering whale like shape of a lone bomber, moving low and fast towards the Royal Navy Cruiser. A tremendous curtain of anti aircraft fire rose from the ships, and seemed to form a tunnel around the bomber, never quite getting close enough to hit. Harriet hit the throttle and pushed it to full. The engine screamed and kicked out even more black smoke as she rocketed after the bomber. The gunner started firing as she closed, and he was on target, his tracers wound around the cockpit and rattled the wings. Harriet knew she'd only have one chance, so she pushed as close as she could, determined to use whatever ammunition she had left wisely. She got so close she could see the gunner reloading in the upper rear turret. She fired, and her bullets found the starboard engine, making it flame with such a long and powerful jet of fire that it immediately engulfed the right wing and most of the right side of the fuselage. A stream of bullets shot out from the rear gunner, rattling her engine and shattering her propeller, then the bomber nosedived into the sea and flipped onto its back, sending a spray of seawater into the air for

Harriet to fly through. She quickly realised how close she was to the waves and pulled up and over the cruiser. She looked over both shoulders, and in the rearview mirror, then took a minute to check how she was doing when she saw she was clear. Her engine was coughing, and she could smell petrol. No sooner had she noticed the smell, the nose of her Hurricane lit up, and a streak of orange flames engulfed the right side of the cockpit and her right wing. The coughing engine and the damage to her propeller were now the least of her worries, she was on fire, and the flames weren't going out. Remembering AP's words, she quickly banked right and aimed for land, desperately hoping to get there before the engine failed or she burned to death, something still preferable to drowning, which was a terrifying death that she'd always feared. She planned to put the Hurricane down somewhere flat as she was too low to jump, and she doubted the engine would manage even a shallow climb to a safe height, it was already a fight just to keep the height she had. The smoke was thickening inside the cockpit as well as outside, but it wasn't so thick that she couldn't see the beach rapidly approaching, the beach packed with soldiers, trucks, guns, and every other bit of kit the army had managed to withdraw with. If she tried to put down there, she'd almost certainly kill herself in the process, and at the same time kill many soldiers who'd already had a bad enough time of things. She pushed on the rudder bar and tilted the stick slightly to give her a slow and shallow turn to port which made the Hurricane shudder so much she thought it was going to stall, so she eased the stick back and shallowed the turn. She could see the soldiers below, their faces looking upwards and watching as she sailed over their heads. A screeching metallic grind echoed through the cockpit, and the engine stopped. It was time. She held the nose up and felt herself climbing a little, then pushed down a touch to keep the glide and stop herself stalling altogether. She still had enough airspeed to get clear of the troops. She just had to keep the aeroplane steady. She focused with every ounce of her being as the flames licked at the cockpit and the smell of petrol got stronger. She looked down briefly and watched the sand pass below through the hole in her floor, then noticed the floor was wet with petrol which was slowly creeping towards the hole. Time was running very short, yet every second felt like a year. She checked her mirror, there was nobody behind her, and a quick search of the sky showed that any Germans that may have been around could see she was finished and not worth their efforts to help the inevitable. The soldiers had thinned out after the line of abandoned equipment, which had been formed into a defensive line. There had been nowhere to put down before the perimeter without fear of hitting something or somebody, and after it was a scrapyard of equipment and bomb holes. She couldn't hold it much longer; the flames were melting the canopy, and the cockpit was getting uncomfortably warm. The petrol on the floor of the cockpit hit the hole and met with the flames outside, igniting and spreading flames across the floor and up the control panel. Harriet dropped the Hurricane instantly and hit the sand belly first. She fought to keep the nose up, though it didn't take long for her to realise she had only the slightest control. The flames licking up the side of the cockpit were more of a concern and her boots were already on fire, but there was nothing she could do to get out until the Hurricane stopped. It careered along the hard-packed damp sand, skimming and bouncing like a pebble on the water. She hit a shell hole, and the Hurricane spun into the water, which erupted like a fountain and launched a spray into the air, which temporarily doused the flames from the wing and canopy, though the engine and nose still burned furiously. Water flooded into the cockpit from the hole below, enough to douse the flames on the floor but not those on Harriet's boots, or those burning the control panel and climbing the windscreen. She reached up and pulled at the canopy. It was jammed. She reached forward and put her right hand on the control panel, hoping her gloves and jacket would hold off the flames long enough for her to use all of the strength she had to lever the canopy open. It shifted, a little, then with a scream she rived and pushed, and it flew back. Flames were already back to licking around the cockpit as she released the pin from her harness and stood, but was immediately dragged back by the oxygen tube on her mask. She pulled at the tubes as flames spread up her right arm to her shoulder. Nothing would move, so she pulled off her helmet and threw herself out onto the left wing, the only part of the front half of the Hurricane that wasn't burning. She rolled down into the seawater, where she quickly doused the flames on her boots and jacket before half running, tripping, and crawling through the incoming waves and towards the sand, and away from a Hurricane which could blow up at any minute. She pulled off her jacket as she ran, then stopped and turned to look at the wreck briefly, then threw the jacket down on the sand as she ran up the beach and into the dunes, where she collapsed and kicked off her boots as she lay on her back and stared up at the rainbow of colours lighting up the evening sky. Her lungs burned, her eyes burned, everything burned. A rumbling explosion from the direction of the water had her sitting briefly to look over the dune at her Hurricane. It was burning fiercely in the orange and purple sky. It had finally succumbed, as had she. They had finally got her. She lay her head down again and stared at the sky. The first twinkling of stars in the royal blue sky mesmerised her as she thought of the only thing her mind would stick to, Nicole. She'd experienced her own burning cockpit not five minutes earlier, and it was terrifying, and she just hoped and prayed that Nicole had been shot and killed before she burned. Her thoughts spun and then faded as her eyes closed.

Harriet's dreams were distant. She was in blackness mostly, with the occasional flashback to trying to fight her way out of a burning cockpit. Her brain would then add a twist and put her on the outside, leaving her to look in through the blistering Perspex of the canopy windows as Nicole screamed and burned to death, begging Harriet to save her while Harriet just watched. It was such a horrendous dream that faded into blackness before starting again, and again, torturing her as she stood helplessly on the burning Hurricane watching her friend burn to death. After the final loop, instead of being enveloped in darkness once again, she heard German voices calling to each other, men's voices. Her German was terrible, it always had been, but she worked out enough to know that they were looking for somebody, looking for the pilot. The pilot. Her eyes opened wide. The sky had turned a little darker in the east and a little redder in the west, but voices were still there. German voices. She lay still for a moment, then put pressure on her arms to lift herself to look around the dune. A sharp pain burned through the middle of her right forearm like it was on fire inside, she let out a yelp and sat grasping her arm to her chest, then let out another yelp when she touched the skin which felt like acid had been poured on it. The German voices became loud and urgent, and she understood enough to know she was in trouble. She did the only thing she could do, raised her left hand in the air and shouted back.

"Nicht sheissen!" Archie's top tip for surviving capture behind enemy lines had been to put your hands up, shout 'don't shoot' in German, and hope for the best. There was no point in running; he'd pointed out if they were close enough to talk to, they were close enough to shoot you, and you weren't a soldier, so it was pointless trying to fight your way out with a pistol against heavily armed soldiers. So the only thing for it was to give yourself up and hope you hadn't shot up one of their friends recently, and that they didn't feel like any bayonet practice. "Nicht sheissen," she repeated as she stood slowly, keeping her one hand in the air and the other across her body. A patrol of German soldiers were already running at her with their rifles at the ready. There were at least ten of them, and they were heavily armed, she wouldn't have been able to fight her way out even if she'd wanted to.

"Hände hoch!" the closest soldier shouted. "Heben, heben." He gestured upwards with his rifle at Harriet's right arm. She nodded nervously and tried to raise it, then let out a yelp as the burning started again and lowered her shoulder in a desperate attempt to make her hand look like it was raising and not annoy him.

"Ist ein Fräuline?" his friend said as he joined him, a statement that even in German, Harriet understood to be 'it's a girl'. She didn't dare roll her eyes, not on the outside at least.

"What's going on?" their Sergeant asked as he joined them. Soon she was virtually surrounded.

"Hans has captured a French farm girl." One of the others laughed, much to the amusement of the others.

"I thought she was the pilot," Hans replied. "It's dark, and it's an easy mistake to make."

"What do you think she's doing out here?" another asked.

"Probably came to see if there was anything to loot out of that Hurricane, food maybe, look at the skinny wretch, she's a mess. Probably a refugee," Hans replied.

"Put your hands down, girl," the Sergeant said in pretty decent French. Harriet was taken aback and looked at him with a raised eyebrow. "It's OK. We won't shoot you. We don't shoot civilians, or girls for that matter," he continued. She nodded and slowly lowered her arms, wincing again. "What have you done to your arm? Let me see." He gestured her out from the dune into the orange post sunset glow. He looked closely, and she followed his eyes. Her shirt was bloody and charred below the elbow and partially stuck to the skin.

"Which village are you from?" he asked as he looked in her eyes, which were wide with fear. She looked inland and then back to him. He nodded and shrugged. "Are you mute?"

"No..." she replied in her best French, which rasped out through her dried out mouth and throat.

"It's OK. We won't harm you. Kurt, get over here, the rest of you keep sweeping forward and see if you can find the pilot." They were joined by a young man carrying a medical pack. "She's burned her arm by the looks of it, and it looks like something is sticking out of the flesh, a bone maybe. Stay here and look after her while we go look for the pilot. We won't be long."

"OK," Kurt replied.

"You'd better come running if you hear any shooting, though!" the Sergeant demanded.

"Of course." The young man took off his helmet to show a mop of light coloured hair. He wasn't old, maybe the same age as Harriet, and wore round wire rimmed glasses. "How did you do this?" he asked in French. Nicole shrugged. "Getting too close to that crashed aeroplane, no doubt?" She shrugged again as he sat her down, then knelt and started to examine her arm while the others swept south along the beach. He cut away her shirt to above the elbow and slowly peeled bits of material from her flesh. He cleaned the wound, trying hard to be as gentle as he could when she flinched and yelped. "So, what do I call you? My name is Kurt."

"Nicole..." she replied without hesitation.

"Nicole, what a beautiful name. I expect there's a beautiful face under all of that dirt, too," he continued pleasantly. She shrugged and looked away. "I'm sorry, I don't mean to be familiar. I realise I'm the enemy, though I hope you can trust I'm not here to hurt you, none of us are, we're just soldiers doing as our Generals tell us. We wouldn't even hurt the pilot if we found him. Unless he tried to hurt us, of course. We'd just take him for questioning and have him put in a prisoner of war camp. One less flyer to shoot and bomb us." He took some tweezers from his pack. "It looks like there's some metal stuck in your arm, I'm going to pull it out, it'll hurt." He grabbed it and pulled, and she felt it grind against the bone and the flesh suck as it popped out. She gritted her teeth and yelled almost silently. "It's OK; it's out." He turned her arm towards the glow of the sky and inspected it. "Cleanly, too. You'll live, Nicole."

"Thank you," she half sobbed.

"Give me a minute, and I'll get it cleaned up for you." He used a wet cloth to clean the wound, carefully, gently moving outwards from the wound and wiping away the grime and dirt. "I don't suppose you saw the pilot, did you?"

"Yes..." she replied cautiously.

"Oh? Where did he go?"

"South. Towards Dunkirk. Some soldiers came for him."

"Soldiers? What soldiers?"

"English, I think. They weren't ours, not French soldiers, and they didn't have German hats. They were round, like dinner plates with a bump in the middle."

"I see. How long ago?"

"I don't know. The sun was still up, just. I saw it crash, and after they left, I went to look."

"Why would you do that? It's very dangerous."

"I don't know. I thought maybe there'd be something useful, some food maybe."

"Burning aeroplanes are dangerous, and you should stay away from them. They're full of petrol and ammunition, and you could have got yourself killed." She winced as he stitched her wound closed.

"It did explode when I got close. It's how I hurt my arm."

"Lucky we found you, then." He pulled a small jar out of his bag and opened it.

"What's that?"

"Honey," he said as he held her wrist and poured the honey over the burned flesh.

"What are you doing?"

"It'll help you heal."

"Honey?"

"Yes, honey. My mother swore by it, honey for a burn." He layered it on thick then wrapped her arm in paper before wrapping that in a bandage and putting the whole lot in a sling. He put the lid back on the jar and handed it to her. "Clean it again three days from now in the evening, and put some more honey on it. Wrap it in paper to stop the skin sticking to the dressing. Do it every three days and keep it clean, and you'll be OK."

"I'm grateful for your help."

"How is she?" the Sergeant asked as he returned with his men.

"She'll live. She burned her arm while trying to find food in that crashed British aeroplane."

"Stupid girl must be starving to go near that thing."

"She said she saw some British soldiers take the pilot away after he landed. Towards Dunkirk…"

"I thought as much. We didn't see them, but there's too much junk further up the beach for us to be safe getting close to their perimeter. We'd better get back and let the Captain know. Maybe we'll assault in the morning if we can get some artillery or a tank forward. Are you finished with her?"

"Yes, just about."

"OK, let's get going."

"What about her?"

The Sergeant knelt and looked Harriet in the eyes. "Don't go near burning aeroplanes, they're dangerous, do you understand?" She nodded and bowed her head shyly. "And don't be hanging around here alone in the middle of a war, I know it's your home, but it's dangerous. All armies have their savages, and some are made worse by war, there's no controlling them. Meet them out here at night, and you'll regret it."

"Yes, Sir," she replied softly.

"Here," he said. She looked up at the bar of chocolate he was holding out. She looked at it and then into his eyes. He was an older man with kind eyes. "Don't wait too long, or I'll put it away again." She reached out and took it from him. "Now get yourself home, and stay there until the fighting has finished."

"Thank you. Thank you all," she said, then quickly stood and ran off across the beach, heading inland towards the bigger dunes and the grass and trees beyond. She ran as fast as she could manage, feeling stones and sharp twigs beneath her feet; then entered the woods and hid behind a tree. She gasped silently for air and waited, then looked back towards the beach and watched the German patrol move back north, silhouetted by the distant low red sky. She watched them all along the beach until they were no more than specks and hadn't been replaced by anyone else. She opened the paper and foil of the large chocolate bar and took a corner. It was strong, bitter, sweet, and luxurious. She sucked on it while she rewrapped the rest and pushed it into her pocket. After looking out and watching for a while she headed back to the beach and searched around the dune where she'd slept. She found her flying jacket and boots, which were a little charred but still wearable, and somehow still had the Major's pistol inside. She heard movement as she pulled them on, and froze. Had the Germans been watching and come back? What would they do if they saw her in flying boots with a jacket at her feet? She thought quickly, maybe she'd seen the pilot hiding them when he crashed and ran off, and she didn't tell the Germans because she wanted them to keep warm? Yes, that was a plausible excuse.

"Hände hoch." A voice whispered quietly from behind her. She slumped backwards in dismay and sat on her feet as she raised her left hand. "Both of them," the voice continued in English.

"I don't understand," she said in French, fearing a trap. "Don't shoot, please, I'm French, I live here." Maybe the Germans had known all along, and by talking to her in English, they were hoping she'd reply, and in doing so give herself away.

"Bloody hell," the voice continued. "Corp, over here."

"What is it?" Came a reply.

"A frog."

"I'm not a frog," Harriet said, as she looked back over her shoulder at the British soldier aiming his rifle at her.

"What? Well, who the hell are you?"

"Who the hell are you?" she replied as she shuffled around to face him. He frowned as he looked at her, unsure of what to make of the situation. The Corporal joined them and stood with his rifle at the ready.

"Well, what have we here?" he asked. "This isn't what I expected when you said you'd found a frog, Jonesy."

"I'm not a frog," Harriet replied.

"Oh? Who are you then?"

"That depends who I'm talking to?"

"Fair enough... Corporal Evans, Royal Signals. Your turn."

"Pilot Officer Cornwall, Royal Air Force."

"Excuse me?"

"You heard me, Corporal," she said confidently.

"Could be a Boche, Corp," Jones said. "A spy or something like that."

"Could well be... I don't suppose you have any identification, do you?" he asked.

"No..." Harriet replied firmly.

"No, of course not. Not even your identity tags, I don't imagine?"

"Not even my identity tags," she replied. "A German patrol came by after I crashed my Hurricane, I buried them with my kit and pretended to be a French peasant."

"A likely story, I'm sure. Jonesy, go get that blue job officer." Jones ran off in the direction of the smouldering Hurricane, while Harriet sat back and looked up at the Corporal.

"I wouldn't hang around for too long. The Germans have only just left, maybe fifteen minutes ago."

"And what were they doing here?"

"Looking for a pilot... What are you doing here?"

"Looking for a pilot..."

"Well, you found one."

"So you tell me."

"Look, we can't sit here all night and debate it, or the Germans will have the lot of us! If you're that worried can you at least take me back to our lines where it's safe, I'm sure there'll be somebody there who can clear this up."

"I'm pretty sure that's exactly where a spy would want to be taken."

"Oh, for God's sake! Do you have to be such an idiot?!" she blustered as loudly as she dared. "I've been shot down, almost burned alive, and captured by Germans! The last thing I need is to sit out here in the dark talking to an idiot who thinks a girl in a British flying jacket a few minutes' walk from a crashed and burned out Hurricane is a German spy!"

"That's the problem, though, isn't it?" he replied. "Girls don't fly Hurricanes."

"Oh, God, give me strength. Just shoot me and have done with it."

"What?"

"You heard, shoot me and bugger off. At least I'll be dead and won't have to idle away my time talking to idiots."

"Well you don't say much, but when you do you sure let rip," a familiar American voice said as more silhouettes joined them.

"Max?" she asked instinctively, as she turned to see him walking closer. "Max, is that you?"

"Hey there, Harry. How's it going?"

"How is this happening? I thought you were... Or am I? Did we both?"

"Don't sweat it," he chuckled. "I was picked up by the army after being shot down, and brought to Dunkirk to be evacuated. I got here this morning."

"Oh God, Max." She stood and gave him a one armed hug, wincing and groaning as she crushed her arm in her enthusiasm. "Am I happy to see you."

"You're a sight for sore eyes, too. I watched you go down after you saved that cruiser. I was worried you'd burned with your kite. These boys volunteered to help me look for you, so don't give them too much of a hard time."

"Sorry..." she said as she turned to the Corporal. "It's been a tough day."

"Don't mention it, Ma'am. We watched you fighting up there, and it's an honour to help."

"I'm grateful."

"Well, let's not stand here yapping," Max said. "We don't want to be shot now we've found you. Lead the way, Corporal, let's get back to relative safety; so the Germans know where to find us when they want to bomb us next."

The group walked slowly through the darkness, making their way up the beach towards the British lines, listening as they went to the distant sounds of battle. They kept quiet as they moved, keen to avoid drawing attention to themselves until finally they reached the perimeter and were allowed to pass by the infantry guarding it. They made their way to a crater in the dunes, and joined a soldier and a couple of RAF airmen waiting inside. Harriet slumped down against the wall of the dune, and Max sat next to her. The Corporal had his men spread out around the small dune, which was quite deep, deep enough to shelter them from the wind and take the beach out of direct view, and for a soldier to hide a fire under a poncho and boil some water.

"I'm guessing that was our squadron that took on the bombers?" Max asked.

"Yes... We were a little outnumbered."

"You don't say. We got a front seat view of the whole show, it looked like hell, but you turned them back."

"We did?"

"Sure. It was pretty spectacular, and the way you hit them head on must have scared the hell out of them, because those that made it past the first scrape soon turned and ran, except that clown you caught taking a run at the cruiser."

"At least we made a difference."

"You can say that again. Brave call taking them head on like that, not usually Singh's style hitting them on the nose."

"It wasn't Singh."

"Oh?"

"He was hit by shrapnel yesterday. He's OK, though. He came to see us off, and he was heading here with the rest of the squadron."

"Who was leading? Archie?"

"Cas."

"Cas? No way! It seems there's life in the old dog yet."

"He's not old."

"Hey, compared to most of us he's ancient, but still a damned good officer, and still a damned good pilot it seems."

"It seems... Did you see anyone else go down?"

"The smoke made it difficult to see, but one for sure. They went down nose first somewhere north of town. Did you see anyone hit up there?"

"Nicole..."

"Oh, Harry, I'm sorry." He put his arm around her shoulder, and she laid her head on him.

"She saved me. She got a 109 off my tail that I hadn't seen. She'd have been OK if she'd turned, but she didn't, she held her course to save me. She knew they were on her tail, but she didn't flinch."

"She's a mighty fine pilot."

"Yes, she is."

"Here you go, Ma'am," the young soldier said as he handed her a tin mug of tea.

"Thank you."

"Sorry about your friend, Ma'am," he added a little awkwardly. Harriet smiled at his kindness, then reached into her pocket and pulled out the large bar of chocolate. She snapped off a few pieces for her and Max, then handed the rest to the soldier.

"Make sure everybody gets some, especially the Corporal." He smiled and hurried around the others, each of whom thanked her gratefully as he shared the chocolate.

"Where was the squadron heading after their patrol?"

"England... We were ordered home after covering the evacuation from the south east, via a sunset patrol here."

"Well, at least that's something."

"Yes... Though everyone else was coming here by train."

"They got here OK," Corporal Evans said.

"Excuse me?" Harriet asked.

"I saw a load of your lot arrive by train this afternoon." Evans continued. I'm pretty sure they were put on that cruiser you saved. It caused a bit of a stir among some of the infantry waiting to get off the beaches, but they got off alright." Harriet smiled and closed her eyes as she sucked on the chocolate between mouthfuls of tea until she fell into a deep sleep.

Fighting continued through the night, and the occasional bomber made an appearance and hit the harbour. The Luftwaffe returned in force at first light, and Harriet found herself pushing tight against the sand wall of what turned out to be a scorched bomb crater that they'd been sleeping in. She prayed they wouldn't be hit as the bombs rained down, followed by the bullets of strafing fighters; who were eventually chased away by the first patrol of the day arriving from England, a squadron of Spitfires which chased the Germans inland and away from the beaches. After a drink of water and thanking the soldiers, Max and Harriet headed off to find the Beach Master, hoping desperately to get off the beach and onto one of the boats. Already lines of men were waiting. Some were queueing out into the water up to the chest, entire battalions of men standing in an orderly column waiting for the small boats that were starting to appear on the horizon to collect them and take them out to the larger ships out in the Channel. Max led Harriet to the harbour and nudged his way through queues of soldiers, many of whom made insulting comments.

"Where's the hurry?" one soldier shouted.

"Must be time for breakfast in the Mess!" another replied.

"First of the RAF that I've seen."

"Must be lost, I didn't even realise they were in this war…"

"Funny how you don't see one for days, then two arrive together, and they're still running in the opposite direction of the Jerries."

They ignored the comments and pushed through to a sandbagged position guarded by a section of marines. An army officer, an older looking Colonel with a grey moustache, walked out of the sandbag walled shell hole and looked at Max and Harriet. "A bit bloody late, aren't you?" he sneered.

"What's that?" Max said, squaring up to the Colonel.

"I said you're a bit bloody late, are you deaf as well as lazy?"

"Look, buddy, I don't know who you think we are, but I can assure you we're not them."

"Don't buddy me, airman, you'll address me as Colonel! As for who I think you are, I know exactly who you are, you're the flyboys who spend their nights in warm beds on safe aerodromes back in England, leaving us to fend for ourselves against the Germans."

"Is that right?"

"That's right."

"And how do you suppose the two of us got here? On a day trip from Dover?"

"It wouldn't surprise me. Come to see what the war is really like, no doubt."

"Why you lousy, jumped up, ignorant son of a bitch. I was shot down a couple of days ago while fighting the Germans miles inland, stopping them even getting as far as the beaches, facing odds four or five to one."

"Well you didn't fight very hard, did you because they're still getting through, aren't they? My unit was attacked just last night by Stukas, and the RAF was nowhere to be seen, again! Quelle surprise. Likely still in their pyjamas getting ready for breakfast! Most of the army here would be hard pushed to know what the RAF even looks like."

"We're fighting the Luftwaffe miles inland to stop them getting this far, asshole, but when they do get close to the beaches, they're shot down by pilots like this one here!" He pointed at Harriet. "Last night she took on overwhelming odds, and even when her Hurricane was burning, she still went after a bomber that was making for a cruiser packed full of troops. She took it down while almost burning to death, before crashing into the sea. You want to know what the RAF looks like, well there you go, take a look, it looks like a young girl who flies head to head with German aces and wins, all so she can risk her neck saving your entitled and stuck up ass."

"A girl?" the Colonel sneered as he looked at Harriet. "Is that the best the RAF can muster? There's no wonder we're in trouble if we've put our fate in the hands of girls and Americans."

Harriet pulled back her arm, then with every ounce of strength she could muster, she threw her fist forward and felt the Colonel's nose crumple beneath it. He staggered back and yelped as blood ran down his face, then became enraged and raised the stick he was carrying, ready to beat Harriet across the face.

"You little bitch, I'll teach you!" he yelled, but before he could swing, Harriet reached into her boot and pulled out the pistol that the German pilot had given her; and pushed the barrel against the Colonel's head.

"That's Pilot Officer Bitch to you," she snarled. Her eyes narrowed as she stared into his, which were full of confusion and fear.

"What the hell is going on out here?" a Royal Navy officer demanded as he stepped out of the bunker. At the same time, a couple of the marine sentries had pulled their rifles at the ready. "I can hardly hear myself think with all your bloody noise. It's quieter in an air raid!"

"This, whatever it is, from the RAF, has just assaulted and threatened a superior officer, Commander!" the Colonel bellowed, a little too excessively, while desperately trying to stop his voice from wobbling too much. "And as you're the Beach Master, I demand you arrest her immediately for insubordination!" The Commander stood between them and waved his marines to lower their weapons, then sucked on his pipe as he looked at them each in turn.

"Did I hear, right?" he asked Harriet. She looked at him and opened her mouth to reply. "You're the pilot who shot down that bomber last night, and stopped it hitting our cruiser?"

"Yes, Sir."

"Yes... Good man, the Captain that is. He took almost two thousand off the beach, army, RAF, nurses even, and many of their injured patients. Packed every square inch of deck space just to get people off the beach, he did. They were fantastically overloaded, but he wouldn't be told when we tried to say he'd already taken enough. 'Just another platoon,' he said. 'Get them on! We'll stand them in the engine room and keep them warm.'" He looked at the Colonel as he blew a cloud of blue smoke from his pipe, then lowered his tone. "If that bomber had got through, there isn't a thing we could have done to save just one of the poor souls on that ship, man or woman, Navy, Army, or Air Force, the lot of them would have been at the bottom of the Channel." He turned to Harriet and his confident charm instantly returned. "What's wrong with your arm?"

"My Hurricane was on fire when I crashed, and the canopy was jammed closed. I got burned while trying to force it open. That and a bit of shrapnel." Harriet replied, having calmed herself enough to talk. He looked her up and down. She was a mess, her flying boots were charred, as were the sleeves of her flying jacket. Her right arm was in a sling, her blue blouse was mostly a smoke stained filthy black, her trousers were grimy with smoke and scorch marks, her face was black with soot and oil, and her hair matted to her head. Mess was an understatement. The Commander nodded slowly.

"Not fun being trapped in an enclosed space full of flames, is it?" he asked.

"No, Sir."

"No Sir, indeed. You ever experienced that, Colonel? Being trapped somewhere tight and narrow, and surrounded by flames? Feeling the air boil and your lungs burn, while your skin singes?"

"What? No..."

"No... Of course not. You wouldn't be half the arse you are if you had."

"How dare you!" the Colonel growled.

"Oh, I dare, Colonel. I dare because as you quite correctly pointed out, I'm the Beach Master. This is my beach, and everything on it belongs to me, including you! Now, I think you'd better hurry back to your unit and hope to God that I forget your face before it comes to your turn to board, or I may just add you to my rear party."

"But she struck a superior officer! That, if nothing else should be dealt with! Whichever uniform we wear, there must be discipline!"

"No, Colonel, she didn't, you're merely senior in rank. The only thing superior on this beach is your sense of entitlement, and it could be argued that discipline starts with self. A good officer would know that, whichever uniform they wear... Now, on your way or I'll have my marines shoot you for inciting insubordination on my beach." The Colonel trembled under the Commander's stare. "Assuming that's OK with you?" he asked Harriet with a wink. She nodded and lowered her pistol, letting the Colonel straighten himself before marching off across the sand. "Sorry about that," the Commander said casually while sucking on his pipe. "This beach can fray the nerves a little; even good men are susceptible to the odd wobble." He turned and headed back into his sandbagged bunker. "Do come in." Max and Harriet followed into his small command post, which was staffed by a couple of sailors. "Petty Officer Wilkins?"

"Sir?" A bearded sailor replied.

"What have we got that's about to leave?"

"The Magpie, Sir. A minesweeper."

"Is she full?"

"Packed, Sir. Ready to push off any minute."

"I see. Anything else?"

"There's a small Dutch trawler bringing in some medical supplies after taking a load off last night, and she's due alongside any minute. As soon as she's unloaded, we'll be filling her up and sending her back. She's only small, so it won't take long to load, maybe a platoon at the most. We should get her away before the sun's too far over the horizon."

"OK, good show. Take our friends from the RAF and put them on it, would you?"

"Yes, Sir."

"My direct orders, they're to be taken back as a matter of priority, so they can get back in the air and keep the Luftwaffe at bay. Understand?"

"Yes, Sir!"

The Commander turned to Harriet and Max, who were standing in shock. "Your tickets home, with the compliments and heartfelt thanks of the Royal Navy for your services," he smirked. "Now, don't make a liar of me. Make sure you're back in the air as soon as you can, we need you, genuinely, and tell your friends we appreciate their endeavours."

"We can't thank you enough," Max said.

"Don't mention it. I'm getting everyone off this beach sooner or later anyway, even fools like the Colonel. You're just going sooner, that's all."

"I kinda feel bad asking, but I don't suppose you've got space on that trawler for a few more?"

"More? Pilots?"

"No... Soldiers. They took me out beyond the perimeter last night to rescue my friend here after she was shot down. Without them, we might both still be out there, or on our way to a German prison camp." At that, the artillery guns sounded heavy in the near distance, and the machine gun fire seemed closer than it had in the night. The Commander walked past them and stepped out on the beach to look north. The dark pre dawn sky was flashing with shell and shot, something being repeated over to the east.

"Dawn chorus... They're at it early this morning. I'd imagine another raid will be due in at sun up," he said as if talking to himself. He took another drag off his pipe, then turned back to Harriet and Max. "How many?"

"Seven in total."

"Well, you'd better go and fetch them. We need to get you on board before we embark others from the queue, or there'll be no space. Will five minutes do you?"

"It sure will. Wait here, Harry, I'll be back in no time." Max took off across the beach, while the Commander reached into his pocket and pulled out a silver flask.

"Not the most traditional of breakfasts, but it'll keep you warm." He handed Harriet the flask. She took it gratefully and sipped the thick and warming dark rum. "Typical of the RAF." He raised an eyebrow as she winced and coughed when the rum hit the back of her throat; which had been burned by the smoke and heat of the burning Hurricane, as had her lips.

"Sorry, I wasn't expecting it to burn so much, I think it's the smoke from the aeroplane fire," she quickly said to excuse herself.

"Oh, don't be silly," he laughed. "No apologies needed. If the air was that hot, it'd have scorched your lungs, and it'll take a while to recover."

"Oh..."

"I meant you. It's typical of the RAF to have a female pilot. I've been saying for years that the Navy needs to make better use of female sailors, but it's always been resisted and pushed back. Often for the most outdated and ridiculous of reasons, of course; and now the RAF have gone and beaten us to it, again! They did it the same with foreigners too, you know? The RAF was the first to invite flyers from other countries to serve. If I remember right there was even a Japanese pilot in the old Royal Flying Corps during the last war, I remember a friend talking of him, incredibly brave chap. Now that's progress. The Navy gets there eventually, of course; they just need a bit of encouragement, and maybe time to see the air force do it first so they can avoid the more obvious mistakes your chaps make," he said as he gave her a wink. "Still, better late than never, the reverse of what the army seem to believe... They're always the last to catch on." Harriet smirked. "I can only hope we get somebody like you when we finally let ladies fly in the navy... I don't suppose I can convince you to switch teams, could I?"

"I can't... I get seasick." Harriet replied sheepishly.

"What, every time?"

"We'll soon find out, I suppose."

"You mean...?"

"My parents brought me to France on a ferry when I was young. I was sick the entire time, and the sea was calmer than it is today."

"Oh dear."

"Quite."

"I suppose you'd better stick with your aeroplanes in that case. The navy can get funny about that sort of thing, too much mess can be a frightful chore to clean when at sea."

"I can only imagine."

"Speaking of aeroplanes, is that the dawn patrol I hear?" he looked up into the dark sky, which was lightening by the minute as dawn spread from the east.

"No..." Harriet replied

"Oh?"

"The engines. They're not Merlins, they're... Stukas, look!" She was pointing at the Stuka diving out of the cloud above the town, followed by another and another. The screeching of their sirens sounded just seconds later, as they steepened their angle of attack and dived at the beach. They screeched so loud they could be heard over the rumble of anti aircraft guns, which scattered fluffy black dots against the heavy grey background of the clouds. The beach lit up as soldiers fired rifles and machine guns at the diving Stukas, far out of range for accurate shots, but perhaps enough to put the pilot off his aim. The beach erupted in bright flashes of explosions as the first bombs ripped through a long snaking column of soldiers which had formed to wait for the smaller boats picking up off the beach. More bombs followed, and the beach turned into a haze of chaos and screams, shrouded in smoke and sand while more bombs fell.

"PO Wilkins!" the Commander shouted. The young seaman quickly appeared. "Get our friend here onto the Magpie right away. No hanging about now."

"But Max..." Harriet protested.

"I'll put him on the Dutch boat as promised. Now get yourself off my beach, Miss...?"

"Cornwall. Pilot Officer Harriet Cornwall."

"It's been a pleasure." He shook her hand as an explosion blasted a little closer than was comfortable, and showered them in sand. "Today, Wilkins!" he called, and the Petty Officer grabbed Harriet's arm and pulled her. She glanced back as the Commander shouted instructions to other personnel, then turned and focused, and ran through the chaos. The petty officer pulled her along, running past soldiers lying on their backs and shooting up at the diving Stukas which appeared to be filling the air for the length of the beach. She was led to the concrete harbour, which was being used to load troops onto ships, and through a small side gate at the water's edge guarded by marines. From there, they ran along a small concrete path which was slippery with seaweed and shells, that ran the length of the bottom of the wall. They climbed a rickety iron staircase and came out at the end of the concrete pier ahead of the barricade guarded by marines and the boarding officer, who turned and shouted them over. Just the other side of the pier was the minesweeper, its engines running and making lots of thick brown and black smoke, and its decks packed with the green and brown mass of the army.

"What's happening, PO?" the officer demanded.

"The Commander sends his regards, Sir, and asks if you can find space for this pilot on the Magpie."

"She's about to leave, and gangways are being pulled up."

"She's the pilot who saved the Kingston yesterday, Sir."

"Chief put a plank across," the Captain shouted. They marched Harriet over to the ship side of the pier, where she stared down at the long wooden plank that had been laid across to the deck. "It's now or never," he said. A statement supported by the Magpie sounding its horn! She nodded, took a breath, then took a few steps back before running and jumping full speed along the plank. She leapt over the side of the ship, and a group of soldiers grabbed her and pulled her aboard. Almost immediately, the minesweeper pulled away from the wall and vibrations shook the deck as they started making way. She stood among the soldiers and waved at the Captain and PO, both of whom waved back before returning to their work.

"Close thing, blue job. Another minute and you'd have missed the bus," the Sergeant who'd caught her said. She nodded and smiled, then they all turned to look as explosions erupted amidst the queue of troops on the concrete pier they'd just left.

"Close thing for all of us, by the looks of it..." Harriet replied.

"Yeah... Nothing we can do for them. Why don't you get yourself up front and try to find some space? There are some medics up there." He looked down and nodded at her slung arm. She smiled and thanked him for helping her aboard, then she made her way along the crowded decks towards the front of the ship, and immediately wished she hadn't. All of the deck space was covered with stretchers, and sitting around the edges in their bloodied bandages were the walking wounded. Medics tended to them as best they could, while sailors handed out tea and sandwiches.

"Have a seat," a sailor said as he approached her. "A medic will have a look at you in a minute."

"I... it's OK. I'll be OK."

"Here," he said as he lifted a large buoy out of a small alcove and threw it over the side with the large coil of rope that it was attached to, and sat her down in its place. It was narrow and a tight squeeze, but just about the right size for her. He grabbed a tin mug of tea and a sandwich from one of his passing shipmates and handed them to her. She shook her head at first. "Get it down you. You'll feel better for it. Don't worry; we'll be home before you know it."

"How long?"

"Well, the Germans have set up artillery batteries to the north and south, and it'll be daylight soon, so we'll be taking the scenic route. Four hours, maybe five at the most. We'll have you back at your squadron before nightfall." He gave her a reassuring wink which made her smile a little. At that, the scream of a Stuka filled the air. Harriet's heart skipped, and she looked up to see the dive bomber's black angular shape against the lightening pre dawn sky. Her stomach churned as she watched it diving; it was almost right on target. The ship's guns rattled and thudded and filled the sky with explosions and long crisscrossing trails of tracer, as the Stuka screeched closer undeterred. A pair of black spheres detached, one from under each wing as it pulled up from the dive. "Oh shit" the sailor shouted, then quickly crouched over Harriet and pushed his torso tight over hers. The high pitched whistle of the bombs cut through the terrific orchestra of the ship's guns and the attacking Stuka, and then the ship rocked as the pair exploded in unison and a wave of seawater was sprayed over the ship. The sailor half stood, and Harriet looked up at his frowning face.

"Did they hit us?" she asked.

"Yeah... somewhere aft I think," he replied. She leant forward a little and could see black smoke coming from the back of the ship.

"Look!" she said as she looked up again. Two more Stukas were heading for the ship, this time from the south and right in Harriet's line of sight.

"Jesus," he gasped. The ship's guns continued their roar after the Stuka that had just attacked, and nobody had seen the other two. "Starboard!" he started yelling. "Guns starboard!" She watched as he ran off and climbed a ladder up to the bridge, screaming as he went. His message must have got through because the main gun quickly started firing in the direction of the Stukas, which looked set to start diving. The whole crowded forward deck looked up and watched as the leader tipped its nose to dive. The sirens started, then without warning the inky black angular shadow sparkled with silver, gold, and bronze flickers in an almost magical way. Harriet found it captivating, almost warming, because she knew in her heart what was coming next. A long golden orange jet of flame extended the length of the Stuka and beyond, and as the ship turned hard to port to avoid any bombs, the Stuka straightened into its dive. It was heading nose down in flames, with the unique and unmistakeable elliptical wings of a Spitfire hard on its tail, firing streams of light from its wings and into the Stuka, making it sparkle among the flames as it screeched downwards out of control. Harriet couldn't help herself, the excitement of watching the Spitfires in action sent adrenaline flowing through her veins, and she stood to watch the fight, despite being shouted at to take cover. Just seconds later, the second Stuka lit up the sky when it turned into a sun like ball of flames as another Spitfire hit home. The ship banked right, and the sparkling Stuka hit the sea close enough to send a wave over the side of the ship and soak the cheering passengers and crew, Harriet included. The rest of the Spitfire squadron roared out of the clouds, headed for the beach. Another pair broke off to deal with the first Stuka, which was shot down into the sea with ease. The pair then flew low over the ship, the pilots waved, and Harriet almost jumped overboard with excitement as she waved back. The guns silenced, and the ship sounded its whistle while everyone cheered. Harriet kept her eyes on the Spitfires as they arrived over the beach and quickly dealt with the remaining bombers, then started in on the fighter cover that had been hovering high above. The creeping dawn lit up the eastern sky and made the perfect backdrop for the battle. She was smiling, proud of the RAF. She thought of the Colonel and his offensive comments and hoped he'd been watching.

The smile faded when she caught sight of the rear of the ship. It was smoking quite badly right about where she'd jumped aboard, and it had been packed with soldiers, some of whom were now in the water, splashing and screaming for help. Sailors were throwing ropes and life belts into the water, while others lowered a cargo net over the side and climbed down to help the stricken soldiers back aboard. Some were already face down, some she watched sink under the weight of their clothing and equipment, only the luckiest and strongest stood a chance. She turned and sunk back into her alcove and pulled the straps of her yellow Mae West life jacket just a little tighter under her slung arm. The excitement and elation of seeing the Spitfires in action were replaced by the heart wrenching misery of seeing soldiers drown after being bombed off the ship that was taking them home. They'd survived being overrun by the Germans, and fought their way back to the beaches where they'd been bombed day and night, only to be killed in the most horrible way when they'd finally got a place on a ship home. They'd spent weeks of escaping death, only to drown five hours away from home, practically within sight of England. She thought back to the Colonel and his nasty comments directed at the RAF, and those she'd heard from the soldiers on the beach, and she started to see why they'd think the way they did. The RAF was hardly visible to the troops on the ground, as they were either inland stopping the Germans getting to the coast, or high above at twenty thousand feet and practically invisible. Then, when they did arrive in their Spitfires or Hurricanes, they had less than a quarter of a minute of ammunition. Meaning that any dogfights witnessed by the army were over in a matter of minutes; then the surviving fighters had to leave. Not through choice, but because they were mostly useless without bullets. She knew the pilots were working hard, and she knew they were fighting hard, and that they were dying hard; and she knew that a one hour patrol and combat was as physically and mentally draining as anything else anyone could ever do, if not more so. She'd flown four in a day, with combat, and literally passed out with exhaustion. She also knew that the life expectancy of new pilots was ridiculously low. She'd been in her squadron less than two weeks, and she'd lost count of the faces that had come and gone, not to mention the old hands, the senior and more experienced pilots they'd lost. The soldiers probably wouldn't care, though, they didn't see it, and if they didn't see it, there's no way that they could understand it.

"Here you go, get that in you," the sailor who'd found her a seat said as he appeared in front of her carrying a tin cup.

"I really couldn't," she replied as politely as she could.

"Captain's orders."

"What do you mean?"

"Well, by the looks of you, you're a pilot of some sort. RAF?"

"Yes... But what's that got to do with anything?"

"Everything. The skipper sends his compliments and thanks on behalf of the navy, along with some of his rum. It's the good stuff from his own personal bottle." She smiled and took it from him before he walked away. She sipped the rum, and it burned her lips, mouth, and throat as though she was drinking acid. She coughed and spluttered, then picked up what was left of the cool tea she'd been given before the bombing and took a sip. It eased some of the burning, but not by much.

"Here you go," the sailor pointed an army doctor down to her.

"Cheers," the medic replied, before kneeling down and looking Harriet over.

"Now then, what happened to you?"

"I was burned," she replied bluntly.

"I'd say so. You're more black than anything else. Anything you need help with?"

"I don't think so..." she coughed.

"Arm OK?" He gestured to the sling, and she nodded in reply.

"Yeah..."

"OK, well I'll leave you to it, I suppose."

"There is one thing."

"What's that?"

"I can't swallow anything. My mouth and throat hurt if I try."

"OK, well let's have a look, shall we?" She nodded, and he moved closer. "Right, tilt back your head and open wide." She did as she was told and he peered into her mouth, then pulled a dental mirror from his pocket and put it in her mouth and looked around. "This fire that burned you..." he asked as he moved back and replaced the mirror.

"Yes?"

"Enclosed space?"

"Cockpit of an aeroplane."

"Makes sense..." He pulled out his water canteen and handed it to her. "Take a sip."

"What makes sense?" she asked after spluttering as the cool water kissed her throat, initially shocking her but soon starting to soothe.

"The air will have been superheated, and when you inhaled it, you'll have scorched your airways. Your throat is raw, and your mouth blistered, you're lucky you can still breathe."

"What can I do?"

"Not much until we get to England... I'll give you some pills for the pain, but otherwise just keep drinking cold water, it'll help in the long run." She nodded, and he handed her a couple of pills. "Keep the water bottle, and keep sipping. Maybe don't try the tea, and if you're hungry, try and wet the bread a little first. It'll make it less scratchy. I've no idea how long the cruise will be, but when we dock in England, I'll make sure you're checked over." She nodded and smiled painfully, then forced the tablets down and sipped the water. "Right, I'll leave you to it. Shout if you need anything, I'm not far."

"Thank you. Oh, here." She handed him the mug of rum. "It's rum."

"I see..."

"I can't drink it, it burns too much, but maybe some of the wounded could use it?" He nodded and smiled then took the cup.

"You know that you're one of the wounded, don't you?" She smiled and shook her head.

"I'm alright."

"Yes. Yes, you are."

She closed her eyes and tried hard to focus on the sound of the engines, trying to ignore the moans and groans of the wounded and dying on the deck. The vibrations and the swaying, which was progressively increasing as a strengthening south westerly wind whipped up the waves and rocked the little minesweeper, soon became therapeutic enough to send her to sleep. England wasn't far, and while it wasn't what she knew to be home, it was safe.

The dreams were bad, again, with the new addition of being trapped in a burning Hurricane. A dream that could be expected considering recent events, but a dream she couldn't escape from. Instead, she just went around and around, crashing and burning, burning and crashing, and feeling the skin burn from her face, then watching it from outside the canopy once again. Kicking and screaming as she tried to pull it open while Nicole burned in front of her. The only escape from her nightmares came when she was thrown into the air then crashed down into the deck, which was at an angle and quickly flooding with seawater. The wounded were sliding on their stretchers, and the medics and orderlies tried to steady them. Harriet looked around in amazement. She'd been dragged from her nightmares into something much worse. She was fighting to squeeze into her alcove as the bow and stern of the ship started lifting more while the smoking and burning centre bubbled with water and slowly sunk. The sailor who'd brought her the rum appeared and pulled her to her feet, then held her upright while supporting himself. Without talking, he urgently searched for the valve on her Mae West and quickly started blowing into it hard while simultaneously looking around and watching the angle of the deck increase.

"What's happening?" she asked as she started to gather her senses.

"You're going to have to trust me!" he replied. She nodded, and he picked her up then without warning threw her overboard. She hit the water with a gasp as she sunk below the surface just for a moment, and the ice cold water covered her head and slipped down her back, shocking her and making her gulp a mouthful. Seconds later she was back on the surface, her Mae West was keeping her afloat, and the sailor was beside her. "Kick your legs," he shouted as he grabbed the collar of her jacket and started swimming hard, dragging her through the water. She did as he said and kicked as hard as she could while looking back at the ship over the tops of the choppy waves, which would hide the scene from her temporarily, leaving only a wall of water topped with a column of black smoke mixed with white steam. Then the full scene would be revealed again as they passed over a wave top. The bow and stern were already high, and both started to sink quickly. There were bodies in the water and bodies jumping, but it was going fast. It didn't take long until it was gone. The bow was the last part to sink beneath the waves in a fury of bubbles and steam, immediately extinguishing all smoke and sound.

"It's gone," she said. The sailor kept swimming. "It's gone," she repeated, louder this time as they dipped between the waves again. The sailor slowed and stopped, almost exhausted, then paddled and treaded water beside her, joining her in looking back where the ship was. The water was full of debris, but no boats. They were far from where the ship had gone down, the wind and hard tide combined with the sailor's hard swimming had made sure of it. "I can't see anyone..."

"They'll have been sucked under when it went down if they couldn't get away quick enough," he said as he floated behind her, and held onto her Mae West. "You don't need to kick. Save your energy."

"What happened?"

"Torpedoed."

"Will they come for us?"

"Who?"

"Somebody? Anybody?"

"Of course they will... The navy will know exactly what course we were on, and our speed; and the radio room will have got a message off to the Admiralty before she went down. They'll be on their way already, but you've got to stay awake until they get here, OK?"

"OK..."

"I mean it."

"I know... I'm so tired, though..." She felt the sea lapping at her face as she eased over the waves. She wasn't cold anymore, or scared, and her arm and face had finally stopped hurting; she was just so tired that she couldn't even keep her eyes open. She blinked and looked at Cas' watch. The rising sun made the pearlescent colours ripple across the white face, it wasn't even half past six and the day was only just starting, but already she was so tired. As her arm sunk back into the water, she looked up at the white clouds in the blue skies above. It was beautiful, just like when she'd laid in the grass with Nicole at Claude's airfield. The warming sun on her face made her smile as she closed her eyes and smelled the sweet grass again, mixed with the unmistakable aroma of aeroplane oil. She looked to her side, and into Nicole's hazel brown eyes. "I'll be fine in a while, Nicole. I'm just so very tired. I'll just close my eyes for a minute."

The End

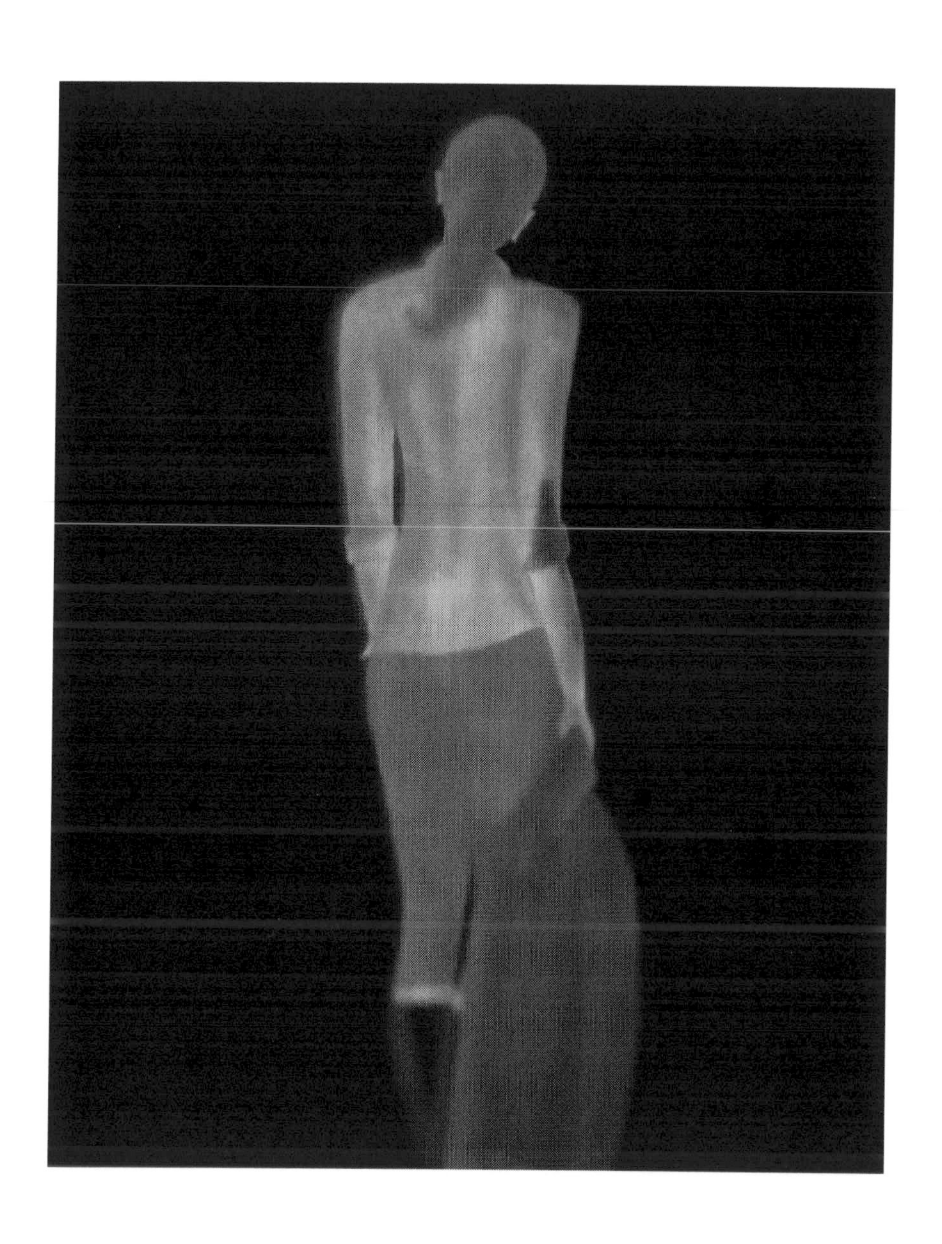

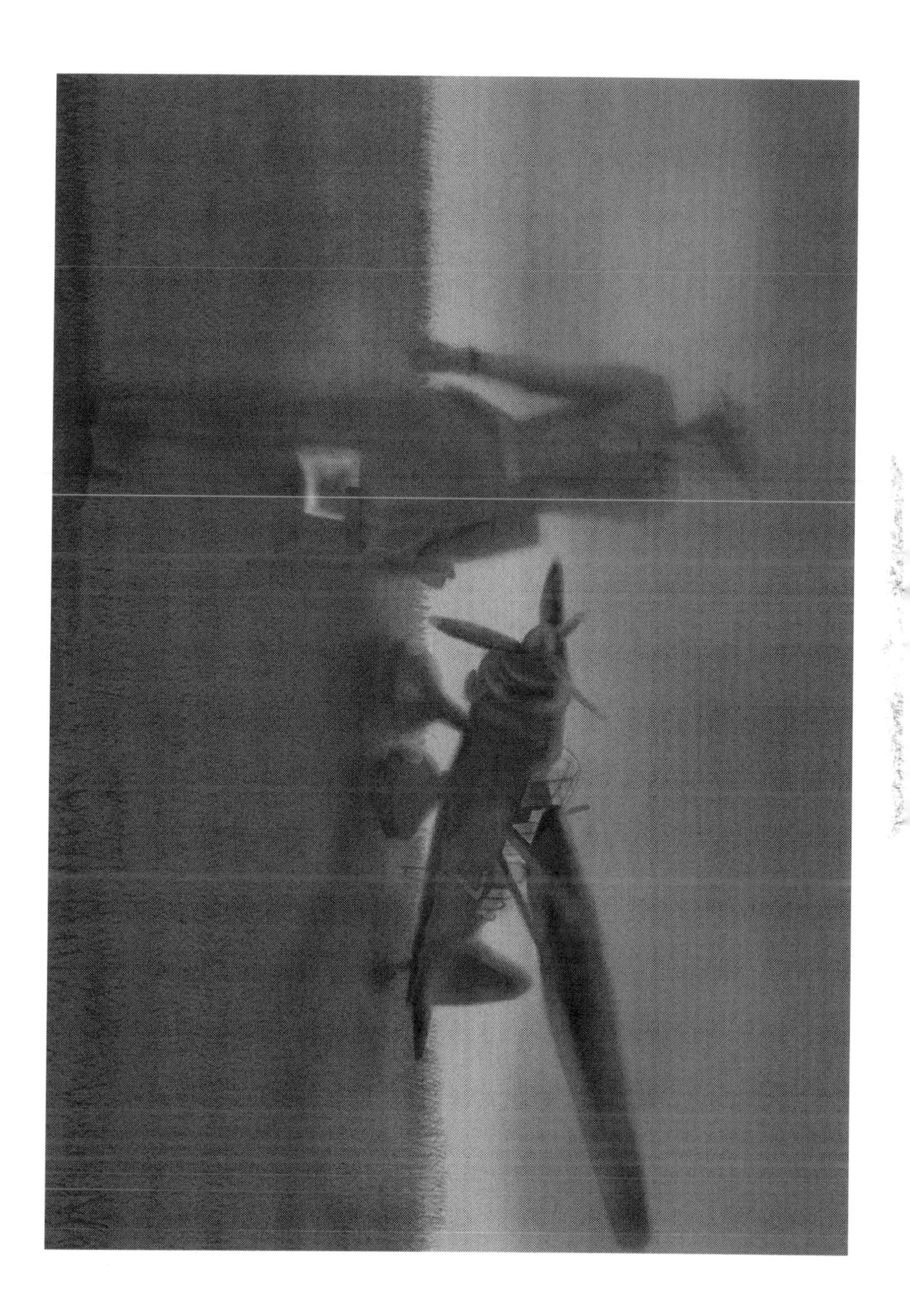

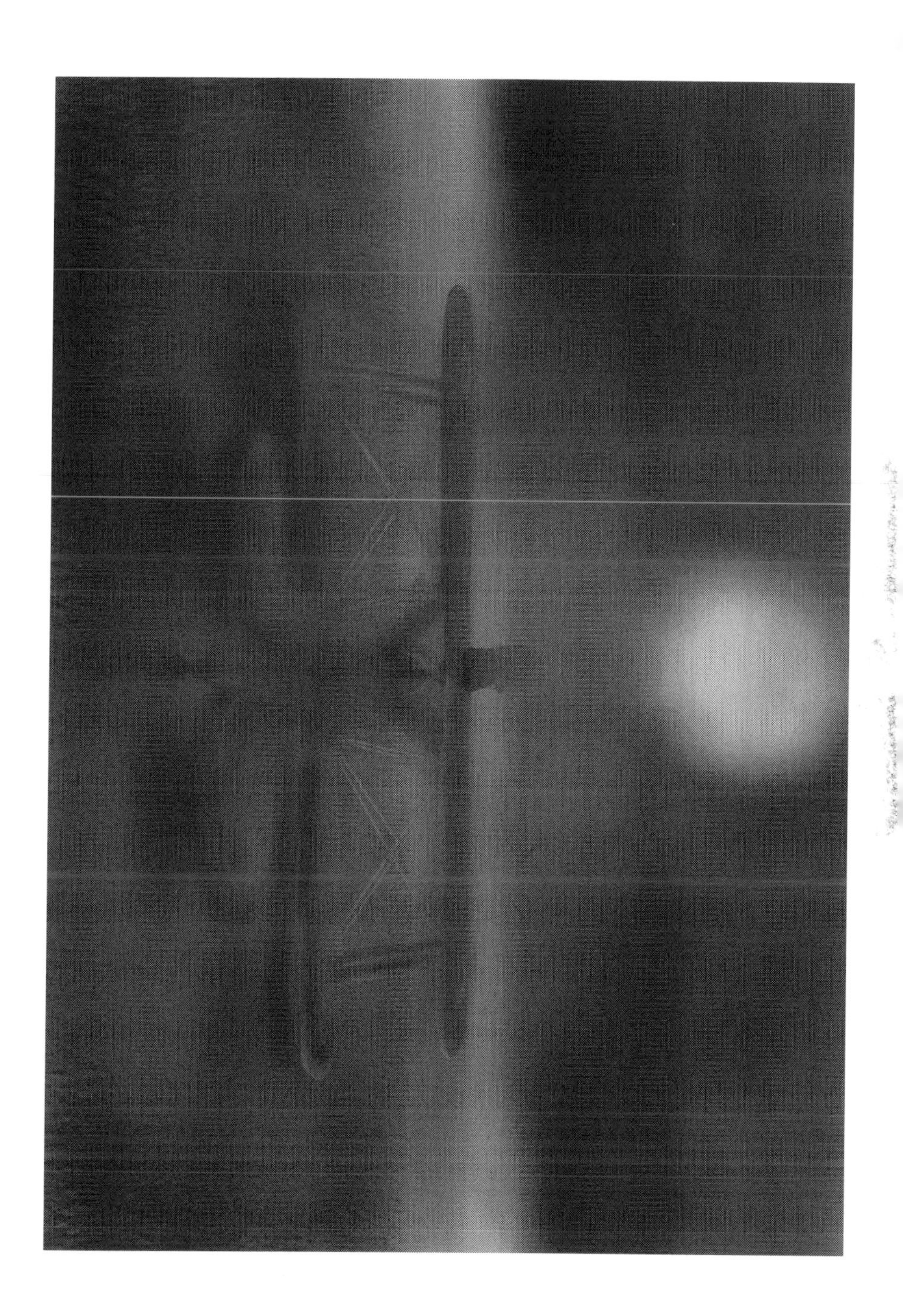

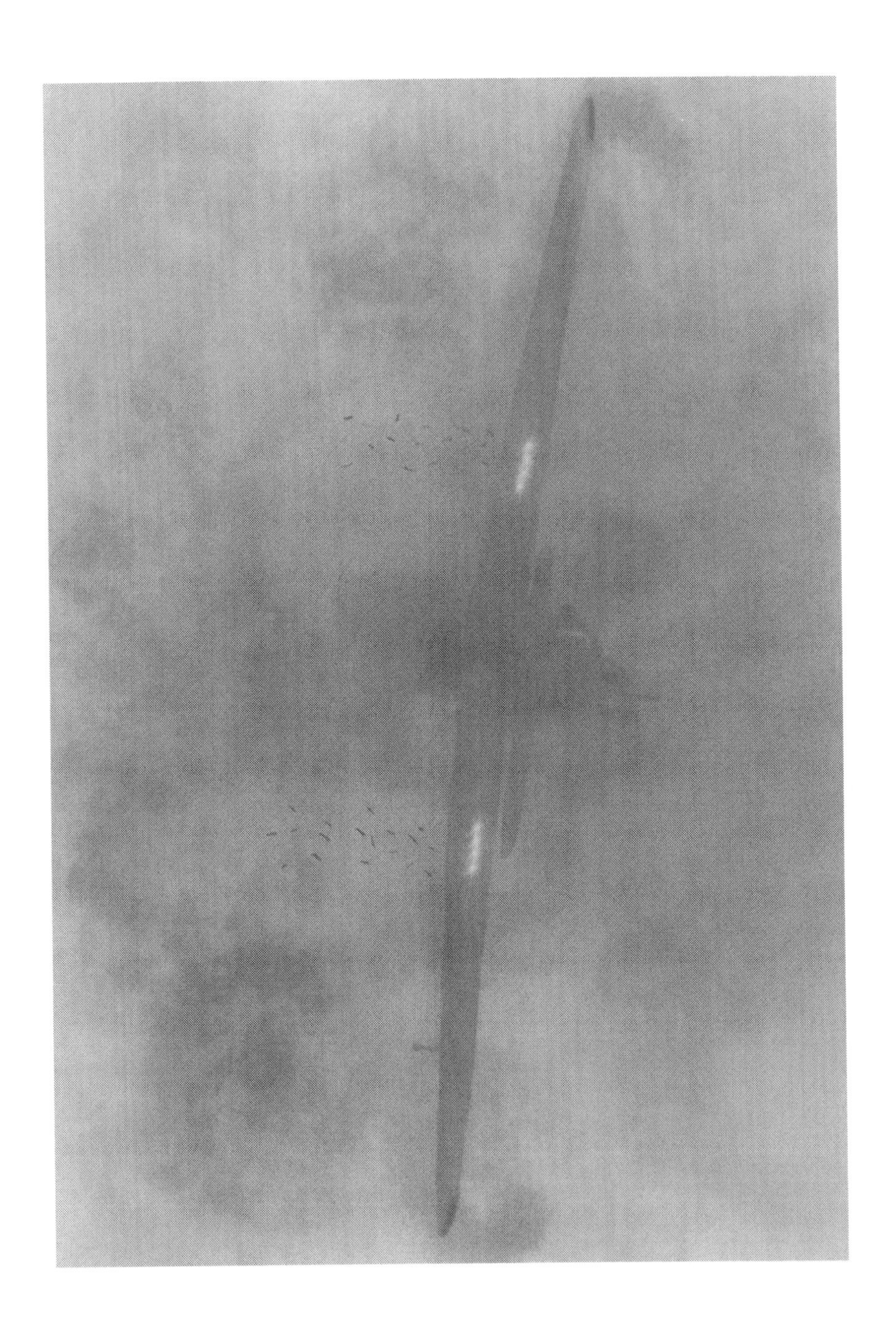

Thank you...

Many people have provided inspiration and motivation through the long months of researching, writing, and editing this book, not least the men and women whose stories of selflessness and heroism in the world's darkest hours are the foundations of Harriet's story. To thank them all personally would be impossible, but perhaps by inspiring even one person who reads this book to learn more about their incredible and at times almost unbelievable stories, the facts behind the fiction, we can offer the greatest thanks of all in keeping their memory alive.

In addition to those who inspired my writing through their actions, there are many others who have touched my life in some way and made the story possible, and for their support I'm truly grateful. Whether they've read my work through, suggested corrections, insisted that I write, dared me to learn how to draw so I could create my own cover and illustrations, or even just showed me an element of humanity that inspired a thought, a moment, or even a character, without them the book would never have been printed. Even those who tease, mock, and work hard to keep me grounded have been invaluable, in their own special way...

Last, but certainly not least, I'd like to thank Harriet, the mischievous figment of my imagination who's given me so much enjoyment in my writing.

Karl

Printed in Great Britain
by Amazon

59912703R00241